Shad

# of Trinity

(Eighth Book of the Kahana Chronicles)

A Family Historical Novel

Allen Goldenthal

Eloquent Books
New York, New York

Eloquent Books
An imprint of AEG Publishing Group
845 Third Avenue, 6th Floor — #6016
New York, NY 10022
www.eloquentbooks.com

ISBN: 978-1-60693-333-6
SKU: 1-60693-333-7

Printed in the United States of America

Hear my voice Lord and listen to your humble servant, son of Abraham, Isaac, and Jacob. Son of Aaron and son of Zadok. Let me walk in your footsteps and guide my path with righteousness...

—Beginning of 8th century Kahana prayer

Prologue

The constable dismounted from his ancient gray gelding, its dappled hide a series of undulating proud flesh and melanomas. As if part of a matching set, the leather saddle was also well seasoned, tattered and torn across its length and breadth. Both were now in the possession of the third man to hold the rank of city constable. A job obviously valued more for its title than for the salary and working conditions.

This particular evening had begun like every other, but by dusk stories of inhuman wails and strange shadows flittering across rooftop skylights had made their way to the patrolling officer's home. The time was almost half past midnight and he found himself dressed in his blue military uniform, searching for a ghost as he crisscrossed the endless labyrinth of streets that transected the south-west district.

His crossbow was held firmly in his left hand. It comforted him as he watched the early morning fog float eerily along the cobblestone paths as if it too was searching for something or someone. The manner in which the mist weaved through the streets made him think that it was possessed of a life-force of its own. He tried to dismiss the foolishness from his mind but no matter how hard he tried, he could not. Too late, he had fallen victim to the myths and legends of the night that frightened both young and old. Instead of fleeing, he found his grip on the crossbow tightening involuntarily. It was a useful weapon. Not suitable for hunting because of its small design to be easily transported on hip or saddle but at close range it could send one of its foot long bolts through a man before he even had time to utter a scream. But to be used at short range meant that he had to get close to whatever it was that had been haunting the nights these past few months. Far too close as far as he was concerned.

Early reports had been filed under flights of imagination; overzealous parents attempting to discipline their children through tales of goblins and demons or by men that had drunk far too much in the inns and brothels to separate myth from reality. But then the deaths and disappearances began. People from all walks of life with nothing in common; totally unrelated. Random by nature, yet always confined to the central district. Clergy, politicians, merchants, bankers, not a single identifiable relationship accept that they represented the wealthier, more affluent classes. Usually by the time the reports were submitted, it was already days since the disappearance and any trail had long grown cold.

But these alleged crimes had heightened the worst fears of the residents throughout the city and now that it had seemingly struck in the heart of the ghetto of the southern district, he found himself on his first hot trail since it all began. People in this district were not willing to tolerate the mayhem that plagued their despised neighbors in the central districts. The rich and powerful were meaningless to them. Here they only wanted to live a quiet life and be left alone. Now that had become seemingly impossible. The contagion of death had spread into their homes and they wanted the problem resolved immediately. When the common people band together, what begins as a simple search party, soon turns into vigilantism, then a mob, and ultimately a revolution. That could not be tolerated, because when it reaches the boil, there'd be far more at stake than a priest or a banker losing their lives. The rabble would bring down anyone in power and at that critical point the Emperor would be most susceptible. The constable understood his orders. Insurrection was to be avoided at all costs!

The murders had to be resolved tonight! There would be no tomorrows if the seething anger of the populace wasn't kept under control. One way or another it was going to end, and he had no intention of letting the mysterious stalker inflict another night of sleeplessness on the citizenry of Prague.

But where was he to start? How do you chase a phantom in a city where demons were considered part of the everyday landscape? Every shadow, every gargoyle sitting on a cornice, every shrill sound that pierced the blackness represented a potential threat. With reins in hand, the constable walked on with his horse close behind. He could sense he was drawing close. There was something different in the air, though he couldn't determine exactly what it might have been. A smell, a feel, an electricity which defied description. It was here, there, had to be, somewhere hiding in the darkness, concealed from view. Holding his crossbow level with his chest, he wheeled about, aiming the bolt in a sweeping circle with the hope that he'd lock on to an invisible target.

A deafening silence settled over the alley. All of time had ground to a stop, and existence became suspended between the beat of seconds. The rustle of leaves caught in a gust of wind pierced the unbearable silence. He edged closer to the entrance into the alleyway. With every step forward he was beaten back by the unworldly odor that surged from the empty blackness. The sweat rolled down his arm and on to the wooden stock of the crossbow. Whatever his prey might be, he had it cornered. It could not be seen, it could not be heard, but he could feel its overwhelming presence crawling over his flesh. Standing at the edge of the alley, he prepared to take that fateful step into the beckoning maw.

Too slow! Like a coiled cobra it lunged at his face, knocking him backwards against the wall. His entire body stiffened in response to the unrelenting pressure around his throat. It was not human; a force exerted by a steel grip lifting him from his feet and pinning him to the stone wall at his back. At first his legs flailed but now they just hung lifeless from his waist as if made from lead. He knew it was over. By morning all would know that the creature that haunted their nightmares had claimed yet another victim. Only this time it would be the man that they had appointed to protect them. In all his mercy, God failed to answer their desperate prayers.

A low guttural sound surfaced on fetid breath. They were words, but not like any he had heard before. As his consciousness faded he imagined that he was hearing the sounds made by an animal attempting to speak, as if that could ever be possible. But all things were possible in a city like Prague!

"Why you bother me? I must hurt you," it croaked in feral tones.

The constable still struggled to determine if the voice was real or merely the tricks of a mind deprived of oxygen. All was going black and the last thing he could recall was his body slumping heavily against the hard ground. He had found the monster that had been terrorizing the night, or more correctly it had found him. A final tear streamed down the side of his face.

1

Hastings; Present

It was time for me to search through my corridor of memories yet once again. Calmly closing my eyes, I leaned back into the chair, the cushions firmly cradling my head. This was going to take a lot out of me. I could feel it; I knew it.

"Well John, I'm not going to let you interrupt this story until I'm finished."

"That's a change!" Pearce commented. "Why are you suddenly changing your style?"

"Because it's my story!"

Pearce sighed, resigned to the fact that he had to abide my whims if he wanted his byline. "They're all your stories, what makes this one so different?"

"Are you actually challenging me John? Since when did you make this part of our game?"

"You asked me to fly down to New Zealand if you recall. I was perfectly happy back at home, taking care of business, without the discomfort of a twenty-one hour flight."

"Ah, come on John, you can admit it. Whatever you were doing was pretty boring and you were praying by the telephone that I'd give you a call that I had something new to report."

"That's not the point!"

"That's exactly the point. You haven't exactly brought any best sellers in to the publishing house lately, have you?"

"Bit of a dry spell, but they pass. They always do."

"I'm sure it will. And this will be the story that does it for you."

"What makes you so certain?"

"Because I've met someone…"

"Do I really want to know about this? And what about your wife?" John appeared quite upset by my revelation. Having met Margaret on several occasions, I believe he was actually feeling quite concerned for her.

"Oh, please," I dismissed him. "I mean I met someone like me."

"There's another one?" he asked quite excitedly.

"Yes," I reassured him, "though she doesn't actually realize it completely as yet. But it's dawning on her slowly."

"What's that supposed to mean?"

"Just what I said. She's actually resisting the eventuality. I think it scares her a bit."

"How can you be so certain she has it? Has she told you anything? Can she do what you do? What's her story?"

"See, now you're interested. The answers to your questions are no, no, no and no. But does she have it, that's a big affirmative yes."

"I thought you said that the only way you can have this genetically linked memory is through generations of inbreeding?

"I did."

"So how could you find someone else with that kind of genealogical history in New Zealand? Is she an immigrant here?"

"One hundred percent Kiwi," I responded knowing I had him on the hook. In fact she's part Maori."

"Well, this isn't making much sense, is it?"

"Perfect sense! I've already talked with her about her family details. I knew immediately that she was descended from tribal chieftains. And that meant that there was a pretty limited gene pool that she was descended from. Chieftains in Maoridom were similar to those in most other tribal cultures. They were the shamans, the spiritual guides. They ruled by mysticism, not force. So that part is very similar to my own familial history.

"But you're the product of over three thousand years of inbreeding. What could she possibly be; eight hundred at the most?"

"That's why I'm saying I'm not certain how good at it she'll actually be."

"So does this Maori princess have a name?"

"Yes, Mandy."

"Mandy?

"Yes, Mandy."

"What kind of Maori name is that?"

"Modern Maori," I snarled. "What's it really matter. The fact is she shares the ability to see things from the past."

"But she doesn't want to, is that what you said?"

"She's resisting. She doesn't tell me that but I can feel it. I think it scares her. Some people are afraid to be different. Fact is she's always been different and she knows it. And that's made her work all the harder to hide her differences."

"She couldn't have hidden it that well, after all, you two found each other."

"Remember what I told you a long time ago. How I said we all tend to gravitate towards people that are familiar, even if that familiarity is derived from memories that aren't even ours but belonged to ancestors hundreds of years in the past."

"Yes."

"Well we gravitated. One of the first conversations we ever had she started telling me that she has these different thoughts on how the world works. That there's a different reality that she can relate to but if she told anyone, they'd think she was nuts."

"But she told you!"

"Exactly. She suddenly tells a perfect stranger that she is in possession of weird ideas and thoughts and she probably couldn't even explain at the time why she felt compelled to tell me that. Other than it was perfectly comfortable to do so. Like taking a walk in the park, it was that easy. No stress, no worries. She knew instinctively that I would understand and I'd believe her."

"So you had a friendly face. It doesn't confirm anything about her. Lots of people have weird ideas. You told me that the first time we met. Most of them were crazies you said. Remember?"

"Yes, but I also told you that there are the other ones that aren't. The ones like me. And of course there's more than that. After all, I'm the one that over analyzes everything, in case you forgot. We started connecting. And get that look off your face; it's not what you're thinking."

"What…?"

"Don't give me that innocent look. Get your mind out of the gutter and focus on what I'm telling you. GLEEM is not just a lot of floating memories that surface and haunt your dreams. In order to process these memories, your mind has to work in a different way. I told you that a long time ago. But for your mind to have the ability to process them means that there has to be a part of your brain that is functioning differently from Joe Average."

"Yea, you told me, so what of it?"

"The memories that are passed on are those that had a high emotional toll on the person involved. I explained all that. And I told you there had to be a trigger; a trigger that released them in the descendant that was now carrying those memories. Well that trigger is also tied up in emotions. There's an empathy that runs on high in those with GLEEM. We know instinctively how anyone else with the gift is feeling and that sets in motion what can only be described as a psychic link."

"So after all these years, you're telling me you're a psychic. Is that it? Okay, I have a number between one and a thousand. Tell me what I'm thinking."

"I didn't say a telepathic link, I said psychic. In this case empathic. I don't read minds, I read emotions. Big difference! But you probably wouldn't understand that."

"Well Doc, it is a bit much to swallow you have to admit."

"This might be a waste of time Pearce, but I'll try to explain it to you. We link. Mandy and I link. It's like a drug. You feed off it. You can be sitting there and all of a sudden you know that something really good has just happened to the other person, or something terrible. And you actually share that high or that low. You can't tell exactly what it is, but you can feel it. You can taste it. It can be overpowering. You can visualize their happiness or sorrow and you have an urge to call them to find out exactly what occurred. And these urges are real. Most time you actually restrain yourself from doing so because you'd end up monopolizing so much of each other's life. So you wait until you finally meet again and then you raise it and the next thing you're talking for hours about an episode you shared through this connection. And it's as if the rest of the world didn't exist for that time you're together. Because that's your time; time to laugh, to cry, to resolve whatever the problem might be."

"I don't know Doc, sounds an awful lot like sex to me."

"That's because you're at an age where you're not getting any and it's all you can think about Pearce. You want to know the truth even though it's going to hurt you." I leaned forward towards Pearce with the pretense of passing on a great secret. "It's better than sex. Sex is only on a physical plane. This link that I'm trying to explain to you is euphoric. It's like your batteries getting recharged. And no matter what language I try to frame it in for you, I will never do it justice. You will never fully understand."

"Okay, I'll take your word for it. So you and this Mandy person share this emotional link, that has nothing to do with a real relationship but you play out scenes and events in your head. Do I have that right?"

"How do you manage to make that sound dirty too?"

"I don't know Doc, maybe because that's how we mere mortals would think about two people that spend a lot of time thinking about each other during their daydreams."

"Too bad for you Pearce because you'll obviously misconstrue my next point when I talk about the merging of souls and feeling as if your part of the same being. I know if Mandy was here, she'd probably describe it in a similar fashion. It's as if you part of something greater. Like a jigsaw puzzle, you're two pieces that actually interconnect, but there's still a hundred other pieces to make up the full picture. And for your information, I am not talking about an orgy!"

"Okay, I'll take your word for it. So this Mandy gave you the story that you're about to tell me. Is that it?"

"No, but she did trigger it. This one was buried so deep in the recesses of my mind that I never would have pulled it out on my own. But she has so much unbridled energy, that she doesn't know how to control yet, and doesn't know how to use, that I think I actually tapped into it and for lack of a better word; literally fed off it."

"Hmm, that sounds interesting."

"What will be interesting is if I bring it up one day in discussion with her and see if she actually sensed anything.

"Such as. .?"

"I don't know. It doesn't seem possible that I could draw off that much energy without her being aware of it. It would have to manifest itself in some form…a dream possibly. I can't say for sure."

"So this story your about to tell me, she actually released it."

"In the sense that she was the trigger: absolutely!"

"And it's a good one."

"Oh yes. That's why I have to tell it without interruption. It's like a video's playing in my head. I'm seeing places, people, names, the whole shebang. And I feel that if I don't get it out in one shot my head's going to explode. So do you understand now?"

"The readers have always enjoyed the explanations that were provided in your past stories. You know that you swamp them in so many details that if you didn't take the time to understand the actual connections with real history, you would have lost them."

"Don't take it so hard, John. Some of my stories are self-explanatory and don't require a running commentary."

"That would be a first," he remarked snidely.

"Oh, aren't we witty today. The fact is, that the story I'm about to tell you has been more of a legend than an actual history. Some even describe it as a myth. Now I can actually tell you that it was a story of my family. Won't be like the other stories. There aren't going to be any major archeological breakthroughs that suddenly prove that everything I told you was the truth. This one you're going to have to accept entirely on faith. Whether it happened as I tell you, or involved events that were entirely different, no one will ever prove. Of all the family tales, this one's the enigma. Because why would I have such a story buried so deep in my memory if it wasn't preserving a kernel of truth? Yet, if it was true, how could such a fantastic legend not have been recorded elsewhere. It had all the makings of a great epic, yet now, the recounting is so shattered it's barely recognizable. Nothing more than a story of a boogey man used to frighten misbehaving children."

"But obviously someone in your family preserved the story."

"Yes and that's why I'm able to tell it to you today. I'm certain there's someone that has a full account recorded somewhere. There were other families involved. And no matter how many lies are used to cover up the truth, even the greatest of liars leaves a record of what they've done. So I think though this recollection is unique only to myself there's a written record somewhere out there."

"But there has to be something."

"There is. Definitely! There are a couple of statues and a tale in Czechoslovakian lore that renders it nothing more than an enchanting fairy tale. But this time I'm going to give your readers something different. I'm going to bring that fairy tale to life!"

§ § § § § §

Rome; September, 1588

The columned halls were illuminated by hundreds of flickering-torches, lit with great pomp and ceremony by the monks that miraculously appeared from the emptiness that rang hollow with each footstep. At the end of the great hall were rows of chairs, dominated by the papal throne that sat much higher and perpendicular to the others upon its own semi-circular purple dais. Beside these was a golden laver created by the hands of a master artisan so precise that it appeared to be floating in mid air with no visible means of support. Upon closer examination, one could see that it was an optical illusion. The laver stand cut to the same design as the pulpit that was immediately behind it. But to those standing but a few yards away, the stand was virtually invisible.

The pontiff waited impatiently, his back to the guards while they led their prisoner into his presence.

"Bow to his holiness," one of the guards commanded as he struck the well-dressed stranger on the back with his ceremonial staff.

Their prisoner remained upright refusing to bend. In his entire life he had never bowed to any man and he was determined that he was certainly not about to start. Not under these circumstances.

The next blow from the staff struck him across the back of the neck and he began to swagger dizzily. The gravelly voice of the guard barked out another command but by this time his charge could barely discern what he said. It was laced with insults but that didn't matter to him. His eyes were rotating wildly but he could ascertain from the moving shadows that another strike was about to rain down. He braced himself for the next blow, withdrawing his neck into his shoulders, shielding himself as best as he could, and waiting for the inevitable. Only when the sting of the metal didn't come to pass, did he open his eyes to see what had gone right.

The guard's arm remained motionless in mid flight; the supreme pontiff having interceded with a stern command.

"This man is our guest and I need him alive," the Pope exclaimed. He leaned over the stooped figure and extended his hand upon the shoulder, more as a gesture of steadying the prisoner than any act of mercy or sympathy.

"May all your guests be so graciously entertained," the captive responded.

"Be grateful for the mercies I extend to you. You are hardly in a position to refuse them," the aged pontiff cautioned with the wave of a gnarled finger.

"Should I have the opportunity to extend the same hospitality to you in the future, be assured you will not find me wanting."

With a wave of his hand, the Pope instructed his guard to finish the delivery of the restrained blow. There would be no tolerance for discourtesy.

The malicious force caused the prisoner to drop to his knees, but no sooner did he touch the marbled floor, he was scrambling to rise once again.

"You know, none of this is necessary, if you would just agree to accept the mission that I propose to you," Sixtus advised. "Truly it would be in your best interest, Caesar, and all this can be avoided and ended agreeably."

"You abduct me from my home in the middle of the night, transport me across the border into Italy, keep me prisoner for a crime that I never committed, and demand that I agree to a task that you refuse to tell me. I can't see how any of this has been in my best interest," Caesar summarized his situation sarcastically.

"Did I ever tell you that when I was a young boy, I had met your father," Pope Sixtus reminisced. "I bet you didn't know that. Your father had come to Italy for reasons unknown to me and I, as a young friar, was merely walking humbly along the road. When we passed, he stared musingly at me and cried out that one day I would be Pope."

"And you resent my father for telling you your future?"

"No, I resent your father, Michel Nostradamus, for having a gift that he did not deserve. God's gifts should be given only to those that are believers. Those that merit them, not to some carnival master who performed parlor tricks for the aristocracy and the wealthy."

"My father had a different version of that story."

"Pray tell."

"He told me that he was traveling on the road when he saw the young Franciscan monk, Felice Peretti. He was so grieved to see that he would become Pope one day that he knelt before him and started to cry. And when you asked him why he was crying, it was due he said, "Because you would become Pope one day." Trust me, those weren't tears of joy."

"And that is exactly why a non-believer should never be granted such a rare gift."

"My father was most definitely a believer in God."

"But who's God? I know that Nostradamus still practiced Judaism. Which means that you are probably guilty of the same heresies?"

"Surely, you did not drag me hundreds of miles to accuse me of being a Jew. The diocese in St. Remy would have verified my devoutness as a Catholic and saved you this trouble."

"If your Jewishness was a concern to me, I would have had tried and executed in your home town in France. Obviously, it is not why I had my men retrieve you and bring you to Rome." Sixtus spat out the words contemptuously.

"Considering the execution of a convert would have disastrous effects on your future attempts to persuade others to join the Church, I hardly believe my death would have benefited you. Those that are non-Christians cannot be accused of heresy and punished by the Church. But should they convert and then you accuse them of heresy, then you are within your power to kill them. By punishing me, you would destroy any chance of convincing others to convert. That would be too great a loss of fortune, even for you!"

"Why do you continue to antagonize me? Why can't you trust me?"

"Trust? This requested by the man who asked the people to trust him to bring the lawlessness of the bandits to an end and make the road safe for passage? How many bandits did you kill in the process? Ten thousand; perhaps fifteen thousand?"

"I have been told that it was closer to twenty-seven thousand by my inquisitors."

"My humble apologies for underestimating the number," Caesar apologized facetiously. "A few hundred bandits on the roads and you've exterminated the equivalent of an entire town. And then you confiscated their property to pay for your debts. So how can you speak of trust?"

"Merely the malicious wagging of malodorous tongues," Sixtus countered, his voice now crackling with anger.

"But true enough, nonetheless."

"Do not try my patience, Caesar. My generosity does have limits."

"As does my patience," Caesar warned. "Or have you forgotten the deal we have?"

"A deal that my predecessors should never had made. One does not deal with the devil, nor should I say, the son of the devil. You have used your threat of publication of your father's letters for over twenty years now. It's time to give it a rest."

"Should anything happen to me, my father's remaining quatrains will be published. The documents are lodged with people that will see to it."

"Of that I have no doubt. Your father was clear that he had predictions regarding the future of the Church. Dire predictions that would spell our demise or so he claimed. But your threat grows hollow with time. Soon, no one will care what Nostradamus had said or didn't say.

You won't be able to hold your precious letters over our head when that day comes."

"Then I will ensure that I leave at least two marks to my church for my entombment."

"Ha," Sixtus laughed at Caesar's sheer audacity. "That is at least one more than you father left it.

Caesar smiled in return. "I would not want it said that I was a miser compared to my father."

"A little joke by your father as I understood it," the Pope smirked. "He had them build a fabulous tomb into the church wall with the promise of a worthy donation, and he leaves them a single mark. But you, he left a sizable fortune as well as his writings. You've lived your entire life as a mere shadow of your father. He knew you had no special gifts. He had to protect you and so he left the publishing of his papers to you. The only way he could secure your life and protect you from the reach of the Church. But he failed. For all of his ability to see the future, he forgot one thing; that time is the enemy to all of us. In time we are all forgotten. And when Michel Nostradamus is forgotten, then he can no longer protect his beloved son!"

"That day will be a long time in coming when the world forgets the words of my father!"

"It needs not come to that," Sixtus suggested. "If you do this task, I will provide you with the Church's protection. No man will challenge your fortune afterwards. You will be given eternal clemency and a position as a magistrate that you may be a guardian unto yourself. A papal edict will enforce it and you will carry it with you always."

"And if I don't agree?"

"Then I will take my chance that time has already buried the words of your father and I will take everything from you. All that Michel Nostradamus was and that you are will belong to the Church. And his joke of a single mark will not be so funny when I take all that you own and add it to the Vatican coffers. Who will be laughing then?"

"So, why pick me for this task?"

"Because the prophecies have called for a failed prophet!"

"I don't understand."

"You don't have to.

"And if I do this thing, how do I know you will keep your word?"

"The same way that I must trust you not to publish your father's remaining quatrains."

"But you said that it didn't matter anymore; that the world has forgotten my father in the intervening years. So that can no longer be reassuring to me."

"I said that we can surmise that the world has lost its taste for magicians and seers. But if you were to succeed in this mission, then suddenly you will have turned the table completely. Once again the name of Nostradamus will be on everyone's lips and whatever they had forgotten will be refreshed. Once again you will hold the sword of Damocles over the head of the Vatican. And it will be I that has to trust you to keep your word."

"And if I was to fail in this mission of yours?"

"If you were to fail, then there would be no need for either of us to be concerned with issues of betrayal. You will be dead, and I will probably be soon to follow you into the afterlife."

Caesar looked discomforted by the Pontiff's reply. "So my choice is to either undertake a mission which clearly must be dangerous as my only options are to succeed or die, or to refuse you and have my life ruined by the Church as you steal my possessions and leave me destitute."

"Finally, you understand."

"And what mission could be so great that you are willing to gamble its success or failure on such an unworthy soul, as myself?"

"I am having you escorted to Prague. There you will be met by others that will share the mission with you. The details will be explained to you along the way. But in order for you to have an estimation of the significance of your mission, I'm asking you to stop Armageddon."

"Is that all?" Caesar laughed sarcastically. "You have me kidnapped, beaten, threatened, and now you want me to save the world. I believe you must have me mistaken for someone that can work miracles."

"If there were any others, any one from my own enclave that I could entrust with this mission, I swear to you I would gladly lay this at their feet than have to rely on the likes of you and the others that will await you in Bohemia. It actually sickens me to think that should you succeed this Church will have to be beholding to you."

"Sick enough to die?"

"I could not live in a world that would acclaim you and the others as its saviors. The vomit already surges in my throat when I think about it."

"Good! I'll do it."

2

Prague: September, 1588

A mailed fist hammered against the solid oak door.

"Go away!" the voice screamed back in annoyance.

The soldier was ordered to knock once more.

"What part of go away don't you understand?" the corporal-less voice emanated from behind the wooden door.

Dressed in a purple and gold ruffled shirt and pantaloons, the man obviously in charge of the garrison ordered the soldiers to kick the door in. Two of the soldiers, using their pikes to balance upon raised their steel clad feet and struck the door like twin battering rams. The lock splintered, held momentarily and then gave way, the door swinging inwards and exposing the shadowed interior of the candle-lit room.

The man in the bed, sprung up immediately, angry at the intrusion and seemingly oblivious to the fact that he was naked. The two women in the bed with him squirmed nervously, wrestling with the blankets in a vain attempt to cover their nude bodies.

The leader of the garrison moved his head from side to side, surveying the three of them in the bed, shaking it in an obvious display of disapproval. The two women were natural redheads, sisters if the uncanny resemblance meant anything. Somewhere between eighteen and twenty years of age judging by the firmness of their bodies, he guessed.

"Excellency, I did not know it was you," the man apologized. The man in the bed was dark in complexion, forty at most, thin of build but his eyes glistened brightly, even in the dimly lit room. The thin lips of his mouth spread into a hugely broad smile and the whites of his teeth contrasted sharply with the swarthiness of his skin.

"And had you known it was me Giordano?"

"Then I would have left the door unlocked," he gloated joyfully.

Sitting on the corner of the mattress, the extravagantly clad leader positioned his large frame awkwardly at right angles to the inhabitants of the bed. The women shook nervously beneath the covers that they had finally wrestled to cover their nakedness.

"Are you ever going to behave properly, my friend?" he asked Giordano.

"When I grow up," he quipped.

"And when will that ever be? Or is that a question to which there is no answer and I should know better?"

"Excellency, God has made man in a multitude of characters so that we will always remain unpredictable. How utterly boring life would be if we were all cut from the same cloth."

"Are you now going to preach to me your philosophies on life and design of the universe?"

"Your Highness, I am sitting here naked, half spent, and my manhood throbbing like a cork on a fishing line. There are two beautiful women in my bed and ten lancers in fall armor between myself and every exit in this room. On the corner of my bed sits the Holy Roman Emperor himself. If that isn't a sublime representation of the universe and the paradox that is life itself, then I don't know what is!"

"Giordano, you must try to behave in a manner far more acceptable to your position."

"And how should I do that, pray tell? I am merely a single thought in all of creation; nothing more than a mere moment in time, coming and going in the blink of an eye in comparison to the entire span of existence. How I behave, or how I conduct myself is meaningless in the overall scheme of things."

"Normally I would appreciate the glibness of your tongue, but it's time you start taking matters more seriously. You, my friend are in a lot of trouble, and you're not helping yourself by this cavalier behavior. How long do you think I can protect you?"

"Estimating from the suddenness of your intrusion this evening, I would guess not very long," Giordano responded wryly.

"One of us has to take our positions seriously," the Emperor sighed. "Even kings have to be responsible to others."

"And by others, you mean the Pope," Giordano countered.

"By others, I mean the obligations that come with our positions."

"And in this case your majesty, the Pope."

"Why do you insist on vexing me? I am heir to the throne of Europe. All men bend to my will. Nations lay down before me. The name of Rudolf is known throughout the world. I have no master save myself."

"Except the Pope," Giordano insisted, a huge smile upon his face.

Exacerbated, the Emperor released a huge sigh. "Yes, except the Pope. The man is a constant thorn in my side. He insists I do what he says, or else he'll give the throne to my brother. Every week I receive messages from him inquiring when I intend to start his war against the Turks. The man is an absolute troglodyte. He still fashions himself as a crusader, destined to free the Holy Land from the Muslims. Bohemia has become one of the richest nations in the world because of the peace and trade I share with my neighbors to the East and he's insisting I paint a red cross upon my forehead and I attack the very people that have helped make this country prosperous. Everywhere I look I find his menials insidiously spreading rumors and innuendo throughout the land, calling for my head. And I in turn am defenseless, unable to touch him because he is protected by God."

"Or so he claims."

"Claims or not, the truth is that he's untouchable; even from the hands of the Emperor."

"He is despised by the people. Given enough rope, he will hang himself. He will not be the first Pope to be forcibly dragged from his pulpit by the people of Rome and flailed to within an inch of his death."

"And when will that be? How many thousands of his enemies and detractors has he killed by accusing them of being brigands? Soon there will be no one left to oppose him."

"And this has something to do with why you are here?" Giordano inquired. "Am I the latest of his detractors to make his list for execution? Has he grown so powerful that you have come to do his handiwork?"

Rudolf shot from the bed, angrily shaking a fist. "Do not accuse me of being so immoral that I could turn so easily upon a friend. I am no Judas."

"But nevertheless, this does have something to do with a demand of you by Sixtus."

"Yes! But it's not in the manner which you think. Get dressed and I will tell you of it."

"And the girls?"

"Send them home. You are finished for the night. We have much to talk about."

Giordano rose from the bed and walked over to the dressing table that held a porcelain laver filled with water. He splashed the water on his face and then toweled himself dry. Looking to the floor he found his frock and pulled it over his head. The hood hung loosely over his back and with the tasseled cord, he tied the cloak firmly around his waist.

Rudolf looked at his friend with amusement as he watched him straighten his mantle. "Are you certain you're a priest?" he jested.

"The Lord forgives you for your doubts, my son," Giordano made the sign of the cross in the air as he spoke.

"You never cease to amaze me Giordano. How many sins can you commit in a single night?"

"You can hardly fault me for desiring a close relationship with my parishioners. There is no sin for seeking heaven on earth." Giordano turned to the two women that had emerged from behind the covers, their heads peeking sheepishly above the sheets and winked affectionately at them both.

"And this is why you are constantly in trouble with the Church. They say you dishonor the robes you wear and you don't seem to care."

"I don't care and that is the truth of the matter. I don't believe Christ denied himself the pleasure of life, so why should I?"

"Then why be a priest at all?"

"We have been over this many times. In order to receive a university education, it was necessary that I join the Dominican order. In Italy, the Church has a monopoly on advanced education. What was I to do? My mind sought to be nourished by the fount of knowledge and this was the only way that I could do so. But it is not a fraternity one can join without a price. Once you have entered you cannot leave. To do so brands you a heretic, and for that they will burn you at the stake. So I must stay within the order, but it does not mean that I must live the life they chose for me."

"How long have you been on the run? How long have you been unable to set foot in your homeland? Unable to see your family? Unable to take joy in the fruits of your labors?"

"And you think they will let me do so, if I start behaving in a manner that meets their approval?"

"Could you at least try to act more appropriately?"

"I am acting appropriately. Man is meant to have heirs. I'm ensuring that there is a balance."

Rudolf winced slightly at the barb he knew was directed at him and the life-style he had chosen.

"Could you not leave it to someone else to ensure that the balance is maintained?"

"It is the least I can do for a friend," Giordano smiled.

As the two men were escorted from the room by the garrison, the Emperor's face transformed dramatically. Now grave and serious, Rudolf was not about to condone any further attempts at frivolous humor from the wayward priest.

"Giordano, they are willing to give you another chance."

"And to what do I owe this act of mercy?"

"I think I may have been responsible and I hope you will forgive me."

"Now I know I'm in trouble. When it is necessary to forgive you for obtaining my clemency then this can only be bad."

"The killings in the city have reached the ears of the Vatican. They are very concerned. Several of the victims as you know have been clergy. They believe the attacks are directed against the Church. The Bishop that was killed was Sixtus's nephew. He has come to the conclusion that these aren't random killings but assassinations commissioned and condoned by me."

"So how have I become involved?"

"Of course I denied their accusations. Just as many magistrates in the city have disappeared as did clergy and it is foolish to think that I would do away with my own people. But the Pope is not convinced. He would be delighted if he could bring down my reign and so he asked for a test of faith."

"Are you asking me to hear your confession?"

"Oh, if it was only that simple! His Holiness has come to the belief that if it isn't my doing outright, then it must be the result of some offense I have committed. His advisors have convinced him that this all stems from my relationship with you."

"I'm sorry," Giordano apologized.

"I'm not. You have been a good friend and teacher. At least they did not accuse our relationship of being a physical one. I'd hate to ruin your reputation," the Emperor laughed.

"It is good to see that you can still laugh at your predicament."

"That is the crux of the matter. It is not so much my predicament as it is yours. The Pope believes that the only result that can come from a friendship between a Holy Roman Emperor and a heretic priest is the end of the world. This stalker in the night he blames on us."

"And so?"

"And so he wants you to put an end to it."

"Me?"

"Try to understand Giordano; there are some ancient texts in their library that speak of these events. To counter doomsday a renegade priest is required. I do not know the full details but others are being sent to aid you. Together you will face the devil and destroy him."

"So there's a happy ending to this story."

"You will either destroy him or perish yourselves. But to fail means the end of God's kingdom on earth."

"And the down side is…"

"I have placed my head on the chopping block. Should you fail, I have agreed to abdicate. They will plunge this world into endless bloodshed as soon as they have a new Emperor that kneels before them. Thousands, hundreds of thousands will die and we all will be plunged back into the dark ages after so many years of clawing our way out of the abyss. You are a man of letters, just like me. All those lives lost would be tragic, but the loss of knowledge, just as we're on the verge of understanding, that would be too horrific to bear."

Giordano nodded his head. "If I fail they will bring on Armageddon through their own stupidity. I cannot let that happen."

"So you will do this?"

"You are the light to guide this empire out from the darkness that has consumed us for so long. How often do you think enlightened Emperors come along? I can't afford to have you replaced by someone inferior like your brother. I will be your champion."

"Do you realize that we don't even know what you're facing? Several nights ago my city constable became the latest victim of this demon. This was a man experienced in all manner of weaponry. They say that when they found the pieces of his body there was no evidence that he had even landed a single blow. I do not know what this bodes for you, my friend."

"And they promised my absolution if I succeed?"

"It was one of the conditions I insisted upon. It is only fitting that if you save the world, you should have the opportunity to return to you home as a free man."

"I will not fail you, Excellency. You have given me a reason to believe."

"And Giordano…"

"Yes, your Majesty."

"Try to behave."

3

Brody; September 1588

The patrol descended upon the city of Brody like a plague of angry ants, swarming through the town center with little regard to the people fleeing from their path. “Make way for the embassage of his Holiness, Pope Sixtus,” they bellowed as they used their lances to clear a path for the sinister black carriage that rolled quietly behind. The men in their black cloaked garments and feathered hats all in black were a strange sight to all that witnessed their arrival through partially barred doors and shuttered windows. Brody was a merchant town, established on the main corridor of goods passing between east and west. As such, it had no allegiance to any particular state or ruler. Tribute was paid to the Polish King, but even he made no official claim to Brody. That was the way it had always been since its inception credited five hundred years earlier. The first waves of merchants and businessmen had made that a major point in the town’s constitution. In order to be a safe for the trade routes running from east to west and in the opposite direction as well, then it could not be anything but a universal city dominated by no particular faith, creed or government. A free city as the townspeople referred to it. Free of the inquisition or so they thought until this day when the riders in their black dress, carrying the Vatican insignia on their standards, strode on horseback through their downtown corridor.

Asking for directions from a young boy that revealed no apparent fear of the platoon, choosing instead to parade along side in the pretense of being a soldier, they were shunted towards the main road leading to the western half of the city. The lead rider tossed the boy a silver coin in appreciation, chuckling to himself as he watched the lad trying to retrieve it from the pile of dung in which it had landed.

The route pointed to by the boy drew them into the southern quarter of the city. With the crossing of the bridge over a small stream that traversed the length of the city, the patrol reacted as if they had entered another country. Everything was suddenly different. Whereas the north quarter flourished with open market places, this southern quarter had only shops and stores, all with signs in Hebrew script that meant nothing to an outsider. The lavish fountains and ornate statues of the other quarters were visibly absent, leaving only a large, barren central plaza that served as the front courtyard to the synagogue that dominated this district. Its high gates and high walls gave it the appearance of a castle more than a house of prayer.

Adjoining the massive stone wall that encircled the synagogue was an equally impressive home, with its turrets and high portico through which the horsemen and the carriage easily passed. Tying their horses to the posts in the front yard, the platoon leader strode to the front door accompanied by his two standard bearers. The large brass ring on the oak door boomed like a drum as the commander struck it against the block three times.

The ornate wooden door rolled back on its hinges and the commander was greeted by a sexagenarian, easily a head shorter in height. Dressed in a blue velvet robe with a matching four cornered hat, his prayer shawl over his shoulders, the owner of the house looked his uninvited guest up and down and then at the two men beside him but did not say a word.

"Are you the leader of the Jewish Community in Brody?"

"I am him."

"I was told that you would be a younger man; a man in his forties."

"You asked for their spiritual leader and I am he."

As if that was his signal, the passenger in the carriage opened the door and stepped down from his conveyance. Similar in height and appearance to the owner of the house, the contrast of his red velvet robes, covered by a black embroidered cloak of impeccable taste and his red hat gave the appearance of two opposing chess pieces. The Cardinal stood behind his commander and looked squarely at the man in the blue robes.

"This cannot be him," the Cardinal openly voiced his opinion.

"I can assure you that it is true. Anyone in the city will confirm it."

"You are their Prince. The one they call Yakov Kahana?"

"You asked for the leader of this community. Not for some pretender to a failed promise. You want to deliver a message to the leader of this community then you deliver it to me.

Motioning his right hand in a half forward circle, the Cardinal instructed his commander to deliver another kind of message.

With almost sublime ease, the commander's fist raked across the face of the older man.

"Is that message clear enough for you?" the Cardinal inquired.

Spitting out the blood that painted his teeth from a cut lip, Ben Shakna held up his hand to stave off any further blows. "He cannot help you. He holds no power here."

"Either bring me to him, or suffer another example of my growing impatience."

"My son-in-law is of no use to you. He knows nothing that would be considered of value to you."

"He has something that we require. It is not for you to decide what he does or doesn't possess."

"The fool doesn't have anything of value that he owns. If it wasn't for me providing him with money now and then, he'd probably let my daughter starve along with her children."

"Hit him again."

The blow came so swiftly that no one could actually say they saw the commander's arm move.

"What was that for?"

"For allowing your daughter to live in poverty while it is obvious from your surrounding that you have no lack of comforts. And for letting a man whose bootstraps you aren't even fit to tie, live in the shadow of your contempt."

"I will take you to him, but mark my words; he will be of no value to you. I am the leader of the community, not him."

"No, you are nothing more than an overstuffed peacock. For all your sakes, you better hope he knows far more than you are willing to acknowledge."

"He's a philosopher, a dreamer. Most times he doesn't even appear to live in this world."

"Be it so, it seems strange that you'd marry your daughter to such a man if he had so little worth."

"In order to neutralize the threat, I'd marry all my daughters to him if it would eliminate the hold his family has on the minds of the naïve."

"So you acknowledge that he has some power over the people. And the truth of the matter is that you married your daughter to him in order to legitimize any authority you believe you have over this community."

"I said no such thing. Only that the stories and legends about his ancestors still fills gullible minds with unrealistic nonsense about the kingdom to come. Men who believe in such things will do foolish things that will ultimately harm us all. By keeping him close I can see to it that he causes us no harm."

"What a noble sacrifice; your daughter's life in order to keep his corrupting influence ineffectual. Or would it be more likely that you fear his very essence and the blood he contains within. Use your daughter as a vessel to contain that power in descendants of your own and then you could wield the magic. Is that not the more likely scenario?"

"I am a man of God, what beliefs would I have concerning magic. There's no such thing."

"You are a filthy Jew and power is all that your kind ever seeks. And we know you well, Israel ben Shakna. You were a disappointment to your father and whatever biblical commentaries you have published they were plagiarized from your father's notes."

"How dare you say that? My father wrote nothing. All of the tractates are my own."

"Do not mistake us for fools. Though we care little for you as a people, we can still appreciate your genius in biblical understanding. We actually collect and review everything you rabbis publish. And in your case, we knew your father's teachings well. Shalom Shakna was too modest to publish and too humble to consider himself worthy of any praise. But his oral teachings were recorded by our own people that we employ for such service. People who actually live within your own community. And remarkably, everything you have published under your own name matches our records of your father's teachings."

"That is slander! I will not permit it in my own house! You can all leave now!" Ben Shakna attempted to close the door but the commander's heavy leather boot placed strategically within the door frame prevented that from occurring. He then pushed the door open, tossing ben Shakna off balance so that he stumbled backwards a couple of steps.

"Hit him again," the Cardinal ordered.

This time he was struck in the midriff with enough force that he buckled over from the blow.

"Do not dare to be so presumptuous to tell me what you will or will not permit. Now where is your son-in-law?"

With tears in his eyes, and gasping wildly for his breath, Israel ben Shakna motioned with his outstretched arm for the Vatican delegates to follow. Holding his belly, his legs visibly trembling, he attempted to walk the length of the hallway to the rear of the house. Exiting into the rear courtyard, he pointed towards a crumbling hut, easily mistaken as nothing more than a dilapidated shed."

"In there?" the Cardinal questioned angrily.

Israel ben Shakna nodded his head.

"How dare you treat a prince of the blood in such a manner? Hit him again!"

Now relishing in his work, the commander unleashed a stunning blow to the back of the Rabbi's head, knocking him off his feet and he toppled to the ground.

"Hit him again and you will not find what you seek," stated the tall man with a short spikard black beard as he emerged from the structure.

"Why protect him? Look how he treats you. He has made you live in this sty while he lives in luxury just yards away from you."

"It's a stable," blurted out one of the accompanying priests.

"What?" the Cardinal responded to the interruption.

"A stable Excellency! Look, just like in the gospels!" An observation which suddenly set the rest of the Vatican contingent murmuring with excitement.

The Cardinal looked at the structure and realized that his young priest was correct. It was an old stable that had been purposely renovated into a home.

"It is my home," the man commented calmly, his voice rising just above the chatter of everyone else. "It is where my wife and children live. Call it what you like but it is our home."

"It still does not make it right," the Cardinal exclaimed.

"And that is my father-in-law," he pointed at ben Shakna. "The father of my wife and as the grandfather of my children, he deserves our respect."

"And I am Guillermo Calabrese, senior cardinal and advisor to his holiness, Pope Sixtus. And as an advisor I can tell you that man shows no respect to anyone."

"And how does the perpetration of evil against him justify the punishment of a perceived evil?"

"There are times when it is necessary to use evil in order to achieve a greater good," Guillermo responded.

"But this is not that time!" the son-in-law shouted.

"I will defer to your greater wisdom," the Cardinal bowed. "You are obviously Yakov Kahana, whom I've been sent to find.

"I am."

"Then you must know that our presence here is a sign of the final days."

"I know your presence here can only mean that the worst is yet to come. Your kind has always cut a very wide swath."

"We must do what is necessary in order save mankind."

"Yes, I know…the performance of evil in order to achieve a greater good. You have already told me that. So what evil can I expect to befall us?"

"It is one that you have the power to prevent."

"So tell me what it is I'm preventing."

"I have been instructed to tell you that should you fail to comply, that this will be the last Jewish New Year your community celebrates. If you do not accept or you fail, then in one year's time we will send an army against this quarter of the city and we will utterly destroy it."

From behind the drapes leading into the other half of the building, a woman gasped in horror.

"This is how you ask for my help. If I decline to help you, or even if I accept but fail, you will destroy all that I love and hold dear. Cardinal Calabrese, you have a very peculiar manner of asking for help. Already you have frightened my wife half to death."

"My apologies if I've upset your wife. These are matters of grave import and his Holiness is not to be deterred in restoring the balance of the universe."

"Ah, the balance," Yakov sighed. "Always the balance! Good versus evil! Evil versus good! But how is it that it's Jewish lives that are always weighing in the balance?"

"That too is part of the universal law. It is your fate, you cannot deny it."

"It is only our fate because men of your kind keep holding a blade to our necks."

"Then here is your chance to change that. Pope Sixtus offers you the opportunity to save your people from disaster."

"A potential disaster that only exists because your Pope has threatened to make it happen in the first place."

"It matters not. If not him, then another pope, or a king, or even one of your own like Reubeni. It is the way it will always be. But not if you accept this mission and stave off the pending disaster."

"I have no choice then but to accept," Yakov responded in exasperation.

"Not so quickly," Calabrese hesitated. "I have to make certain that you are the right one. His Holiness has provided me with several questions to test you first."

"Ask what you will."

"The Pope asks you to explain the Trinity." Guillermo Calabrese's tone became quite challenging.

"What nonsense is this?" ben Shakna interjected. "What would he, or for that matter any Jew know about your Catholic Trinity?"

With a backwards wave of his hand, Guillermo dismissed the comment while his commander made a threatening gesture that silenced the Rabbi immediately.

"If he is the one to save you, then he knows," the Cardinal provided an explanation, more so for himself than for the benefit of Israel ben Shakna.

"Command your guard to step away from him or else I will tell you nothing."

"Very well…" With a nod of his head the cardinal shunted his man to the other side of the room, "…there it is done, now tell me the answer."

"What you seek is not as you know it but rather as it once was. Before the one that became three, there were the three that became one."

A look of delightful surprise spread over the Cardinal's face. "You know, don't you?"

Once again ben Shakna cried out from his protected corner. "What nonsense is this? I've heard nothing of this before."

The commander began to move towards the other side of the room but was quickly stopped by the icy stare from his master.

Ben Shakna slithered back into the corner.

"Yes, I know what it is you seek."

"Tell me then. Who were they?"

"The Creator, the Avenger, and the Fool."

A wave of pure excitement flushed over Guillermo. "Who then was the most high?"

Yakov smiled at the eagerness of his inquisitor. "The Fool of course, for He created the earth and all that's upon it. He gave man the breath of life and set us apart from all other living things."

Guillermo shook his head in utter amazement. "How can you possibly know these things? They were the secrets that Jesus shared with his disciples alone. And the heirs of Peter have inherited them in their due course."

"No," Yakov corrected him, "these are the secrets that Jesus shared with the apostle that he trusted and in so doing betrayed the secrets of his family."

"Why are you saying such a thing?"

"Because I too am from the house of Phiabi; the same house that sprouted Jesus. And the secrets were never intended to set foot out of our house!"

"I am a servant to you, just as the Holy Father has instructed me to be. Verily, he said to me, seek this man out and if he is truly who he claims to be, then he will know the secrets that have been entrusted to us. And so it would appear to be that you are this man!"

"I have not denied that I am him that you seek."

"But that is not the same as having proved yourself now. And that trusted disciple that you spoke of. Do you know which one it was by chance?"

"Certainly not the one that your Church pays homage to since he was the one that actually betrayed Jesus and then slew the one that was trusted because he feared what he might say."

The expression on Guillermo's face grew fierce and terrible. "These things are not to be spoken of!"

"Yet you asked and I merely told you what you already knew."

The cardinal bowed with great respect. "You are the one we seek and you are the one that must help us in our time of need."

"This mission that you spoke of…this quest that threatens the very existence of my people should I refuse. Why do you need me so badly?"

"Because you are the one!" Calabrese shouted. "You cannot refuse!"

"Yet still you threaten the existence of my entire community."

"As the chosen one you cannot fail."

"There are no certainties in the divine scheme of things. That is exactly why it was the Fool that took it upon himself to create the universe. Until he merged with the Creator and the Avenger, he had not

the omnipotence to determine the outcomes of all events. And for that reason, man has been left to his own devices."

"Are you refusing the quest?"

"I have no choice but to accept. But should I fail and your Holy Father dares to lay a hand upon my people, then I will become like the vengeful harpy and will bring down the walls of the Holy See. Do we understand each other?"

"What is every one talking about?" ben Shakna shouted from his protected position in the corner of the room.

"Your son-in-law has agreed to save your worthless hide. Though I have no tolerance for you Jews, he alone is worthy of my appreciation. He is marked with a sign from above. His is the sacred blood as you well know. And that is all you have to know for now!"

"My son-in-law is a fool. Everyone knows that. A dreamer who lives in a world that died over a thousand years ago. If this community has to depend on him for its salvations then we are already doomed."

"Please let me have this pestilence that torments you, killed," Guillermo begged Yakov.

"No one is to die in my community. I have said so."

"So be it but remember that I have offered."

"No killing! If I am to go on your mission, then promise me that we have that understanding."

"Alright, but let's be off before I begin to regret my commitment to serve you."

"And exactly where do you plan on going," ben Shakna chose to interrupt into the conversation once more, ignoring all the previous warnings to remain silent.

"He is off to Prague," the cardinal responded, "and you will prepare his bags and see to it that he has enough funds to cover all his expenses."

"I will not," ben Shakna stamped his foot defiantly.

"You will take from your synagogue treasury whatever funds we require!" Guillermo ordered.

"The elders of the community will not agree to it! I do not agree to it!"

"I can suffer this man no longer," Guillermo turned to Yakov, both vexed and exasperated. "Seize ben Shakna," he ordered his commander. "I am sorry Yakov Kahana, but this man is a pariah on the face of mankind. My guards will escort him into the synagogue and the treasury will provide the money for your journey. If he refuses, then my guards will beat him severely until he complies. And if we do

so in front of all your elders then I apologize for the effrontery, but it is his own disrespect and defiance that would bring it bout. The choice is his; my men will seize the funds regardless. I do believe I am being quite reasonable. The end is his choosing, so I do not believe I will be abrogating our agreement. Now be off with him," Guillermo commanded his men.

"He is not to be hurt!" Yakov insisted.

"I know this type of man, Yakov Kahana. Trust me, he will cooperate. He values himself far above anyone else and therefore will sacrifice everyone and anything for his own self-preservation."

"He will hate me even more for this."

"He hates you enough already," Guillermo reassured. "More will not make a difference."

"And in Prague, what is it you expect from me."

"All will be explained in due time."

"Give me some time. I have to say goodbye to my wife and family."

"Ah yes, the woman behind the curtains…take your time, I will wait outside. Close up your affairs for now."

Yakov waited until the cardinal had left his home.

"Raisa, you can come out now. They are all gone."

Her eyes swollen with tears, the dark haired beauty passed though the partition in the drapes and wrapped her arms around her husband. She was easily fifteen years younger than her husband but in each other's arms, the age difference appeared meaningless. "Must you go away Kova," she asked, half begging that he would stay.

'You know it is my destiny, my darling. We knew this day would come."

"Why must it be this day? How can you be so certain that this is the destiny you were meant for?"

"How could I be anything but certain? Could there be any greater threat than the destruction of this community? Would not the saving of ten thousand people not be considered significant enough to require a savior?"

"I know you arc right but right now I am so afraid that I will not see you again. Your children might not see you again."

"Nothing short of death will keep me away from you."

"But that is what I'm so afraid of."

"Am I not the eighteenth generation since the last savior in my family? Whatever end God foresees for me, it is still with the blessing of the eighteenth. We must have faith."

"How can you be so certain of which generation you are? The records are blurred. Even you said that you could not be certain if you were the eighteenth since Mar Rav Hilai."

"Everything that is happening now suggests that I am."

"But you can't be certain, Kova."

"They're talking about the end of the world Raisa. If I am able to stop this disaster, then surely it would confirm that I must be the one."

"But what about us? How am I to go on without you?"

Yakov hugged and kissed his wife repeatedly. "You must. And I must go. But whatever happens, don't let little Yusef and Tanit forget about me. Don't let your father take my memory away from them."

"I will never let them forget you. You will see, when you return they will know everything there is about their father. I need you to come back to me. Please, come back to me."

"I will never leave you Raisa." He tapped on her chest lightly. "I will always be here. No matter how far away or how long, this is where I live."

"And this is where I live," she tapped him back on his chest, holding back the gush of tears that would follow.

4

Prague: November 1588

"Are these them?" Rudolf inquired as he looked down from his ornate throne upon the two men standing beside his friend, Giordano.

"Yes, your Highness," the Cardinal responded.

"They don't look like much," Rudolf laughed. "Are you certain that these three are going to stop the demon?"

"Wiser men than us, your highness have gone through the prophecies in the Vatican library. These are the ones."

"Have you had a chance to meet your comrades Giordano?"

"Your Majesty, not only haven't I met them, the Church in its wisdom hasn't even bothered to tell me who they are and why they're special to this mission."

Rudolf turned on Guillermo de Calabrese. "Is that true?"

"Your Highness, I cannot speak for my brethren in the Church. I have spent the last month on the road with my charge, and it is only now that I myself have laid my eyes on these other two. If brother Bruno was not told anything, it may have only been out of respect for me, that they had waited until I could tell him myself."

"It would appear to be a plausible explanation," Rudolf nodded to his friend. "Clandestine as it would appear to be, it is probably best that the three of you heard it once from the same source. So go on, Cardinal Calabrese, tell these gentlemen why they are here."

"Your Highness, this man here is Yakov Kahana; a nobleman from amongst the Jews."

"A nobleman you say?" the Emperor questioned. "I didn't think they had such a thing. Explain this to me further."

"He is descendent of Aaron and of David," the Cardinal cleared his throat in an attempt to disguise his words.

"Did I hear you right? A descendant of David?"

"Only through his female line," the Cardinal was quick to explain as if that made it insignificant.

Rudolf rubbed his forehead, appearing quite perplexed by the explanation. "I thought you clergy teach that the line of David is no more. That Jesus was the last of it."

"That is true, your Highness."

"Yet here in front of me stands a contradiction to that truth."

"Because of the female line only!" the Cardinal persisted.

"Male, female, what's the difference? Does he, or does he not have the blood of David in him?"

"Yes, but…"

"But nothing, Cardinal Calabrese. Standing here before me is living proof to the contrary of what you preach. And why is he dressed like some commoner? Couldn't you find a descent set of clothes for him? This will not do." Looking directly into Yakov's eyes, Rudolf addressed him. "Are you able to understand German?"

"I am fluent in the language, your Majesty."

Rudolf clapped his hands with delight. "Oh, good! We are going to have so much to talk about. And do not address me as your majesty. I believe you outrank me in birth."

"Nonsense your Majesty, I am nothing but a humble philosopher."

"Nonsense yourself! You are a king and a high priest of the old temple. No matter what that person over there says," he pointed directly at Guillermo, "none of us are fit to carry your shoes."

Yakov bowed his head in humility.

"Never apologize for who you are," the Emperor instructed. "Lord knows if I started doing that, there'd be no end to it. These Catholics know that I have as little to do with the religion as possible, which serves to drive them absolutely insane, since I'm their Holy Roman Emperor. But then they're their own worst enemies, aren't they. Parade you in here and announce that you are King of the Jews."

"I did not say that," Calabrese was quick to refute.

"Oh, yes you did. Not exactly in those words, but you did say it," Rudolf corrected him. "And if he is the King of the Jews as you proclaimed, then you have some serious explaining to do about Jesus."

"Give me the chance to explain, your Highness."

"Explain what, Cardinal? That your kind has preached a pack of lies for years, and meanwhile all the time you knew where this man was. I think that is explanation enough. So how do they call you, Yakov Kahana."

"Just that, your Majesty."

"We'll have to work on that; too long and too difficult! And who is this other one?"

Looking somewhat sheepish, the Cardinal announced quietly, "Caesar de Nostradame."

"Caesar de Nostradame…Caesar de Nostradame…why is that name so familiar?"

"Probably because of my father, your Highness."

"You speak German as well. How absolutely glorious! Even if there is a heavy French accent I detect. So who was your father?"

"Michel de Nostradame, your Majesty. The one called Nostradamus."

"My lord, you're the son of Nostradamus. Why do you look like you've been sleeping in your clothes for a month? And they're tattered. I heard that your family was of some substance. Has something terrible befallen you?"

"Nothing but the Church, your Majesty. I did not leave France under the best of terms. In fact I was kidnapped to Rome, beaten, and put on the road exactly as they found me that night in September. I really wasn't given the opportunity to change my clothes."

"This is not acceptable, Cardinal!" he roared. "I do not like what I am seeing here." Rudolf's puffy face began to glower with pending rage.

"Your Majesty, Master Nostradamus tends to exaggerate somewhat in his telling of the events."

"No, I don't think so," Caesar commented. "Let me think about it for the moment. Kidnapped, beaten, threatened, transported to Prague without a single mark in my pocket, no that seems to sum it up pretty accurately."

Guillermo laughed nervously. "He has such a clever wit," he remarked. "I'm certain it wasn't exactly as he described, after all, he did volunteer to come on this mission."

"And did you volunteer as well," Rudolf inquired of Yakov.

"Only after the Cardinal threatened to kill my entire community if I did not agree. But what he did not realize, had he asked me to come on this mission without the threat, I would have agreed regardless."

"And why was that?"

"Because it is my destiny!"

"And of what community do you speak? Is it with my domain that I can offer it my protection?"

"I am from Brody, in Galicia, your Highness."

"Brody. I have heard of it. But it is beyond my borders. Is it a significant sized community?"

"We refer to it as the New Jerusalem, for never have so many Jews been gathered in a place where we live in virtual peace and harmony."

"Until this threat!"

"Yes, until now."

"And what about you Caesar?"

"Without the threats I would have come too. My father had predicted it so."

"Do you know that when I was a young man, twenty-five years ago, your father sent me a horoscope he personally prepared for me? I did not understand most of it back then, but this evening much of it is becoming clear to me. Giordano, what do you make out of all of this?"

"Excellency, I can only say that we are in fine company. Except for maybe Cardinal Calabrese over there."

"I agree with you totally," Rudolf nodded in compliance. "You may leave us now Cardinal."

"I don't think that is wise your Highness. There is still the matter of explaining the full breadth of the mission to these men. And the Pope has asked me personally to stay with them for the entirety of the mission."

"Unless you were thinking of accompanying them on their task and placing yourself in danger Cardinal Calabrese, I cannot think of what possible value you could be to them from this point onwards. And since I know of this mission in far greater detail than you do, I don't see why I can't tell them of it. Do not be offended. They will report to you regularly so you can send word back to your superiors, but for now you are dismissed."

"Your Highness, this is most unwise."

Sitting up straight in his throne, Rudolf grew a head taller. He was a big man in weight and size, but the change of color in his ruddy complexion made him appear huge by comparison to everyone else in the chamber. "Leave now Cardinal or I will have you escorted out!"

Stamping his foot, Calabrese swirled about on his heels and stormed from the chamber.

"Good, now we can talk freely," Rudolf advised them. "My apologies to you all for the circumstances that have brought you together but these are not good times. Would you not agree Giordano?"

"No definitely not. I now understand what the Holy Father is up to and I can't say I like it all."

"Forgive me for not understanding it myself sooner but even I have to be answerable to the Church at times. As few times as that might be, this was one of them."

"Your Majesty, I'm afraid I'm still at a loss," Caesar interjected.

"Please stop this 'your Majesty' political correctness nonsense. We are all friends here. I don't think Giordano has referred to me in that manner in years now except when we're in public. One of the reasons I moved my capital from Vienna to Prague was to do away with all the formalities. They're stifling at times. Just call me Rudolf."

"I don't know if I can do that," Caesar replied.

"Try it, say Rudolf."

"Rudolf."

"Again!"

"Rudolf."

"See that wasn't so difficult." The four of them laughed at the emperor's commonality. "Good, now that we are friends, let me explain. I have a dilemma. There is some creature that moves through the night and kills my people at liberty. At first it seemed directed at people that one might describe as deserving of it; criminals, bullies, thieves, and the like. Wasn't even murder at first! Just physical assaults but none of them could describe their assailant accept in terms of a ghost, or specter. It would strike them in dark alleys and out of sight of anyone else, so we never had any place to look for the criminal. But then something changed. The attacks became more vicious and it was no longer directed at the criminal element. They suddenly involved leading members of the City and the Church and then one day a priest was killed. Before long it was children and then a bishop. That is when I received notification from the Holy See that they considered that I was somehow in league with this night prowler. It was fairly obvious that I have never been a great supporter of the Catholic Church. In fact, I would not even describe myself as a good Catholic. And that is part of the problem. Even monarchs can find themselves bearing the wrath of the Church. I'm not prepared to go the route of Henry over in England, though I must admit I applaud him for it. I was faced with several choices, abdicate in favor of my brother or lead a crusade against the Turks on behalf of the Church, even though the Turkish Sultan is one of my closest allies. I choose to do neither, but instead used my offices to magnify the threat that this killer presents to the Church. At least that was my intent. To make it appear that the greatest enemy the Vatican was not the Sultan of Turkey but this demon incarnate that will destroy the house that Peter built if left to its own devices."

"Rudolf," Giordano smiled, "Your forgetting to mention the best part."

"I was getting to it," the Emperor insisted. "There were some ancient texts in the Hapsburg library that described the end of days."

"And…" Giordano Bruno prodded.

"I'm getting there. I had several scholars translate them in context of the current events of the city. They were about the Antichrist. I was able to convince the Pope that these were the days of Armageddon. And this night creature was Satan's emissary preparing the way for the coming of the Antichrist."

Yakov and Caesar stared at each other sharing the same thought simultaneously. As incredulous as it all seemed, they had been brought together because of an intentional misrepresentation of the facts.

"I know what you're thinking," Giordano dissected their train of thoughts. "Both of you have been made to suffer because of a deceit designed to trick a stupid old man sitting in Rome. But I don't think that's true any longer." Bruno held out his hand for Rudolf to finish his explanation.

"Yes, we had some ancient documents that were intentionally interpreted to my advantage. But when I started to explain it to Giordano after I set it into motion, it started to take on a life of its own. The prophesy called for a false Christ to take on the minion of the Antichrist. There would be three in this poor man's trinity; a heretic priest, a false prophet, and a king without a kingdom. The first one was easy. I had my own heretic priest that the Church has been trying to bring down for years. It took nothing for me to convince them that Giordano was that priest in the description. But the other two, I had no idea that they could be found. I had thought it would take them years of discussion, and arguing amongst themselves before they could even attempt to find two candidates to fill those shoes. In the meantime the night prowler has become even bolder in his attacks. It was almost as if it knew that I had escalated the affair to a much grander scale. Almost as if in response it did likewise increasing its range of terror within the city, going after my own magistrates, and now as I mentioned, it's begun to attack children. A reign of terror has begun and my people are growing more afraid every day."

"It is true," Bruno interceded. "It is almost as if the Emperor was meant to find those ancient documents. That what had begun merely as an attempt to dupe the Vatican into perceiving a greater threat and putting them off their pursuit of war in the east, actually became the nightmare that the scholars had described."

"And the presence of you two in this room at this moment in time," Rudolf continued is proof of the prophecy in those documents. How else could you explain that I have a false prophet and kingdomless ruler standing before me, just as the prophecy described."

"Not to mention a heretic priest as well," Giordano included himself.

"I have to disagree with you," Caesar spoke up. "It was my father that the Church referred to as a false prophet. I cannot claim that title. I have no such powers. As much as I tried, and as much as my father thought I would follow in his footsteps when he handed me his astrolabe, I have no abilities."

"But you have all of your father's writings in your possession, is that not correct."

"Yes."

"And you've already published some."

"I don't see your point."

"Your father never released his predictions to the public. It was always to select individuals, and usually only to the aristocracy. It was you that made some of his predictions available to the populace. Is that not so?"

"That is true but I'm still not following you."

"You are the false prophet. You are the one releasing the predictions and they're not even yours. If that's not a false prophet, then I don't know what is."

Caesar was left momentarily speechless. The logic was impeccable. He had never thought of it in that way, only thinking of himself as a failed prophet.

"And is it necessary that I explain your role in all this Yakov," the Emperor inquired.

"No," Yakov shook his head. "It will not be necessary. I am the one in the prophecy. That has always been without contention. From the time I was a young child I knew that I would be sent on a mission of grave importance. I cannot escape that destiny. What you thought was your own duplicity in creating an illusion was in fact your being part of that same destiny. You did what you did, not of your own accord but because you were part of a much larger scheme in the universe."

"I think you are right, Yakov."

"Kova."

"Huh…" the emperor responded in a somewhat Bohemian fashion.

"Kova. If I am to call you Rudolf, then you can call me Kova."

"Kova it is then," Rudolf slapped his thighs. "I like you King of the Jews. We will have much to talk about. I want you all to stay in my palace. The further I keep you away from the clutches of the Church the better off for all of us. Do you have any belongings that I need to bring here?"

Looking dejected, Yakov stared down at the floor before responding. "The Cardinal is holding on to all that is mine. Even the money that he took from the synagogue treasury, which belonged to the people of my community he is holding in his own keeping."

"That certainly will not do," Rudolf replied, the broad smile on his face reassuring Yakov that the matter would be dealt with properly. "The Cardinal will be informed that all your expenses will be taken care of by me. The money will be recovered from him and returned to your community by my own couriers. I will not permit a guest of mine to be treated in this manner."

"Thank you, your Majesty.

"Rudolf, remember!"

"To act so magnanimously, such an act can only be described in terms of your Majesty. Rudolf will not do."

"I will accept that. But only this once. It's Rudolf from now on. And Caesar, what about you?"

"Other than this shirt on my back and this tattered cloak, I have no possessions to worry about. I traveled light," he mused.

"That is good," the Emperor commented. "It means I can have my tailors attire you properly. Consider it payment for your father's horoscope that he sent me. He said that I would be meeting you. I wonder how he knew these things."

"My father was unique among men. I knew what he did and what he said in order to see his visions, but I have never been able to repeat them myself."

"Do you really believe it was the ritual that gave him his power?" Giordano challenged.

"I'm not following your question," Caesar responded.

"I perform a little magic myself. The ritual I do is entirely for show. To help those that are unable to comprehend my tricks to believe what they wish to believe."

"My father was not trickster."

"No, but he was a showman. And the gift must often be disguised so that a skeptical world will actually believe without question," Giordano expressed his opinion.

"And what do you think it was then, priest."

"Tsk, tsk. No need to get upset," Bruno waved his index finger back and forth in front of his face. And don't let my frock mislead you. It is part of the disguise that hides my gift; my gift of science and alchemy. It is my understanding that these gifts, or talents, or powers that might be, though they seem strange and unusual are nothing more than the soul that animates us."

"Now you are sounding like a priest," Caesar mocked.

"Accept that the soul to me is nothing more than an energy that binds all living things together. Find how to channel that energy and you have the powers and the intellect of which we speak."

"Be assured," Rudolf added further comment. "Giordano is a great scientist. Of that I can certainly attest to. But for now, let my steward show you to your accommodations. You must be tired and we will have a long day tomorrow."

"The Cardinal will be back tomorrow and he will come with a show of force," Yakov predicted.

"So he will," the Emperor agreed. "But when last I checked, I am still the supreme authority in Prague. Let tomorrow take care of itself."

5

Prague: The Castle

It came like a whisper in the night, silently creeping through the carpeted halls and vestibules, an early morning mist that had made its way into the castle during the dead of night. No one could hear it, none could see it, but it flowed nevertheless like an endless river, reaching with its tendrils into every room causing a mild chill to what had been a pleasant autumn night.

Settling over the three recently arrived guests at the castle, it nestled over their beds in an invisible shroud, perceived only in their dreams which now had fallen prey to its malevolent presence. Haunting shadows stole whatever free thought any of them may have had earlier that night, leaving only the corrupted horror of demonic visions. Each of them felt the heavy hand of mystic possession tormenting their uneasy slumbers.

Giordano Bruno, a man of science, a cynic of anything supernatural, could not escape the feeling that some force was physically reaching inside his chest and squeezing his beating heart within its slender fingers. No matter how he strived to rationalize the experience within his dream state, to explain even to his sleeping self in terms that he could deal with, he could not override the fact that what was occurring defied his defined reality. The visions of torture and suffering were overwhelming. He could feel the fire licking at the souls of his feet and the invisible flames consuming his flesh piece by piece; all that he was, all that he wanted to be, melted away like the wax of a spent candle. His conscious awareness screamed for him to wake up, to free himself of the horrible nightmare but whatever had seized hold of him would not permit him to stir, would not allow him to rise, only to suffer continuously into the small hours of the morning until such time that he awoke naturally.

Caesar cried through his sleep, overcome with the fear of failure, all the while tossing and turning in his bed, never to find respite or comfort. In the recesses of his mind he could see and hear his father looking down upon him disapprovingly. A father disappointed that his son never measured up to his expectations as either a seer or a man; a son that evaporated into nothing more than smoke in the presence of his father's greatness. He tried to call out to Michel de Nostradame, but each time his father would simply turn his head away, ashamed to acknowledge the flesh of his own body. This was not a new dream but an old familiar nightmare that he had experienced many times before, but at no time had it caused such pain and torment as it did this night. Trapped within his own feelings of impotency and inadequacy. It left him totally demoralized and devastated this particular night, at a time when he was finally on the verge of creating and accomplishing his own legacy. In the past, the nightmare had come and gone, but this night the looming face of his father hung above his bed, taunting and baiting him, criticizing the entirety of his existence.

From the distance he could hear Raisa's voice calling to him, though from where exactly, he could not determine, having lost any sense of direction. Everywhere he looked was black, bottomless, and empty. As far as he could sense, there was nothing below him, as he was set adrift into the emptiness, with no anchor to this or any other world. Only his wife's voice provided the frailest sense of connection as he drifted aimlessly but it soon faded more and more into the ever increasing distance. He was lost, gone, paled by insignificance within the void that engulfed him. Was this how it would end? Life ending in a meaningless absence without any concrete purpose; nothing more than mediocrity. The one fear that he could admit to experiencing; to leave the world without having accomplished anything of permanent value. No historical record of his being left behind. It had haunted him all his life and now he was being subjected to its expression. No matter how hard he sought to find any object within the vast void to tether to, the only sensation passing through his fingers was one of nothingness. Slowly he was becoming indistinguishable from the black abyss into which he was falling. It would eventually devour his essence as if he had never been. That particular thought scared him more than death itself. And when he felt himself to be all but lost, he awoke, his body soaked with sweat in a room that was only partially illuminated by the rising sun. He sighed with relief. He had made it through the night.

§ § § § § §

That morning the three guests at the Castle sat hunched over their breakfast of cheese and bread served to them in the dining hall, without passing a single word between them. The toasts and marmalades would have been a veritable feast for Caesar and Yakov, whom ate only a Spartan diet on their journey to Prague, but this morning they had absolutely no appetite. They had acknowledged each other's presence through grunts and nods, an observation that was quickly noted by their host.

"Good morning," Rudolf strode cheerfully into the dining hall. He was about to say, 'I trust you all had a good night's sleep,' but thought better of it when he saw the dropped chins and darkened bags beneath their eyes. "I guess the night did not pass well for any of you?" he rhetorically questioned and as anticipated he received no answer. "Well, I for one slept like a baby. Was there a problem with the beds?"

Finally Giordano Bruno spoke, breaking the self imposed silence. "No, the beds were fine. In my case it was my dreams that were not."

His attention piqued by the priest's remark, Caesar looked up from his plate, quite interested to hear what Bruno had to say. "How odd, I had my worst night of dreams as well."

"They weren't dreams, I'm afraid," Yakov finally spoke up. "They were warnings and we have to take them very seriously."

"Then you had them too," Caesar sat straight up like an arrow poised for the release.

"Warnings from whom," Bruno questioned in a tone not willing to admit that he could have experienced a mystic visitation.

"That is what we must find out gentlemen. That is where the answer to this mission will lie." No sooner had Yakov said these words then his head dropped down, to stare with closed lids at an empty plate. His mind was deep in thought, searching for an answer though to the rest it appeared as if he had fallen back to sleep at the table.

"I know that I may be speaking out of turn," the Emperor interjected, "But as the only one that appears to be somewhat in control of my faculties this morning, I think it's imperative that we pursue that line of thinking. Perhaps if each of us talks about what they saw in their dreams we can find the common denominator. If everyone is in favor, then let's begin with you Caesar. What did you see?"

"I really don't want to talk about it," Caesar refused to relate his dream sequence.

"But if you don't tell us, then we won't be able to help each other overcome this dilemma," Rudolf advised.

"Alright! It was my father," Caesar blurted, embarrassed to even talk about it. "He would not speak to me. In fact he condemned me as a disappointment."

"Is that all?" Bruno ridiculed the already agitated Caesar de Nostradame.

"Why, is that not enough for you," Caesar scowled. "My father was everything to me and I fear that I was nothing to him. But you wouldn't know anything about that. You have your vows to keep you warm at night along with your brethren."

"What are you implying by that?"

"Nothing unless there's something you'd like to tell us."

Both Caesar and Giordano lifted themselves slightly out of their chairs leaning towards each other as if to resolve their differences physically.

"Gentlemen, gentlemen, if I could kindly have your attention please." Rudolf attempted to calm the situation. "None of you are working on a full night's rest and as a result your tempers are short fused. But one thing I will not tolerate in my palace is violence of any kind. Do I make myself understood?"

"My apologies," Caesar bowed humbly, "but this priest has no right to question my relationship with my father."

"To refer to Giordano as a priest is doing him a disservice," Rudolf consoled Caesar. "I often think of him as a pain in my derrière. I am certain you will come to that same resolution in time as well."

"That's me," Bruno gloated proudly. "I'm the pain in your backside, but you will come to appreciate me."

"I somehow doubt that," Caesar commented coolly.

"Is that your greatest trepidation?" Yakov inquired, lifting his chin from his chest once more.

"Why do you want to know?" Caesar grew angry by the continual line of questioning.

"Because it is important!"

"If you insist on knowing, then yes. I have always been loath to live in the shadow of my illustrious father. Are you satisfied now?"

"Yes, I am," Yakov slowly rose from the table and then began pacing around the room while his mind digested the information.

"My greatest fear is losing my anchorage in this world. Actually separating myself from the reality of what you would refer to as our physical world. My family is all that binds me to the present. Lose them and I'm adrift in a world of dreams and historical events."

"I don't understand," Bruno responded.

"I think I do," Rudolf added. "I think any of us that come from a long line rulers have the sensation that we're always being judged against the actions of our ancestors."

"In my case it is a little more severe than just judgment by the performance of my predecessors. There are times that I cannot separate my life from theirs. I live more through them than through myself at times and that places my sanity at risk. The loss of my own persona, my own identity, my own consciousness, that is and always has been my greatest fear."

"How strange," Bruno contemplated. "That all three of us would suffer nightmares based on our greatest fears. "I am only a priest because it gave me the means to pursue my education. Otherwise I cannot claim to be the most religious of people. Science is my religion. Exploring the universe is my passion, and these two entirely opposed existences will be my doom. The more I pursue my scientific fields, the more the Church tries to condemn me and punish me for perceived crimes against my vows. Sadly, it would appear that they're winning. But I will not give up my search for truths. Dogma and myths have no place in today's world. I have no room for mystical ideals and magical beliefs in my reality. In fact I perform magical feats just for the entertainment value of showing my audience how I was able to confuse and dupe them merely through trickery based on scientific principles."

"That's very nice, but what about your fear," Caesar grew bored with Bruno's dissertation.

"I was getting to that. What if I'm wrong? What if magic does exist? What if science can't explain everything in this world? Everything I believe in would suddenly be refuted and the lies that I have fought so hard to disprove would then become the truths and I would be the liar. It was magic that assailed me last night. I swear a presence beyond scientific principle that actually entered into my body and tried to destroy me from within."

"It was a dream," Caesar reminded him.

"No, it wasn't," Bruno retorted, his voice rising by an octave. "It was more than a dream. I knew it was happening. I tried to wake up but it wouldn't let me. If it was a dream, then one cannot know while experiencing it that it's not a dream. It meant that I had to be consciously aware of what was happening and I was unable to resist it. Something was there; in my room, in my mind, squeezing the life from my body like an overripe fruit!"

"Interesting," Yakov commented, still pacing about the room as he analyzed everyone's experience from the previous night.

"What are you thinking, Kova?" Rudolf questioned.

"To have three people all experiencing dreams based on their worst fears on the same night is not a random event. For those same three people to be sharing a mission together, and have such dreams can only mean that there is a force that obviously feels threatened by our presence. Whether we choose to believe in the supernatural or not, does not discount what we experienced. Our enemy is quite real and he knows we're here to stop him. This was his first attempt to make us abandon all hope and flee from here."

"You're asking me to believe in things I cannot rationally accept," Bruno replied, extremely discomforted by the explanation.

"Who says the world must always be rational? I do not discount your science, but even science is nothing more than another means of making miracles happen. It is but an infant compared to the mystical studies that have been refined over the past millennia. Given time, it may have all the answers, but for now we must deal with the old beliefs."

"Meaning?"

"Meaning if we have an enemy that is convinced that they have power through mystical means, who are we to say that their reality cannot be manifested?"

Rudolf rolled over the logic, recognizing it as a philosophical argument. "So, what you're saying is that if it occurs, even though we believe it can't, then we must be wrong in our evaluation because we cannot deny it did occur."

"Exactly! Just because we can't explain it doesn't mean it didn't happen. It just suggests we lack the tools to explain it, not that it can't occur."

"A scientific argument," Bruno interjected.

"Now you should be able to deal with it," Yakov advised.

"I can accept that. There may still be a scientific explanation but I just don't have the tools to analyze it yet. So we're dealing with someone with skills that are beyond our understanding at this time."

"Oh great! You're telling us that we're up against a wizard and we're hapless against him."

"Who said we're hapless," Yakov challenged. "Whoever it is fears us more than we can appreciate. The message sent to us last night didn't destroy us and certainly hasn't made any of us turn around and run back to our homes. In fact, I think we've become wiser for it. We have taken the measure of our enemy and found him lacking."

"Who's to say that wasn't some infinitesimally small demonstration of his ability last night and the worst is yet to come," Caesar panicked slightly.

"Because if I was in possession of power of this magnitude, I would not have let my adversaries live through the night," Bruno answered. "That's what you're implying, isn't it," he turned to Yakov.

"I concur," Yakov agreed.

"Me too," Rudolf added his opinion. "Those that have power abuse power to its fullest. Mercy is not one of their attributes."

"Personal experience," Bruno inquired jokingly.

"You would know," the emperor answered his friend.

"There is far more to learn from this," Yakov continued. "If we examine this correctly I believe will have our first clues to follow."

"What do you need from me," Rudolf offered.

"A model map of the city to begin with. That will give us our first indication of where to look. And then I'll need the map marked wherever this thing has attacked someone. If we separate the attacks into those that survived and those that were killed, it might give us a pattern to work with. And dates. I'll need to know what dates the attacks occurred."

"That won't be a problem. My constabularies have all that information. I'll set up one of the rooms in the palace as your base. We can work from there. Is there anything else?"

"Histories of the people that were attacked. There has to be something which links them all together."

"Now this, I can get in to," Bruno became excited. "We treat this like a mathematical problem and we'll arrive at an answer."

"And what else?" Rudolf felt himself being caught up in the excitement.

"The most difficult items to procure, I'm afraid. I'll need whatever reports the Church has gathered on the three of us. Are you able to obtain those?"

Rubbing his hands gleefully together, the emperor nodded in confirmation. "Leave that to me."

6

Prague: Cathedral of St. Vitus

"I don't see why we couldn't meet in your palace," Cardinal Calabrese commented indignantly.

"What is the difference? Here or there is only a matter of several hundred feet. And I personally felt like going for a walk," the Emperor replied.

"When are you ever going to finish this cathedral?" Another barb perfectly shot in Rudolf's direction.

"Why does it matter to you? You live in Rome, not Prague."

"Because the fire took place over forty-seven years ago and there is still a gaping hole in the tower roof."

"It has always been my intention to have a fifty year celebration of the great fire. I think the unveiling of the repaired cathedral that year would be a great attraction for the people. That has always been my intent. I've never said otherwise."

"Hrrmph," the Cardinal snorted, disgusted in the fact that he was going nowhere in his conversation with the emperor. "Why aren't you letting me see the three of them?"

"There's nothing to see. Once they have had a chance to evaluate the situation, you'll be one of the first to know what they intend to do."

"I am the Pope's official advisor. I have been put in charge of this mission and therefore I demand to see my charges."

"And I am His Holy Roman Emperor, and I say there's no reason to see them at this time."

"It is clear that we're going to be at odds over the direction this mission is going to take," Guillermo observed. "I have been talking with these august men assembled here and they have provided me with some very disturbing news, your Highness." The Cardinal acknowledged the archbishop and the clergy seated around the outside of the hall. "Your personal habits would appear to be antagonistic to the Church teachings."

Rudolf puffed up his bulk, appearing far more ominous than usual. A big man, he tended to be overweight this latter part of his life, but he never let anyone assume that his now jovial appearance meant that he was weak. "Cardinal, if there is something about my lifestyle that offends you, then come out and say it directly to me. If it is a matter of the friends I keep, then I can only remind you that the Church has no business in my bed chamber. The archbishop has made these accusations numerous times in the past and if there isn't anything new to add to your repertoire of complaints I would suggest you trod carefully. In case you haven't noticed, the Catholic Church is not as powerful as it once was. There are other denominations in Christianity now, and the people find them far more appealing. I would not be the first monarch to suggest a reformation within my own realm. You can't afford to lose another so soon."

"Is your highness seriously threatening the Roman Catholic Church?"

"Where did you get that idea from Cardinal? If anyone was being threatened, I thought it was me."

"You do not appear to grasp the gravity of the situation," Guillermo warned.

"Which situation are you referring to now? You seem to have so many that you want me to be aware of."

"This world is facing annihilation at the hands of the Antichrist! Your own scholars were the ones to find the interpretation in the documents. Our researchers have confirmed it. This is a matter to be handled by the Church! This is a matter of religious significance, and as you have freely admitted on numerous occasions, you are not religious. In fact atheist is a word that comes to mind."

"I wouldn't exactly call myself an atheist," Rudolf protested.

"Perhaps I should use a far worse term. Considering the painting you had commissioned by Giuseppe Arcimboldo portraying you as a Roman god, makes the term heretic comes to mind."

"He painted me as a bunch of fruit," the emperor felt compelled to defend himself. "It's his style; no one looks into it further than that."

"You're the Holy Roman Emperor. You had yourself painted as the god Vertumnus. A man in your position does so in defiance of the Almighty. It was a sign of disrespect and blasphemy. Do you think you could withstand the Court of the Inquisition on this matter alone?"

Even Rudolf knew that an Emperor's powers were not limitless. Others had been taken before the Inquisition and been condemned for lesser crimes. "Perhaps we should re-examine our roles in this affair," Rudolf suggested. "I am not saying that you are not in charge of the three guests in my palace. I only think that it would be wise to give them the opportunity to get to know each other without any interference. As the ancient documents suggested, in order to succeed the three must become as one. That will only be achieved if they can find a commonality amongst themselves. Let that be my undertaking, to see that they do unite in this endeavor. Then, when they are ready, they will report directly to you and be under your instruction."

"I will indulge you for now," the Cardinal smirked; satisfied that he had found the Emperor's weakness and was able to exploit it. "I will give them three days and then I will have them moved to rooms in the abbey, where they can be more acutely instructed."

"The move may not be accomplished that easily," the Emperor attempted to reassert his self. He was well aware that the use of the term 'instructed' by anyone belonging to the Church was synonymous with 'controlled.' "You have a fallen priest, a seer that if I recall correctly, the Church in the past has condemned his father as a practicing Jew who only pretended to be a Catholic, and finally a Jewish holy man of sacred blood, that would probably set the walls and foundations of the abbey trembling if you tried to make him pass through its gates. Might I suggest the Lichten Palace be set up for them as a residence? A far more neutral accommodation, both outside my palace and the Cathedral grounds but still in walking distance for either of us. You can have your own men stationed in the palace as servants and guards, and you won't have to worry about any consequences regarding their presence being dangerous to your structures."

Guillermo was about to object, but the muttering of the archbishop and his clergy suggested that they were very much believers in such superstition, and at that time he required their full support if he was to suppress Rudolf's interference. "Okay then, they will stay at the Lichten Palace off Nerudova under the care of my men. But I will have my belongings moved there as well!"

"One more thing! I will need the files that you have assembled on each of them."

"Pray tell why you would need those," Guillermo responded, obviously annoyed by the request.

"It is for Yakov Kahana. He needs to know whom he's dealing with if he is to succeed."

"I don't see the need."

"It has to do with the flux in the world stone," Rudolf hastily fabricated a story based on some of the information he had been told was in the ancient documents. It obviously struck the right cord, because the archbishop nodded anxiously to the Cardinal.

"Fine, I will send it over to you."

"I don't mind waiting for it now. I'll take them over immediately as there is an urgency that was expressed to me by Yakov. Already he appears to have some answers and he needs to confirm his suspicions.'

Guillermo motioned for his secretary to bring over the documents and lay them out on the table before the Emperor.

"There they are. Take them with you. But remember, in three days they will be delivered to the Lichten Palace and any information they might have is to be given directly to me."

"Of course," Rudolf agreed. "We are in agreement!"

7

Prague: The Castle

"How did you get these," Bruno seemed quite surprised.

"I told you I would," Rudolf boasted. "If you're going to work together, then it's important that you learn to trust each other completely."

"Then having these may not be such a good idea," Bruno suggested.

"Why would you say that? Do you know what I had to suffer through in order to get them? He was threatening to bring me in front of the Inquisition on charges of heresy."

"Oh don't be ridiculous,' Bruno critiqued his friend. "They'd excommunicate you long before they'd bring you up on charges of that nature."

"Oh great, that makes me feel so much better. I'm glad you think it's such a big joke."

"Listen, if anyone deserves to be in front of the Inquisition, it's me, and they haven't done that yet, have they. Don't let them play games with your mind. They're infamous for doing that."

"I don't know how you've been able to withstand their attacks on you all these years, Giordano. Why you haven't handed in your cassock and declared yourself a Protestant, or any other kind of free thinker, I don't know. You'd be free of their persecution if you did that."

"I explained it all to you before, Rudolf. I'm not ashamed of who I am or what I am. But at some time in my life I want to go home. I want to return to Naples and the only way I'll ever be able to do that is by remaining a Catholic. Going home someday is worth all the persecution."

"I hope so, for your sake Giordano."

"But back to the Church descriptions of the three of us. They say a lot of things in here that might just make us turn around and go back to wherever we came from. I would suggest that you have your staff edit them and remove anything offensive. Once they've been edited, then it would be okay for the others to see them."

"Is there anything I should know from those documents?"

"I'm certain you will read them at some point. But if there is anything of immediate interest it might be the fact that Caesar de Nostradame is sitting on a pile of prophecies from his father. He's been using them for years as leverage to stave off the Church. They leave him alone and in exchange he doesn't publish the prophecies."

"You think some of those prophecies pertain to what's happening now."

"I'm not a believer in his father but whether Caesar de Nostradame is aware of them or not, I'm not to certain. I think he's correct when he claimed he didn't inherit his father's gift but according to this Church document on him, he may have some other ability. They've remarked that he's more intuitive than most. That's why they've had such a difficult time trying to lay charges against him in the past. Seems every time they think they can prove he's violated some Church or civil doctrine, he has this uncanny ability to beat them to the punch by publicly releasing an explanation that clearly shows he hasn't breached any of their doctrine or legislation. Could just be coincidence but then again…," Giordano suggested.

"Why would the Cardinal give me a document that is so potentially damning?"

"Well, how did you ask for it?

"I told him that Yakov needed it."

"And that was all?"

"I said he needed it to stop a flux in the world stone."

"Interesting," Bruno pondered his friend's words. "If the world stone or foundation stone is dislodged from its perch under the altar of the Temple, then the earth would be plunged into another deluge. Or so the tradition goes. But there is no Temple any more, and when facing Armageddon, does it really matter if the earth is threatened by another flood of forty days and forty nights?"

"What do you make out of all that?"

"I think that there's more to this Yakov Kahana than meets the eye. Let's look at some of the information written in the Church report." Bruno carefully sifted through the documents, making a variety of gestures and sounds as he perused through it. "Do you know whom we're dealing with?"

"I thought I knew as much as you, but obviously not, now that you've had a chance to read through the document."

"They say here, that Yakov is descended from one of the oldest families on record. That not only is he this priest-king that the Cardinal spoke of, but his family was directly involved with Jesus Christ. I haven't had a chance to read all of it, but that's the general concept. Though they don't come out and say it directly, I think they fear him most of all. Some bit about his knowing the true story about how things were meant to be. That sounds a bit ominous, don't you think? How things were meant to be! That would suggest to me that we've been living in a world of 'How things were not meant to be.' There's also a section here on how a line from Yakov's family ended up ruling out of Narbonne in southern France and if the Church hadn't gone out of its way to eliminate this family, they may have taken over all of France. But they didn't get all of them, and there's a comment here that Nostradamus may have been from that line too. Now isn't that something. Caesar and Yakov might actually be related. I guess that makes me the outsider."

"Giordano, you have always been the outsider," Rudolf reminded him.

"Good to know that you feel that way, my good and trusted friend. But anyway, none of this is making any sense. It goes on and on about how Yakov can reveal the hidden history, which they can't afford to let happen. Does this sound like a document you would hand over to the person that is the subject of your hostility?"

"Doesn't make any sense!"

"Unless…hold on a minute." Bruno buried his face back into the document, his index finger quickly skimming over the lines. "Ah, there it is!"

"What?" The Emperor was eager to know what he discovered.

"In their commentary about myself, they have accused me of being a servant of the Devil. Apparently my science is sorcery and my teachings are designed to tear down the foundations of Catholicism."

"So what's that mean?"

"If I'm the servant of the Devil, and Caesar is a mystic capable of blurring the Church doctrines, which would leave Yakov as the one that can bring in a new world order."

"But that is how John in Revelations described the coming of the Antichrist. First the minions would arrive that would confuse and mislead the people, set them upon each other in a great war, and then the Antichrist would resolve all that through his New Order and bring a false peace through a universal truth."

"Now you're catching on my friend. They don't see us as the saviors to this little problem you're having here in Prague. They see us as the cause. By gathering us all here, they plan on bringing about the end of the old world by forcing Armageddon to occur."

"But that makes no sense at all? Why cause the end of the world if you want to avoid it."

"That's where you're wrong. They don't want to avoid it! They believe it has to happen. Otherwise they can't defeat the Antichrist and bring in their total domination of the world as was promised in Revelations. Get rid of all Kings, all Emperors, all rulers and aristocrats of any kind. That leaves only the Church to be in charge of ruling all mankind."

"Then it would be foolish to have revealed all this to us. It doesn't make any sense at all." Rudolf was totally confused by the statements being made by his friend.

"It makes perfect sense. They're exposing their hand. They're letting us know exactly what is going to happen and what they intend to do."

"But why?"

"Because they want Yakov to know that they think he's the Antichrist."

"Now you have lost me completely." Rudolf rubbed his forehead, totally perplexed by the argument.

"What do you know about the Antichrist that they haven't told you?"

"There is nothing else but what they tell us!" Rudolf admitted.

"Let me explain the Antichrist to you. Look what is written about him. It's all there in Revelations. I know it by heart. Chapter 3, to the people of Philadelphia, a name which in itself signifies harmony and brotherly love, 'Those that are of the Synagogue of Satan that say they are Jews but they are not Jews. I shall make them bow at your feet and keep you from the hour of temptation that they bring upon all the world that tries and binds all that dwell upon the world.' Do you see the connection?"

"They would be the Jews that are really not Jews," Rudolf guessed but didn't really know.

"Yes! A priest-king of the old lineage by definition cannot be a Jew. And a Catholic from a converted Jewish family that still practices some form of Judaism. But the promise is that the Church will bring them to heel, even though they are the ones that bring the world together in unity."

Rudolf contemplated his interpretation. "I can see that."

"There's more. 'Hold fast that no man takes thy Crown.' That's a warning that the rule of the Church is threatened by this man. But there's a contradiction that the one that overcometh will be made a pillar in the Temple of the New Jerusalem. But the New Jerusalem is built by this Antichrist. And what did Yakov call his city."

"The New Jerusalem!"

"Correct! The New Jerusalem! Another coincidence if you believe in such things. It's all there. Then next chapter is even more explicit. The four beasts come. The first is like a lion. The second is like calf. The third is like a man and the fourth a flying eagle. And those beasts shout out the name of God in Heaven and all the elders of the world bow down upon hearing it."

"But isn't that talking about Jesus and the Father up in heaven. Why would the beasts be associated with the Antichrist?"

"That's what I'm trying to explain to you. Now listen to me! Like it says, 'those that have ears, hear.' It's a warning that everything is mixed up. What's up is down, what's down is up. Good is evil, evil is good. He tells the Church to get eye salve because they're blind. They can't see that what they're preaching is wrong. But the four beasts see clearly; the Lion of Judah, the Golden Calf of a false religion, the Man that is all-seeing, and the monarch that has Eagles on his Crest. Do these sound familiar?"

"The last would be me?"

"Yes, the last is you my friend. You are inextricably tied into this as well. Do you not think it odd that the plagues and pestilence unleashed on the world are not by the hand of God or even Satan, but by the Lamb whom opens the seals and releases them? To me I always found that a conundrum. That the devastation is caused by Jesus and the seven angels that heed his commands, but no others. Would that not suggest that the destruction of two thirds of this world is by the hand of the Church which professes to be the word of Jesus?'

"How can you be so certain of this?"

"It says so in the tenth chapter. The seventh angel holds the little book. The book he tells John to eat, which is sweet as honey in the mouth but sours in the stomach and is foul to digest."

"You're going to tell me what that book is, aren't you."

"If the Old Testament is the big book, then the New Testament is the little book. The Church feeds it to us from the day we're born and we think it is sweet to the taste, but all things that our evil, done in God's name are the result of that book being soured in our stomachs. John is told to go out and write a new book, the truth, because the one that is preached is a lie."

"So what are done in Jesus' name are the actions of false preaching and the Antichrist preaches the truth? Is that what you're saying?"

"No. The truth is in Jesus' original teachings but these have been corrupted. It would take someone that knew the original teachings to set the world straight. Rather than say Antichrist, let's think of him as anti-church. Now remember what they wrote about Yakov. They say he's in possession of old knowledge, of the truth about Jesus. That he knows secrets that they have kept buried for almost two millennia."

"And in their own documents they admit as much, that Yakov knows the original teachings through his esoteric gifts." Rudolf finally put together exactly what Giordano was attempting to explain. "But in order for him to succeed, you're suggesting the Church has purposely brought us all together. Why have us succeed if it means the end of their reign over the minds and hearts of men?"

"Because that's how it has been prophesized. There has to be the final battle, if they're going to try and defeat the new order and continue to dominate the world."

"This is all mixed up."

"Precisely! That which is first comes last, that which is last is to come first. Isn't that the key which is written into the Gospels? It's always been there, but so few have bothered to look for it. Now we have a chance to try and see that it succeeds as it was intended to."

"But by giving us this document, aren't they afraid that they've revealed their intentions and now we'll be wise to their plans?"

"They obviously are afraid that Yakov has not realized his role in the greater scheme of things. I think the Cardinal is calculating that by giving him this information, Yakov will pick up the gauntlet and accept the challenge. Something that Yakov said in your throne room struck a peculiar chord. He said he would have taken up this mission even if the Pope had not threatened to destroy his city. It was his destiny he claimed. If that's true, then providing him with this information would only convince him more that his destiny lies here."

"But we're not going to provide these documents to him?"

"Not as they're written, no! These are the ranting of men drunk on the wine of prophesy. A man like Yakov would not tolerate men blinded by their faith into performing irrational acts. He's cut from a different cloth. He sits in judgment and I think he would consider their actions to be lunacy. In order to thwart their plans he'd merely pack his bags and return home because it's obvious they intend to destroy him and his community regardless of the outcome. I'm going to need your staff to do a lot of modifications."

"So why not let him?" Rudolf suggested. "If we all walk away from this, it defuses all of the Church's plans. No Armageddon. No final battles. Everything just stays as it is."

"Because I believe in one respect the Cardinal might be right. I think we were intended to come together and bring about this change. I don't believe in coincidence. There is a thread of fate that has bound us all together and I believe we must see this through to the end. But in the end we must succeed in order to bring about a better world. It's clear to me now. This murderer running rampant in your city has been portrayed as Satan's chief servant. A creature bent on bringing Hell's domination over the world. The Church will ensure that everyone becomes aware of this and in so doing they will cause their own undoing. If the three of us actually succeed in destroying this murderous creature, and we make certain everyone in the empire knows of us and our part in this deed, then we become the heroes that they heed and follow. We can bring about this New Order, a better world where all men are created and treated as equals. Yours will be the greatest kingdom that has ever existed on earth!"

"You think we can do this?"

"Only if we can stay alive."

8

Hradcany: Lichten Palace

"I don't see why it was necessary to move us," Caesar complained. "And furthermore, I'm very uncomfortable with all these Vatican guards stationed here. Is it their purpose to keep unwanted visitors out or to keep us in?"

"I'd say a little of both," Giordano Bruno responded as he walked past carrying some of his bags and overhearing part of the conversation Caesar was having with Yakov. He continued on his way towards the room he had been assigned.

"I do not know if I trust that man. I have this feeling that he knows far more than he's letting on."

Yakov dismissed the comment with a shrug of his shoulders. "I've had the opportunity to read the file they keep on all of us. Trust me, he can be trusted. He is more of a thorn in the side of the Church than either you or I."

"But he's not like one of us."

"I don't believe he's particularly like anyone else. He lives in a world entirely of his own creation. His mind stretches far beyond this time."

"But so does yours," Caesar was quick to remind Yakov.

"Differently though; mine reaches into the past, his into the future. He can never be comfortable with us, and no one of our time is truly comfortable with him. How sad that he must travel his path all alone."

"If you say he can be trusted then I will accept that but I still sense something isn't right."

"You must rely on your senses. You would have come to that same conclusion with time that he is with us, but he can never be one of us."

"What do you mean one of us? How are we different?"

"Something else I read in their papers. It would appear that they think you and I are distantly related."

"Because I am descended from Jews?"

"No, it's because part of my family traveled westward to France seven centuries ago and ruled a kingdom in Narbonne."

Caesars face became white as a ghost. "Those are things my father would have never spoken of with the Church."

"They are very thorough in their research. After all, they've confiscated all the books from all the libraries within the realm. Even my family is still aware of some of the legends regarding the Kahana of Narbonne."

"Long ago my family moved from Septimania to Provence. We buried any traces of that past. My father would say that they would never let us alone if they knew. I guess he was correct. It would help explain why they despise us so."

"They despise you because you have something they cannot have; a gift from God. Envy is the greatest sin that leads all men astray. Of the seven deadly sins, it is the deadliest."

Two burly porters carried in a large trunk into the main hall, dropping it heavily on the stone tiled floor.

"Hey, careful with that," Giordano shouted from the second floor balcony. "Are you trying to kill us all? Just take it over to that far wall and leave it there before you cause a disaster!"

The two men did as they were told and quickly fled from the palace, fearful of what Bruno might have hidden within the chest. They heard stories of his evil sorcery and they were genuinely afraid of the man.

"Well that's reassuring," Caesar chastised Giordano. "You've brought something into this palace that could destroy us?"

Descending the winding flight of marble stairs, Bruno joined his colleagues. "Only if they were to fall into the wrong hands!" he explained.

"Being?"

"I think we're all aware of whom that might be," Bruno winked. "Come on over here and let me show you what I have." Withdrawing a key on a letter strap that he kept hidden beneath his cassock, Bruno removed it from behind his neck and thrust it into the lock. The clasp withdrew from the shackle bolt with a loud click. Lifting the lid he urged the two of them to step forward and peer within at the contents.

"You collect little glass balls," Caesar commented sarcastically.

"It's what I seal into these balls that's important. These are how we're going to take down our adversary."

"I'd like to hear more," Yakov was keenly interested in Giordano's crystal orbs.

"Rudolf's relationship with the Turks has some benefits," Giordano continued. Their science is far in advance of ours. This was something I picked up from one of their apothecaries. If you add oil of vitriol to wine it will produce a third layer that the Moors call oleum vitrioli dulce verum."

"Oil of the sweet truth," Yakov translated.

"I wasn't aware you knew Latin," Bruno was quite surprised not having read that fact in the Vatican's report.

"I don't think I do," Yakov explained. "I hear languages and somehow my brain is able to translate them even though I've never been formally trained in them. Not all languages and it doesn't happen all the time. A family gift, my father called it."

"Impressive," was Giordano's only response. "But even though this dulce verum has been around for over three hundred years, it wasn't until recently another apothecary discovered that if you happen to leave equal parts of the wine and the oil of vitriol in contact for at least two months and then distill them in a water bath, the dulce verum takes on an added property. It knocks you out."

"No," Caesar gasped in astonishment.

"Yes, really," Bruno eagerly informed him. The oleum vitreoli dulce verum in these glass balls will start to evaporate when the glass is broken. Breathe in the vapors and it puts you right out."

"That is fantastic," Yakov looked back and forth between the glass orbs and Giordano. "So how do you intend to use them?"

"If we get close enough to our prey, all we have to do is throw the balls at him, have them smash against his chest, and in a minute he should be completely out. Then we can capture him."

"So why the two colored balls," Caesar inquired, noticing that besides the blue ones, there were a fewer number of red ones.

"Ah! Those are some of my own inventions. They may look like a single ball, but there are actually three smaller chambers in each one of them. One chamber contains salt Peter, the second naphtha, and the third has sulfur in it." Bruno paused as if expected some bright light of realization to shine down upon his two companions.

"Go on," Yakov urged.

"It's a weapon. You throw the ball, the inner chambers break and the contents mix, and then burst into flames."

"I don't get it. So you're going to try and burn the creature to death." Caesar shook his head, offended by the thought.

"No, of course not! But let's say we find ourselves in danger, or surrounded by enemies of some nature, we can set up a wall of fire between us and them and make good our escape."

Yakov cocked his head on an angle as if to say that the red orbs were interesting but he didn't see them as being practical on their mission.

"Well, anyway, they're here, and who knows, maybe we will find a use for them."

"What about the rest of these objects," Caesar pointed to the remaining items in the chest.

"You'd probably not be interested in them," Bruno was quite huffy with his colleague.

"I'm certain we would both be fascinated," Yakov soothed Giordano's hurt pride. "I know that I'm intrigued. Please go on."

Bruno bowed graciously to Yakov. "At least someone here is interested in the science of learning." Though the barb was intended to sting, it slid easily off Caesar's back. "These little vials are some medications that I derived from various plants. I consider myself to be quite the herbalogist. If we should have need of any treatments, I'm well prepared."

"Well prepared for what exactly?" Caesar inquired.

"I thought these might be of interest to you. After all, they say your father was quite the herbalogist as well."

"He was a doctor, a medical practitioner. That is somewhat different from a potion maker."

"Yes and no," Bruno disagreed. The understanding of the purpose of the plant is quite the same. The difference being that as a doctor, your father would make the diagnosis first and then prescribe the treatment. My potions as you call them are not necessarily for the treatment of disease. For example this one, a vial etched in the glass with the number eight." Bruno held up the small vial for all to see.

"That is oil crushed from the seeds of the curcas bean. If any of us should be poisoned then a small sip of this and within a short time, we'll vomit the offending toxin from our stomachs. Very effective and also very flavorful. You really have to be careful that you only take a sip. This one is particularly fascinating. Vial number three." This time Bruno held up another vial, slowly moving it to and thro in front of his face. It's merely the water from the vases in which Lilly of the Valley are kept. For those that suffer from a failing heart, it helps strengthen their rhythm and sustain its function. Quite a marvelous drug when you consider where it came from. Oh, and here's another interesting one. These vials etched with the number fifteen contain the powdered roots of Monkshood. I believe you might call it wolfbane where you're from Yakov."

"Kova, please. My friends call me Kova," Yakov insisted.

Bruno was pleased to hear that. Though he did not know why it was important to him, he desperately wanted to be considered a friend by Yakov. "I will remember that," he smiled. "A nasty little root if I might say so. It can be absorbed right through the skin if you handle it. It makes the blood in your veins feel as cold as ice. But if you're careful and you just open the vial a small bit so the aperture allows the fumes out, it will give you a feeling of giddiness when you inhale it. A very happy feeling I might add, but if you begin to see a green tinge to everything it's time to put it away."

"You've tried this?" Yakov was unnerved by the description.

"I've tried all my potions at some time. How else would I know how to use them properly? Take this one for example, this is ergot of rye. A very useful elixir when taken after giving birth as it helps the uterus return to normal, preventing the retention of any placental materials."

"So are you suggesting this worked for you?" Caesar couldn't restrain himself from taking the opportunity to poke fun at Bruno.

Bruno ignored the remark, preferring to continue with his dissertation on the benefits of ergot. "But what most don't recognize is that this drug also treats those people that have constant headaches that reach the point of being unbearable. And if you must know, for those like myself that get repeated outbreaks of little ulcers on my lips, I merely have to rub some of this on the ulcer and it clears them up quickly. I bet your father didn't even know that!"

"A very impressive collection of medications, Giordano," Yakov congratulated his colleague. "It is not so much the manufacture of these substances that I find impressive but your ability to handle them properly. I can see why this chest falling into the wrong hands would be a worry to you. But it is those other items, your inventions that most intrigue me. Those spools of filament; what are those? I've never seen anything like it." Yakov pointed towards a collection of tailor spools, each holding a different diameter of a thread, but he knew they were unlike any thread he had ever seen before.

"You've noticed them. For lack of a better name, I call it Brunon, after myself. I think of them as liquid steel." A slight blush spread across Giordano's face. "I've always been fascinated by soap making. I would watch the monks for hours while they made their soaps and candles from tallow. And whenever I would get the chance, I would scrape the flakes off the sides of the barrels because I always thought that I'd be able to use them in some of my experiments. I would make mixtures of a variety of chemicals in the hope that one of them would prove useful. One day I added some of the soap flakes to a mixture of wood alcohol and ground apatite powder. Then I added some nitrite and water. I thought I could see something change in the nature of the mixture. As if the solution was a liquid glass. I don't know why I did what I did next, but then I added the dye extract from oysters and that liquid glass became a layer on top of the solution. I wanted to pull it out, to examine it more closely, so I took a wire and tried to lift it out of the container. But instead of peeling off like a layer, it came out as a single strand. I wound and wound for what seemed ages, until it was all out. The strand was still unstable, being quite malleable and fragile, so I rinsed it off with ethanol in order to clean it. And then the most miraculous event occurred. The strand became solid and formed a strong filament. I found by altering the amount of chemicals I could make the strands as thin as a hair or as thick as a cello string. They're light, practically see through, and as strong as steel. The thickest filament I made was a quarter of an inch in diameter and it was strong enough to pull a table across the floor."

"A table!" Yakov was impressed.

"How big a table?" Caesar countered somewhat less impressed.

"A big one," Bruno stamped his foot.

Nodding his head Caesar had to admit, "That is impressive."

"I can see that it's important we don't let this chest out of your control. I suggest we carry it up to your room and put it out of sight. I guarantee that privacy will be an issue while we're guests here."

Between the three of them, there was little problem lifting the trunk up the stairway and into Giordano's room. The few times that they missed placing their feet properly and the balance shifted, rocking the chest precariously, Bruno, tensed hearing the sharp tinkle of glass striking glass. It was enough to remind the other two how serious their predicament would be should they drop the chest.

Once they had safely tucked the chest into a small alcove that was built into the eastern wall of Giordano's room, they all sighed simultaneously and upon hearing each other's sense of relief they burst into laughter.

"I think you will end up killing us long before we encounter this creature,' Caesar jibed.

Finding the comment uproariously funny, Bruno burst into another wave of laughter and slapped his companion on the back. The gesture was well received by its recipient. "Truce?"

Caesar shook his head. "No, better than that, friends."

"And better than that," Yakov held out his right arm stiffly, encouraging the others to do likewise. "Knuckles to knuckles, please." The three of them untied their fists into the shape of a triangle. "An old war cry of my family's. Repeat after me. One heart, one soul, one mind, we three of a kind."

"One heart, one soul, one mind, we three of a kind," they repeated.

"Yes, I believe we are," Yakov smiled. "But Giordano…"

"Yes Yakov."

"Remember, Kova from now on."

"Yes Kova."

"You will let me know when you intend to use any of these little vials of yours."

"Whatever do you mean?"

"Just for your own safety. I wouldn't want you hurting yourself."

"I'm very judicious in my use of them," he explained, carefully watching Yakov's facial lines to try and determine exactly what intent was being hinted at.

"Of course you are."

9

Prague; The Central Town

It was early morning as they strolled down the frosty December streets, the usual crowd consisting of the wretched and desperate shuffling to and thro in their morning rituals. So preoccupied were the townspeople in the routineness of their everyday lives, that no one paid much attention to the three strangers; one dressed in monk's cassock, another in the typically frilled blouse under tight short jacket of the French, and the third in a blend of styles that crossed all boundaries between east and west. By themselves, none would have been overly unique in this internationally flavored city, but together they formed a most incongruous trio. It had been three days since they first relocated into the Lichten Palace and this was the first day that they had any chance to explore the city together and most unexpectedly, alone.

Most of all, it was an opportunity to escape from the weighty pressures placed on their shoulders by a relentless Cardinal Calabrese, who pushed them for answers where there were none. A model of the city had been built by the Emperor's architects and erected in the main foyer of the Lichten Palace. Exact in every detail, Yakov felt that he could navigate every building and alleyway that existed in Prague. The miniature civic buildings stood out as giants amongst the row upon row of two and three storey residential buildings. Even the bridges that crossed over the river Vlatava were perfect down to the finest detail. At every site where an encounter, injury or death occurred after confrontation with the murderous creature, a tiny figure of a man or woman was placed on the city model along with a flag. There were nine such figurines placed upon the map already.

For hours the three of them would stare at the positions of the little clay victims and as if on cue for the striking of each hour, Guillermo Calabrese would ask if they had found the answer yet. And each time Yakov would say 'come back later.'

Though frustrated and angry, the Cardinal would storm from the foyer, but methodically returned on the hour, only to be told to go away again.

By the third day, Calabrese was becoming more belligerent and critical, accusing the three of them of being uncooperative and incompetent, yet he still continued to leave each time Yakov Kahana sent him away.

"You must have some magic spell you've woven around Monsieur Calabrese," Caesar suggested to Yakov.

"Why would you think that?"

"Because he listens to you like a whipped puppy. You tell him to leave and he goes. No matter how much he apparently dislikes it, he still does it. You can see it in his face that he doesn't want to abide, but he still goes! That can only be magic."

"It's true," Bruno interjected. "I've never seen anything like it. I think he fears you."

"I'd like to think he respects me," Yakov corrected them.

"No fears," Bruno repeated. "That man doesn't' respect anyone. Don't be fooled."

"I agree, fears," Caesar corroborated Giordano's assessment.

"What would a man of his power have to fear from someone like me," Yakov laughed at himself.

"Obviously there are matters that go well beyond power and position. I would have to suspect it has to do with knowledge and the birthright you possess."

"What knowledge could a humble peasant like myself from Galicia possess Giordano, that the cardinal, such a learned and educated man, wouldn't already know or need to know?"

"Therein lays the rub. He is educated and he is knowledgeable. He knows it but then there's you. And because he knows that you are in possession of esoteric secrets that aren't available to him, it must be driving him mad."

"So now my knowledge is of an esoteric nature. How does one jump so easily from the concrete to the sublime. You ask for a leap of faith that is not supported."

"That's it!" Caesar blurted excitedly. "You are in possession of knowledge of the faith. He must feel his faith is being challenged. In fact, what's worse, you are able to challenge all his beliefs and prevail. It's not respect, it's resentment but mixed with both awe and fear."

"I thought you said you had none of your father's abilities?" Giordano questioned while simultaneously applauding Caesar's intuitiveness.

"I don't, I think it's just plain logical. It makes sense that is the reason for Cardinal Calabrese's behavior. So am I right?"

"The Cardinal is a torn man," Yakov conceded. "He wants to do what is right, but is unwilling to open his mind to the possibility of failure. That troubles him."

"What is that supposed to mean?" Giordano bore a puzzled look upon his face.

"Just what I said. In time you will come to understand it. But more importantly, I have a hunch about the murders. We need to venture to the heart of the city to see if I'm right."

"Why not tell us now?" they asked.

"No, tomorrow! In the morning. Away from here and away from the Cardinal. If I happen to be right then I think I might just be playing into his hands. We can't afford to let that happen. So until the times right, he is not to know."

"And you think he's just going to let us walk out of here in the morning, without an escort, without telling him anything?" Bruno retorted, mystified by Yakov's naïve belief.

"As you just said, he listens to me. Just leave it with me," Yakov reassured them both.

§ § § § § §

Now that the morning had come and they were walking towards the town center, without an escort, and not even a trace of anyone following behind in the shadows, they were compelled to ask the question that had been plaguing them from the moment they stepped outside the palace.

"Alright. I give up. How did you get him to agree, Kova?" Giordano Bruno had run out of possibilities that he had been mulling over in his mind and finally conceded defeat.

"As I told you yesterday, he listens to me."

"But that doesn't tell us why he listened to you," Bruno challenged the response. "It's definitely something you're holding over his head. I know it. I just can't figure out what it is. How else do you explain his leaving us all alone like this?"

"Oh I assure you, we are not alone. He's had two men following us from the moment we've left the palace."

Caesar looked quickly to either side and then behind. "I can't see anyone, let alone two."

"If you saw them," Yakov mused, "then they wouldn't really be any good at their job, now, would they? But they're there. Trying very hard to act non-conspicuous and doing it rather well I must say."

"But not well enough, you saw them," Caesar indicated.

"As long as they can't overhear us, I don't mind if they follow us to the end of the earth."

"And the hold that I spoke of," Bruno directed Yakov back to the original conversation.

"It is knowledge. You were right before. It is words and letters that cannot be erased but can bring about the ruin of his world. Or at least he believes it can!"

"Wait," Caesar exclaimed.

"Wait for what," Bruno wanted to know what was happening as he watched Caesar stroke the side of his head as if he was in pain.

"I've heard this all before. My father spoke of it in one of his quatrains. Give me a second. It's as if it's trying to force its way into my head. '*Oh mighty Rome, thy ruin approaches. Not by your walls, but of your blood and substance. The sharpness of words and letters shall make so horrible a cut, like an iron blade thrust in all the way to the shaft.*' Do you see? It makes perfect sense now."

"No, it's just another riddle," Bruno said exasperated.

"But they're the same words Kova used!"

"Those that have ears, let them hear," Yakov winked at Caesar.

"Now you're quoting the Gospels to me and mocking me with them," Bruno criticized them both. "I used that same expression with the Emperor. Now I'm hearing it from a Jew?"

"Karaite, please! There is a distinct difference. But you wanted to know my hold over your cardinal, and it's quite simple. It's through your own Gospels; as they are written, but more so by what was not written. There just may be more to Caesar's father than you ever expected. He obviously knew what I was going to say. Now finish off the quote that I just made to you," he instructed Giordano.

"What's to finish, that was all of it."

"Was it Giordano? Think again and then tell me that was all of it. I believe Michel de Nostradame used the same instruction to those that read any of his predictions."

Caesar nodded in confirmation.

"Those that have ears let them hear. That's all of it. There was nothing more." Bruno scratched his head, trying hard to understand what Yakov was pointing at. "No wait…it's incomplete. Or at least you're suggesting it's incomplete. He's telling us to use all our senses. To hear what's behind the words. I think I might understand it now. Those that have eyes let them see. Am I right? He's telling us that we have to go beyond what was written and decipher the hidden meaning. That would suggest there must be a key to unlock it."

"Now you understand."

"Are you that key?"

"The key was already inserted into the books. You have to look deep but it's there. My family had the advantage of being there at the time Jesus walked this earth. We knew what really happened. What the Cardinal fears the most is that someday I might have the opportunity to tell the world where to look for the key and that would tear apart his straw house. Or as Caesar has mentioned, put the fatal knife in and twist it all the way to the shaft."

"I don't claim to be the most devout Roman Catholic," Caesar exclaimed, "but you've totally lost me on how one person could be in possession of knowledge that could bring down the Church. You are just one man."

"As was your father just one man, but he made the foundations of the Vatican tremble in his wake. That particular quatrain could have just as easily applied to him as it does to me. You've used that to your advantage."

"Care to explain?" Caesar pretended he didn't know what Yakov was referring to.

"Explain that you are in possession of your father's books and have agreed not to release them in a deal for immunity from the Church. Why should I explain what you already know?"

Caesar felt compelled to defend his actions. "But what you probably don't know is that they say they no longer fear my father's words and that is why they abducted me and forced me onto this mission."

"Fools will always feast upon their own ignorance," Yakov spouted. "You are more dangerous now than ever!"

"Now you're even sounding like my father. But if everything my father said is to come true, then are we to assume that we're are nothing more than role players fulfilling parts of a play that has already been written."

"No," both Yakov and Bruno turned to their companion and stated simultaneously and emphatically. "God gave us the gift of self determination," Bruno continued.

"Why not just tell everyone what you know?" Bruno continued to pry. "If you know the where to find the key then you should just tell everyone."

"I wouldn't because no one will believe what I say but if I should point them in the direction of what your own saints actually said, then they will tend to believe that. Just as stated in the quatrain, cut down by words and letters. How much more ironic could it be if it was through their own letters?"

"I wouldn't mind hearing this story of yours."

"And me too," Caesar added.

"Don't worry, our mission here is likely to be a long one. We'll have plenty of time to discuss these matters more fully. Now we must deal with the problem at hand by exploring the old city."

"Care to tell us yet where we're heading?"

"To Stare Mesto."

"All the way over there," Bruno groaned, familiar with the layout of the city having resided in Prague for a year already. "Why did we not just take a carriage? We'll be exhausted by the time we reach the district."

"Have you not noticed yet how much attention the three of us garner, just by walking together?" Yakov replied, answering the question with a further question.

"So what of it?"

"Now try to imagine how much attention we'd gather if the three of us stepped out of a sedan together. What do you think the townspeople would be thinking then?" Not waiting for a response, Yakov set about immediately answering his own question. "They'd be thinking, 'government agents here to spy on the people and dressed ridiculously as camouflage. That would hinder our mission tremendously since everyone would be afraid of talking to us. This way we only look like a group of eccentrics from across Europe, journeying across the continent on a grand adventure, and that would hardly terrify anyone. The fact that we are walking suggests we have limited funds. That we are together is more chance circumstance than intentional."

Bruno looked at his companions and himself, assessing Yakov's comments. "I guess we do look a bit incongruous. Especially you," he pointed at Caesar. "Why do you French insist on dressing so pompously? You look like a floral arrangement with all those frills and cuffs."

"Me? What about you? You're a priest, walking around in a dingy monk's habit, and you are the least Godly man I have ever encountered."

"Thank you, I'll take that as a compliment."

"And so will I," Caesar smiled back at his companion.

"So why Stare Mesto?" Bruno abruptly changed topics, acknowledging that Yakov was probably right in his assessment of the general response of the populace. "There weren't any victims in Stare Mesto reported thus far."

"Precisely! Why is that? If I'm to guess correctly, it is because no one wishes to dump their bedpan in their own backyard."

"So you think the killer is concealed somewhere in the neighborhood. It's a fairly large area to cover. You're looking for a needle in a haystack."

"I think I can narrow it down," Yakov indicated. "And with the help of our intuitive friend here," indicating Caesar, "I would not be surprised if we could reduce our hunt to a few city blocks."

"What do you need me to do?"

"Open your mind for us. Nothing more, nothing less. Though we are not merely actors in a play as you suggested, we have all been brought together for a purpose. That was not chance or mere happenstance. You're father did see that clearly. But you are in possession of abilities far greater than you realize."

"I told you already, I have none of my father's abilities. I disappointed him and now you'll probably find I will do the same to you."

"Look me in the eyes Caesar, what do you see?"

Caesar stopped by the rail alongside the river and gazed earnestly into Yakov's eyes. "I see the reflection of myself," he shrugged.

"Look deeper."

Caesar obeyed the command and concentrated. Locked into a gaze, he let his mind open up to Yakov's power of suggestion. "I see…I see myself…as you see me. I'm different. Why do you believe in me so much? How is this even possible?" Caesar's jaw dropped open until he was able to break free of the gaze.

"Think of me as a mirror. But I reflect who you are, not as the world has come to see you. You are what you have seen. It has been one of my cursed blessings that people around me tend to see their true selves."

"Hey, can I try that," Bruno interjected thinking this would be great fun.

"No. You will probably not be happy with what you see."

"Oh, thank you very much!"

"I do not mean it as an insult, Giordano; merely as a warning. You thrive on how others see you. You wear that façade well, and that gives you your strength. But to be confronted with your own self doubts, that permeate your true nature, I do not think you're prepared for that."

"Kova, just tell me then what you see. I'm a big boy, I can take it."

"You're standing at a precipice, my friend. Your spirit has sailed far beyond this time and place. You know of things that are not of this world and you can never be content in living the lie. When a man can glimpse of a better future, how can he ever be content with the reality of the present?"

"Enough, enough," Bruno cried out. "I shouldn't have asked you. I have to hope that my life can get better than this. I have to get home, to see family and friends. I don't want to be an outcast for the rest of my life!"

"You must first deal with the darkness before you can step into the light. Do you understand what I'm saying?"

Bruno looked like he was about to weep. Whatever chord Yakov had plucked from within his soul wailed too deeply upon the string, leaving him pale and weak kneed as he gripped the riverside rails for support.

"Then just one more question, please," Bruno insisted. "Will I ever step into the light you spoke about? You know whether I do or not. I know you know this."

Yakov smiled compassionately at his companion. "Be contented to know that in the end, you will find it. Though it will bring you to harm, you will be satisfied in spirit and soul to exit this world in the knowledge that you have found that which most men never find."

Bruno bowed his head as a cold shudder ran through the length of his body. He was better off not knowing, he thought.

Standing at the edge of the Vltova River, at the broad entrance to the Karlov Bridge, the three companions took in the breathtaking view of the massive structure that joined the two banks of the city.

"Now Caesar, what did your father say about this?" Yakov challenged his abilities as if it was a sporting game.

"He talked about events, about wars," Caesar protested, "he didn't write about mundane things like a bridge."

"This bridge is a turning point. It has to be important. Think harder," Yakov encouraged him. "Remember what you saw of yourself. You have the ability to see what your father saw, but more importantly, to know how it was to be applied."

Shutting his eyes, Caesar stood upon the causeway, motionless, deep in thought under the heavy burden of so many quatrains to search through in his mind. Suddenly his eyes shot open like two great fiery orbs. A look of pain crossed over his face, contorting it for the moment. *'Pass over the bridge and come near to the rose gardens. We arrive too late but much sooner than he thought. The coming of the new Spaniards to Besiers, who shall chase this hunting undertaking.'*

"Well done," Yakov congratulated him.

"Does that really mean something to you?" Caesar asked. 'I don't know why I felt that I had to say it, but I can't see it telling us too much."

"It does and it confirms we are moving in the right direction. You know that once we cross this bridge, there will be no turning back. Your father was giving us that warning. Our destinies will be sealed. If you have any doubts or any cause to wish to turn back now is the time to do so."

Bruno immediately held out his hand for the others to do likewise, his knuckles squarely in line with his body. It was a sign that he was not prepared to turn back. There was only one direction as far as he was concerned. Caesar and Yakov held out their fists so that knuckles to knuckles they formed a small triangle. "One heart, one soul one mind, we three of kind," they swore in unison, breaking off their pledge of allegiance with the laughter of their unique friendship.

"Then let's cross the bridge," Yakov suggested to them. "Time is wasting. We're too late to stop what has already happened, according to Michel de Nostradame, but we're well ahead of schedule to stop the next attack."

"And the rest of the quatrain?"

"That I'm certain Caesar can explain."

As he walked, Caesar's hands became fully animated as if they could tell the story all on their own. He didn't understand how or why, but he knew Yakov was correct in implying he'd understand his father's quatrain fully now. Bruno was impressed by the sudden change in his companion. It was as if a great weight had been lifted and now Caesar had become possessed with a sense of purpose. There was even an air of dignity that surrounded him as he spoke, and Bruno could only wonder what was this amazing ability Yakov had that could influence so many people so dramatically.

"The history of Beziers is quite unique. Though everyone in Southern France is aware of it, few outside the province know anything about it. They say that after the fall of Jerusalem to the Babylonians, there came a fleet of Jewish and Phoenician ships that set up a colony that existed uninterrupted until the time of the Romans."

"And precisely what does any of that have to do with us?" Bruno sounded quite skeptical.

"I can see clearly it's meaning," Caesar continued not allowing Bruno to interrupt his story further. "The history of my family and Kova's in Narbonne is tied directly to the events that happened. We ruled the land as a distinct Jewish kingdom and because of it, the Church attempted to exterminate us. The New Spaniards is in reference to the term used for Sephardim or the Jews that inhabit that area. Did you know that the land was called Sepharad long before it was shortened to Spain. The name was changed to erase its original Jewish heritage. The Carthaginians were of the same stock, Phoenician by origin."

"So why the mention of the New Spaniards going to Beziers then? What does that have to do with any of this?"

"I would think you of all people would know the answer to that, Giordano. After all, as a priest you would have studied that part of Church history."

"The Cathars?" Bruno guessed correctly.

"Precisely."

"But your ancient kingdom was gone by then. And what does the massacre of heretics have to do with what we're involved with now? This isn't clear to me even though you say you can see it," he turned beseechingly to Yakov for an explanation but Yakov tossed the matter back towards Caesar.

"The kingdom was gone, but not the people. You can kill and eliminate a royal family, but what about the people they ruled. What was it the Church said about the Cathars? A population of heretics found to be sharing beliefs from Persia with a concept of a God as the creator in constant battle with his evil nemesis for the domination of men's souls. No Son of God, no gospels, no priesthood, merely the Ten

Commandments to guide their lives and an overwhelming belief in the equality of the sexes. What does that sound like to you?"

"Jews," Bruno responded.

"No, not Jews," Yakov corrected him. "Karaites! By the time we're finished together, I swear you will know the difference. These Cathars believed each person had to work out their own relationship with God. Therefore they had no formal places of worship. A select group of individuals would lead their lives according to strict biblical requirements, but this would free up the rest of the populace from having to bear the burden of strict religious instruction."

"And exactly why would you, no offense, have knowledge of Cathars?"

"Because of what happened to them. It's as if I can still hear the echoes of their cries for help. As if there's a wave of emotion that carries on long after the event and I am somehow receptive to it."

"And by what happened, you mean their execution," Bruno was irritated by the accusation that had been leveled at the Church for so long.

"Hardly an execution," Caesar quickly reasserted his dominance into the conversation. "Not unless you consider the slaughter of over twenty-thousand people a mere execution."

"There's never been any proof of that," Bruno took the public stance of the Vatican, as if their crimes of the past were his to bear and defend.

"Come on now. The records show the numbers clearly. How does that ballad of the Crusade go? Oh yes, "The lords from France and Pairs, clergymen and laymen, princes and marquieses, all agreed that at every castle the army besieged, any garrison that refused to surrender, should be slaughtered wholesale, once the castle had been taken by force.' Of course it rhymed better in French. Wasn't it the Pope's own Cistercian abbot-commander that wrote back to Rome, 'Today your Holiness, twenty thousand citizens were put to the sword, regardless of rank, age or sex.' Not to mention his now infamous comment when his forces had found over seven thousand people locked inside the church and his officers questioned as to how they would separate out the Cathars from good Catholics, 'Put the church to the torch, kill them all. The Lord will recognize his own.' I would consider that as being proof enough, wouldn't you?"

"It was all so long ago. Two hundred and eighty years to be exact. The Church was out of control at the time," Bruno tried to justify the Church's position.

"I do recall recently Sixtus reminding me that his number of bandit executions back in Italy has now reached approximately twenty-seven thousand people. Do you really believe that much has changed over three centuries?"

"No," Bruno shook his head. "And that is why I am the man that I am. Torn between what I believe and what really is. Unfortunately, because of what I have become, I am tainted by the same brush."

Yakov placed his hands over Giordano's shoulder to comfort him. "When the time comes for you to look into my eyes and see yourself, you will recognize that it is not true."

Caesar agreed completely with the sentiment expressed. "Coedite eos. Novit enim Dominus qui sunt eius. That much is true. The Lord will recognize his own. It is why we are here. To ensure that another Beziers doesn't occur in Kova's city and to undertake the hunting of the predator. To cross this bridge and ensure there are no more holy crusades against innocent people. Now all we have to do is find those rose gardens."

"Then we head to the district of Josefov," Bruno instructed, looking up from his moment of self-deprecation and feeling imbued with a stronger sense of purpose."

"You know this area?" Yakov questioned.

"And so will you when you see it," Bruno advised. "It's the Jewish Quarter."

"And how do you know where we'll find this garden?"

"By the Klausen Synagogue, where the path leads to the cemetery, you will find some of the most beautiful rose gardens anywhere in Europe. They say that the flowers are fed by the spirit of love of those that rest there. Even those that are not Jews come from all over to admire the gardens."

Yakov reached into the folds of his outer robe that he wore over his woven tunic and balloon pant-legged trousers, and withdrew a piece of paper he had made a sketch upon. "Here, show me on this map we're we are heading."

Bruno took the paper into his hand, quickly assessing the lines and drawings and the few names scribbled around them and then pointed to the spot he was talking about. "Here at the intersections of Siroka and Ostapadu. That's where the gardens start and then spread out towards Parizska. But how is possible that you would already have drawn a map of the area, when it's just now that Caesar has recalled his father's quatrain and I have just told you the location of the gardens?"

"To that there is no great secret. The model map of the city that we have been reviewing in the palace has provided me with the clues necessary to lead us to that place. But it was yours and Caesar's input that was required to ensure that I was on the right track."

"I've looked at that model a hundred times and have seen nothing," Bruno scratched his head again.

"Ah, but did you happen to gaze down upon it from the second landing like I did?" Yakov looked at their blank faces. "I did not think so! After we placed the flags demarcating the sites of each one of the creature's victims, I happened to go up the flight of stairs to return to my room. For whatever the reason, I wanted to take one last look at the model which to that point had been defying me. Nothing appeared to make any sense. Every victim seemed to be selected at random. At locations that had no connection other than that they could be found there. Yes, there were people of high standing and clergy, but what does that tell us. Nothing more than there is a grudge against both the municipality and the Church. That would leave us with a few hundred thousand suspects. But from the balcony, when I gazed downward, there was a discernable pattern. An unmistakable pattern! The first victim was by a park in Letna. A man of means, that sat on the city council. No surprise really. Anyone foolhardy to walk alone through the park displaying his wealth invites attack. But most criminals tend to perform their first crime close to their hideout. In that way they can escape easily and gauge the successfulness of their activity. The next time they will venture out further and further until they roam freely wherever they wish to go."

"If that's the case, then Letna had to be close to where he started from," Caesar surmised.

"But that was only after you discarded a lot of earlier attacks," Bruno criticized.

"I never believed they were part of this investigation. Even when Rudolf first mentioned that the earlier attacks were all upon thieves and robbers, those deserving of punishment, I had my doubts as to their connection. The criminal we seek has no idealism that would first motivate him. His crimes are distinct and therefore I concluded had nothing to do with those other attacks. A city of this size has more than its share of murderers."

"So let's say you're right, then what?"

"The next attack was at Stromovka, a little further north but still similar to the first with a park and a rich individual strolling through it at night. Apparently unconnected, as neither man had anything to do with the other, at least superficially."

"Perhaps more confidence building, learning the ropes so to speak?"

"Precisely. And then the next attack was by the bridge head at Stvanice Island. A little further away but still close. The one victim that didn't appear to have anything in common with the rest; a youth, a teenage boy, known throughout the neighborhood as a bully and gang leader. It would appear that he deserved what he got, unlike most of the others."

"But why would you not think this boy was part of that earlier group that you discarded. Or perhaps he was the one that performed the first attack. The constable reported that he was known to prey on the rich as they walked alone, crossing the bridges at night."

"Because in all the attacks perpetrated by this bully, he never tried to strangle any of his victims. I read the police reports. Our assailant always goes for the neck; either strangling his victims or breaking their necks. It takes a lot of power to kill in that manner. The boy didn't have that kind of strength and it wasn't the trademark of any of the other crimes I've excluded either."

"Good point," Bruno concurred.

"Then the fourth attack. This time it occurs in a park by Pernerova; a young couple in love. Both were from wealthy families and living on estates outside the city. Two families that could not tolerate each other yet their offspring had somehow come together. He's a paraplegic as a result of the attack, and she lost her sanity from the brutal attack she suffered. What had they to do with any of this? That is still for us to find out."

"Maybe nothing," Caesar suggested.

"A case of being in the wrong place at the wrong time," Bruno added.

"Perhaps, but fortunately from their attack we get the first description of our mysterious assailant. A creature, not quite human, but resembling a man, except that he has no discernable features, his body nothing more than scaled skin, hard to the touch and resistant to any blows the young man hit him with. Now that this man is able to talk again, we must question him about his details."

"So where next?"

"The streets of Vinohrady."

"A very prominent district where some of the chief magistrates reside," Bruno clarified.

"Exactly! That's when the stories started to receive some credence. Attack the best in society and the wheels of justice begin to turn. They finally assigned a unit to patrol the streets from my understanding," Yakov pieced together the bits of information he had uncovered.

"Yes, but only because of the disappearance of the young girl. Those that witnessed the kidnapping said that she was actually carried aloft along the rooftops by her kidnapper. It was so unreal from the description. Nothing could move like what they described. It wasn't human."

"Or so they say," Yakov played down the description. "That which terrifies us often beggars description. That is how our mind best handles the unknown."

"So what do you make from it?"

"It's a turning point. Prior to that, our assailant is operating in a manner that is somewhat predictable. He attacks, he maims, and he kills. But he never kidnaps. The child is unique in that respect. Why not demand a ransom? The family is wealthy and prominent in Prague. They would have paid any amount. Why not kill the child? Why take her with? And if you take her, then where do you go?"

"Obviously back to you hideout," Bruno concluded.

"I don't think so. It would be too hard to conceal the child in your normal day to day routines. The girl would become a severe liability. And if you recall, there was a long delay between the abduction and the next attack. I think that was significant. Something occurred that caused the cessation."

"Such as…"

"I think the child was kept alive for a while. That her continued existence, which was probably only temporary, kept our attacker occupied for some time. There was no intention of ransom, or murder. This was a crime of passion of sorts."

"But he still would have had to hide her for that time."

"But not in his usual place of hiding. Somewhere else; somewhere where only he had access to. Someplace which we'll have to find if we want to even understand how his mind works. But either through neglect or misfortune, the child meets her demise as well, which sends him into a rage which explains the next crime."

"The banker," exclaimed Bruno.

"What does a banker mean to you?"

"Wealth," guessed Bruno.

"Lending, usury," Caesar added.

"What else?" Bruno inquired.

"The attack on the banker was one of hate. Not only was he killed by snapping his neck, but his body was mutilated horribly. As if by a pack of dogs, the report claimed. Why hate a banker to that extreme?"

"Because you had a personal vendetta," proclaimed Caesar.

"Never doubt your intuition," Yakov congratulated him. "I think you must be correct. We need to see the bank records this banker was handling. Whom he may have been involved with is of prime importance. Any businesses or homes he may have been foreclosing on. Something of significance that one would despise him for. If you're already upset and enraged by the death of the child, then you will empty that pent up rage on your next victim. Find the connection and it may just lead us to our prey."

"And the fact that it happened out by Strasnicka?"

"All part of what I saw from that second floor landing. It represented the furthest point that the attacks occurred from the initial attack at Letna. The assailant is now bolder, more likely to feel invulnerable. The attack on the banker was not random, it was preplanned. And I think all to follow were preconceived as well. It's almost as if he were now convinced that he could attack anyone he wanted with impunity. The first were merely an exercise to see if it would work. Now that it had been proven it was time to unleash the master plan."

"So the seventh attack was also preplanned?" Bruno was beginning to understand where this was leading.

"Fugnerovo was no accident and no coincidence. They had to know exactly when the priest would be leaving the Bethlem Chapel and what route he'd be taking. The attack took place several blocks away to the east. Planning something of that magnitude takes precision."

"And that obviously disturbs you," Bruno commented, studying how Yakov's face became contorted by the retelling of his thoughts.

"Nothing prior would suggest this murderer is capable of such a detailed plan. In fact, the exact opposite is true. He's described as an animal because he behaves like one. How then could he mastermind such a scheme?"

"You think there's someone else involved." Bruno watched the flicker in Yakov's eyes. "Of course you do! You've already come to this conclusion."

"Everything suggests this killer works on baser instincts. The murder of Taddeush, this priest of the chapel, was too complex for a person working purely through primal qualities."

"Taddeush was part of the inquisition," Bruno clarified. "I for one couldn't be bothered to shed a tear for him. You didn't have to be a genius to find a way to kill him. There were a lot of people looking for the opportunity."

"But to know that he would be passing through Fugnerovo, that did take a strategist," Yakov corrected him.

"What's so special about Fugnerovo?"

"Location! Fugnerovo was necessary in order to murder the bishop at St. Peter's and Paul's Cathedral in Vysehraq."

"The Pope's nephew," Bruno added.

'By way of the desert of freedom and ferocity. The nephew of the Pope will come to wander. Overwhelmed by seven with a heavy stump, By those that afterwards take over the cipher.' The Quatrain leaped from Caesar's lips as if it had a life of its own, his brain feeling as if it was on fire as he recited the words.

"What was that all about," Bruno asked Caesar.

"I don't know, it just popped into my head."

"You don't know?"

"Well, I do know because if was one of my father's quatrains but I don't know why it suddenly appeared in my thoughts," Caesar tried to explain himself. "All I do know is that every time I recite one of these damn things I get the most terrible headache. Then as soon as I finish it, the ache is gone. This is getting annoying Kova. Why is this happening to me?"

"I think it's obvious," Yakov postulated. "Your father had prepared you for this event, long ago. You just didn't realize it then. He's planted these memories, his prophecies into your mind and our coming together has merely acted as a trigger to release your latent abilities. There must be code words that we are using that are now causing the visions to manifest themselves."

"This is getting too weird for me," Bruno sighed. "I'm sorry, but I find this difficult to believe."

"Difficult or not, Caesar has stored in his mind secrets that will help us solve these murders. Your being forced to come here by the Vatican was not a random event. Your father knew it was going to be so and he prepared you for this. So what more can you tell me about your father's prophecy."

"Nothing. I just remember it was Century VI, Quatrain eighty-two, that's all.

"Six and eighty-two. By my additions, that makes it this year or 1588. You see, your father knew you'd be here."

"Okay, so what's it mean?" Bruno interrupted. "Even if I was going to believe in this power of suggestion by your father, why are you telling us this quatrain now?"

"I told you, I don't know."

"It's a key to unlocking the mystery," Yakov explained to his two companions. "What does it tell us? In my interpretation its saying, if we trust in your father's quatrains, he will help us. This was just a confirmation. Numbers don't lie. They're a universal truth. He's given us the year. He's told us that the nephew dies after seven have already been attacked. And the attack is part of some master plan that we have to unravel. Primarily, he's telling me that I'm right in trusting your instincts Caesar. He's also telling me that I'm correct in my line of thinking."

"And exactly what is that?" Bruno inquired.

"That there was a sequence of events that were being followed at specific locations."

"And how can you know that?"

"Because as I was in the process of explaining to you, I saw it! The ninth attack at Palakeho Bridge was all part of a much larger design. Again, just a prominent man of the town, the city constable, but he wasn't selected by chance. He had to be eliminated. They couldn't afford to let him get too close. He was probably even lured to the location."

"What exactly did you see from the second landing?"

"What I saw is the reason we're heading to Josefov district. I noticed once perched high above the model, if you started to join all the flags we placed on the map, they start to form a twelve pointed star. A Star of David!"

"You're kidding," was Caesar's only comment upon hearing the revelation.

"I wish I was. But it was clear to see from up there. Who's ever behind this, I'm afraid is connected to the Jewish community."

"I can't believe I didn't see it?" Bruno pounded his right fist into his left palm.

"It wasn't obvious. When you look at the map at ground level there's no evidence of a pattern. It appears to be entirely random."

"Those dreams that we had in which we felt like we were being attacked during the night would suggest we're probably dealing with a Jewish mystic," Caesar guessed.

"A cabbalist, more than likely. And he's probably more dangerous than whomever he has perpetrating these murders."

"You're still insistent that there's more than one involved," Bruno half stated and half questioned.

"Even if I wasn't aware of what was said in Nostradamus's prophecy, I'm convinced there's more than two as well. How many is something we'll have to find out."

"What are we going to do?" Bruno suddenly sounded lost by the revelation. "Who will we talk to? Better yet, who will even talk to us? No one there is going to help us!"

"Today we just look around. That's all. Strolling the streets. Familiarize ourselves with the territory so to speak. After all, we still have our two unwanted friends in the shadows behind us. I don't want to provide them with any clues. As far as they're concerned, we're nothing but tourists today examining the sights of the Jewish Quarter. It's our job to make it look like that, so when they report back to the Cardinal, there's nothing of value to offer him."

"A twelve pointed star," the truth hit Bruno like a thunderbolt. "There are three more murders being planned."

"We have to work fast gentlemen!"

10

Prague: The King's Forest

"We need a way to do our work undetected by Calabrese's spies," Bruno explained to the Emperor.

"Is that all?" Rudolf's eyes rolled back in his head as if to say he could wish for the same thing, but it wasn't about to happen.

"No, we also need documents from the bank that the banker was in charge of."

"Now you're asking for things that even God might not be able to provide to you," Rudolf huffed. "There's a reason why people lock things away in banks. It's to keep people like us from getting our hands on them. Getting rid of Calabrese's spies would take a miracle, getting the bank papers is merely impossible."

"It's important. We wouldn't ask if we didn't think it was essential to the case."

"So are you going to tell me what all this is about?"

"Kova has an idea where the killer might be hiding out."

"Well good, then let me know and I'll have him arrested. In fact, tell Calabrese's spies and let them do the work for you. After all, that's what everybody wants, isn't it."

"It's not that easy. There may be others that are providing him with a place to hide."

"Then I'll have them arrested too!"

"That also might be a problem."

"Giordano, are you purposely making this difficult for me? Am I going to have to force every answer from you in order to find out what is going on?"

"It's complicated. We may be looking at an entire community. If news was to get out of this nature, you'd have riots in the streets. People will start murdering others wantonly without any cause or proof. Mass hysteria turning Prague into a blood bath"

"Oh…I see. I definitely wouldn't want that," Rudolf sounded reluctant as he retreated back into his chair.

"If Calabrese finds out what we're thinking, then that's exactly what you're going to have. He'll whip up a mob into a murderous frenzy and before you know it, all our heads will be on the chopping block. They'll lead the inquisition right to your door; a bloody crusade against your own people. The streets of Prague will be running knee deep in blood!"

"Enough, I get the picture already. We can't let the Cardinal know of any of this, so in that case we will have to find a way to free you of his tracking dogs. So who are these citizens of mine that you're suspecting of doing all these crimes."

"I think it best that Kova tells you himself."

"And where is he now?"

"Back at the Lichten Palace. We thought if the Cardinal saw us all leave and head to your palace he'd become suspicious and try to join us. This way, when only one of us leaves at a time, he wouldn't suspect we had anything of importance to convey. Not to mention, when that one person leaving happens to be myself, he's probably relieved to be rid of me for the time being."

"Of that I am certain," Rudolf mocked in jest. "So how do we arrange that I talk with Kova now?"

"I will return to the palace and pass the word to him that he will meet with you. Then he'll come on his own."

"That would appear highly suspicious," the emperor nay-said the plan. "It's one thing, like you said for you to take off on your own and come see me, but for Kova to do so would be completely out of character. They'd know immediately that it was a purposely arranged. I have a better idea. We will all go hunting this afternoon."

"I don't hunt."

"Well guess what, neither does the Cardinal. You'll just have to keep him company while the rest of us go into the forest. Tell everyone that I'll be there with my party just before noon. And Giordano…"

"Yes…"

"Dress accordingly, will you? We're going hunting, not for midnight mass."

§ § § § § §

By noon, the party waiting in the main foyer of the Lichten Palace had grown to a score of people. When Rudolf arrived, accompanied by his stewards and personal guard, there was barely enough room to negotiate through the corridors.

"What is all this?" he bellowed.

"Merely my fellow clergy and a few personal escorts for protection," the Cardinal answered calmly.

"My good Cardinal, we are going hunting, not on an expedition to the heart of Africa. What do you believe are in my forest that you need protection from? Perhaps a rutting stag or two, but that is about as dangerous as it will get. Now, any one that wants to hunt, they can come with, but the rest can go home. This is not the royal ball. If you want to stand around and talk, then attend a mass, but not my hunt."

"But your majesty, we don't hunt," Calabrese pleaded.

"Then don't come," Rudolf rebuffed him abruptly.

Guillermo Calabrese dismissed most of his fellow clergy but insisted that his personal guards attend to his safety. Yakov smiled broadly at the two men, the same two that had been following him the day before. Neither returned the offering, content to turn away from his prying eyes.

"Well gentlemen, our coaches wait,' the Emperor instructed them. Outside, the three coaches, impressive structures of black ebony wood with ornate brass hardware on every bit that moved or rotated in even the slightest manner. Rudolf made certain that Yakov accompanied him in his personal coach, along with two of his security force, abruptly closing the door on the Cardinal when he made an attempt to climb on board. "Sorry, Guillermo," he apologized, "but these coaches have only been built to accommodate four passengers. I know you understand. Why don't you ride along with Giordano and Caesar? I'm certain that they'd welcome your company. That is if you're comfortable having your own guards ride in a coach by themselves along with some of my other guests."

Calabrese was left with no choice but to smile uncomfortably and acquiesce to the Emperor's wishes. He stepped down from the carriage stoop but instead of climbing into the coach with Bruno and Nostradame, he instead chose to ride with his own men in the last coach.

"Good riddance," Rudolf cursed as his coach got underway. "The man is like lichen, no matter how hard you try to weed the garden he always seems to be underfoot."

"He has a job to do," was Yakov's only response.

"You still fail to realize that man would be very happy to see your demise."

"I'm perfectly aware of that," Yakov acknowledged, "but like I said, he has a job to do."

"How can you be so nonchalant about such a matter? Egads man, if it wasn't for the fact they needed you, they'd be burning everyone in your town at the stake this very moment."

"But they do have need of me, and what they intend to do and what will happen are two entirely different matters."

"You're sounding fairly confident!"

"We all have destinies to fulfill. This is mine. Of that I have no doubt," Yakov articulated with extreme confidence.

"No doubt," Rudolf repeated. "I hear you have had somewhat of a breakthrough regarding this creature loose in my city."

"Hardly a breakthrough," Yakov corrected him. "More of a revelation courtesy of the map and Caesar's intuition."

"And are you going to be cagey like Giordano and keep it all a secret from me too?"

"I don't believe that was Giordano's intention. Because of the sensitivity of the situation he thought it best that you discuss my findings directly with me. If my hunches are correct, then decisions will have to be made that I believe will fall directly into your lap. And they may not always be easy ones for you to make. They could reflect badly on you."

"What makes you believe that any decisions an emperor has to make are easy ones? There is always something major hanging in the balance. But be reassured, I will do my best to make the right ones."

"Of that I have no doubt. Hopefully I will be proven wrong, but I don't think so. Yesterday as you know, the three of us ventured to Josefov with the Cardinal's two security men tailing us up and down everywhere. There was no point in trying to lose them, but what I made certain was that we did not spend too much time in any one place. Nothing to make them think I had uncovered any details of any importance. I'm certain they had no inclination that my interest lay with the Jewish cemetery we passed."

"So you are telling me that therefore you were interested in it. Is Caesar able to commune with the dead?" Rudolf jested.

"No, but you'd find it interesting how much the dead have to say to us, if only we'd open our eyes."

"I presume you are talking from your own experiences, Kova?"

"A curse I'm afraid in my family. The memories of my ancestors do not tend to fade once they're laid into the grave. They persist from generation to generation to the point of madness and distraction. Are you aware that it is written in the Old Testament that my family is forbidden to set foot in cemeteries? There is an ancient belief that if we should pass over the roots of trees that all pass through the graves of the dead, then the spirits have a direct link to commune with us. And since communion with the dead is forbidden, we are rendered unclean for thirty days. I know you must be thinking, 'what a foolish belief' but if it was so foolish, then why would Moses have included it in his sacred texts?

"But you said you went to the cemetery!"

"But I did not enter it. No, that I left to Giordano and Caesar. I wanted to know if the roses passed close to any graves in particular."

"The roses? Kova, is this intended to make any sense? If it's an appreciation of flowers you have, then I have my own gardens at the castle."

"A message form Caesar's father brought us there. It would appear that he knew that the three of us would be on this mission together this specific year."

"Which would also explain why he requested in his horoscope he prepared for me that I watch over the safety of his son. I try not to believe in the supernatural but his father would be hard to explain otherwise. And what did Nostradamus have to say about the roses?"

"Only that they would put me on the trail of this killer."

"And did they?"

"Perhaps? There is a secluded part of the cemetery with a private gravesite. It would appear the Maisel family has purchased the plots in that area."

"Not surprising," Rudolf responded. "They are a very wealthy family that could easily afford to have the best location, even for their dead."

"Did you know he lost a daughter over a year ago?"

"A very tragic occurrence," Rudolf shook his head in regretful sympathy. "Apparently she was caught in a riot. Trampled by the crowd from what I understand."

"And a monarch would know about the death of a Jewish child because..."

"Marcus Maisel is well known by me. He has been both advisor and financial donator to many projects in this city. Many of these projects have nothing to do with the Jewish community."

"So when you say he's wealthy...?"

"Immeasurable!"

"How does one accumulate such vast wealth?"

"To be perfectly honest, I don't know. "

"But surely there must be some record of financial investment. A business that suddenly took off? An inheritance? There would be a record," Yakov persisted.

"It wasn't from his father Samuel, that I can assure you," Rudolf stated. "The family had something to do with publishing, but it was a small community business. The son must have invested wisely."

"It must have been a very exclusive investment if even your financial advisors weren't aware of it," Yakov smiled.

"Are you insinuating that there's something afoot?"

"The grave had been freshly turned over. Last few weeks by my estimation."

"Perhaps the family plans on a big planting at the site?"

"I thought about that," Yakov contemplated. "But that should have occurred at the one year anniversary of her death. This is more recent than that. And if there was to be a planting, then where are the flowers?"

"It is winter after all," the Emperor mused. "Hard to find anything that would grow this time of the year," he laughed.

"Then why dig it up at all? The ground would be hard. Any groundskeeper would have known that."

"Hardly worth worrying yourself over. People do strange things."

"You have enough strange events happening already in your city without others arising. Fabulous wealth appearing out of the ether is cryptic as well," Yakov insinuated to Rudolf. "It may be nothing, but at the same time, anything unusual could be important. I wouldn't mind the opportunity to meet this Maisel family if it could be arranged."

"Of what use would it be being the Emperor if I couldn't arrange a simple meeting," Rudolf replied jovially, his girth rumbling with his satisfaction with his own wit. "It just so happens that my city councilors have a meeting arranged to discuss his latest building project this very week, which you obviously must have seen when you walked through Josefov. "

"You're referring to the new synagogue I saw being built as a memorial to his dead daughter. A magnificent structure from what I could tell." Yakov's eyes squinted as if what he had just said had awakened a new awareness.

"Yes, exactly."

"In fact, I'd like to meet most of the families that have encountered this killer. I need to find out if there's a connection between any of them."

"That shouldn't be a problem either."

"And I need to get into the bank records. I can't believe the banker was chosen at random."

"I can't see why he wouldn't have been. This killer doesn't appear to have any logic in his choice of victims."

"At least nothing apparent yet," Yakov advised.

§ § § § § §

The King's Forest loomed menacingly at the edge of the ravine, shrouded in shadow cast by the dense apron of ancient trees that dwarfed all that entered into its hallowed domain.

"Preferred weapons, gentlemen?" the Emperor questioned his guests.

"You highness, as I explained, I don't hunt," the Cardinal reminded Rudolf.

"Too bad, Guillermo. I'm certain you won't mind waiting by the carriages then. Can't have people just aimlessly walking through the forest now, could we. You'd either be mistaken for the prey and wounded or you would simply frighten away all the animals. I can't permit that."

"I will keep him company," Bruno suggested. "After all, you know I'm certainly no hunter myself."

"And arc you going to tell me that you don't hunt either now, Kova?"

"No, that will not be an issue," Yakov replied.

"And here I have a Jew that hunts, and a group of priests that don't. My how the world has flipped completely upside down over the years. I thought Jews were dissuaded from hunting or is that just another rumor spread against your people?"

"A misconception, that has been further perpetrated by the Rabbis I'm afraid. In our prime, we were once great hunters. Just look in the bible and you can see it was a way of life. David took down lions with a mere sling. With all the wars we fought over time, there was barely a Jewish child that didn't know how to use a variety of arms. But with the fall of the Kingdom, the Rabbis gained power and convinced the people that there was no place in our society for such pastimes."

"But yet you still managed to learn to hunt."

"Once again everyone seems to forget, that I am a Karaite. We still remember many of the old ways."

"So what shall it be? My orderly has brought a fine collection of wheellocks for us to try; much easier to handle than the old flint-locks."

"A crossbow will do fine. I have no interest in firearms. They make too much noise and make the hunt an uneven match of animal wit against skill."

"Obviously you haven't tried them or else you would know that the animal stands a far better chance with the firearms. At least when I'm hunting," Rudolf belched out a laugh. "Can't get the blasted things to shoot straight no matter how many times I try."

"I'll be content with the crossbow," Yakov reassured him.

"Have it your way. What about you Master Caesar? Care to give an invention of modern science a go?"

"Don't mind if I do. I never had the opportunity to try one before. It should be most interesting."

"Good then, we'll be off. I've heard tale that this year there are stags in the forest with antlers as large as cedar bushes. With the mild winter we've had so far they should be big and fat. Well worth the effort."

Leading his party, Rudolf took off into the forest, followed closely by his guests and his security guards, leaving behind the clergymen and the Cardinal's own guards.

"Should we follow them, sir," one of the guards ran up to Guillermo before the Emperor's party departed.

"The old goat would only find a way to elude you any way. It's obvious that he has made today as difficult as possible for us. He's up to something, I know it! What have you say to that Bruno?"

"Yes, most definitely," Bruno agreed. "He's up to hunting and we would just be a burden to him."

"Don't be coy with me Giordano. You three are on to something and I think it best you disclose it to me now!"

"Excellency, if we were on to something, your men would have reported their findings back to you by now. Let us do our job and perhaps we will find out what is transpiring but if you continue to harass us with these two men of yours, you will only interfere with any success we do achieve."

"Giordano, you do not seem to comprehend the gravity of this situation. The fate of mankind is resting on your shoulders. We need results and we need them quickly."

"And we need time in order to resolve this mystery," Bruno challenged back.

"Time is not on your side. We are on your side. And you must remember whose side you are on."

"And what exactly does that mean?"

"It means you work for us. You seek absolution. You wish to return home to Naples. You want the Church to overlook your indiscretions. These are all things that we are willing to grant you as long as you realize where your loyalties must lie."

"I have done nothing to betray those loyalties."

"You have done nothing to demonstrate them either. Tell me, did you find out anything on your journey through town yesterday?"

"What did you expect us to find in the Jewish Quarter?"

"There was a reason you went," the Cardinal stammered the point home reacting to Bruno's impertinence.

"Yakov Kahana is a Jew. Jews like to be around Jews. Nostradamus and I tagged along to see something other than the four walls of our rooms."

"And you discovered nothing…?"

"I discovered Jewish towns are noisy places; lots of screaming and haggling in the streets. Different smells as well as food that is often fried in oil. I didn't like it much."

"Are you trying to anger me, Giordano?"

"You asked me, I told you."

"Then why did you visit the cemetery and spend so long in there according to my men?"

"Because Yakov couldn't enter into the cemetery because of some obscure law in his family and we were trying to find the names of relatives that he believed were buried there, and neither Caesar's nor my Hebrew was that good that we could read the headstones without struggling."

"Well that is of interest to know that Caesar can read Hebrew. I knew his father could but didn't realize he had bothered to teach his son."

"Is that a crime?"

"It is when you think someone is hiding the fact that they are a heretic and furthermore a practicing Jew."

"Then my day wasn't a total waste if you are happy with that little tidbit of information," Bruno said laconically.

"Remember what I've told you Giordano. If you wish for us to provide you with forgiveness, then you must help us resolve this situation to our advantage."

"And exactly how is this to be resolved?"

"It must never be made public that we required a so-called King of the Jews and a half-Jewish prophet to save us from Armageddon. We must see to it that the killings stop, but not at any price. Rudolf is not to gain from this episode either. At best, he is an atheist garbed as the Holy Roman Emperor. That is enough already to make our detractors look at the Church with revulsion. No, all this must end as a moral victory for the Church and it is up to you to see that happens."

"But if Yakov does solve the murders, how are you to stop the fame he would justly reap as his reward?"

"He will not succeed. There was a part of the prophecy that Rudolf had not uncovered because it was not contained in the documents in his possession. They were safely tucked away in the Vatican library, and we were not about to share that information."

"You wish him to stop the end of the world and yet you are not about to provide him with the information to do so. That would mean that you're sealing the destruction of all of us."

"All we need from Yakov Kahana is for him to identify the demon servant that is causing the deaths. We have our own men that will deal with the creature from that point onwards. We will remove Yakov and Caesar from the equation at that time and none will be the wiser to their involvement."

"And you'll be able to do this because we don't have the information you spoke of?"

"We will be able to do this precisely because of that information which has made it clear that the three of you would be incapable of dealing with the demon because none of you are pure enough to complete the task. You are all tainted and that makes it impossible for you to succeed."

"You have brought the three of us together to save the world, yet you know that we are incapable of doing so. Why bother to bring us here in the first place?"

"It was clear in the writings uncovered by Rudolf's researchers that the only way we would ever find the demon is through the three of you. The parchments never claimed that it would be you three to bring about its downfall. That according to our documents would take men of virtue and sanctity that were free of any trace of the seven deadly sins."

"That is the missing piece of information you have held back?"

"Would any of you have accepted if you knew from the onset you were doomed to failure? Be honest with yourself Giordano. Of the sins of pride, envy, gluttony, lust, anger, greed and sloth, can you say that you and your colleagues are free of any of them? You, yourself are so filled with lust that you'd contaminate the others merely by being in their presence. And Yakov Kahana, what man of his birth could not be guilty of pride? But with that pride comes envy for he is a king without a country. All other monarchs he would be envious of. And what about Caesar de Nostradame, such anger he harbors against all of us in the Church, mixed with the greed that he inherited from his father who contributed nothing of any value to the Church upon his death, even after his local parish built him such a fabulous tomb."

"You forgot gluttony and sloth," Bruno ridiculed him.

"You have allied yourself with Rudolf have you not? Those sins he has anointed you with as part of his own guilt. So as you see, it is very clear. None of you are qualified to be the hero as in Dante's little play. You were doomed from the start. Work with me and I'll see to it that you'll be rewarded."

"And you are certain that these sins play a role in the success of this mission?"

"It was clearly stated in the documents we held in our possession. 'In order to succeed against the demons of Armageddon, you must first conquer each of the deadly sins.' Of that it was emphatic. Since I know you are incapable of curing your own self of these sins, there's no reason to conceal the truth from you."

"So it did not read that the sins were possessed by those that would undertake this mission."

"I don't see your point," the Cardinal questioned Bruno's statement. "It is obvious that the four of you have manifestations of all the sins, therefore you will not prevail. Is that so difficult to understand?"

"No, Excellency. There is no problem. Your point is perfectly clear," Bruno conceded.

§ § § § § §

From their perch behind the bushes by the small glade, the Emperor and his guests watched patiently as the buck strode into the clearing completely unaware that it was being watched.

"Incredible! A truly amazing animal, is it not, Kova? The size of his antlers alone staggers the imagination. Only a few dozen yards more and he'll be in range. We'll have him."

"Yes, a truly amazing animal," Yakov agreed.

Rudolf held out his open palm for his orderly to place the rosewood handled pistol into it. Already cocked and loaded, the wheel lock pistol was the latest firearm to be invented. No longer relying on a piece of flint to spark the gunpowder, the wheellock was more reliable, firing a good percentage of the time the trigger was pulled.

Caesar carefully examined the matching pistol that was handed to him. The ornate brass fittings with their scrolled handiwork were pieces of art, brought together into an invention designed to kill and destroy. He thought about the irony, but just for a moment before he practiced balancing it in his hand, attempting to use the sites along the top-plate and muzzle to line up his quarry.

There was a loud bang and a black puff of smoke as Rudolf pulled the trigger. The crack of the lead ball hitting the tree to the rear of the buck about ten feet above the ground before it buried itself into the trunk was enough to start the Emperor cursing under his breath. "Quick Caesar, take your shot before he makes a run for it."

Doing as he was told, Caesar's shot fell well short of the intended target burrowing itself into the ground several yards away. "Damn," Rudolf bellowed. "Now he'll know the direction we're coming from," as a puff of dirt and dust rose from the ground where the shot had dug in. With the adrenalin surging, the deer was leaping as fast as it could towards the dense forest brush. Yakov had already moved in the same direction anticipating the flight path of the animal. Raising his crossbow to shoulder level he took a deep breath and steadied his aim. The resonating twang of the bow string meant the bolt was well on its way before the rest of the hunting party knew what was happening. As if guided by an unseen hand, the bolt sunk into the chest, almost to the end of the shaft. The buck continued onwards towards the forest, and Yakov let the bow sink back to his side, too late to take a second shot. 'Missed,' he thought to himself, thinking that the bolt had not hit anything vital but after traveling fifty or so yards the buck slowed to a walk and then crumbled on to its front knees. Rolling on to its side, it took several heavy gasps before it closed its eyes, succumbing to a final full body shiver before it breathed its last.

Scurrying towards their prey, the hunting party pulled up alongside the animal, pausing to admire its size and beauty. "Truly outstanding," Rudolf slapped Yakov across the back. "I've never seen anyone take one of these down on the run with a crossbow. Absolutely stupendous shot Kova. I never took you for being such a marksman. Where did you ever learn to shoot like that?"

"A gift from my ancestors," Yakov replied humbly.

11

Prague: Oak Tree Tavern

It was most opportune that the drainpipe ran down the outside corner of the room to the palace gardens below. From the window, if he stretched out far enough, Bruno was just able to grasp the framing hook on the downspout. It meant for the moment he was suspended high above the ground by only one arm, madly seeking a foothold in order to secure himself firmly around the pipe, but he had been in much tighter spots in the past. He remembered one night back in Vilna, a young countess he recalled fondly had got him into a similar situation when her husband came home from the wars unexpectedly. What was her name, he desperately tried to remember as his left hand found a firm grip on the other side of the framing hook. The rest was easy, simply sliding the length of the pipe, and using the trellis as a ladder until the final drop to the soft ground.

From the cushioned landing in the gardens to the kitchen staffing gates of the palace was a simple stroll. All of the Cardinal's men were on watch in the main foyer and hall of the palace portico. They never would have suspected that Giordano Bruno would leave in such an ungentlemanly manner. He'd worry about how he would get back into the palace at a later time, thinking to himself no one would be looking that closely at someone entering the palace when their instructions instead were clearly to prevent anyone from leaving.

The cool kiss of the night air caressed his face as he strode down the street toward the town. It had been some time since he had tasted the night. It was sweet, just as he remembered it. The lights along the main road attracted him like the flies in summer. Wherever the lights were, that's where he'd find what he was looking for.

It wasn't long until one place caught his interest. Not far from the palace, just a couple of miles to the south on Ujezd, at the crossroads to the bridge that joined Strelecky Island to the mainland. The tavern lights were burning brightly, indicating a lively crowd that would suit him nicely. The tavern goers were already bursting to the seams, with the patrons falling out on to the pavement where they had a little more room to spread their wings and crow at the sun due to rise in several more hours.

"Father, have you come to save our souls," a one-eyed man with a crooked nose and coal black teeth roared with cherry mirth upon spotting the cowled priest standing at the entrance.

"No my son," Bruno answered him, "I've come to drink my fill, like everyone else in this tavern. So who will by me a drink for a blessing in return?" It was an offer few men could resist. Life was hard enough without seeking a little help from the Almighty. At the price of a cool ale, the grace of God had come cheap. They cleared a table as if it was an alter and gathered around Giordano who sat like the Pope himself before them, and one by one they stood in front of him and confessed their greatest desires in hopes of receiving a divine blessing. It was a horrible sin to take advantage of their misery in such a fashion, Bruno thought to himself, but only momentarily, as he quickly dispelled any guilt with a quick downing of their beer offerings. Each tale of misfortune and tragedy reminded him of how hard life could be for those not born with a name that commanded wealth or respect. The last century had been particularly cruel, with wars and the remnants of the plague taking the last of its victims. Few families had survived unscathed and these poor wretched souls were the remains of what was left. Yet, even in the hardness of their lives they could find kernels of hope that they tried to grow into gardens of happiness over and over again in the stony soil. Who was he to deny them a little happiness with a simple blessing? Certainly not he!

The last few hours of the night were upon them when finally the one that Giordano had been seeking rested upon one knee before him and made his request. "Father, I have no need of a blessing. Instead I would prefer that you offer me a curse that will lay low those that have offended me."

"Tell me more, my son," Bruno encouraged him.

"I am not a man of little substance. I do have some coin to back my family name. And a good name it is and has been for a long time in this district. For five generations my family has been grain merchants to this community. We have fed them in times of famine, we kept them alive during times of siege, but do you think they remember any of that. No, we filled their bellies and they were never grateful. There is a woman, Sophia Commencu that comes into my family's store. I have known her for years and have desired her for just as long. When she would come in to buy my grain, I would always give her fair weight, nor would I ever haggle price, always giving her the market rate. You would think that she would appreciate that." He waited for a response from Bruno.

Nodding his head in an attentive manner, his bottom lip curled outwards, Bruno gave careful consideration to the words of the young man. "So in other words you never tried to take advantage of her and cheat her."

"Never Father! I always was fair and honest with her."

"Unlike your other customers?"

The man blushed a bit ashamedly. "It is not unusual to make a little extra profit where one can," he quickly justified. "A business cannot be successful if it doesn't try to make a profit. We've been here for five generations. Longer than most because we have been successful."

"In both famine and siege," Bruno added as if to say that was quite an achievement. "So what is the problem you have with this woman that has obviously offended you?"

"The Commencus are a poor family. They have nothing to speak of. Her father is a laborer in the sewers and is well past his prime. Her mother is still a maid to one of the families that resides on the hill. She has no dowry, no lineage, no inheritance to speak of, nothing that would make her attractive to any man."

"But if I may be so bold to intercede here, I'm assuming that you are attracted to her. Would that not be unusual considering what you've told me?"

"I could give her things she could never dream of having. I would do this for her, even though others may scorn me for choosing such a lowly woman. I would even give her my name which commands a lot of respect in this neighborhood as I told you. In time she could forget where she came from. She could erase that from her memory and pretend that she was something more than she is."

"And let me guess, she wasn't interested?"

"I went to her home; her shambles of an abode that bore the stench of the poor and profane. I was embarrassed to even knock on her door in case someone would look out their window and see me standing there. How much I had to swallow my pride to be there. To go as a beggar to beggars. Can you even imagine that?"

"Oh, I'm definitely trying," Bruno answered.

"And when her father answered the door, he didn't even bother to ask me in, instead inquiring what my purpose was while I was still standing in the street."

"Terrible," scoffed Bruno.

"As if I was nothing, he made me stand in the street and ask him if I could have his daughter."

"And he did not give her to you?"

"No! He actually asked me who I was and what business I had to do with his daughter. Can you imagine, he didn't even know who I was? Was he blind and stupid? Everyone knows my family in these parts. How could he not have possibly known?"

"Impossible!" Bruno exclaimed.

"And I actually lowered myself to explain to him who I was, as appalling as that was. Then I repeated again, that I wanted his daughter to be mine and that I would take her away from the squalor and give her a much better life than she had ever known."

"How could he have refused you?" Bruno repeatedly made a tsk-tsk sound to emphasize his disbelief.

"Exactly! What better could she have ever done? But he didn't even give my request consideration, telling me instead that she was already betrothed and that I should be gone from his step or else he would have me escorted away by the constable, as if I was nothing more than a stray dog."

"So this curse you spoke of?"

"I want them to suffer. All of them for the humiliation they have done me. To even suggest that she was better off with someone else compared to the life that I could have offered is offensive. They have offended my family name. They have spat in my face. I want them punished. I want God to make them suffer for the harm they have done me."

"Surely they are ripe for it," Bruno evaluated his request. "Already they have raised themselves to the pinnacle of arrogance. It is often said that God let's a man be most proud before he leads him to his downfall. They have had their moment to lord themselves above you. Their downfall is imminent. Come with me. Help me from this chair back towards my lodging for I have had too much to drink and I think my legs will not support me all the way on my own."

"Will you meet my request, Father?"

"How could I refuse, dear boy. Now help me up."

The young man eagerly helped Bruno to his feet and led him towards the tavern exit. "Will you pronounce the curse upon them now?"

Bruno strolled down the street towards the large city parkland of Mala Strana without responding. The young man kept pace with him waiting for the priest's answer to his question. It wasn't until they actually reached the entrance to the park that Bruno stopped and turned to the man.

"Better than that," Bruno proclaimed. "Those of us in the order have mastered the fine art of herbs and fungi. There are certain plants that are endowed with almost magical gifts that are ours for the taking. Some give us longevity, some great strength. Others provide us with unparalleled wisdom and vision, but there are even others that make us irresistible to the opposite sex. Imagine what you could do with such a potion. You could stand before her when next she comes into your storehouse and she will beg you to take her. And you will have the great pleasure to refuse her, to make her suffer, to make her beg. She will crawl on the ground, clutching at your legs as you drag her across the floor in an effort to break free from her desperate plea. All will see her humbling herself before you, so not even her fiancé would want her any longer. She will be reduced to the level of insignificance that you have always seen her at, and in her despair she may even contemplate suicide, an act so vile that her family would be disgraced as well. I could give you that power, but such a thing would be cruel, and a man like yourself would not wish to reduce even someone as vile as this Sophia Commencu to such a level, no matter how much she might deserve it."

"Like you said, she would deserve it," he beseeched Bruno. "It would be for all the right reasons. To teach her and her family their proper place in life. I could pay you if that's what you want. You must give it to me."

"Are you certain," Bruno acted coyly. "I don't think you should ask for this without careful consideration."

"Yes, yes, I am most certain."

"I warn you, there is no turning back once you make this decision."

"Give it to me," the young man betrayed a tone of frustration in his voice as he stared sternly at Bruno, tired of his bantering. Holding out his hand he practically forced the decision on the drink-weary priest.

"Very well then…here it is. Take only a little swallow as it's quite potent." Bruno removed the vial from beneath his hassock. "It is a potion made from aminita panterina, the beautiful panther mushroom that few have mastered the properties of."

The young man whipped it from Bruno's hand and had the top of the vial removed and the potion pouring down his throat in one full sweeping arc of his arm. Bruno, slightly alarmed, had to seize the lad's elbow and force his hand away from his mouth before he completely finished the bottle of elixir.

"I think that is enough," he advised, removing the vial from the clutches of the man and replacing the stopper before squirreling it away in the folds of his clothes once more.

"I can feel it doing something," the man responded. "It's like a tingling all over. Like the blood is racing throughout my body. I feel powerful!"

Bruno smiled devilishly, suggesting to the young man that he sat down before the drug took full effect. Following the priest's instruction, he sat against one of the garden trellises that marked the four entry paths into the park.

"That's strange," he remarked to Bruno, "my limbs feel suddenly numb." His speech had become slurred and his eyes stared out blankly from their orbits. "Something's happening…" were the last of the words he uttered before Bruno braced the man's back more solidly up against the trellis framework.

"Do not worry," Bruno consoled the man. "It is not permanent. You will experience this sleeping death for about a week. Though you will be unable to move, or talk, you will hear everything, and you're unblinking eyes will see everything. I think you will be quite surprised to witness what people have to say about someone when they believe they're on their death bed. It will be a humbling experience, and humility is a virtue you sorely lack. Your hubris has been your undoing. Such false pride could not go unpunished. To suffer such pride to the extent that you would wish ill on others simply for not sharing in such a high opinion of yourself could not be left unpunished. I hope you understand. In the morning your family will likely send out a search party and they will find you. They will carry you back to your home and lay you in a bed in preparation for you death. The doctors will come and they will pronounce you have fallen to the palsy. Only you will be the wiser but when the week is over, and the illness passes, I think you'll be far happier to rejoice in your recovery than try and pursue some imaginary priest that poisoned you in your delirium. That is how your doctors will view it, so don't waste your time trying to convince them otherwise. Use your time wisely sir and learn from this experience. When the week has expired, I hope that you will be a better man. I know not your name and I care not, I have called you PRIDE, and you are the first of the deadly sins that have fallen in Prague."

12

Hradcany: Lichten Palace

"Brother Bruno, it was good to see you in morning mass in the cathedral," the Cardinal commented as the priest returned to the palace, where the others sat around the main foyer. "You must have been up early this morning, as no one saw you arrive."

"Nor would they as I was present before any of the monks had even risen. I must say, they are a slack bunch at St. Vitus. In my day, my cloister was all up before dawn and had their chores done before the morning bells. You really should look into that Guillermo. If you start letting them away with it, before long they'll start using their native tongues to perform mass instead of the Latin."

"I assure you, Brother Bruno, that day will not come. "Not if I can help it!"

"Some things not even you have the power to stop," Bruno replied smugly, the grin almost menacing as he bared the points of his teeth.

"The only failure I can see is your own. The three of you failed to stop another attack last night. The son of a grain merchant, left in a catatonic state after his attack. Where are any of you when you're needed?"

"Are we here to stop the attacks or stop the killer?" Yakov whom had remained silent thus far challenged the cardinal.

"Is there a difference?"

"Only if you consider the situation no different from a runaway horse. In its effort to escape, it may run down several people, but in the end the horse will be caught and killed for the terror it caused. But even so, the finality of its demise does not erase the fact that it has wreaked a path of devastation prior to its death."

"In case you have not recognized the difference Master Kahana, we have not brought you all this way to stop a horse."

"Ah…but that is where you are wrong," Yakov wagged his index finger in front of Calabrese. "What we are searching for is no different than that horse. An animal that has been let loose on the city and is wreaking a path of destruction."

"And when do you plan on stopping this horse?" the Cardinal's words dripped with acid.

"When he strikes again," Yakov advised.

"Were you not listening? I just told you, he has struck again."

"A merchant's son, you say. And where did this crime occur?"

"By the park in Mala Strana," the Cardinal stamped his foot in a fit of anger.

"And the bruising around the man's neck…"

"There was no bruising! I told you, he's in a state of shock; unable to move or speak. It's as if he's dead but he still breathes."

"Then this was not our killer, Cardinal. One does not have to be a professional to see that. Our killer physically disables his victims. Always goes for the neck. Read the reports! And the victims he is choosing now have a higher profile than some merchant's son."

"And based on that you feel confident enough to state emphatically that it is not our killer…hmmph." Calabrese folded his arms in disapproval. "That is not enough to draw a conclusion."

Yakov stared directly into the Cardinal's black eyes, sending a noticeable shiver down his adversary's spine. "It's the wrong area. Unless you've found another body lying in Holeckova, it doesn't correlate to the pattern!"

"Pattern? What pattern?" Calabrese stuttered anxious to hear more.

"The one that the killer is using."

Both Caesar and Giordano displayed obvious looks of bewilderment as they overheard Yakov reveal the information they so carefully concealed as he toyed with the Cardinal.

"When were you going to tell me about this pattern?"

"After we caught the killer," Yakov responded. "I shouldn't even tell you now, because you'll try to send in your men to pre-empt the attack and you will fail, and all it will do is let our prey know that we are on to their intentions and they will abandon their plan."

"You said their! Are you implying that we are dealing with more than one killer? I demand to know everything immediately." He stamped his foot another time.

"You can have your men follow us, but I will let you know everything when the time is right. Until then you will bear with me and you will not interfere."

"Just who do you think you are to tell me what to do?" the hackles rose on the back of the Cardinal's neck as he prepared to fight Yakov on this issue.

Rising out of his chair, Yakov approached the Cardinal until he was standing mere inches from his face. Calabrese felt compelled to take a step backwards as he appreciated for the first time that Yakov's height actually towered over him.

"You will not interfere," Yakov repeated as he hovered intensely in front of the Cardinal.

"I will not interfere," Calabrese found himself saying involuntarily.

"Now let us do our work," Yakov instructed him. "Your men can come with us, rather than follow behind. Today I have asked the Emperor to arrange several introductions for me within the Jewish community. I will be seeking their help in solving these killings."

"What could they possibly offer you?" the Cardinal was curious.

"Perhaps nothing. But if that should be the case, then at least I will know that I must look in another area."

"Another waste of time," the Cardinal criticized. "They will not help. After all, it is not their religious leaders that are being attacked!"

"All the more reason that they will help," Yakov corrected him. "History has shown them that whenever Christians are attacked, Jews have always been incorrectly blamed and suffered for it. With that threat hanging over their heads, they will be more than willing to provide me with any information they might have. Now if you don't mind, Cardinal Calabrese, we will be on our way and I'll take your two agents with me."

Providing a gesture of salutation, Yakov paraded from the foyer towards the entrance of the castle accompanied by Giordano and Caesar.

Waiting until he felt he was out of earshot from the Cardinal, Bruno spoke quietly to Yakov. "You must really show me how you do that."

"Do what?"

"That mind thing, where you can convince Calabrese to do what you want. It is very impressive."

"They have to have a reason to fear you," Yakov parroted Giardano's own suggestion.

"Well then at least tell me what he's afraid of so I can use it too," Bruno grinned.

"In time," was all that Yakov had to say on that matter.

§ § § § § §

"What is it you're hiding from me," the Cardinal muttered over and over again as he walked to the map model in the center of the floor and scrutinized it meticulously, looking from anything that may have escaped him in the past. "You think you're so smart Yakov Kahana, but I will find what it is you are not revealing and when I do, I will take control of the situation once and for all!"

Picking up two of the marking flags that Yakov had used to mark the location of the victims, Calabrese leaned over the map and placed them precisely on two spots; the park at Mala Strana where the merchant's son was found and the second at Holeckova, the name that Yakov had mysteriously mentioned. "What is it you see, you son of a bitch!" the cardinal cursed. The evidence of any pattern still eluded him. "Augustine," he shouted to one of his aides, "fetch me some string." The monk scurried off on his assigned errand, returning in a few minutes with the ball of wound cotton.

Starting with the flag that marked the first attack, the cardinal tied the string to the point of the pole and then slowly unraveled the twine until he wrapped it around the flag at the second attack. Then the third followed by the fourth and so on, until he interconnected all eleven flags in that manner. Standing back from his handiwork he gazed upon the pattern outlined by the string. "Blame the Jews falsely my ass!" he cried out. "Quickly Augustine, assemble the archbishop and the priests at once and have them brought here immediately. I think we have solved this crime!"

§ § § § § §

By midday the arrangements had been made through the offices of the Emperor for Yakov to visit the fabulous home situated on Siroka Street. As beautiful as the other homes located in the neighborhood may have been, none compared to the magnificence of this particular home that they entered. Yakov requested that the Cardinal's agents remain outside in the courtyard, a request that they appeared most happy to honor, having no desire to be seen in the home of a Jew, even one that from the outside must have been incredibly wealthy.

Summoned by his butler, the owner of the home came to the vestibule to greet his distinguished guests. A man of some importance, his balding pate covered sporadically by the strands of silver-grey hair that still remained, and the protruding belly demonstrating that he rarely had suffered a missed meal in his sixty odd years. Mordecai Maisel appeared for all intents and purpose an earnest and generous fellow. “May I have refreshments brought out for you,” he inquired, pointing with his hand to the parlor on the right side that connected to the central vestibule. His guests followed his instruction and moved gingerly into the adjoining room avoiding knocking any of the priceless figurines along the way. Nodding to his butler, Maisel silently ordered him to bring in the refreshments from the galley.

“This is a great honor gentlemen. For the courtesan of the Emperor to contact me personally, how could I possibly refuse to see you? But he did not tell me much, and I must admit, the three of you appear somewhat different than I expected.”

The remark was not without foundation but betrayed a malevolent and deprecating side to the man.

“I am Marcus Maisel, as you obviously know, the mayor of this community and it is a privilege to have you visit us. But how may I be of service to you?”

Each introduced themselves separately, starting with Bruno. “I am Giordano Bruno, an ordained priest of the Dominican order. I am Napolese by birth but here in Prague as a guest of the Emperor to teach the sciences at the university.”

“I have heard of you Father Bruno, although not necessarily in a favorable fashion. They say that some of your writings on man and the universe challenge the very fabric of our beliefs.”

“True,” Bruno agreed. “But if beliefs are worth having then they are worth challenging to see if they can withstand the stigma of criticism.”

“I’m afraid I find that quite hard to accept, coming from a priest,” Maisel beamed, his cherubic appearance made even more round as he puffed out his cheeks.

“That is what my order says as well,” Bruno responded in return, the four of them sharing a strained laugh before Caesar introduced himself.

“I am Caesar de Nostradame, son of Michel de Nostradame, the one called Nostradamus.”

The name did not register at all with Mordecai Maisel. Caesar waited, cocking his head slightly anticipating a response at any moment but still nothing was forthcoming.

"The seer," Caesar added.

Maisel gave a courteous nod as if to agree, but still no indication of recognition.

"The famous prophet and psychic to King Henry of France!"

"Oh," was all that Maisel had to say, but it was clearly evident that he had never heard of Nostradamus nor knew of any of his writings.

"A most famous man in certain communities," Bruno came to the defense of his colleague.

"Of that I am certain," the mayor responded.

"And I am Yakov Kahana of Brody."

Upon hearing the name Maisel momentarily froze and the expression on his face changed in character from the warm angelic features that had greeted them initially to on far more grim and revealing of the real man.

"You have obviously heard of me," Yakov continued.

"Yes," the answer was short and curt.

"And therefore you know that my being here is not by accident."

Even the timbre of the mayor's voice changed from being melodic to gravelly. "For the so-called Karaite prince to be in my house can only result in complications. If anyone was to see us together they might suspect I have abandoned my faith."

"That should not be a worry," Yakov assured him. "I had the privilege of walking through your community and saw the most magnificent synagogue you were building nearby. How could anyone doubt your commitment to your faith upon seeing that monument of bricks and mortar to it?"

"I thank you for your compliments for the synagogue, but you must understand my reluctance to be seen with you. After all, this is a very traditional community and the teachings of your people challenge those very foundations."

"My people are your people. Are we to become like the Christian Church with their differentiation between Catholics and Anglicans? Cannot two sides of coin share the same metal they are imprinted upon?"

"See, that is the problem," the mayor pointed out. "You Karaites try to make it sound so simple, as if there were no differences. But there are, and they are like night and day."

"Both the night and day share the same twenty-four hour period that God created. One cannot exist without the other."

Maisel turned beseechingly to Bruno. "Can you not see the problem I'm dealing with? He tries to convince us that you can have two sets of rules for the same thing. How can one be a Jew if his teachings are contradictory to what the Rabbis teach?"

"I wouldn't know," Bruno answered, "but then again, I'm not a Jew. It made sense to me."

The mayor made a gesture of disgust as he threw up his hand and then crossed them quickly, brushing aside the air as he did so. "Two sets of rules cannot occupy the same space," he said exasperatedly.

"Which came first," Bruno inquired as he winked at Yakov.

"That does not matter," Maisel brushed the question aside. "First, second is not the issue. What is important is what is right."

"Yes, I agree," Yakov interjected. "And that is exactly what the teaching of Karaism is about. Did not Anan ben David state that one should read the book and if how one interprets the teachings for themselves appears correct to them, then it is right!"

"Of course you would say that," Maisel stated somewhat contemptuously. "He was your ancestor. Why would you disagree with him? But the rest of us do."

"And if you feel you are correct in doing so, then you too are right," Yakov tutored.

"It cannot be that way."

"It can, but I am not here to convince you , so rest assured I will let everyone know that should inquire that you have defended your faith admirably. And as I mentioned previously, the synagogue you are building in your own name is a testimonial to your faith."

"Of that we are in agreement," the mayor nodded.

"Even from my view, which is alien to your culture, I am awestruck by its beauty," Bruno added. "It rivals any cathedral I have ever visited. How one man could even afford to build such a structure on their own is incredible."

Maisel basked in the praise that Bruno effused for him. Once again his facial features reverted to the cherubic visage they had first viewed. Seeing the change, Bruno turned on the praise even stronger, continuing with one complement after another.

"Most kings would not even dare to build such an edifice, afraid that they would risk everything they possessed in the attempt," Bruno suggested.

"True, very true," Maisel confirmed. "But for God, I would gladly donate my entire fortune. For the people I govern over, I consider it my privilege, and for my daughter, whom was taken away from me, I owe it to her memory."

"I am so sorry," Bruno apologized. "I did not mean to stir any sorrowful memories."

"It's okay," Maisel patted the air in front of him. "I know you meant no harm."

At that precise moment an extremely attractive young woman entered the room carrying a tray with an assortment of juices in very expensive Venetian glass.

"What happened to Karlov?" Maisel inquired.

"I heard we had guests, Mordecai. It was only proper that I came out to greet them."

"Gentlemen, my wife Frema," the mayor introduced. "That is Master Caesar, and Father Bruno, and Yakov Kahana," he said the last name with a slight note of contempt.

Upon hearing Yakov's name pronounced, the woman froze slightly, which did not go unnoticed by Yakov. The motion did not betray any sign of contempt, but more one of awe. Yakov then examined the beautifully interwoven skirt she wore, a mixture of brown, gold and crimson threads. A skirt that was very familiar to him.

"A pleasure to meet you, Frema Maisel," Yakov smiled at her.

Hearing her name caused her to blush, and she quickly tried to hide the fact that she did so by standing behind her husband's chair where he could not see her.

"We are discussing the synagogue, dear wife," Maisel informed her. "I was just telling the gentlemen how I was dedicating it to our daughter."

Upon hearing that, Frema turned pale. "I'm sorry, I have to leave. I have a difficult time talking about my daughter. Forgive me." She ran hurriedly from the room.

Thumbing his mouth and chin, Yakov analyzed what had just happened. It was obvious that Maisel was well aware of the reaction he would get from his wife as soon as he broached the topic of their dead daughter. Why raise it unless he wanted his wife to leave. What better way to do so, than to make it appear to be an oversight on his part.

"I am sorry if we upset your wife," Yakov apologized.

"She has not taken our daughter's death well. I cannot blame her. It was a horrible death."

"Would it be rude to inquire how she died?" Bruno asked.

"I'm afraid it was one of your own that was responsible," the mayor indicated by pointing at Bruno's cassock. "He incited the populace to attack the Jewish Quarter. In the ensuing panic, people were blind to their own actions. She was trampled by the crowds trying to flee from their attackers."

"Most horrible," Bruno hung his head, "and I am ashamed of anyone that wears these robes and dishonors them with hate and malice."

"I hear that justice has been served," Maisel commented. "God works in mysterious ways and the priest responsible was punished by being attacked and killed by an unknown assailant."

"If you speak of Taddeush, then I feel even more shame for I am glad that he was made to suffer. As a priest I should not say such things."

"I cannot agree with you more," the mayor found comfort in Bruno's words. "Though I am ashamed to say it myself, I am glad he suffered too."

"Death is hard for any of us to accept. Especially for a mother," Yakov turned the conversation back to Frema. "Though it is said we all return to the Shekinah, it is little comfort to those of us still alive."

"Only if you believe in your teachings," the mayor argued. "We would like to believe there is a heaven that welcomes us. That is where I'd like to believe my daughter is."

"Whichever place, I hope that your wife understands that both offer a continuance."

"Why would you say that?" the consternation appearing on Maisel's face showing that Yakov had struck a chord.

"Only because I thought your wife might be a Karaite," Yakov suggested. "The dress was unique to our weavers in Moldavia."

"I have traveled a lot," Maisel countered. "I bring gifts back. I like to give gifts to my wife. You are wrong!"

"I appreciate your pointing out my error. It is a beautiful dress. You have good taste. Would you mind if I used your water closet. I'm afraid that the walk over here has left me in need."

"Where is Karlov when you need him? Oh, never mind! Just go down that hallway past the kitchen. It will be the first door on your left."

Rising from the brocade couch, Yakov bowed to his host and followed his directions. Before disappearing from the room he winked at Bruno and Caesar, and immediately Giordano began asking questions about the synagogue again.

Moving down the hallway, Yakov stopped in front of the doorway into the big galley kitchen where he found Frema slumping over one of the food preparation counters, oblivious to his presence.

"Forgive me," he broke the silence, I was seeking your water closet."

She turned to face him, tears welling up in her eyes. Pointing to the right beyond the archway, she indicated it was further down the hall.

"Actually, that was not completely true. I was looking for an opportunity to speak with you."

"Why would you want to speak with me, Mar Kahana?"

"Because you know who I am."

She nodded accordingly. "You are the Makhir."

"And you are one of my people."

Again she confirmed his statement.

"I am truly sorry about your daughter. But if you are one of us, then you know that there is no finality in death. Though we suffer for their loss, they do not. There is peace in knowing that."

"Master, I no longer know what to believe," she cried. "My husband says that she is gone. Her spirit is departed forever and that all I have to look forward to now is to grow old and childless."

"Harsh words. Perhaps said out of grief? So often we want to punish those that are not responsible."

"But I am," she burst into tears. "I let go of her hand. When the people were surging in the streets, I let go of her hand and she was trampled to death."

"Look at me Frema!" Yakov commanded her.

She turned away trying to avoid his stare.

"Look at me!" he insisted.

She felt compelled to do as he commanded.

"You know who I am. You know I can see what others cannot see. From God, through my ancestors the word has come down to man since the beginning of time, and I would not conceal from you what He has seen."

Frema was mesmerized by his stare. She could not break the contact, sensing that Yakov was probing through her mind, searching her thoughts and memories.

"You were knocked over yourself," Yakov recalled the event for her. "You were in danger yourself of dying in the panic. Your guilt is not that you let go, for no person could have held on to your daughter that day. Your guilt is that you remained alive. She would not have wanted you to die. She loved you too much for that to happen. Live for her sake. That is how she would want it." Breaking the connection, Yakov reached out to steady Frema as her legs felt week and began to fold beneath her.

It took a few seconds but then she felt the strength return to her limbs. She was no longer crying. The tears had dried and she could feel no reason to shed any more. She returned Yakov's smile. "Thank you Makhir. I can see her smiling. She is smiling at me."

"She is happy for you if you can give up your sadness. You must do it for her."

"I will try."

"That is all she wants."

"How can I repay you," Frema insisted. "You have come all this way to help one of your people and you don't even know me."

"We are all part of the same family. The Kahana are here to serve for you are all known to us. But I must confess, I had not come here originally to help you. I am here on another mission. I need to know about strange events occurring in this city. Of a silent killer that stalks the night. Do you know of anything that might help in our search?"

"Why would we know of such things Makhir?"

"The why and the how are merely matters of perception. Things that do not appear right can often lead to clues and discoveries that weren't even conceived of. It is obvious your husband cannot tolerate Karaites, yet here I find he is married to one. He is a man well advanced in age, you are young and comely, but somehow the two of you have come together. He builds a monument that staggers the imagination from his own personal funds, yet no one knows how he came in possession of such a vast fortune. Perhaps if I can shed some light on these mysteries, perhaps I will find my way clearer on other matters."

Frema reacted nervously, biting her lower lip subconsciously. "I cannot help you, Makhir."

"Cannot or will not," Yakov inquired placidly.

"Please, he is my husband. Does there have to be an explanation why two people come together?"

"Usually there is. And for a rabbinical Jew of his stature and power, to marry a Karaite Jewess there would have to be a very interesting story."

"What is going on here," the voice was angry and threatening as Mordecai Maisel entered into the kitchen and found Yakov with his hands firmly wrapped around Frema's outstretched arms.

"Your wife was despondent and crying when I found her," Yakov answered truthfully, "and I managed to calm her."

"How dare you sequester yourself away with my wife! Who the hell do you think you are? Get your hands off her this instant!" Maisel waved his fists threateningly as he glanced around the room in search of a utensil, any instrument that would be suitable to use as a weapon.

"I am her Prince, the Nasi, as you well know. Why should I not feel entitled to speak with any of my subjects?"

"I told you, she is not one of you any longer. Now get away from her."

"He has not done anything, husband, but help me shed my grief," Frema defended her Makhir.

"Since when are you entitled to speak out against me? Know your place woman!" Maisel shouted hysterically.

"She knows her place," Yakov informed her husband. "As a Karaite woman she is your equal in every facet. She does not need your permission to speak."

"How dare you come into my house and destroy its harmony! I will see to it that you are charged for this."

"When you manage to think of the crime of which to charge me, then I'm more than willing to face your prosecution. But remember this Mordecai Maisel, you have already lied to me on one occasion and that only makes me more curious as to what else you have lied about. I am the Emperor's agent in case you have forgotten and I will be investigating this further."

"Get out," he screamed wildly as he chased the three visitors from his home, slamming the door behind them as they left.

"Well, that went well," Bruno commented sarcastically.

"Could have been better," Yakov answered. "What do you think Caesar?"

"I did as you instructed, Kova. I concentrated on a focal point in the room, all the time that he spoke."

"And?"

"He was hiding a lot from us. He knew far more about the priest's murder than he was letting on. And when he talked about the sums of money that he was spending on the synagogue, it was almost as if he was hiding the biggest secret of all."

"And what about his wife? How does he feel about her?"

"He hates her," Caesar answered.

"Good," Yakov commented. "That gives us something to work with."

13

Prague Castle: December 1588

"What am I supposed to do with you?" Rudolf proposed the questions to the three of them standing in front of his throne, summoned for chastisement. "I arrange to have you visit one of the most prominent men in all of Prague, a man whom I should remind you donates thousands of florins every year to this city for public works, and you go and insult him in a few short minutes after your arrival. Do any of you have an explanation for what I've been hearing?"

"If I could just speak for a moment," Bruno partially raised his hand like a scolded schoolboy.

"Now if it was you, Giordano, I would not be surprised at all. Sequestering yourself away with someone's wife is something you do all the time. But you, Kova? That I find hard to believe!"

"It wasn't what you think, Rudi," Bruno practically pleaded.

"Then enlighten me, but not you, him!" The Emperor pointed an empowering finger directly at Yakov.

"If I have caused you embarrassment, Excellency, then I beg your pardon. But if you are willing to support us fully in our efforts to find the night stalker, then understand that what we did, what I have done, was solely in the pursuit of that end."

"Being caught, practically in an embrace, with the young, beautiful wife of Prague's most affluent man is all part of the effort in finding a killer? Then this I've got to hear!"

"Me too," Calabrese voiced his opinion from the side of the throne room where he was standing surrounded by his cronies.

"There is a connection," Yakov insisted.

"He is right," the Cardinal declared in full support of Yakov, a move which surprised everyone except the Catholic clergy assembled formally for this hearing.

The three of them looked sidewise at the Cardinal, perplexed as to his motives. Whatever it was could be to no one's good.

"I have broken your code, Yakov Kahana. I have seen what you have been hiding from me. And I am not surprised that you have done so. In your situation, I probably would have done likewise. Your majesty, there is a pattern to the killings; a Star of David. You can see it clearly on the map. The demon stalking your city at night and killing your citizens, my churchmen, is none other than a Jew."

"I thought you were convinced that we were dealing with some demon sent by the Devil to herald the end of the world, Guillermo."

"Demon, Jew, there is no difference. Both are bent on our destruction and bringing about the end of the world.

"Is this true, Kova? Have you been concealing this information from us? Is the killer in Josefov?" Rudolf had to pretend he had not even the slightest revelation that Yakov had spoken to him earlier about.

"Your majesty, if I may," Yakov's attempt to explain was done quite sheepishly, not knowing how the Emperor would intentionally react. "The three of us were assembled in Prague in order to find the killer that is terrorizing your city. For that purpose we all have unique abilities which are guiding us to that end. And truthfully, I did not reveal my findings thus far to the Cardinal, simply because I knew he would jump to hasty conclusions, as he's already done, and brand the entire community guilty of a crime we are still investigating. There is reason to believe that the answers lie in Josefov. And every fiber of my being tells me that the mayor of Josefov knows far more about what is transpiring than he is willing to say."

"Then let's bring him in," interrupted the Cardinal. "We have ways to make him confess."

"You see, your Majesty, that is exactly what I have been trying to avoid. On a rack, hot brands applied to the body, a man would be willing to say anything. I don't want a confession, I want the truth, and I think that you would want the same thing."

"I want an end to these killings Kova and if you think this man is responsible, friend or no friend of the Court, I'll have him brought in for questioning."

"He is not the killer," Yakov was adamant. "Does he know the killer, possibly? Will he tell us, no! But his wife is an entirely different matter. She knows far more than anyone, and I need to pluck that information from her, but delicately."

"Perhaps you want to peel back the leaves and succor the fruit," Calabrese ridiculed. "Honestly, she is a woman. Whatever she knows, or what you think she knows will be of little value. And she certainly isn't the killer!"

"I merely need time," Yakov pleaded to the Emperor. "She is one of my own, a Karaite, she will reveal all to me but in time."

"Time is a luxury we have very little of," Rudolf warned. "We need results. I can dismiss the charges against you laid by the mayor but I cannot obviously request that he makes his wife available to you. Either he is guilty, and I bring them all in to the armory for questioning, or he isn't, and then our hands are tied and we can do nothing. Nothing! Do you understand, Kova? You cannot harass him or his wife if you say he is not guilty."

"Of the actual performance of the murders, he is not guilty. Of other crimes that may be related, I will need time to prove. I cannot brand a man with guilt unless I am certain."

"Do what you must to be certain, but tread carefully. There are laws that govern society, and not even I can protect you if you choose to transgress them. Do you understand?"

"Have no fear," Yakov reassured Rudolf, "I will not compromise your authority."

"But your majesty," the Cardinal interceded once again. "There is this map and it is a certainty. Whoever is doing this is connected to the Jewish community. We cannot ignore that."

"What are you suggesting Cardinal? That I arrest fifty thousand people and torture each of them until one confesses."

"If that is what it takes, yes!"

"That will not happen in my city!"

"I have already dispatched a summary of our findings to the Pope and I'm certain he will make recommendations as to how this should be handled."

"And I'm certain he will," Rudolf corroborated, "but this is still my city and no one will harm the Jews unless it is by my command."

Calabrese slithered forward in his black robes, his feet not visible as he moved so he appeared to float above the ground. "Do not make me add Judaizer to the list of your indiscretions," he warned. Any power and authority you have has been invested in you by the papacy. It would be best if you remembered that."

"It would be best if you leave this chamber now Cardinal before you see me lose my temper." Rudolf rose out of the throne and his imposing frame dwarfed the cardinal.

"We will await His Excellency's response to my dispatch," Calabrese compromised, withdrawing back towards his clergy as he escaped from the overpowering shadow that Rudolf had cast upon him.

"See to it that you do wait," he was instructed. "I do not want to hear of any incidents in the Jewish town resulting from your secret police confronting the people in the meantime. Otherwise, Pope or no Pope, I will have you all arrested and charged for disturbing the peace!"

Calabrese didn't even bother to respond, turning his back on the Emperor and leaving the hall, his entourage of priests and monks traipsing behind him.

"Good riddance," Rudolf puffed as he let himself slump back into his chair.

"You put him in his place," Bruno congratulated the Emperor.

"I did nothing," Rudolf sighed. "Nothing but make him more determined than ever to see me removed from this throne. And mark my words; they will stop at nothing in order to see that happens. Gentlemen, all our heads are in the noose. You better have more than a hunch!"

"The hunches I leave to Caesar," Yakov responded. "The rest I leave to facts."

Everyone looked to the doors to ensure that the Cardinal had truly left and was not hiding in the wings overhearing their conversation. Convinced that he had gone, Yakov continued his explanation.

"It was not as if we went to the mayor's house without a plan."

"If antagonizing him was your plan, it wasn't a very good one," Rudolf criticized.

"Have you ever questioned where all the money has come from to build that new synagogue?"

"From Maisel and the community I suppose," Rudolf replied.

"They already have three synagogues. The community is definitely not paying for a fourth. All the money is coming from Maisel himself. Giordano can confirm that. He knew exactly what words to stroke Maisel with, and the mayor was more than happy to tell him how much everything was costing him. Do you know that he's imported tapestries that their cost alone could support your entire palace workforce for a year? What kind of man has that amount of money that he can part with so freely without a single thought to his own future needs?"

"A man that has lost his daughter and has no thought of the future any longer. I have had this conversation with Marcus in the past, and he made this point to me quite effectively. He built up his fortune for his family, for their future. Now that he no longer has any offspring, there is no point to hold on to it any longer. This synagogue will be his daughter. All that he would have given her, he will give to it."

"No man gives away everything he has grown accustomed to," Yakov argued. "It is not in the nature of man, and the man I confronted yesterday is no saint. If you haven't noticed, he may be spending millions of florins, but he does not appear to be suffering for it. In fact, I would say that his lifestyle hasn't changed at all. It's as if the money is coming from a bottomless pit. How would one man amass that amount of money and no one noticed?"

"You Jews do tend to be a secretive lot," Rudolf suggested.

'Not even the Jews in the community seem to know how he acquired so much money," Bruno felt compelled to comment. "The pay for being mayor is nominal. The family printing presses were productive, but certainly not to the degree of some of the other publishing houses. And if the other publishers didn't accumulate the same level of wealth from their businesses, then how could he?"

"What are you suggesting then? That he's an alchemist that has learned to turn base metals into gold?"

"If it was possible, I'd know that secret before anyone else,' Bruno declared.

"There's no alchemy involved, I can assure you," Yakov removed a piece of parchment paper from his robe. "I've recorded the amounts that Giordano remembered from his conversation. The total is staggering. There's only one place you'd find a sum of money like this and that's in a bank."

Rudolf raised his index to his finger in recognition of Yakov's deduction. "Aha! And you are going to tell me you found a connection between Maisel and the dead banker?"

"No, but I was going to say that I believe we will find a connection if we dig deep enough."

"Another hunch," the Emperor remarked condescendingly.

"A hunch that Caesar agrees with."

"Oh, Caesar agrees with it. Well that must make it true then," Rudolf repeated cynically as he lowered his head into the palms of his hands.

"Not only me, but my father as well."

Upon hearing that comment from Caesar, the Emperor raised himself to sit erect and fully attentive. "That is a different matter. If your father had something to say about this, then please tell me."

"As I sat in the mayor's house I could not help but recall a particular quatrain that my father wrote. Century VIII, Quatrain ninety-six to be exact. In it he said, *'The synagogue sterile without any fruit, It will be received into the infidels, From Babylon the daughter of the persecuted, Miserable and grieved, her wings are cut.'*

"And you believe your father was talking about this particular synagogue?" Rudolf requested an explanation.

"He's building the synagogue in the name of his daughter," Caesar exclaimed, "A daughter who is no longer alive. His family tree is cut down. It will bear no fruit, it is finished. But it will be built, and it will be finished, but when that happens, it is going to be expropriated by the state."

"Just how did you come to that conclusion," the emperor could not follow the explanation past that point.

"If my father wanted to say that it was taken over in an anti-Jewish riot, than he would have used much different language. Language that was far more violent in nature and far more aggressive. He only used the term infidels for non-Jews and non-Christians but he always indicated where they were from. He'd say Asia or Africa at some point in the quatrain. He doesn't do that this time. Therefore he implies that the handing over of the synagogue is an internal matter. The state is the only non-religious organization in this country to have the authority to seize a synagogue as an asset."

"And why would I have the courts do such a thing?"

"Exactly, why would you do such a thing," Yakov redirected the question back to Rudolf.

Taking a moment to think about the answer, Rudolf replied enthusiastically as he slapped his thighs, "Only if the property and building was in default of a loan or if the possession was proven not to be legal and had to be settled in a court of law."

"Precisely my point, but carry on Caesar. There was more."

"I did not quite understand the latter two lines until we found out what Kova was up to in the kitchen. Once I realized that the mayor's wife was one of Kova's people and I saw how even amongst the Jews, his beliefs and teaching were persecuted, then I knew my father was pointing the wife out as a key to our mystery."

"But the last line," Rudolf pleaded for the final explanation.

"Without her daughter she has nothing to live for. Any relationship she may have had with her husband revolved around her daughter. Now she is nothing to him. She has nowhere to go, no life to live. In essence her wings are cut."

"Your father was an amazing man." Rudolf praised Caesar.

"No, Caesar is an amazing man," Yakov was quick to correct Rudolf. "God adorns the heavens with stars and in their entirety they tell a story of the past, the present and the future. But it's not God but the astrologer that reveals their meaning to us. In that case, who is the more amazing?"

"So what are we to do next?" Rudolf was quick to throw his lot back in with the chosen three.

Yakov pounded his right fist into his left palm. "I need to see the banker's records. There has to be something there that shows the connection."

"I don't have any authority over private banks. I've already told you that. There's nothing I can do?"

"Perhaps there is," Bruno suggested grinning from ear to ear. "You can open an account."

14

Strasnicka: Korunni Bank

"But we have a letter," Caesar argued with the clerk blocking their way at the door which he was half way through before the stout, pig-faced man tried to force it closed by bringing the metal grill across and locking it in place with a hasp.

"I don't care if you have a letter from the Emperor, himself," the man squealed as he placed the greater portion of his bulk against the flat of the iron bars.

"We do have a letter from the Emperor you paper pushing bureaucrat!" Caesar screamed as he quickly lost his temper.

"Then take it to the Koenigsbank, he doesn't do any of his business here," the man huffed under the strain of holding the metal grill still as it rattled on its hinges from the force of Caesar's thrusts.

"Let me talk to him," Yakov suggested from behind Caesar, who was still caught halfway between the door frame and the edge of the bars, neither able to move forward or back because of the locked hasp.

"Just wait Kova. Let me get my hands around his ruddy neck and then you can talk to him all you want."

"That won't be necessary Caesar; he wants to talk with me."

"I want to talk with you? Who the hell are you," the man questioned. "You're dressed up like some pompous potentate from Turkey. We don't let you Mohammedans in here let alone talk to you."

"I assure you, I am not Turkish, but you do want to talk to me. It is in your own best interest."

"Are you threatening me?"

"No, I am here to protect you," Yakov insisted. "I am here about the missing money. The Emperor through our empowerment is here about the missing money. No one wants any trouble. Especially if your clients should find out that their savings have disappeared; evaporated without a trace. They would be very upset and start demanding that the Crown make good on its promise of compensatory insurance for bank fraud."

The sweat began to roll down the forehead and on to the fleshy cheeks of the man. "There's been no fraud here!" he was practically shouting now.

"But there is money missing."

"Yes, that is true, but I'm looking in to the matter. That is why I have closed the premises until I complete the audit. I don't know how this happened. How did the Emperor find out? I just discovered it myself but a few weeks ago?"

"Do you think anything of this magnitude could go undetected in Prague without his Excellency knowing," Yakov pointed an accusatory finger at the man. "He knows everything and he is not happy with what has occurred."

"Please, please, you have to understand,' the sweat now poured profusely until the clerk's shirt collar was soaked, "I had nothing to do with this. It had to do with Master Korunni and he's dead now, and with him he has taken the secret of where the money is."

"Then for your sake, I hope you can séance with dead, because we need to hold someone accountable for the loss, and right now I don't see anyone else in your bank except you," Yakov winked at the man.

"You have to believe me. You have to help me."

"Right now you have my associate trapped in your security door. I would suggest you release the hasp-lock so that he can extricate himself, and then you let us in so we can hopefully find a solution to your dilemma."

The man did as Yakov suggested, opening the grill so that the two of them were able to pass through the doorway and into the banks exchange room. Caesar whispered into Yakov's ear as they entered. "You can be a very dangerous man."

"Whatever it takes," Yakov replied in a voice inaudible to the clerk. "So that I can fill in my report when this is all done, what is your name? And whatever you do, don't provide me with a false name, because the Emperor's men will find you if our investigation points in your direction."

"Porcenski, sir," he quivered and shook, terrified at the thought of being blamed for the bank's mysterious loss.

"Well then, Master Porcenski, we will be joined shortly by another colleague; a priest. If you have anything to confess to, he will provide you with your rights if you should happen to be a Catholic. Are you a Catholic, Master Porcenski."

The clerk nodded vigorously. "Yes, yes, I am. Not like my employer," he added. "I have no idea what Master Korruni was, but he wasn't a Catholic. I never trusted the man. He was from somewhere in White Russia. And you know what those Russians are like. They're all thieves and liars. Everyone knows that."

"From Moldavia?" Yakov inquired.

"I don't know. Somewhere like that. Around the Black Sea I think. He talked about it, but I never really listened."

"Perhaps you should have, Master Porcenski. I know something about those Moldavians. You're right; they hide a lot of secrets."

"Precisely," the clerk hastily agreed, "Matters that he would never discuss with me. But he lived such a frugal life. I never suspected he was taking money from the bank."

"So how did you become aware of the sums missing in the first place?"

"One of our clients," he answered in a halting voice. "He came in and wanted to close his account. We never have anyone closing their account, but he wanted to. He had managed to save a small fortune over the years and he wanted to withdraw it all at once. So I took his receipt for the amount he had last recorded and then went down to the records room to check the balance." At that point he stopped in his tracks and refused to say any more.

"It's alright. We're here to help," Caesar urged him to continue, feeling very comfortable with their charade.

"I don't think I can say," the clerk resisted.

"And why is that?" Yakov looked sternly into his small black eyes.

"If I say anymore, then you will know that there was an illegal activity being perpetrated."

"My good man, we already know there was an illegal activity going on here. You're missing an obscene amount of money and that implies that someone was perpetrating an illegal activity, wouldn't you think?"

The clerk rung his hands nervously, the sweat now evident streaming down his arms and under his sleeves. "I think I should have the bank solicitor here, before I say any more."

"If you bring in a solicitor, I am certain the Emperor will be very angry," Yakov told him quite implicitly. "We don't want to raise the profile of your problem more than is necessary. You understand? A solicitor would only indicate that you have something to hide. Only a guilty man has to hide the evidence."

"The records didn't match. That's all I'm willing to say. Now please, you must leave and let me finish my audit. You must go now. I don't want to talk to you any more!"

At that precise moment, Giordano Bruno arrived at the bank and entered into the foyer. "Am I missing something?"

"Master Porcenski, your confessor is here now," Yakov waved his hand towards Bruno. "If it makes you feel better, you can tell Father Bruno everything and you know that everything you say will remain in the strictest confidence. Is that not true Father Bruno?"

"Of course," Giordano responded automatically. "What is it that we're confessing to?"

"The disappearance of a huge sum of money and the manipulation of bank records to cover up that disappearance."

"Oh, is that so," Bruno shrugged. "It seems to be a common confession nowadays. I've had several thieves do so in the past few weeks."

"I am not a thief!" Porcenski denied vehemently.

"Of course not, my son. All of us make a mistake once or twice. We should not be immediately labeled by a rare indiscretion."

"No, seriously, I am not a thief," he reiterated. "I'm certain it was my former employer, but he's dead now, and I can't prove it."

"Master Porcenski won't provide us with the opportunity to help him Father. Although he says he's aware of how the crime may have been perpetrated, he no longer wishes to cooperate. I'm not certain how we can help him if he won't allow us. Especially if he won't show us the altered records he referred to."

"We must not allow a false sense of loyalty to the dead cloud our judgment, my son," Bruno advised.

The clerk appeared to be partially regaining his composure, analyzing the events since their arrival and rethinking his options, none of which included cooperating any further. "Father, I do not wish to offend a man of the cloth, but I have nothing to confess to, and now that I'm thinking about it, this is more likely a legal matter that will require an investigation by the courts. I'm sorry gentlemen, but whether the Emperor likes it or not, this will have to come out into the open."

"I can understand perfectly," Bruno appeared to be agreeing with the clerk's opinion. "I think we may have stressed you enough. A man of your girth often can suffer terribly from the stress my colleagues may have caused you. I am a bit of a medical man, as are many of the clergy, and we are aware that the heart of a large man like yourself may not withstand the pressures of such events. Profuse sweating is a common sign. You're not feeling faint are you? Shortness of breath perhaps?"

The clerk nodded, wiping his brow and growing even more stressed when he assessed the amount of sweat that was streaming down his face. He placed his right hand over his chest, worriedly checking on his heart to see that all was right. "I think it may be fluttering," he commented to Bruno in a distressed voice.

"Oh, that is not good. Not good at all. Do your legs feel weak? Any dizziness?"

Suddenly the clerk felt his legs bend beneath him and he momentarily felt as if he was going to lose his balance. "I think I may not be well. I have to sit down."

"By all means, please do, my son," Bruno prescribed. "Let me fix you a pot of herbal tea. You do have a cook stove where I can boil some water?"

The clerk pointed at the small potbellied stove over in the corner of the foyer that served not only as the heater for the winter days but also as their hot plate. A copper teapot sat on the floor beside it.

"I'll just be a moment. Don't you worry! We'll have you fixed up in no time," Bruno patted him comfortingly on the shoulder.

Yakov and Caesar looked at each other, both baffled and amused; having no idea what Bruno was planning as they watched the priest preparing a tea from a small pouch he withdrew from his frock. The water once boiled was poured into the ceramic cup that the clerk kept by the pot and Bruno gently mixed the tea, humming softly as he did so.

"Here, drink this," he placed the cup into his hands, helping fold the clerk's fingers around its base so that he held it firmly.

"Thank you," Porcenski bowed his head in gratitude as he sat down to have his drink.

"If you still feel like your heart is perhaps failing, then I would suggest you drink quickly so that we can arrest the symptoms before they become too pronounced."

Troubled by what Bruno may have done, Yakov reached out and grasped Giordano's arm.

"Don't worry, he'll be all right," Bruno assured Yakov but at the same time pretending to be concerned for the clerk's well being. Yakov took a moment before he was satisfied by his companion's reassurance and then released his grip.

"I don't think it's working," Porcenski informed Bruno. "My head is still spinning and my heart is feeling even more restless."

"You must give it time to work, my son. A man in your condition should take better care of yourself. You should know that palpitations are common to someone of your size and this matter with the bank was not going to do you any good."

"You're right father, but what am I to do. Someone has to take care of this mess that Master Korunni has left me."

"Yes, I understand, and we will not trouble you any longer. We will find another way to deal with this matter that clears your name and identifies the true culprit."

"Thank you father, thank you." Feeling a spasmodic reflux in his throat, Porcenski had to gulp repeatedly in an effort to steady his stomach. "I think I'm feeling sick," he muttered.

"Oh, this is not good," Bruno instructed him. "If you don't keep the tea down, it will do you no good. "

"I'm sorry father but I don't think I can. I have to go." Cupping one hand over his mouth and the other seizing his protruding stomach, Porcenski ran to the water closet to the rear of the bank and outside in the alleyway. Caesar and Yakov watched as he was able to move his impressive bulk with amazing speed and agility, practically leaping over the railings that divided the various accounting desks that lined the hallway to the rear exit.

"Well gentlemen, I think you have some time to do whatever it is you're supposed to do," Bruno commented.

"What did you do to him," Caesar felt compelled to ask.

"Merely a little recipe of mine for such an occasion. I made him a nice cup of baneberry tea. At first it causes some of the symptoms I described for a failing heart, but then it affects the intestinal tract. He'll vomit at first and then have stomach cramps and severe diarrhea for a few days, but what better way to treat a glutton. He'll probably thank me for the weight he'll lose."

"You're certain he'll be all right. He'll recover?" Yakov sought a further reassurance.

"He'll be fine. Better than fine even. It will probably affect his appetite for quite some time, even after it has completely passed from his body. You know gluttony is one of the seven deadly sins. I have probably cured him."

"Good, as long as he'll survive."

"Go! Go do what it is in here. You probably have half an hour at most until he's able to return."

"What about your visit to the victim that survived," Caesar inquired."

"I'll tell you later. Now go! I'll keep a lookout for our fat friend."

Relying on Bruno to give them sufficient time to cover their actions, both Yakov and Caesar raced down the step into the basement where the clerk indicated the bank held the records. They were in luck; the door was unlocked, probably because the clerk himself was frantically looking for information before they had interrupted him with their arrival.

"So where do we start," Caesar whined, glancing around him at all the boxes brimming full of papers stacked around the perimeter of the room.

"There's got to be some sort of indexing system. It can't be random! Look for anything familiar. A name, a place, anything!"

"They appear to be packed by dates," Caesar groaned. "There's like a hundred years here."

"Focus on the last ten. If the crime was being committed somehow by Maisel, then it couldn't be much longer than that. Have you found anything yet?"

"I'm looking, I'm looking!"

"Wait, here's something. Fifteen seventy-nine." Yakov opened the lid to the box. "We're in luck, at least all the accounts are alphabetical."

"Did you find his name?"

"Better yet, his family business. His printery is a client here. Not a very rich client from the looks of it, no wait…change of fortune midyear. There's a large sum of money coming in every month from then on. That's strange. The entry clerk's name for each deposit is F. Rofe."

"What's so strange about that?"

"Ha Rofe is a Karaite name; a very notable family actually. But it's not the banker's. Therefore I'd have to conclude that there were others working here."

"So he had his family and relatives working in the bank, what's the big deal?"

"Our mayor doesn't like Karaites. If his reaction to me was any example, you might even say he hates us. So why bank at a Karaite establishment? It doesn't make sense."

"Hey, Kova, in case you haven't noticed, a lot of this doesn't make sense. We're actually breaking into the records of a bank. Does that make sense to you that we've just made ourselves into criminals?"

"Only if we're caught," Yakov corrected him.

"Well the way we're going, that's only going to be a matter of time."

"There's got to be more. Just the fact that there's a flow of money into the account doesn't prove anything. It could be legitimate. The only way we'd know for certain would be by tracing back the source of the funds each month. But without knowledge of how they work their system here, that could take a lifetime."

"Well then, the only one that's going to know is F. Rofe, so why don't we find him and get him to tell us."

"I think you might be right," Yakov agreed. "We'll never get through all these records, but the clerk that appears to be the signing authority on every transaction would know what occurred without even having to review the records. If it was illegal, I don't think he'd be about to forget. Let's get back up top before we're discovered."

"Too bad my father didn't give us a better clue where to look."

"What was that?"

"My father. He talked about this. I was just thinking about it and then another of his quatrains popped into my head with a blinding headache I might add."

"And what did he say?"

"It was Century VI, *Quatrain* nine."

"And....?"

'There will be a great scandal about the holy temple. The one that will be given our honors and admiration. By the one that makes graven medals of silver and gold, the end of it will come in very strange torment.'

"Most curious," Yakov agreed. "It's as if you're father knows the building of the synagogue was pivotal to everything that's happened so far."

"We're obviously on the right trail," Caesar added.

"Yes and no. I think your father is suggesting that it runs even deeper. He's agreed that we'll uncover a great scandal surrounding this synagogue, but this bank doesn't make the coins, it only handles them. The graven image refers the Emperor's portrait and that only comes from the Royal Mint. What's the connection?" Yakov drummed his fingers along the tops of the boxes. "There has to be a connection. Then there's the bit about the strange torments. Who? The mayor? He's already suffered the loss of his daughter. Is he going to suffer more? Why call that strange?"

"I think my father was referring to something far more excruciating."

"Any ideas?"

Caesar grew acutely silent.

"What are you thinking?"

He hesitated before answering, clearly avoiding Yakov's probing question. "I'm not certain yet. I have an idea, but I'll need time to sort it out."

"Time my friend is a luxury that none of us have and which everyone keeps reminding us. Let's get out of here before we get caught red handed."

They had just reached the top of the stairs at the very moment the clerk was coming through the back door.

"Thanks for the advance warning," Caesar grumbled to Giordano.

"What did you want me to do? Yell out, 'Get the hell out of there, he's back.' I think that might have been a bit risky. If you hadn't come up when you did, I was prepared to use one of my blue globes."

"You actually carry those on you?"

"Always."

While the two of them debated the issue of how they were going to extricate themselves from a situation had it gone bad, Yakov intercepted the clerk before he had progressed very far down the hallway. "Are you feeling better Master Porcenski?"

"Better sir, but my belly is at war with me. I don't think I can make it through the rest of the day. I must close the bank, so if you don't mind, everyone must leave."

"We will not keep you any longer. I fear it may be more than your heart. I hope it is nothing contagious. Just in case we will report back to the Court Magistrar and he'll monitor you over the next few days in case the Treasury feels it necessary to assume control of your bank while you recover."

The thought of court appointed agents crawling all over every file and document in the bank made him feel even sicker. Porcenski grabbed his stomach again and groaned loudly.

"Do you not have anyone else that works here that can perform your duties?"

"No," he grunted between spasms of pain. "There used to be another clerk."

"Well give me his name and I'll see to it that they are appointed to fill in for any absence you might have."

"It was years ago."

"Who was he?"

"It wasn't a he."

"A woman? The other clerk was a woman?"

"She is no longer in town as far as I know. No one has seen her for years. Perhaps Master Korunni knew where she went, but he's dead and she's lost."

"What was her name? Perhaps I can find her?"

"What good will that do you? I told you, no one has seen her for years. She's probably dead too."

"Her name!"

"Rofe. I think I remember it was Rofe. Now please go, I have to lock up. I'm feeling sick." The clerk turned away from Yakov to wretch on the hallway floor.

They did not stay to see what happened next.

15

Prague: Venceslas Square

"Perhaps we should have found a more secluded place," Bruno suggested as the three of them stood in Venceslas Square while teams of people passed to and fro all around them. The market stood to the west, the municipal buildings to the south, the Tyne cathedral and its domain to the east and the clutter of the over congested residential area to the north. Where they stood was the heart of Prague, the essence of a people, and to those that lived in the Old City, the center of the universe.

"If you want to hide," Yakov advised them, "then do it in a crowd."

"Where did you learn that?"

"My grandfather used to tell me that. One of his old family stories about when we fought the Romans at the time the Temple was still standing. The sicarii would hide amongst the crowds with their long curved knives tucked under their robes. They'd move quickly and quietly through the masses of people, leaving behind a trail of dead Roman soldiers in their wake. No one would see it happen. No one could recall seeing anything unusual. In a crowd, no one is looking."

"It doesn't get much more crowded than here then," Bruno reaffirmed. "This is the center of Prague. But why are we hiding?"

"Just to buy us some time before the Cardinal's men catch up to us."

"The Emperor said that they wouldn't be bothering us any longer that he convinced Calabrese to let us do our job without interference," Caesar piped in. "I haven't seen them at all."

"Just because Calabrese agrees doesn't mean he's going to do it. Why should he? He has far more at stake now than we do. I think he must have berated his men severely for being observed the last time. They won't repeat that mistake again. But why would he give up now? What an opportunity for him if he can lay an accusation against the entire Jewish community. And he's hoping we'll lead him to the evidence that will allow him to do that."

"But he already knows about the bank. Everyone knew the banker's name that was killed. So why are we hiding?" Bruno appeared confused by Yakov's attempt to hide. He ran his fingers through his thick black hair, an indicator to all that knew him well that he had been unable to fully comprehend an event or answer.

"Because it will look like we're concealing something."

"Oh, now I understand," Bruno mockingly retorted.

"It's actually quite simple," Yakov added. "When it comes to accessing the bank records, we're pretty much at a dead end. But if we can convince Calabrese's men that there's far more going on in that bank than banking, then he might use whatever contacts and influence he has to look deeper into the matter."

"But what more could he find out," Bruno was bemused by the concept.

"It probably won't be much, but the length of time it takes him to realize that means he'll be off our backs. Either way we win."

"You are devious one, Kova."

"I'll take that as a compliment."

"So in the meantime we can find out where the clerk on the records is living. He may still be around," Caesar suggested.

"He's actually a she," he was corrected.

"How do you know that?"

"Porcenski told me that Rolfe was a woman."

"A woman?" both Caesar and Giordano responded simultaneously, legitimately astonished by the revelation.

"It's really not that difficult to believe," Yakov calmed them. "Just like the Cathars we discussed, Karaites extend equality to woman. They have the same rights to own property, engage in contracts, and even work in jobs normally reserved for men."

"Ridiculous," Bruno exclaimed. "Why not just let them run governments too while you're at it?"

"That day will come," Yakov assured him.

"I hope that I never see that day!"

"It's instructed in the Bible."

"Where?"

"In Numbers. You may recall the chapter where Moses was allocating land and there were these daughters of the one tribal leader that had died. They claimed the right to possess his share and Moses awarded it to them. From that, we've interpreted that woman are entitled to all the same rights as men."

"That's not reasonable," Bruno protested.

"Why not?" Yakov challenged.

"Just because!"

"You argue the same way the Rabbis do. No justification, just emotion. Look beyond your sexual prejudice and tell me why women shouldn't be equal to men?"

"Because," grumbled Bruno, "they can't be."

"I thought so. You have no arguments, just blindness produced by your testicles. Now you know why your mother told you if you play with yourself you'll go blind."

Caesar burst into a fit of laughter.

"What are you laughing at," Bruno shouted at him. "Such rules would affect you as well."

"I don't have to worry about it," Caesar still laughed. "My father gave the lion share of his inheritance to both my sisters. "

"That doesn't surprise me, after all, you are related to Kova." he sneered.

"So let's find this woman," Caesar returned to the original subject matter.

"We already found her," Yakov responded to his request.

"We already found her?"

"The name on the account cards was F. Rolfe. Our missing clerk is none other than Frema Rolfe. Wife of the Mordecai Maisel."

"How can you be so sure?" Bruno inquired.

"It all falls into place." Yakov looked around searching the crowd for the cardinal's two spies. "Good, they're still not around. I wouldn't want them overhearing any of this."

Still the skeptic, Bruno argued, "It still doesn't add up. Give me a good reason why his wife would be this clerk."

"Because she is a Karaite. The banking establishment was Karaite. The clerk was female that served as a signatory link between Maisel and the bank. And Maisel hates her. I'm willing to bet that her maiden name was Rolfe. That gives me enough to go on."

Bruno ran his hand through his hair once more. "Presuming that her last name is Rolfe, and the entire scenario you pictured is correct, I'm still failing to see the connection surrounding the money."

"Tell me what you know of how a bank operates and I'll then tell you ten good reasons why it's her and how they worked their scheme."

Bruno thought hard about what he was going to say. Not being majorly interested in accounting, he never volunteered to work in the abbey's money room, leaving that to the other priests and monks more suitably inclined to the task. "I can't tell you anything more than you probably already know."

"What about you Caesar, what can you tell me?"

"In that matter I will have a little more knowledge than Giordano. My father saw to that."

"Alright then, tell us already," Bruno grew impatient.

"A depositor comes into the bank. He provides either a letter of credit from his employer or actual coin to the bank agent. In return for his deposit he receives a banker's bond updating how much he has in his account at that time."

"What then," Yakov urged him to continue.

"Well then…all the letters of credit are recovered from the issuing banks and exchanged into actual currency. But banks are only allowed to hold so much currency in their vaults at any one time. Usually only about a fifth of the money held on record."

"Is there a point to all this," Bruno growled.

"Just be patient and wait for it! What else can you tell us Caesar?"

"The hard currency is sent to the Royal Mint and in return the mint issues a treasury note."

"And that is the key point!" Yakov shouted.

"That's what?" Giordano looked lost.

"That's how I knew," Yakov teased him, delighted with the fact that he had confounded Bruno even further. "That's how I knew the wife was the clerk. That's when I knew how their entire operation worked. That's how I knew what they did!"

"Well why don't you enlighten the rest of us?"

"Think Giordano, it's obvious. The bank account for Maisel was in the name of the family business. It's a printery. They can print almost anything. Perhaps everything!"

At that moment the light switched on in Bruno's mind. "Even treasury notes."

"A good forger with a printing press could do it with ease," Yakov congratulated his colleague's enlightenment. "An auditor from treasury would never spot the difference. His role when he visits once or twice a year is to sum up all the treasury notes in the bank and make a statement that the bank's reserve value is equal to the total value of the notes. Since most people let their money accumulate in the bank, it's a rare event when a bank has to actually cash in some of its treasury notes. Normally it's the other way around with the bank acquiring more."

"So if I wanted to steal money from the bank, all I need to do is funnel the value into an account and issue a false treasury note every so often to cover the total value stolen." Bruno marveled at the overall simplicity of the scheme. "The auditor comes in, counts up the false notes with the real ones, credits the bank with more money than it's really worth and no one is the wiser. Absolutely brilliant! So where did it go wrong?"

"They got greedy," Yakov surmised. "They had to be taking so much money out that even if the forged notes were perfect, an auditor would have found it incredulous that they would have had so many. He would have been forced to check their numbers against the issuing records back at the mint and would have realized they were fake."

"And the only reason you'd have generated that many notes would be for the building of something so enormous that it would have exceeded a king's ransom. Like a monumental synagogue."

"Exactly, Yakov confirmed.

"So if I think I may have reached the saturation point of using my fake notes, I need to find another way to move money that wouldn't be detected by the treasury auditor."

"Now you see it," Yakov was jubilant.

Bruno continued his train of thought. "So instead, I start moving funds between accounts, so that I'm relying on internal resources which would go undetected by the treasury auditors."

"Unless, by some rare occurrence, one of your larger patrons decides to close their account, a rare occurrence for any bank, and you discover that your record of the account doesn't come close to covering the withdrawal amount identified on their credit note issued by your own bank. That's the point at which Master Porcenski obviously became aware of the problem. He probably checked a few more of the larger accounts and found the same thing."

"And then Korunni turns up dead," Caesar punctuated into the conversation.

"Coincidence?" Yakov asked rhetorically, then answered his own question. "I don't think so. I think Korunni was confronted by Porcenski, and in a panic ran to Maisel and demanded that he return some of the money so that he could cover the withdrawal. Maisel refused for whatever reason, most probably because he didn't have it any more and Korunni threatened to go to the authorities and plea bargain."

"And if Korunni turns up dead, then the trail is dead as well. It would look like the guilty party through some quirky twist of fate received divine punishment by falling victim to the creature stalking the night."

"But why not make it look like suicide? That would be the smarter move!" Analyzing the possibilities and mulling over the number of different vials that he had in his possession, Bruno knew how easy it could have been.

"Because whatever this creature is, subtlety is not one of its strengths. It was trained to kill in a most violent fashion. That's all it knows how to do. But since we're on the topic of the creature, what did you find out."

While Caesar and Yakov had gone directly to the bank, Bruno had gone to visit the home of the fourth victim in the district of Pernerova. "His family would like to blame the girl involved, that much was clear. They'd swear up and down it was one of her ex-lovers exacting revenge."

"But the boy, he knows better."

"He claims that it happened so fast that he can remember very little. Judging from his current condition, I'd say the creature struck from behind. Broke his neck cleanly but fortunately did not sever the cord completely."

"And that you consider fortunate?" Caesar interjected.

"Though my medical training is limited, I think there might still be a chance that the he can partially heal."

"And then what, he crawls around on all fours for the rest of his life." Caesar was tormented by the thought of the young man incapacitated in that way.

"This obviously troubles you," Yakov consoled him, "but we are lucky that the boy survived. It's important we know what we're dealing with."

"My apologies, Giordano. Something else I can blame my father for. He would often describe to me in horrific detail some of his patients. Often he would tell me how much better they'd be off dead. It's something he never should have discussed with a young child."

"Your apology is accepted Caesar. And you're right; he never should have used you as a confidant for such discussions. Children are too impressionable."

"Let's discuss the creature gentlemen."

"He recalls the stench; the absolute mixture of stale musk and acid. He said it was overpowering and almost caused him to pass out on its own. And the size! He remembers that it was huge, lifting him completely off the ground bringing him level to its mouth."

'How big was the boy?" Yakov was trying to picture the attack.

Bruno drew a blank. "I don't really know, he was always sitting down."

"Imagine him standing up," Yakov instructed him.

"Six feet maybe."

"How does he know that he was level with his mouth if attacked from behind?"

"He said he could feel its breath on his ears; hot, moist, stinking breath."

"To lift him off the ground level to his mouth would suggest that the creature had to be at least a foot taller because it only works if the boy's shoulders were at least level with the creature's elbows. The creature would then swing his arms up until its own hands were level with its mouth. That would make the distance raised at the minimum equal to the distance between the creature's own elbow and shoulder." Yakov demonstrated the motion he had just described to prove his point.

"A foot if a normal sized man," Bruno gesticulated, marking out the distance on his own arm, but if we're talking about something bigger than that, then the distance would also be greater."

"Over seven feet! Wow!" Caesar expressed his concern when he imagined it. "We're going up against a giant."

"A giant what is more to the point," Bruno continued. "The lad said he tried to fight back but he could not grip his opponent anywhere. Its skin was covered in hard scales, impossible to grip on to as they were smooth to the touch. Each plate was overlapped by the next so that there was not a single chink that could be penetrated. He insisted that the shell was the actual skin of the creature."

"Most interesting," Yakov put his hand up to his head and subconsciously drummed his fingers against his temple.

"What are you thinking, Kova," Giordano inquired.

"Probably the same as you, Giordano, that the creature was wearing armor. Obviously not metal, but something else. But what?"

"Cuirboulli," Giordano practically shouted. "It was cuirboulli! How could I not realize that?"

"You just did," Yakov praised him. "So what's cuirboulli?"

"It's a process to harden leather. The leather is already vegetable tanned, so it's hard already, but this way you make it a little more flexible, yet almost impossible to cut through."

"So what do you have to do," Caesar asked genuinely interested.

"It's actually quite simple. You soak the leather in lime juice until for about ten minutes. Then you put it into a pot of heated water that is close to boiling but hasn't boiled yet until the leather starts to turn black and starts to curl. Perhaps thirty seconds at the most. Pull it out, stretch it into shape and let it harden. It would be easy to from armor plating out of it. Pretty simple when you think about it."

"It would definitely explain the acrid smell as well." Yakov nodded in agreement with everything Giordano had explained. "So we have a giant covered in leather plating. That is significant. Since nothing suggests the creature is intelligent enough to create his own armor then it must be concluded someone else has done it for him. Where does one find someone that works with this cuirboulli method you described?"

"A shoemaker! They use it for making the souls of shoes." Bruno was electrified by the revelation he had just pronounced. "Find the shoemaker and we're one step closer to finding the creature."

"Here's the plan." Yakov leaned forward and closer to his companions whom did likewise. Speaking in hushed tones, he set out their next destinations. "I'm presuming that by now, the Cardinal's men have discovered our whereabouts. If they didn't think we had anything to hide before, they certainly will now. We're going to separate and head in different directions. They can't follow all three of us, so I'm counting on one of them at least following me. I'm going to go visit the mayor's house again, see if I can get an audience with his wife. You, Giordano are going to go back to the cemetery and see what you can find. We have to find out why that grave was redug. Speak to anyone you can find that might have some knowledge about it. Caesar, of all of us, you're the only one that looks like he'd be prepared to buy a pair of expensive shoes. Find a shoemaker in Josefov that makes the best shoes. I doubt very much our friend the mayor would just wear a pair of cheap leather shoes. See if you can find who makes his shoes. That's the person we want to talk to!"

16

Prague: Josefov

As Yakov had predicted, he was being trailed by one of the Cardinal's agents. He smiled inwardly to himself knowing that it meant that either Bruno or Nostradame was free to do their part without being observed. Whichever it was would mean that the reports back to Calabrese would be incomplete. That in turn would cause the Cardinal to fret uncontrollably, which he had already assessed was the Cardinal's nature. Then Calabrese would resort to trying to play his trump card over Bruno, which would provide the perfect opportunity to feed him false information. Ever since Giordano had informed him of how Calabrese was trying to use him as an insider to report back on the mission, Yakov had considered this as having excellent potential, fortuitously designed to be turned to his advantage. It was only a matter of deciding what the nature of the lie should be.

By the time he reached the path to the mayor's front door, he knew that the agent was looking for a perch from which he could peer into a window or opening to observe his prey. It wouldn't matter. Having played out the scene in his own mind, Yakov knew exactly how the reception at the Maisel household would play out. The encounter would be brief. It was the aftermath he was more interested in and for that he'd have to wait several days to find out. In the meantime, he'd give something more for Calabrese to puzzle over.

Even before he could knock on the door it had already swung open and Karlov was standing in the opening, blocking his way. "The master will not see you. He requests that you go away and never return to this house."

"I have neither intention nor desire to see your master." Yakov watched as the manservant's face remained expressionless. "But if you should happen to care for your mistress, I would ask that you give to her this letter." Withdrawing the rolled piece of parchment from his cuff, Yakov placed it into Karlov's outstretched fingers. When the butler attempted to withdraw his hand, Yakov refused to let go immediately. "Remember, if you do care for your mistress, you will ensure that she gets this. Have I made myself clear?"

"Entirely, Sir. Now if you don't mind, I have my chores to do."

No sooner did Yakov release his grip on the letter, the door swung closed in his face. It didn't bother him. Everything had gone as expected. He pulled out the rough map he had drawn earlier based on the model that stood in the center of the hall back at the castle. Looking over the web of streets that interlaced the Jewish Quarter, he identified the longest route that would take him back to the palace but ensure that he did not cross paths with his two companions. Selecting the path that looked the most promising, Yakov began his long walk towards the Stefanikov Bridge, whistling a sprightly tune as he did so.

§ § § § §

Kanprova Avenue had the most merchants Caesar reckoned. That being the case, then it was also the most likely place in Josefov to find the most affluent stores. The fact that most of the signs were in Hebrew lettering didn't bother him. He was fluent in the language having been taught by his father, whom himself would often write his notes in Hebrew letters in order to safeguard his secrets from prying eyes. But this was Yiddish, even easier to translate since it was merely a German dialect written in the Hebraic alphabet. The only problem he encountered was that there were several stores hanging a sign that read 'shumacher.' That being the case, he relied on his superior judgment for fashion, a gift that came naturally for a Frenchman. Yakov had made it clear that Mordecai Maisel would buy only from the best. Of course, money being no object, especially when it may have been someone else's money, dictated extravagance. It was only after carefully examining the merchandise in several windows that Caesar came across what he believed was a master craftsman.

Entering the shop, he rolled the shoes over and over so that he could examine the stitching from heel to toe. He was satisfied with whomever made this pair of shoes was an artist. He rapped his knuckles against the souls, listening for that wood like echo that told him the leather had been hardened to perfection.

"They are a magnificent pair of shoes," the man behind the counter stated proudly. He was short of stature but his features were long and weedy, with thin face and arms that hung loosely at his side. He was probably only around forty years of age, but his balding head made him appear much older. He wore a traditional skullcap, but even that was too small to cover his hair loss. The untrimmed beard and side-locks told Caesar immediately that the man belonged to one of the more extreme groups of orthodoxy that had sprung up over the last century. Even in France they were becoming more prevalent, insisting that theirs was the one true faith to counter the growing tide of assimilation that had become prevalent in the progressive countries of Europe. Amongst the Jewish communities the rift was evident in numerous ways besides hairstyles and clothing. Where once upon a time a single synagogue was sufficient for a Jewish Quarter, now several would exist, standing practically side by side, each catering to a different sect, that interpreted the Old Testament in a slightly different manner, but different enough that they could not bear to sit alongside anyone that did not share the same interpretation of a passage. Almost a mirror image to what was happening in the Christian world; Judaism was fragmenting into several competing denominations each striving for the hearts and souls of the people. But unlike Christianity, the multiplicity of Jewish beliefs hadn't yet reached the bottom of the crucible, where brother had taken up arms against brother in order to establish which one held the one true faith. At least not yet.

"That they are," Caesar lauded. "Did you make them?"

"They were my greatest challenge. I wanted to design a pair that could withstand a tremendous journey. One immediately thinks it is the soul of the shoe that must be made to take the impact and therefore be most durable, but that is not the case at all. If a shoe is to last them its longevity is entirely determined by the stitching. Notice how every seam is triple stitched, and the middle seam uses an interlocking pattern so that even if one stitch breaks, it will not cause the others to unravel."

"I can see that! They are absolutely beautiful. I can see how you would be proud of them. I would guess that you couldn't find this quality at too many of the other establishments."

The shoemaker's face turned dour upon hearing Caesar's comment. "You will not find that quality at any of the other shops. They are all saddlers pretending to be cobblers. Their shoes barely last a season. If that's the quality you're looking for then I suggest you look elsewhere; you won't find it in my store."

"No, I assure you, I'm looking for a superior quality. Especially when preparing the soul. In fact it might not even be available in your country. Back home we refer to it as cuirboulli."

"Bah! Cuirboulli, shmaboulli! What you're holding there can't even be reproduced through the cuirboulli process. They only use lemon juice in the preparation. I use tea. The result is a much harder leather but less prone to cracking. That's my little secret, so don't you go telling anyone."

"You must have gone through a tremendous amount of leather in your research."

The shoemaker liked the sound of the word research. Yes, that is exactly what it was he thought to himself. Research! He had experimented over and over until he finally arrived at his formula. He was a researcher and a good one at that. "Yes," he replied, "my research was quite extensive. But I had a benefactor that helped support it; otherwise it might not have been possible."

"Then you are a very lucky man," Caesar complimented him. "To have someone believe in your work so much that they'd be willing to fund your research."

"He is a very wealthy man, and he has benefited from my work, so I am certain that he has no complaints."

"I'm certain he must be wearing your finest work of all."

The shoemaker thought for a moment how he was going to answer that. "If you asked him, he would probably agree."

"He must be very pleased then. As only a man in government could be."

"Why did you say that?

"Say what?"

"That he was a man in government. How would you know that?"

"Wouldn't it be obvious," Caesar toyed with the man. "The shoes in my hand are likely a fortune, for your benefactor to have a pair that is even better than these could only mean that he would be a leading member in the community. Leading members of the community usually go into politics. Probably the richest man in the community too. Rich, prominent, I bet it could even be your mayor. Am I correct?"

"I think you ask too many questions stranger. That's what I think." Looking around the top of his desk the shoemaker found an awl and gripped it tightly in his hand. The threatening motion did not go unnoticed by Caesar. He could sense that the man was prepared to use the instrument if he thought he had too.

"If I don't ask the questions, how do I know if I want to buy your shoes? I know if I was a shoemaker and the mayor was a patron of mine, I'd want to shout it from the rooftops. What better way to show everyone the quality of my work."

"I never said the mayor was a patron of mine."

"But you never denied it either," Caesar pointed out. "Personally I think it's wonderful that he's a client of yours. If your shoes are good enough for your mayor then they're certainly good enough for me."

"What would a stranger know of our mayor? You come from some other country and you want to talk about the mayor of the Jewish Quarter of Prague. That is not normal. I don't know who you are or what your purpose is, but I think it's best that you leave my premises now!"

"Is that anyway to sell me a pair of shoes?"

"I mean now!"

Caesar watched as the shoemaker's grip tightened further over the handle of the awl. He knew from the deliberate and threatening action that he had worn out his welcome. "They really are a beautiful pair of shoes. Too bad you don't want to sell them to me. Perhaps next time?"

Exiting the shop, Caesar was satisfied that he had identified the likely manufacturer of the armor the creature was wearing. He was even more satisfied that he could tell Bruno he was wrong. That it wasn't cuirboulli leather at all but something even better; a process that he as a scientist failed to find himself. Holding that over Bruno would only be temporary at best, until the Bruno swagger took over and he said something biting and sarcastic back to Caesar, but even if it lasted only for a minute it would be well worth it. Afterward they could get down to the hard stuff. What they would have to do to force the shoemaker to lead them to the creature.

§ § § § § §

Standing by the gravesite, Bruno spoke quietly to the headstone, almost expecting it to answer back. "I don't know what your secret is, but one way or another I'm going to find out." he whispered, ignoring the stares of a family of Jews gathered around a grave site several hundred yards away. It was not going to be easy finding anyone to talk about the cemetery. Standing there in his flowing dark robes of a Dominican priest, he could not be viewed as anything else but a threat to these people. They probably felt he was there to steal the souls of the dead through some mysterious means, even though the idea was entirely ludicrous. But he understood their fears and resentment. The competition for souls was fierce amongst the religions, let alone between God and Satan. How could he even explain to them that personally he had his doubts as to whether or not the concept of a soul being judged as to whether it was sent to heaven or hell even existed? Here he was, an ordained priest, doubting the promise of an eternal afterlife, and there in the distance were people willing to sacrifice their own lives to guarantee their right to secure that very promise according to their own beliefs. Everything really has turned upside down, he thought to himself.

Deciding that he could do no more standing at the grave of Maisel's daughter, Bruno decided to investigate the rest of the cemetery. Perhaps there was a clue somewhere else that would help him with the riddle of the turned over soil. Even one other site where there was an internment from a while ago having the sod turned over would indicate that the Maisel gravesite was not unique. He was hoping he would find another grave in exactly the same state because then he could avoid what he knew would be the next step. Exhume the grave to see why it had been redug. By all intents and purposes even that was too ghoulish for him to stomach.

He nodded courteously as he passed the ceremony being held that day, the family and friends of the deceased pretending to ignore him completely but in reality all eyes watched him very closely. Funny, he thought to himself, all the differences, the accusations and the prejudices that would be tossed back and forth between the two religions and yet, when it came to this point in life, or death to be more precise, when it was all over, what did it really matter?

In one of the distant corners of the cemetery, Bruno found what he was looking for. A freshly dug grave but according to the headstone the original occupant had been there for well over fifty years. And the second occupant which was below his name and sharing the headstone was his wife, whom died almost fifteen years later. This latest occupant was their son, his name freshly engraved on the headstone and his death occurring almost forty years to the day after his mother's. That's the secret, he realized. Whether it was common practice for all Jewish cemeteries, or just this one because of its limited size, they bury their dead in layers. One family could occupy a single grave site, but each member would be interred at a different level, the original grave being dug ten, fifteen, or even more feet below the surface.

It would explain the grave he had just examined, but how would it apply to the grave of Maisel's daughter? He knew if he could unravel that question he would have the answer to one of the riddles that he and his companions were facing. Exactly which riddle he didn't' know as yet, but it definitely had to be one of them. He rose from in front of the stone and felt uneasy as if someone was watching him, studying his motives, calculating his next move. He swung around in a complete circle but couldn't see any one, yet he knew instinctively that he was being studied. He could feel the piercing stare burning his flesh. Time to go, he thought to himself before an ugly incident occurs. Finding a priest dead in a Jewish cemetery would do nothing for interdenominational relations. Plus, Kova would be very displeased, he laughed to himself.

17

Josefov: Kozi Street

“I’m telling you, they know what we’ve done,” the shoemaker in his high pitched voice squeaked as he paced back and forth about the room.

“Nonsense, they know nothing,” Maisel confronted him. “They want you to think that.”

“Well they’re doing a very convincing job if you ask me.”

“No one’s asked you Eidelman. Now sit down and be quiet. We have to think this out logically.” Mordecai Maisel appeared to be clearly in charge of the meeting taking place in the old three storey home. The room was large, filled with an endless row of book cases, every shelf completely filled with tomes that far outdated the dust that had settled upon them. The illumination from the candlelight danced with the distorted shadows of the people huddled nervously around the flickering flames.

“Whatever they’re up to cannot be good,” one man spoke out, his clothes grimed and frayed at the cuffs and hems. “I was watching that priest this afternoon and he knows something. I would swear on it.”

“So, he visited my daughter’s grave, what of it?” Maisel spat in disgust at the thought of a priest having set foot near the grave. “You can’t tell anything. And he can’t do anything to it without being charged with desecration. Not even a Catholic priest would have the gall to defile the dead. I believe they have their own laws against it punishable by death.”

"Everything they don't like is punishable by death," a deep voice surfaced from the shadows in one darkened corner. "They worship death. It is the great equalizer to them. Their entire religion focuses on the End of Days. Death is their salvation."

"You see," the caretaker pointed his gnarled finger at Maisel. "He doesn't fear death so why would he care if he desecrates the grave or not."

"Gruenberg, I can assure you, all men fear death. It humbles the bravest of men. But what do you possibly think he could have seen that would be of any great help to him in the cemetery. There's nothing!"

"I don't' know," he answered. "I'm just telling you, he saw something that started him thinking. I've been the custodian for that cemetery for over forty years now. I've seen people come and go from there for more funerals than I'd wish to count. You can always tell when someone is standing by the grave and a last message or lost memory pops back into their head. You see it in their eyes or the smile that crawls across their face. That's what I saw today. He figured something out!"

"Ridiculous," Maisel blurted out. "Nothing happened and nothing will happen. You're letting your imagination run wild. Both of you! You're acting like frightened children."

"Well, what about the one in my shoe store today," Eidelman demanded to know. "They say that Frenchman has some sort of magical power. He wasn't there to buy shoes, that much was obvious. He specifically asked me about cuirboulli leather. Why would anyone ask about that? It was like he could read my mind! Then he wanted to know about quantities of leather I might have used in my perfecting the process. And after that he was asking about you Mordecai. Don't you think that's a little too coincidental? He was putting it all together I tell you. He's some sort of magician!"

"Friends, friends, relax. They're on a fishing expedition. The only thing they suspect is that I took money from the bank. So let them. Now sit down and let's discuss this rationally and come up with a plan." Maisel motioned with his hands for them to sit but they were slow to respond.

"We're dealing with forces here that are beyond our comprehension," Eidelmen panicked. "Look at them. I'm telling you, they have powers. They have a Nasi with them, Mordecai. How can we possibly overcome our own Nasi?"

"He is not a Nasi! How many times do I have to tell you that? Nasis are gone, they're history, extinct! We don't have Nasis any longer."

"He can trace himself back over two thousand years, Mordecai! If that doesn't make him a Nasi, what does?"

"He's nothing! Today that so-called Karaite prince came to my house and tried to pass a note to my wife. Does that sound like the Prince of Power? How stupid is that to think that my butler wouldn't give it to me. He wrote in it that he knows her name used to be Frema Rolfe and that she worked as a clerk at the Korunni bank. He asked her to meet him so that she could answer a few questions. How foolish is that, I ask? To actually ask someone to come forward and incriminate themselves, unbelievable! I tell you, the man has nothing."

"Don't be fooled by him, he has power," the mysterious voice from the shadows reentered the conversation. He is the Karaite prince, your wife is a Karaite. That is enough. Had she received the message she would have gone and met him and answered his questions. Don't underestimate the power he holds over his people. That is his real strength."

"My wife would not be that stupid, I can assure you. She would be giving up everything she has gained from me."

"You know nothing of these Karaites otherwise you would fear him as much as I do. He is the rod and the scepter combined in one. That means that whether you like it or not, he is protected by an ancient covenant from God."

"See, I told you so!" Eidelman shouted. "We are dealing with magic!"

"Ancient covenants from ancient times," Maisel dismissed the claim. "That is not magic. Miracles don't happen anymore! His family lost any right to lord over us when the Temple was destroyed. God saw to it that a new religion rose out of the ashes, and there was no place for priests or kings. We're talking about now, and that means he is nothing but an anomaly from our past. Isn't that how his own father-in-law described him to you, Rabbi? Didn't he send you that letter to say that you should see to it that he doesn't return home and you'd be doing everyone a favor?"

"Israel ben Shakna should know when to keep his mouth shut," the voice from the shadows advised. "Whether you choose to believe in the ancient traditions or not, there are people that still want to do so. There are those that believe we cannot exist if the descendants of Aaron and David disappear completely. Why would we do anything to pander to that fear? No, for ben Shakna to write such a thing was foolish and incriminating. We will not lay a hand on this Yakov Kahana."

"Maybe he just understands better than most that we don't need these people any longer?" Maisel exclaimed.

"Have heed for what I tell you if you care for your own life. You will not physically harm Yakov Kahana. To do so would bring doom upon us all."

"How can you say that?"

"Because there are things you do not know and things we Rabbis do but tend not to tell our congregations so as not to stress you beyond your day to day realities."

"So you're actually stating that the Karaites are correct in what they have claimed; that they are the true standard bearers of the faith!"

"I have said no such thing. The Karaites are a plague upon us all. They divide us and thereby make us weak. They preach a Judaism where individuality is highly sought after, and we would never have survived if they had been successful. Our strength came from the unity of our viewing our world not as individuals but as a single entity. We survive the persecutions and the pogroms because we have not selected our own paths but like bees in a hive have worked for the common good. Had the Karaites succeeded in capturing the hearts and minds of the greater number of adherents we would have become extinct as a people, erased from the face of the earth like a thousand other civilizations that have gone before us. We live because they failed!"

"Then do away with him and then we can all live in peace!" Maisel was still insistent that Yakov Kahana had to be eliminated.

"No! You still do not understand. The Karaites whether they survive or not matters little, but that man is more than just another Karaite. He is the living proof of God's intervention in mankind. He is from the house of Phiabi; the family whose ancestors have viewed the face of God and still lived. The divine spirit is upon them."

"So we just let him uncover what we have done and we do nothing about it?" Maisel slammed his meaty fists against the surface of the table startling everyone in the room and causing them to jump backwards. "We are all in this situation because of your insistence. Or should I remind you of who wanted this new synagogue in the first place. Or better yet, who was it that was rejected by the religious council for the position of chief rabbi of Prague and made to look foolish as a result of that? You!" Maisel answered his own question, "The famous cabbalist, unable to even control your own destiny."

"Beware of what you say to me for I too am not powerless." Rising from the shadows, the Rabbi entered into the thin rays of light cast by the burning candles. His attire bore a greater resemblance to those worn by mystics and wizards than to a rabbi of a modern metropolis. The long conical hat on his head was a reminder to all that he was not to be compared to any rabbi they may have been familiar with in the past. He was a cabbalist and that meant he held sway over the four elements through the hidden arcane words of the Torah. Taller than most men, the hat transformed him into a veritable giant and Maisel felt compelled to shrink back as the Rabbi approached and towered over him.

"You were stealing money long before I became involved in your affairs," the Rabbi reminded him. "I at least showed you how you could do some good with your ill-gotten gains and perhaps even buy your way into heaven with your generosity. God may overlook your other discretions in doing so, but otherwise you should remember that you were nothing but a thief!"

"And what about you Rabbi? How will the mighty Judah ben Loew get into heaven when they see how many murders you have been responsible for?"

"The angels will count how many murders I have stopped and weigh that in the balance when it comes to my judgment. I have no worries when that time comes. Or do you forget how this community would cringe in fear every time some priest would arouse the populace against the Jews. And there you'd sit, waiting for the inevitable burning of your houses, raping of your wives and children, not to mention the killing of any of you that resisted. And why, because a Christian child would go missing and that priest would scream out, 'the Jews have taken him and they're draining his blood to make their matzoh!' How many times have you heard them lay that accusation at our feet? And how many of you did nothing until I showed you how to stop it?"

"Will you be able to stop it when they find that young girl's body or will they have their proof this time to support their ridiculous accusations?" Maisel thundered. "The only way to insure that doesn't happen is to remove any threat to us completely!"

"How many of us have lost relatives as the result of their frenzied hatred? How many of you sat in the dark praying that they would pass over your house and spare you your lives? And do you do so now?

No! I have given you a weapon to strike back with. I have given you the means to defend yourself. Yes, a child died, an unfortunate casualty in our war to survive but I have struck at their black hearts and shown them that their venomous priests are not safe from being held accountable for their sins. And now they say not a word but instead send our own to do battle against us. But until that time that we actually confront each other, there is peace between our two communities. So let my deeds be held in the balance when the time comes. I am not ashamed of what I have done. What I have done for you!"

"I still say we must not wait for the battle to come to us." Maisel ran through the strategy he had already prepared in his mind. "We must strike first while they are still weak before they have time to decipher the events that have occurred. Right now, everything they uncover leads to my door. That is too close for any of us to tolerate."

"Yes, and therein lies your urgency," the Rabbi pointed out the folly of his argument. "You're afraid because all of this has come to your door and yours alone. You fear that we will cast you adrift to bear the entire responsibility of our actions." Judah ben Loew had an exasperated look on his face, highlighting Maisel's ignorance. "And that is exactly what our adversaries have calculated on with their separate visits today! You considered Yakov Kahana stupid and yet look at you, all huddled here and wailing like frightened children. He's divided you, turned you against each other like whipped dogs. You have underestimated him and now it is up to me to clean up your mess once again."

"What do you intend to do?" Like a chattering field mouse, Eidelman was hunched over the table to hear the Rabbi's plan.

"I'm going to give him what he seeks," Judah ben Loew grinned wickedly. The points of his teeth were bared like a savage wolf. "That is how you deal with someone like Yakov Kahana. We outsmart him at his own game."

"You're actually thinking of letting him catch the killer? That will leave us defenseless. Without a protector we are doomed. And do you not think that they'll be able to trace him back to us?" Maisel was astounded to think that the Rabbi was even suggesting such an approach. Who's the ignorant one he thought to himself.

"Again you underestimate me. Have you learned nothing since we've merged our talents?" Ben Loew loomed over the stocky mayor. "And I can only hope that the Kahana will do the same and underestimate my abilities. I have no intention of handing my faithful servant over to the authorities. Though I know that even under torture he'd be able to tell them very little, he's still is too valuable to me to let him suffer such a fate. His work is hardly done. I will give them a killer but it will not be this one."

"More of your cabbalistic magics?"

"Not at all! Flesh and blood I will give them. See to it that a message is sent back addressed from your wife. Tomorrow night at the sixth hour, he is to meet her under the bridge in Karov. Tell him to come alone or she will not show herself. Make certain that you are perfectly clear about that."

"What are you planning Rabbi?"

"Better you do not know all the details. That way you are unable to implicate any of us by what you don't know."

18

Prague: The Manesuv Bridge

"I don't think it's a good idea," Bruno warned.

"I agree with Giordano," Caesar confirmed. "Something smells rotten."

"Is that your instincts or just emotions getting in the way?" Yakov asked.

"I definitely think it's my instincts."

"I will keep that in mind but I must go. We have lured the fox out of its den, one way or the other and we cannot stop baiting him now."

"What makes you think that the fox isn't baiting you? Maisel could have men waiting to assault you and you're going there alone." Bruno was certain that nothing good would come of this meeting.

"Why not let the Emperor decide," Yakov suggested. "Should I go or should I stay?"

Sitting pensively on his throne, Rudolf had not said a word throughout the entire conversation. His head resting on his bent arm, he didn't react to Yakov's question, his mind a million miles away.

"Rudolf, are you even listening to us?" Bruno shouted at his friend. "I'm trying to save a life here, and you aren't even listening."

Abruptly raising his head from the top of his balled fist, Rudolf looked about him as if he realized he was in his throne room for the first time. "Of course I was listening. I was just thinking about the best answer. What was the question again?"

"Should Kova go and meet this woman under the bridge or not? I for one don't think she's even there. I think it's a trap."

"A good possibility," Rudolf cleared his throat, "Most likely a trap."

"But I see it as an opportunity," Yakov explained. "When I handed over the letter at the mayor's house, I had no expectation of it being anything other than a declaration of war."

"Yes, a declaration of war," Rudolf repeated.

"There was never a thought that he'd actually give it to his wife. I wanted him to know that I've pieced together the episode at the bank and have sufficient information to implicate him. The fact that I've received a response either tells me his wife was far more involved in his crime than I had originally thought, or that it's not from his wife at all, and they are prepared to gamble all or nothing in an effort to stop me."

"How many millions of florins do you think he forged in treasury notes?" Rudolf finally revealed what he had been concentrating on all this time. It troubled him deeply that it would have been so easy to steal the money directly from the treasury.

Yakov cocked his head to his colleagues as if to suggest that Rudolf wasn't going to be much help in making this decision. "If we calculate that he hasn't touched any of his personal fortune in all these years and has been building his projects completely from treasury funds, then taking into consideration the materials the labor, the furnishings, and all of the artwork and religious artifacts, perhaps thirty million."

"Thirty million! How in the world am I to recover thirty million? Even if I was to raise taxes, it would be years before I could replace that amount. And if someone was to discover that the money didn't even exist to cover the debts, the financing of everything else would become dubious and suspect. Financially, the country could be thrown into turmoil."

"I do believe you might be exaggerating slightly, Rudi," Bruno tried to relax him. "After all, it's only thirty million. You've built museums for more money than that."

"You were never one for finances Giordano." Rudolf had a penchant for finances. A long time ago he learned about balance statements. If he was to become a collector of fine arts and a patron of museums, then it was necessary to always ensure that the balance statements still remained appealing enough to satisfy the court auditors. Any purchase that caused a left shift in the statement without a balancing mark in value on the right was always a bone of contention. There was no balancing mark in the right column for this synagogue; it wasn't crown property. "Perhaps we could seize the synagogue as a crown asset."

"I don't think that would be a good idea," Yakov cautioned. "It would be like seizing the Vatican. You'd have riots and chaos on an enormous scale, not just here, but throughout the empire. Much wiser to seize the synagogue on behalf of the crown and then donate it to the Jewish citizens of Prague. That way it would still be recorded as having been property of the Empire but written off for the public good. You'd be able to market the good will in a variety of ways afterwards."

"Interesting," Rudolf contemplated the suggestion, rolling it through several scenarios. "I hadn't thought of that. I'd also be satisfying Nostradamus's prophecy at the same time. Of course I'd have to be one hundred percent certain that we could prove in a court of law that it was built with stolen funds."

"Which would take years," Yakov advised, "perhaps ten at the most, but at least you'd be able to demonstrate to the Chancellor that you're on top of the situation and that there would be no financial loss to the country once the courts ruled in your favor."

"But only if I win the court case," Rudolf pointed out.

"This is exactly why I need your approval to go to this meeting under the bridge. We must flush everyone out that's a conspirator in this crime and have them all charged with treason against the crown. But we must make certain that they are identified as individuals and not as representatives of the community. Otherwise we'd be inviting the Cardinal to turn the Jewish Quarter into a carnage house."

"Then by all means you must go," Rudolf bellowed. "I want to know the names of every last one of them. I want them all to be brought to justice. So do whatever it is you have to. And God be with you!"

"Then it is settled, I go," Yakov nodded.

"We can hide in the shadows," Caesar offered.

"No! I am to go alone, I must see this through!"

§ § § § § §

"Arriving at the designated sport under the bridge, Yakov found himself shrouded in the blackness of the night, barely a sound breaking the stillness of the air. The Manesuv Bridge wasn't like the other bridges that crossed the river in Prague. Being one of the older structures in the city, they had not bothered to recess lanterns into its brickwork, rendering it unused at night for that very reason. It had a reputation for being the meeting point for the criminal element, prostitutes and those contemplating suicide. At the time, Yakov could only wonder which part of the seedy underworld he was going to encounter that night.

The hour had grown late and there was still no sign of Frema. It wasn't that he had expected her, but he had assumed they would be sending at least someone in her stead. A representative of the cabal that he calculated was masterminding the attacks in the city. It was a natural assumption after Caesar had reported back to them about his episode in the shoemaker's shop. Clearly Maisel wouldn't have used the shoemaker as a confidant. From the description provided by Caesar, it was impossible for him to play either role as the attacker or the strategist. No, there definitely had to be more people involved; people that actually gained from the attacks much in the same way that Mordecai Maisel benefited from the murder of the banker. That's when Yakov started asking more and more questions of his self. What if every attack and murder had been intentional and there were no random victims? What if each victim represented a targeted individual for one of the members of the cabal? The Star of David has twelve points. Could that mean that he would uncover that there were twelve members. The only way that he was going to find out was to flush them from their nest and that's why he knew he had no other choice but to accept their invitation. Foolhardy, reckless, dangerous, he remembered all the adjectives that both Giordano and Caesar had accused him of being in their effort to persuade him not to come alone. At the time, he didn't want to let them know that they were right.

It was then that he thought he heard someone walking along the bridge. Thinking it might be one of the cabal members finally appearing in order to parley, he crawled deeper into the hollow of the bridge trestles. Just in case Caesar had been right and they may be using their meeting as an opportunity to become physical, he wanted the advantage of surprise. From the shadows he would see who was approaching long before they could see him. As he clambered over the bulwark, he suddenly stumbled forward, his foot catching on a wooden object left under the bridge, and hitting the ground with a fairly loud thud. He turned and patted a wide circle on the ground, looking for the wooden box in the darkness. As soon as his hand hit the lid, it made a semi-hollow sound that told him there was something inside. Opening the lid to the box, he scrounged around inside, feeling his way through a pile of papers and parchments. Instinctively, he presumed that the contents would contain details about their group, and most likely a request to negotiate their surrender. They obviously wanted him to find the chest. With the evidence building quickly, he saw it as the only logical thing for them to do. Picking up the box, he began his climb back over the bulwark, retracing his footsteps, when out of nowhere the baton flashed past his eyes and landed squarely on the side of his head, knocking him unconscious.

§§§§§§

"Where is he," Bruno demanded to know.

"I don't know what you're talking about," The Cardinal replied.

"You know everything that's going on, especially when it comes to him. You've been having your men follow him everywhere. It took me a while to figure it out, but then I realized why he wasn't concerned going alone. He knew that you're men would be following him. He figured you'd keep him safe."

"Then he miscalculated," Guillermo feigned a yawn as if he had already grown tired of the conversation.

"You bastard, you're letting this happen," Bruno railed, his temper rising to the boiling point.

"Let me remind you that I am your superior," Calabrese shouted back. "Think of how easy it would be for me to have you disciplined for your impertinence. If I wanted to, I could make you disappear, just like that." The Cardinal snapped his fingers to emphasize the extent of his power. "None of this had to happen. If you had just done your job as we discussed and reported to me everything the three of you were up to, we could have resolved the entire Prague affair to our mutual benefits. Now as it stands, I have to do what is in the Vatican's best interest."

"What is that supposed to mean," Bruno was already afraid of the answer.

"Our entire aim of this exercise was to stave off Armageddon. There were certain conditions to be met. Stop the demon that was terrorizing the city and remove the threat to the Church."

"But that is exactly what we have been working on," Bruno declared. "We were well on our way to achieving that!"

"Perhaps," Calabrese gesticulated with a broad wave of his hand. "But with Yakov gone, you have no way of succeeding and that means we look at the contingency plan."

"What are you talking about?" Bruno was taken completely by surprise. "What contingency plan? No one said anything about a contingency plan!"

"When all else fails, you make a deal with the Devil," Calabrese smirked. "As long as we achieved our end goal, it really doesn't matter how we do it. I would suggest you start packing if you intend to come back with me to Rome and clear your name. Not that I intend to put a good word in for you. As far as I'm concerned, you failed in your mission."

"How can we go to Rome? There's a killer out there. Kova is missing!"

"Everything has been taken care of. There will be no more killings. The threat is over. The city will be at peace and the End of Days will not come."

"I don't understand?"

"Of course not! That is because you have always been at odds with the Church. If you had accepted your role as a priest, you would know exactly what I'm talking about."

"You're sacrificing him! A trade! You traded him for an end to the killings, didn't you. Didn't you?" Bruno raved. "I'll tear you apart, you scumbag."

Bruno lunged but before he could even get a step closer to the Cardinal, the guards had seized him around the waist and shoulders and immobilized him. Still struggling to move forward, his frock began to tear in his effort to break free but the guards tightened their grips, restraining him even more.

"Tsk, tsk. Perhaps it's not a good idea you accompany me to Rome. With this attitude there's absolutely no hope for you. Absolution will not be granted and I will recommend you be condemned as a heretic."

"Give me the chance and I'll tear that black heart out of your chest," Bruno frothed from his mouth, a trail of swearing accompanying his words.

"I don't have to tolerate your profanities, but I must admit I'm enjoying you like this. So let me make this perfectly clear. Your friend, this so called King of the Jews, is as good as dead. He is rotting in a prison as we speak. Your lover, bedmate, whatever he may be, the Emperor is powerless to save him. Did you really think that we wouldn't figure out that the mayor of the ghetto was behind the murders? We knew it from the first day you went to his home. Karaites don't visit mainstream Jewish homes. They've been at each other's throats for fifteen hundred years, so no Jewish King is going to do the honors of sitting with a man like Maisel unless it's to threaten him. Am I not correct?"

Bruno remained silent.

"I thought so. You knew that too. I haven't exactly worked out what the nature of that threat is, but it didn't really matter. You can't threaten a man as powerful as Marcus Maisel without expecting him to exact revenge. He set your friend up by leaving him to find a box full of letters that describe exactly how they planned and conducted their trail of murder. Everything we needed to know was in that box and Yakov Kahana was foolish enough to be found carrying it with him when he was stopped by the village constable."

"It was a setup, you know that."

"Of course it was!" Calabrese agreed. "The constable was told exactly where and when he should go to the bridge if he wanted to catch the man behind the killings. He was even told that he stored the record of his crimes under the bridge too in a strongbox. I guess they thought they'd better include that just in case Yakov was smart enough not to pick up the box, which he obviously wasn't."

"But you can tell him that it's all a lie. Kova wasn't even in the city when the murders took place. You brought him here. He didn't even know what the mission was until you threatened him into coming. You can have him released."

"Why should I do that," Calabrese grinned. "The setup was perfect. Every letter, every document referenced the leader of the Jewish community as the mastermind without giving an actual name; even the letters of correspondence, referred to this mystery man as the, 'rightful leader of the Jewish community.' It was precise. Even if Yakov Kahana was not here at the time, there is no denying by his birthright that he is the rightful leader of the Jews."

"I will tell them what I know."

"It doesn't matter. There has already been a letter sent out by the diocese outlining our suspicions that Yakov Kahana was behind the strange events that threatened the city. Why would anyone believe you when the entire diocese is congratulating the civic and judicial administration on apprehending the mastermind behind the plot?"

"But what about the killer?"

"Like I said, we have made a deal. Maisel will confess that he was forced to be an accomplice by the Kahana and that he had no choice in the matter. In so doing, the courts will grant him blanket amnesty. Privately he's promised that the killer will be dealt with and the problem will be erased. All will be happy in the world."

"And what about Kova?"

"He will die," Calabrese replied coolly without any trace of emotion. "There happened to be some very serious documents in that chest. Arcane magic is suggested. Creating a being out of clay and infusing it with life so that it could go out and slaughter innocent Christians. Using the dark arts is a crime punishable by death. The fact that he ordered the ritual to be performed makes him entirely culpable."

"But he didn't," Bruno insisted. "You know he didn't. You can't put an innocent man to death!"

"Innocent? Do you really believe that the Kahana can be considered innocent? Do you have any idea of whom or what he truly is? Of course you don't. You don't believe in such things, so let me tell you. He is the epitome of all that represents the destruction of our Church. He is the Antichrist! He is the end of you and me and everything we have built in this world!"

"You're mad," Bruno screamed.

"Mad? Is it madness to resent the chosen of God? One who by birth claims to be the equivalent of Jesus Christ? One who's family actually communed with God face to face! The audacity of them! They even called the house they descended from the House of Phiabi. The House that has seen the face of the All-father! That is whom he claims to be. We know about him more than you think. We know he is descended from Martha, the daughter of Elioneai, the son of Joseph Caiaphas. As such he is guilty of the murder of our Lord. How can one guilty of such a crime be deserving of mercy. No, he will die and the End of Days will not happen!"

Giordano Bruno listened to every word that Calabrese was spewing. Every nuance of hate and loathing he used to accent his phrases and in his mind he searched for the true essence of the cardinal's intentions. "You're afraid of him. You may say that you're punishing him for the sins of the past, but you're afraid of what might be done, not what has been done. He possesses something that can destroy the Church and you're trying to stop him for that reason."

"Always the clever one, aren't you Giordano? Yes, you're right. He does possess knowledge that could be trouble to the Church. Why would we want him to set the world back a thousand years now that we have come so far, made so many advances for the betterment of mankind?"

"What power could one man hold that makes you tremble in fear?"

"Better that you should never know! I've had enough of this audience. Take him back to his room," the Cardinal ordered the guards. "And post a guard outside his door. I don't want him leaving that room until I say so. We are done here." Calabrese provided a mocking wave of his hand, as if to bid him farewell.

19

Prague: The Castle

"I am surprised to see you here," Rudolf commented sheepishly. "I thought they had you locked in your quarters."

"I have my ways to get out," Bruno answered.

"Obviously, but it's no good Giordano, I cannot help you."

"You don't even know what I was going to say."

"I can imagine."

"If you can imagine then you know that this isn't right and that I have to do something about it. You should be doing everything within your power to see that it doesn't happen either."

"You are right. You are absolutely right, but I cannot help you. I'm sorry."

"Sorry! Sorry! How is sorry going to help Kova? How is sorry going to help me find him? What is wrong with you? What is wrong with all of you?" Bruno threw up his hands in frustration. "I didn't want to believe Calabrese when he told me, but he said you were powerless. I never thought it could be true."

'Understand Giordano," Rudolf pleaded, "they have signed statements. They have some book of spells for raising some sort of creature out of the earth. They're talking witchcraft and they have references to Kova all over the paperwork. I know none of its true, but they're preparing to tell the people that the felon has been apprehended and the city is safe."

"You're the Emperor. Tell the people it's a mistake, that he's not the one."

"What! And send them all into a panic again. Because that is what will happen, and Calabrese promised me that if I did that he would then tell everyone that it was the Jews that were responsible. And you know what would happen then. Thousands would die and probably in the melee, Kova would die too. So what would be the point?"

"What would be the point? Are you serious? You'd let injustice reign in your city so you can avoid having to deal with a difficult situation. Since when have you become such a coward?"

"Let it go," Rudolf urged. "We have been out done."

"Where is he Rudi?"

"It doesn't matter."

"If it doesn't matter then you'll tell me where he is."

"He's being held at the prison house on Bartolomejska, but it's a big place. How do you expect to find him? And even if you do, there's nothing you can do."

"Do you have a few ducats that you can give me? Or maybe a small bag of thalers? Either will do."

"You can't buy him out of there, Giordano."

"Can you give me some or not?"

"Yes. I'll get you some money. Just don't get yourself thrown into jail as well."

Arranging for his clerk to hand over a small bag of silver thalers to Bruno, no sooner did the priest have the bag in his hand he was out of the castle and heading towards the Karlov Bridge. In the distance the tower clock struck nine o'clock but the streets were empty on a cold winter's night, making it that much easier for Bruno to approach the prison house without the worry of being observed. The massive iron doors at the front of the building swung easily back on their hinges, allowing Bruno to slip through the opening and into the main vestibule. There were no guards posted at the main entrance. Few people ever break into prisons. Guessing that the warden's office would be at the top of the stairwell, Bruno climbed noisily up each step ensuring that his arrival would be announced. As expected, one of the doors opened a crack and Bruno could see dark set eyes watching him closely as he made his way up.

"What is your business here?" a hoarse voice croaked from behind the door.

"I'm here on the Emperor's business," Bruno replied. "I'm sent to see one of your prisoners."

"It's late, come back tomorrow," the man advised.

"I would but it's urgent. The Emperor has said he can make it worth your while if you at least let me come in and talk with you."

The door opened fully upon the promise of possible payment. The man behind the door was short but stocky. The black moustache was thick and bushy, hiding his top lip completely, even when he spoke. "Come in then. I can promise nothing more than we talk."

"I ask nothing more," Giordano answered as he entered the room.

Pointing to a chair across from his desk, the warden intimated for Bruno to sit down. "So what is your business here?"

'There's a prisoner I'd like to see."

"I said we'd talk, I never promised anything more."

"And I said the Emperor would make it worth your while," Bruno jiggled the bag of thalers in his hand, catching the warden's attention.

"Let me see," the warden held out his open hand.

"Un-uh," Bruno shook his head. "You get this if I get the information I want."

"So who are you looking for?"

"Yakov Kahana," Bruno extended the name as he said it, making it sound far more important.

"Don't know that prisoner."

"He would have just been brought here yesterday."

"I have over one hundred prisoners here at any one time, am I supposed to remember all of them?"

Jiggling the bag of money, Bruno taunted the man. "If you want what's inside this bag, you will do your best to remember. You wouldn't have had too many like this man; tall, sharp pointed beard, dressed like an Eastern potentate."

A sign of recollection appeared in the warden's eyes. "You mean the warlock. The man they say created the monster that killed all those people in the city. No one sees him. He's locked away where he can't do any harm and there are strict instructions that he is to see no one."

"Instructions from whom?"

"Practically everyone," the warden responded. "Town mayors, bishops, even the Emperor himself. So if he's the one you want to see, then the Emperor never sent you."

Bruno opened the top of the bag so that the warden can peer inside. "Oh, but he did. Can't you see his face right now?" The thalers bore a strong likeness of Rudolf on the obverse.

"Yes, I think the Emperor might have said you'd be dropping by. But the one you're looking for is being kept in the isolation cells. They're inaccessible, locking from the inside. There are always two guards posted inside and they won't open those doors until feeding time in the morning."

"How can I talk with him?"

"You can't. There isn't any way."

"There's always a way."

The warden paused and thought about it for a few seconds. "Let me have the money and I'll tell you."

Bruno handed over the bag which was snatched greedily by the warden who then poured the coins out into his sweating palm.

"So, how do I speak with him?" Bruno reminded the warden of the reason he was given the money.

"I'm under orders not to let him speak with anyone. You will leave or I'll have you placed under arrest too."

"You lied." Bruno remained calm in his accusation.

"You said you only wanted to talk, we talked," the warden said smugly as he rolled the coins over and over in his hands. In his delight the warden held his cupped hands to his mouth, practically kissing his newly won treasure. "Now you can leave!"

"But what about the antidote?" Bruno inquired menacingly.

"What are you talking about?"

"The antidote for the poison that's coating the surface of the coins! Don't you feel the oil all over your hands now? It's probably on your lips too. It spreads easily, especially at that concentration. That's croton oil. I soaked the thalers in it before I came here. Your hands should be starting to itch just about now. You might even start feeling a burning sensation on your lips. I would expect that you'll be in a coma within the half hour; dead before midnight."

The warden could feel the oil penetrating his skin, the irritation beginning to take hold as the burning sensation spread up his arms. His throat felt painfully dry. "Give me the antidote."

"Tell me how I can see my friend first."

"Go to Husova Street. You'll find a small grate in the curb by the road. That is actually a window into the cell. You can talk to your friend there. Now give me the antidote."

"I lied. There is no antidote. Bye." Bruno flashed a genteel wave of his hand.

The warden tried to get out of his chair but his legs had become too weak to support him and he slumped back into the seat. "What's happening to me?"

"It's beginning to reach your brain and is now shutting down your motor functions. It's painless though, so not to worry."

"Why-y-y," the word trailed off into nothingness as his power of speech slowly decayed.

"Greed is a terrible sin. It makes men do the most foolish of things. As you know, it's listed as one of the seven deadly sins," Bruno rambled on. "I'm sorry but you left me with no other choice. I must save my friend."

Easing himself out of the chair, Bruno walked to the door, looking back as he did so to see the warden sprawled in his seat, unable to move. Silently he turned and closed the door to the office behind him as he left. Racing down the steps he was on to the street in seconds, running the length of Bartolomejska until it met at the corner with Husova heading north. His eyes glued to the curb he was frantic to find the grill set into the road that was the window to Yakov's cell. He was half way up the street before he found it. Kneeling on the light layer of snow that had fallen that night, he tried to peer through the grating but he could only see shadows of the room below.

"Kova, are you in there?" He didn't care if anyone was to pass by and see him head down talking to the cobblestones. They were of no concern when it came to finding his colleague.

"Giordano, how did you find me?"

"That is not important. What's important is that I have found you and now I intend to get you out of there."

"That may prove impossible. My cell is locked and two doors away there is a pair of guards on duty. I don't think they are amenable to your wonderful personality."

"How can you be joking at a time like this?"

"Would it be better if I was praying? I don't think God is listening to me right now."

"Forget about God, I have something better," Bruno tried to cheer up his friend.

"There is something quite absurd about a priest advising me to forget about God. Wouldn't you think so?"

"We'll discuss religion later; tell me about your cell. What can you see?"

"Bars and a locked cell door and beyond that a wooden door leading out to where the guards are staying."

"And beyond the guards? What did you see when they led you in?' There's a stairway that leads up to the street. One of those houses you see isn't a house at all but part of the prison complex."

"So if we get you past the guards then you'll be free." Bruno worked out the plan in his head. "Do you know where the keys to your cell are?"

"They're on a hook on the other side of the cell bars at least ten feet away and therefore impossible to reach."

"Hey, you're talking to Giordano Bruno. Nothing is impossible to a man of science. Take this." Bruno pulled out a metal bar attached to a long line of the substance he named Brunon and handed it through the grill to Yakov on the other side.

"What am I supposed to do with this?" Yakov inquired.

"It's always been my experience that people leave their keys hanging on something so they don't lose them, so I put this together for that contingency. The metal bar has been heated and then hammered repeatedly while in a north-south position. Afterwards I attached a copper lead to one end of the bar and a zinc lead to the other. Then placed the other ends of the leads into a potato while heating and hammering the bar some more."

"Am I to ask you why you would do such a thing?"

"You know how lodestone is attracted to metal. This bar is at least one hundred times more powerful in its attraction. With the cord attached to it, you can toss the bar anywhere close to the keys and it will attach itself to them. Then you just have to pull the keys back to you and unlock the door."

"I still have two guards waiting on the other side of the wooden door!"

"That's why I brought these." Bruno handed Yakov two of his red glass orbs.

"What are you intending for me to do with these?"

"Throw them at the guards of course."

"That might kill them," Yakov protested. "I have a better idea."

"I will trust your judgment Kova, though sometimes we have to do bad things in order to make things right."

"I wish people would stop telling me that. I refuse to believe that. By the way, if the keys weren't hanging on the wall, what would we have done then?"

"As I said, I try to plan for every contingency. I have black-powder with me as well. You would have loaded the locking mechanism with it and then used one of the orbs to blow the door open."

"That would have brought the guards charging in here as soon as they heard the explosion."

"Then you would have had no choice but to throw the other orb at them," Bruno advised with a wink.

"Wait there. Hopefully I'll be joining you soon!" Yakov stood alongside the bars of his cell and stretched his right arm as far as he could extend it towards the far wall. Holding the end of the Brunon cord in his left hand, he flicked his right wrist releasing the metal bar in the direction of the hook. The bar fell far short of its mark and Yakov wound the cord back up. A second toss, this time a little closer, but still too far away. On his third attempt the metal bar flew directly at the key ring hanging on the hook and attached itself. The adhesion was strong, and when Yakov started winding the cord the ring came immediately off the hook and tumbled onto the sand floor with barely a sound. It seemed to take an eternity fumbling with the keys to find the right one that fit the lock but eventually the cell door swung open and it was time for the next phase of the plan.

Putting his ear to the wooden door, Yakov listened for the sounds coming from the other side. They were exactly as he suspected; the soft snoring of a shallow slumber. Guards were no different in Prague than in Brody. Give them what they think is easy duty and they just sit back in their chairs and dose on and off until the end of their shift. But over the years, guards, at least good guards learn to drift off but keep their senses acute, so that any little sound snaps them upright and ready for action. That meant there was no way he could slip past them without being detected, but the plan he devised didn't depend on that.

Instead, Yakov had decided to jolt them awake and rattle their defenses before they had time to think about reacting. Opening the door he looked around for anything that would burn well. Seeing the straw mats that the guards had piled up for use in the cells, he knew they would do nicely. He hurled one of the red globes onto the ground alongside the mats. Immediately upon impact, the chemicals burst into a bright orange flame. The fire roared as it caught hold of the first mat screaming like the wind racing through the forest. "Who dares to lock away the servant of the Lord?" Yakov bellowed in his deepest and loudest voice. The cacophony of sound from smashing glass to roaring flames, to threatening voice jarred the guards from their slumber and practically turned them over in their chairs. "This is my servant! Like Paul before him you dare to lock him in your cells of stone. Your bars are nothing to me, and he will walk free, for so sayeth the Lord. Kneel down before my all consuming flame, lest I be tempted to consume you in my wrath. Kneel down and pray for your souls that I do not damn them for an eternity!"

Their minds still foggy, both guards knelt on the ground and shook nervously. "Forgive us Lord, we did not mean to do your servant harm!" one of the guards wailed.

"Let me pass," Yakov commanded in his normal voice, or else I will bear no responsibility for what happens next." The flames spread to the next few layers of mattresses, the heat generated in the small room practically unbearable, but Yakov stood stoically beside the fire leaving no doubt that they were witnessing the power of God.

"Like Paul of Tarsus, your chains will not hold me, your prisons will not keep me but if you rise up against me your damnation shall be eternal. Now let me pass!"

He could see from the puddle on the ground and the soiling of the pantaloons that one of the guards had moved well beyond fear and was overcome with terror. Meanwhile, the other guard appeared to be reestablishing his composure, and Yakov knew he had to do something quickly. "You in the Dunne overcoat! Your soul is not pure; your heart is not virtuous. I damn you to hell!" he screamed loudly and threw the second globe to the ground in front of the guard. "Let Satan have you!"

All it took was seeing the globe shatter and burst into flames in front of him and the guard was on his feet and fleeing from the room, his screams trailing off as he ran up the stairs and out on to the street though the concealed doorway. No sooner had he taken to flight, the second guard overcame his paralysis and ran screaming from the room on the heels of his companion.

From his position in the street, Bruno watched the spectacle of two guards tearing down the street, running as fast as their stubby legs could carry them.

"Quite amusing," Bruno commented to Yakov as he emerged from the doorway. "What did you do to them?"

"I gave them a revised introduction to the New Testament. The Book of Acts to be precise. I don't think they fully appreciated it."

"Amazing!"

"Yes, your little glass orbs are truly amazing," Yakov agreed.

"No, I mean amazing that you would know the New Testament. I thought you Jews refused to read it."

"How many times do I have to remind you Giordano, I'm a Karaite? We read everything."

"Keep reminding me as we get out of here. Both you and I are fugitives now."

"Let's start walking," Yakov suggested. "I don't think we'll find too many people on the street at this hour. Do you have a destination in mind?"

"If you don't mind the surroundings, I know of this little inn that I've had the pleasure of staying at before. The innkeeper has these two beautiful twin daughters."

"No daughters, Giordano. We have too much to do."

"Okay, we go to the inn, we make our plans and then if I'm still up after you've turned in for the night, you wouldn't mind then, would you?"

Looking searchingly into Bruno's eyes, Yakov burst into laughter. "I can see that there's absolutely no way I'd be able to stop you. Let's go to this inn."

Together they started walking a path that was very familiar to Bruno, staying close to the shadows, just in case someone accidentally stumbled across them.

Yakov was still laughing as they progressed down the road. "Are you certain you're a priest?"

"Why does everyone keep asking me that?"

20

Resslova: L'hotel Cheval Blanc

The innkeeper was fascinated by the stories that Yakov told him about life in Galicia. Having never ventured outside Prague himself, to have another city described in such detail as the trading center of the Eastern Europe was mesmerizing. He had bought the inn, years before, with its French name, thinking that some day he would travel to Paris, but that day never came. Now all he could do was listen to the tales of the travelers that shared his accommodation and dream. With the unexpected death of his wife three years before, he was left to raise his two daughters on his own, and with the attentions afforded them from men like Giordano Bruno, that was becoming a full time occupation.

"You have obviously accepted the fact that Giordano is incorrigible," Yakov alluded to the fact that the girls and Bruno had not yet joined them for breakfast.

"Giordano is a fact of life. At least I know that they are safe with him. He takes good care of them and has helped us out tremendously since the death of their mother. Yes, I know you're thinking to yourself that he has stolen from them their innocence, but in this modern world we live in, that was a given to happen anyway. Better it's with a priest. It means he'll take the proper precautions to see that we have no embarrassments and nothing of permanence to stain their reputations. He is very kind to them."

Yakov tried not to look shocked at the frankness of the innkeeper. "Yes, he's a good man, but as you say, it's a modern world. I don't know if I can accept how fast it's changing."

"As a parent we can do nothing but sit, watch and hope for the best. It's not like it used to be."

Placing his hand on the innkeepers shoulder, Yakov shared his resolve. "But you are right, he is a good man, and who knows, perhaps one day he will give up being a priest."

"Then he'd be like the rest," the innkeeper smiled, "and who would want him for a son-in-law?"

"True. I didn't think of it that way."

"My ears are burning," Bruno announced his arrival into the room, "Time to stop speaking about me."

"Sit down and break some bread with us," the innkeeper invited him over.

Squeezing himself between his two friends, Bruno could not help enjoying the pleasure he felt of being surrounded by such warm affection. "I see you two have become acquainted."

"Master Kahana is a most intriguing gentleman," the innkeeper responded. "I don't get the pleasure of the company of too many Jews in this place. They tend to avoid these establishments, but if they were all like Master Kahana here, then they would be most welcome."

"I think Kova is unique in that respect. But if you don't mind Nickos, we need to discuss matters of a private nature.

"Of course Giordano," the innkeeper excused himself. "Master Kahana, my home is yours, as long as you require it."

Giordano waited until the innkeeper had disappeared through the door into the kitchen. "That means my home is yours as long as you continue to pay. Fortunately, Rudolf had provided me with some funding prior to my leaving the castle."

"If we stay too long we will be endangering these good people," Yakov worried that their whereabouts would eventually be discovered.

"We will stay just long enough," Bruno assured him. "With three groups trying to find us, I think it's imperative that we move quickly and strike back before they have a chance to organize."

"Since when is it three groups," Yakov inquired.

"Since our good friend the Cardinal has decided to form an alliance with the mayor of the Jewish Quarter and my dearest friend Rudi has placed his role of protector of his Empire over that of our friendship. Not that I can blame him too much. Even an Emperor must adhere to the laws he's sworn to uphold. As an escaped felon, you must be apprehended. As the man that assisted your escape, I too must be brought in. That is inevitable. Our only escape is that we expose the entire plot, capture the killer and name everyone involved prior to our arrest."

"We must get word to Caesar."

"Is that wise?"

"We need him. There is more to this plot than you realize."

"You found out more," Bruno leaned closer over the table.

"The box they left for me to find was a good ploy, but it only works if I had remained in prison. Then everything in the documents would be attributed to me, but in so doing they have exposed the mastermind behind this murderous rampage."

"Are you saying it's not the mayor?"

"I always suggested to you that Maisel was merely a tool, a man that was trading his gain for power. But to do so meant he had to resort to dealing with someone even more powerful."

"So tell me already."

"The one behind this is the Maharal."

"The Rabbi Judah ben Loew? How is that possible?"

"The papers in the box were the damning evidence if those that reviewed them had any knowledge on how to interpret them. They're signed off from the Spiritual Leader of the Jewish Community. The reference is local not to the people as a whole. The Tannim used the reference of being spiritual leaders all the time."

"Tannim?"

"The rabbinical sages of a thousand years ago. It was their way of discounting my family and elevating themselves with airs of self importance. They would argue the details of the bible for years, sometimes over a single word. And when they finished their debates then they would tell everyone, this is how it should be interpreted and no other beliefs are accepted."

"Sounds like the Vatican Papal Bulls to me!"

"The very same concept, and for someone to use that reference today would suggest to me that he thinks he is above his counterparts. Self exclaiming that he is superior, more knowledgeable than they are."

"So why Judah ben Loew?"

"The author of those papers was also a Cabbalist. The witchcraft they accused me of was the creation of a Golem; an animated being formed from the clay of the earth in which a Cabbalist has infused into it a captured soul through the use of the magical letters and words hidden in the Torah."

"Fairy tales," Bruno objected as a man of science. "Can't be done!"

"Of course not! But to a superstitious and uneducated mind, they can be convinced of the most absurd of notions."

"But I don't understand why? Why would he be helping Maisel steal the money? Why would he even contemplate letting loose a killer on the streets? It doesn't make sense."

"What do most men crave, Giordano?"

"Power."

"Power," Yakov concurred. "That is what this has all been about. The refusal to make him the Chief Rabbi of Prague had humiliated him. Therefore he swore he'd have his own synagogue, greater than all the rest. Whether by confession, or stealth, he discovered Maisel's secret of stealing money directly from the treasury."

"Blackmail?"

"Perhaps not. After the death of his daughter, Maisel would have been emotionally primed for the taking. "Wouldn't you expect in his situation that you'd go to your religious leader and inquire as to how you could preserve the memory of your child? How you could take out revenge on those that caused your loss? You'd be willing to do anything, wouldn't you?"

"Even build a synagogue."

"Especially if the Rabbi says that the synagogue will be named after your lost daughter and as long as he's made the Rabbi to serve in it for perpetuity, he'd see that the lost life of Maisel's daughter would be exalted and glorified."

"But the killings? How could they have contemplated such a thing?"

"Maisel was a willing accomplice. Revenge is a powerful motivation. In the hands of Judah ben Loew, he would have been easy to manipulate."

"Okay, so you kill Taddeush, what about the others?"

"Some would be done only to prove you were capable of performing the task. Others perhaps accidental like the little girl. And some for no other purpose than to remove anyone that could jeopardize your plan like the banker. He knew he was going to be audited and therefore he would have needed to have a sizable amount of capital to balance the treasury notes in his safe. But Maisel wouldn't have anything to give him. The synagogue would have consumed all of that.

So, if I was the banker, I would threaten him. I'm prepared to turn myself in and name Maisel as the person responsible. It would be believable, since the only one that would appear to be having any benefit from the stolen funds would be the mayor. I suspect that the initial plan had been for Maisel to set the money aside, someplace safe and when the banker retired, he would come to pick up his share. But that was now gone, and I doubt whether the Rabbi was willing to watch his dream of being a chief rabbi in Prague evaporate for the second time."

"So, if there is no Golem, then who is the killer?" It was a logical question and one which Bruno hadn't heard the answer for as yet in Yakov's explanation of events.

"Easy, there is a Golem!"

The quizzical look on Bruno's face suggested that he didn't believe Yakov at all.

"Dress him up in a full body armor of leather, have him swing across the roof tops, grunt like an animal, smell like a cesspool and for all intent, you've created the Golem." Yakov nodded his head and shoulders as if taking a bow.

"But who would do such a thing? Certainly not the Rabbi, and Maisel is too old and portly. From the shoemaker fellow Caesar described, it certainly couldn't be him. So who is it?"

"That is a question we must still find the answer for. What do we know so far? About seven feet tall. Incredible strength. They say he moves like an animal between buildings and climbs like an ape. His arms are apparently disproportionately long. What we have to figure out is how would a man with a description like that hide in broad daylight?"

It only took a moment for Bruno to think it through. "He doesn't. You don't let him out. He stays hidden away from the public."

"Still, someone has to know of a person like this."

"Wait…it's acromegaly!" Bruno couldn't believe how he didn't see it immediately.

"I'm not familiar with that word," Yakov admitted.

"It's Greek. I learned about the disease from my medical training in the order. I've seen it before during my travels. The mother was larger than most women with a longer face than normal and she was mentally a little slow. She had a boy. He was huge, with hands the size of frying pans. His arms practically swung down by his knees. And he was an idiot, barely able to talk."

"What else do you remember?"

"His forehead was extremely high, his ears stuck out like a bat, yet his chin was small and pointed. Very much like an ape, now that I think about it."

"Sounds like a Golem to me."

"So how do we find him?"

"That's where Caesar can help. Whether you believe it or not, he is intuitive. Far more than even he realizes. We have to speak to him about acquiring for us changes of clothing so let's see if we can persuade him to do another job for us. A mission that's more characteristic of his father."

"I'm not wearing any of his fancy namby-pamby clothing," Bruno resisted the thought of Caesar selecting their wardrobe. "He'll have to bring me something I find acceptable."

"We don't have that luxury. If he's to request clothing from the Emperor's tailors and they're anything other than what he's known to wear then he'll raise suspicions. Remember, others will be watching him closely thinking that we'll try to contact him."

"I'll send the girls with our message. Where do you want him to meet us?"

"Obviously far away from here. Somewhere near Kozi Street because that's where I suggest we begin our search."

"Right into the lion's den," Bruno remarked.

"Let's see if God's willing to extend to us the same protection he afforded Daniel. You know this town. Where's a suitable meeting place in that part of the city."

"I usually avoided the Jewish section of the city. As you may have noticed, I don't quite exactly fit in with my attire. But if I was looking for a good place to remain concealed in that area, then I'd suggest we go to this little chapel across from the Spanish Synagogue off Vezenska Street."

"A chapel? Do you think that's wise?"

"The parish priest is probably a worse heretic than I am, not to mention a chronic alcoholic. He and I go back a long way. Plus, he's blind and won't even remember seeing us by the next day."

"It's close enough to where we want to be and doubtful that they'd expect to find me in there....okay, let's meet there." Yakov didn't have a better suggestion to offer and Bruno's instincts for getting out of trouble had proven themselves credible thus far. "So, it's settled, we get the message to him this afternoon and he meets us there once night has fallen. He'll have a better chance of evading anyone following him if he's under cover of night."

§ § § § § §

The door to the chapel creaked loudly on its hinges as Caesar let it swing inward under its own weight. The chapel itself was small, lit by at least two dozen candles, scattered around the perimeter. The impact of his footsteps echoed loudly against the terrazzo floor as he made his way forward, closing the door behind him with a resounding thump.

"Who's there," a man kneeling by the altar broke from the prayer he had been reciting and reached out to grab the corner of the altar to steady himself as he prepared to rise to his feet.

"I am looking for some friends, father," Caesar replied.

"All who come here have a friend in God, my son." the old priest responded, never turning to face Caesar directly.

"My friends are a little more earthly than that," Caesar corrected him.

The priest answered by pointing towards the room in back without saying a word.

"Thank you," Caesar sketched a bow then passed through the curtain behind the altar to where the priest had pointed. Sitting around a small table with a single candle burning in the center, were Yakov and Bruno. Caesar could not hold back his enthusiasm in seeing them. He raced forward and hugged Yakov, practically lifting him from the chair. Then immediately afterwards he ran over to Bruno and did the same. "I never thought I was going to see you again. I was so afraid that they were going to find you and not even bother to bring you back alive." The tears started to well up in his eyes.

"Alright, alright! We missed you too. Now get off me," Bruno lightly pushed Caesar away. "Now let's see the clothes you brought me. And they better not have frills and lace or I can tell you right now, I'm not wearing them."

Still unable to control his jubilation, Caesar hugged his friends another time. "I can't believe your both alive. I thought my father had been right again. But now I know the future can be changed. It doesn't have to be the way he said."

"Let's run this one by me again," Bruno requested

"It was in one of his quatrains. Century I Quatrain seven he described what was going to happen."

"How do you know it was about us?'

"Because that's what happens. I think about an event and one of his quatrains appears painfully in my head. Even if I try to stop it from happening, I can't."

"So what did this one say?" Bruno asked.

'A late arrival, the execution done, a contrary wind, the letters having been taken, fourteen in the sect that conjured the plot, But by the Red One the undertaking will happen.' Caesar looked back and forth at his companions to emphasize his point. "You see, he was wrong. Kova wasn't killed."

"No, he was right," Yakov argued. "You naturally interpreted execution as meaning death. I have come to appreciate your father's technique. He is skilled at placing one riddle inside the next. It's as if he knew you'd solve the first one, but it is the one within that would take all of us to resolve. I did arrive at the destination late that night. I waited even longer than I should have because Frema never showed. I stumbled across the box of letters and I took them. Because of that, everything suddenly changed. We who were the hunters became the hunted. The contrary wind he speaks of. But now I know what we're up against. Fourteen men have conspired against us in total. And the one that I must fear the most is the Red One and he is the most obvious one of all."

"The Cardinal," Bruno cursed under his breath.

"As dangerous as this cabal of Judah ben Loew's might be, they are nothing compared to what Calabrese has in store for me."

"Judah ben Loew?" Caesar was surprised to hear that name.

"Long story Caesar but I've figured out that he is behind the killings in the city. He is the leader of this cabal so it matters not that there may be fourteen involved, cut off the head and the others will fall."

"So my father was right again."

"No, you were right, my friend," Yakov corrected him. "Without you the quatrains are meaningless. You have the ability to apply them where and when they are required. And that is why we need you more than ever."

"We do?" Bruno jested. "I mean, we do," he lowered his voice to create the illusion of seriousness.

"Good, because I brought you some of my favorite clothes with lots of frills, especially for you," Caesar paid him back.

"Anything else your father wished to say to us?" Yakov restored the conversation to their dilemma.

"Actually there is, but this was worse than the last one."

"Tell us and let us be the judge of that," Yakov suggested, decreasing the level of fear by which Caesar had approached the next quatrain.

"Same Century, Quatrain sixty-eight," he informed them. *'Oh, how horrible and terribly sad is their torment, the three innocents that have come to put right, poison is suspected but poorly protected and betrayed, put through horrors by their drunken executioners.'*

"Well that isn't such a big surprise, is it," Giordano turned to Yakov and commented. "We've been betrayed by practically everyone. And the drunkenness, we've already had this conversation before you arrived," he pointed out to Caesar. "It would appear that those that want us dead are drunk on their own power. At least that's how I interpret this quatrain."

Yakov looked contented with the explanation. "That is a fairly descent appraisal of what he had to say. And if that is the worst our enemies can do to us, then I say let's bring the horror back to them!"

"What do you have in mind," Caesar was eager to hear the next step.

"Tonight we watch the Rabbi's house."

"For any particular reason?"

"To catch a Golem, of course?"

"A what?"

"Long story," Bruno repeated.

21

Josefov: Kozi Street

Reluctant to have all three of them isolated at any one time, Yakov devised a strategy that only one of them would stake out the house of Rabbi Loew each night until they had proof of the existence of the Golem. It took some time to explain to Caesar what he suspected the Golem to be, primarily because Bruno felt he had to interrupt repeatedly in order to provide a medical dissertation to support his theory. Then afterwards, Yakov continued to explain why he felt the first night watch should be undertaken by Caesar besides the obvious that Caesar didn't have a warrant out for his arrest.

Suspecting the mind of the creature to be functioning on a more primal and primitive nature, there was a chance that it would be more prone to emit some form of energy that Caesar would be sensitive too. If Caesar's father could somehow tap into energies that permeated the ether, then there was no reason to believe that he hadn't inherited the same ability. As much as Caesar wanted to deny it and protest the fact that he had never had a single forecast of the future that was his own, Yakov insisted that the ability had to be there, even if it was lying dormant. If anything would cause it to manifest itself, then coming in contact with a deranged killer should certainly precipitate a vision.

Reluctantly Caesar accepted the argument, though it meant staying alert through a winter night hidden in shadows, and both Yakov and Bruno returned to the inn. Bruno informed Caesar that he would send the twins early in the morning to retrieve him and bring him back, though he did make the offer to send one that evening to keep Caesar warm through the night. Caesar declined the offer which only prompted Giordano to question what was wrong with everyone that they didn't appreciate the opposite sex for their full potential.

In the shrouded gloom of the alley across from the Rabbi's home, Caesar leaned his back against the wall, wrapped tightly in the fur-lined coat that Rudolf had gifted him when they first met at the castle. Between the coat and the mild winter night he could not feel any chill at all, comfortable at least in knowing he was not going to freeze to death, having accepted to undertake the first night of surveillance at Kova's insistence.

Now that he was alone, he had plenty of time to think over the description that he had been provided about the Golem. Especially what Bruno had to say about the family he once met with the disorder. Graphically, the picture in his mind was horrific; thick, coarse skin that produced an excessive amount of oil resulting in a highly offensive skin odor. That would at least give him his first warning if the Golem had somehow detected him and he had in turn become the prey. The enlarged extremities, including the ears and nose were interesting though not novel. In his lifetime he had come across numerous people sharing those feature and they weren't exactly monsters. A deep, croaking, almost inhuman voice. That would be the most bone chilling feature he thought. Putting all the characteristics together in a single individual, now that would be someone impossible to hide if such a person even existed, he surmised.

But then again, the fact that the creature's mental faculties were limited meant that he would have been treated like any other person of the time that was considered mentally deficient. They had places for those people. He had heard about them, only because people would ask when they saw parents offering up their children to the authorities to be taken away, but he never heard of anyone going to visit those special schools. Large estates, supposedly, way out in the countryside, where these unwanted individuals were locked away so that the public never had to deal with them; in fact never had to admit they even existed. Then his mind started questioning if such places truly existed or were merely tales much like the Golem, used just to keep the public in line.

If this Golem was such a person, then where would they keep him locked away, so the authorities wouldn't come for him? And if a family decided to keep the child, how would they be able keep him secret all this time? These were the questions that would have to be answered if Caesar was to provide Kova with anything useful with which to accuse Judah ben Loew.

As the night wore on, he questioned whether he should have taken Bruno's offer to send one of the inn-keeper's daughters back to keep him warm. The company would have been welcome, the night wearing on without a single noteworthy event. He could feel himself growing tired, and no matter how much he tried to resist the urge to shut his eyes, he could not fight it any longer. In the distance he could hear the bells tolling the midnight hour. Six more hours to go and he'd be able to lie down in a warm bed at the inn. His mind started to wander, walking the fine line between being awake and slumber. That was when he thought he heard it. Howling like a wolf, but definitely neither wolf nor dog, or anything he knew of the four legged variety. Wolves still lived close to the city, inhabiting the woods that surrounded it but this was not a howl. Perhaps it was a wail, or even a cry, but it sounded muffled, stifled, as if penetrating several layers of covers. He kept his eyes closed, remembering what Kova had told him. 'See with your mind, hear with your heart, and feel with your gut.' Doing as instructed, he used his heightened senses to locate the origin of the sounds. An image appeared in his mind of someone or something looking out from a top storey window, and when he opened his eyes he found that he was staring directly at the closed shutters of the attic on the third floor of the Rabbi's home. "Ah, so that's where you are," Caesar said to himself and he was satisfied that this first night was not in vain. Kova would know what to do next.

That's when he felt the pain once again in his head, the experience he so often endured of his father making his presence known. He rubbed the side of his temple but he could not make it go away. 'Damn you father, what is it you want to say now? Can't you see I'm busy?' The numbers were inscribed into his thoughts; Century fourteen, quatrain thirty-four. The full verse began to appear as if written on the insides of his eyelids. *'The bird of prey flies to the window, Before the conflict the Frenchman will see it, The good one accepts it, the other as something sinister, And the weak one takes it for a good sign.'* As quickly as it had come, it disappeared and Caesar was able to stop rubbing the side of his head.

'Thanks for nothing father,' he mouthed inaudibly. 'I had already figured it out without your input, in case you didn't notice.' Having the self-satisfaction of knowing he had superseded his father's warning warmed him even more against the night air. The Frenchman had been able to see it, just as Kova had hoped he would. Even knew that the killer they were hunting was being concealed in the attic room and probably used that shuttered window to exit and return from his excursions. Kova, whom he identified as the good one would be delighted with his progress, but he knew that Giordano with his scientific scrutiny would insist that it wasn't possible, let alone desirable. But his father, whom even from the grave had to deliver one more insult by calling him the weak one, knew that his son would be very pleased with himself. That he had finally awakened his own abilities to pierce the veil of the unknown. Yes, he was very self-satisfied even if his father viewed his pride as a weakness.

§ § § § § §

Sitting in the inn's dining hall, Bruno and Yakov partook in the meal of pheasant that had been prepared that evening by the Nickos. He had been out hunting that morning and returned with a sac of the delectable birds.

"How do you think he's getting on," Bruno asked stuffing his mouth full of white breast meat.

"He'll be fine, stop your worrying about him," Yakov advised.

"Who says I'm worried about him? He could be in trouble though," Giordano garbled the words while he spoke and chewed at the same time.

"He's not in any trouble. He can take care of himself."

"How can you be so certain?"

"Because of the three of us, he is the one that is the most gifted," Yakov replied. "I know you might find that hard to believe, but when Caesar finally comes to peace with his true self, I am certain he'll change the world."

"And why are you so certain that we won't," Bruno questioned as he wrestled the wing off the bird.

"Because neither you nor I play by their rules. We're outsiders and the fact is we both don't mind being outsiders. Caesar knows how to work within their rules. He's part of their world. That makes him more influential and possibly more dangerous than you and I could ever be."

"I never looked at it that way before," he successfully managed to separate the appendage from the breast.

"That's because we neither understand nor care to understand how they see this world. Our view is the only one we pay attention to, which makes them both despise us and fear us."

"Like the Cardinal," Bruno suggested.

"Yes, like Calabrese. You and I probably represent the greatest threat to everything he believes in. The foundations of his entire world can be torn asunder by our refusal to play by his rules."

"I don't know about me, but I definitely know he feels that way about you," Bruno waved the bone about as he spoke. "He revealed some interesting facts about you, without probably even knowing what he said."

"And you want to know if they're true?" Yakov remarked.

"He said you are a descendant of the High Priest Caiaphas and therefore you are indirectly responsible for the murder of Jesus. He also mentioned that your family claims to be the equivalent of that of the Christ; in fact that you've seen God."

"Which would like answered first?" Yakov responded calmly.

"Then you're agreeing that all of it's true," Bruno shuddered at the thought.

"If you're referring to the fact that Jesus of Nazareth was descended from Alcimus, and that my ancestry also goes back to Alcimus, then I guess being from a family equivalent to your Christ is true. It's the same family. His line was through Sadok the son of Alcimus, my maternal line was through Martha the granddaughter of Caiaphas and then through Matthias, the other son of Alcimus."

"That would mean that Caiaphas and Jesus were distant cousins," Bruno ran the family connection through his mind.

"Yes, they were. Why do you think he let Jesus walk so freely through the Temple until he could permit it no longer?"

"I never thought about it."

"One thing we learn as Karaites, ask questions. Never take anything at face value until you're satisfied with the answers. That's why the rabbis detest us so much."

"And the other accusations he made?"

"Your Cardinal is afraid of the knowledge my family carries. He fears all that we've seen over the centuries and all that we've done. If it was to be made known, it would destroy the myths that Christianity holds so dear. The one he worries about most is the Trinity. I knew that from the day we met and he used it to challenge me to confirm my identity. Your Holy See knows the answer to the conundrum but has kept it secret. The fact that I also know the answer threatens the basic belief that they have built their religion around."

"The Trinity is a thorn in many a Christian's side."

"But what if I was to tell you that the belief isn't Christian at all? That it predates your Nicene Creed by two millennia."

"Impossible!," Bruno exclaimed. "The concept of the Trinity has to be unique."

"Has to be? That essentially is the problem. Calabrese knows that it is not. Therefore to claim Christianity is unique by following the concept is a lie. And if the basic tenant of the religion is a lie, what does it render the rest?"

"And this other Trinity, where does it exist?"

"The Trinity is the basis upon which Judaism was founded."

"I don't understand," Bruno gesticulated as he waved the other wing around after tearing it from the bird.

"It's quite simple. Judaism was founded on the concept of three Gods becoming one. All Christianity did was separate them out once more."

"Simple," Bruno parroted. "What are you even talking about?"

"Don't they teach you anything in seminary?"

"Well, certainly not that."

"Okay, let's start at the beginning. Moses has to lead a people out of Egypt and they're as diverse as the flowers in a garden; different customs, different beliefs, different Gods."

"Don't think I've heard this one before."

"Quiet. I'm talking. You asked, so I'll tell you. When you're trying to consolidate a multitude into a single entity then it's necessary to merge their beliefs into a unified system. Elohim is the Hebrew word for God."

"I know that," Bruno was quick to acknowledge, "they did teach us that in seminary."

"Well did they teach you why the word is plural?"

Bruno shook his head. "They skipped over that part."

"The word is plural so that it would be a constant reminder that from many came one. The universe was the result of three gods; the Creator, the Avenger, and the Fool. That is the most ancient of all the beliefs and has been the keystone of all religions that followed. Moses was leading a people that comprised three major religious groups; those that worshipped Isis, those that worshipped Ra and the Midianites that worshipped El-Shaddai. In his wisdom he realized that they were all manifestations of the same God. So he called the people after the unified God. IsRaEl. And that is how we came to be."

"That's not exactly how they teach it," Bruno protested. "What about that story about Jacob wrestling the angel of God. You've overlooked that story from the bible."

"Does that story make any sense to you? That Jacob has a dream where he spends an entire night wrestling with an angel, to achieve absolutely nothing, because you have no idea why they're wrestling in the first place, but nonetheless, he changes his name to Israel, to signify that he wrestled with God, which he never did. And having studied Hebrew, you would know that if that was the case, he would have used the letter 'shin,' instead of 'sin' and would have been called 'Ishrael.' So, recognizing the obvious, that a story had to be fabricated that concealed the fact that the nation was actually formed from the unification of three distinct peoples and beliefs, they developed an interesting fable that has hidden the truth for over twenty-five hundred years."

Bruno stared blankly back at Yakov unable to believe that he actually heard someone of the Jewish faith critique his own origins.

"As difficult as the truth might be, it is as things were."

Snapping out of his stupor, Bruno thought of a question. "But you said that the universe had a Creator god, Avenger god and a Fool. Which is which then?"

"Ra was the creator and is recorded as such in the Egyptian teachings. El-Shaddai was known as the avenger or destroyer. And Isis about who it is said created life, but not without emotional suffering and sharing the hardships of the humans whom she loved was the fool. She dared to feel in order that mankind gained knowledge. She was the mother goddess and around their children, all mothers will at times be foolish."

"How can you so readily accept this?" Bruno was perplexed.

"There is no conflict if that is what you're inferring. All were but manifestations of the one God. Moses made the people realize that. Our God, who has no name, is so, because he has so many names. Hence, the Trinity that your Church prizes as being the key to your salvation is nothing more than a redefining of the essence of Judaism. And that is what your Cardinal objects to so strenuously."

"I think I need a few more drinks in order to take this all in," Bruno reached for the wine cask and filled his clay cup one more time. "If this is true, then there isn't any clear distinction between our beliefs."

"Why do you think it was so easy for the Jews of the first century to become Christians? The lines that are being so clearly drawn in the sand now, didn't exist back then. What was being taught by your early leaders was already in existence in the mainstream. Why else do you think James was able to teach 'the Way' from within the Temple, if it wasn't an accepted belief already?"

Drumming his fingers unconsciously against the table top, Bruno digested what he had been told along with his meal. "I think you're wrong Kova. I think you might actually be the more dangerous one, far more than Caesar could ever be. The knowledge that you possess would be enough to change the world right now!"

"I will accept your point. But remember, knowledge is of little value unless you have a way to teach it to others. But more importantly, the others must be willing to listen."

"Amen to that Kova," Bruno raised his glass of wine, saluting Yakov with it, before he gulped it back. "Perhaps I should send one of the girls to see how he's getting along?"

"He'll be fine Giordano, we've been through this." Yakov was amused at the concern Bruno was displaying for their younger companion. This was a side of the priest that he rarely showed, concealing himself behind a façade of bravado most other times. "More importantly, let's talk about what we shall do tomorrow."

"I'm presuming you've already thought about it."

"Tomorrow we will pay a visit to Frema Maisel once she is alone. I'll need you to stand watch for me to alert me when either her husband or the butler returns to the house. She's carrying a heavy burden of secrets that I wish to relieve her of."

"Are you sure she'll confess to you?"

"She will because whether or not she has adopted the rabbinic teachings, one cannot free themselves of Karaism that easily. To lie to her Nasi, would not be possible. She will tell me everything she knows."

22

Josefov: January 1589

By morning, Caesar was already back at the inn, fast asleep in the room provided, and oblivious to the fact that the sister that had gone to retrieve him was curled up at the foot of the bed like a cat and sleeping there as well. Having returned before either Yakov or Giordano had risen meant that he did not have the opportunity to reveal to them what he uncovered during his night watch. They'd have to wait until later in the day to get the details.

Neither did they think of waking him, considerate of his state of exhaustion from the night's work and knowing that whatever he had uncovered could wait as whatever it might be was not critical to their task that particular day. Bruno complained bitterly after getting dressed that morning about the selection of clothes that Caesar had provided, but after viewing the apparel that Yakov had been given, he thought better of it and was grateful for what he had.

Hiding in the bushes outside the mayor's house, both of them waited what felt like hours until they could confirm that both Mordecai Maisel and the butler were not at home. Maisel had gone to watch over the construction of his synagogue, one of his favorite pastimes, and the butler had gone to procure the household goods and food from the marketplace. Calculating on at least an hour before the butler returned, Yakov was circling the house, looking for an opening into the interior. Checking each door, he considered himself fortunate that by the fourth one, he discovered the entrance into the laundry area was unlocked. He slipped in silently and began he search for the whereabouts of Frema Rofe.

It wasn't until he searched the upstairs parlor that he discovered her sitting at her sewing desk, quietly working on a delicate needlepoint of a bouquet of wild flowers in a wicker basket. "That is very beautiful," he startled her.

The needle point dropped from her hand as she gasped to see him standing there. It took almost a full minute before she caught her breath. "You scared me, Mar Kahana."

"My apologies for doing so. May I sit down?"

She motioned for him to sit on the duvet across from her. "My husband will be very upset to find you here."

"Of that I am certain, since he's probably already very upset that I'm not in the prison he sent me to." He watched her face closely to judge her reaction to what he said. Her full lips pouted which he interpreted as an indication that she had not known what her husband had done. "He sent me a message addressed from you requesting that we meet by the Manesov Bridge."

"I had no idea," she protested, bending over to pick up the needlepoint from the floor. "My husband and I don't talk that much I'm afraid."

"My condolences on your loss. I have experienced with other families how the death of a child can tear the parents apart."

"The death of my daughter only doomed what was already a loveless marriage. Are you married Mar Kahana?"

Yakov realized that Frema was far from being a weak and defenseless woman. The woman he was dealing today was not the same as the one he encountered previously in the kitchen. She was far more complex than he first presumed. Beauty was often combined with frailty, but he quickly assessed that in Frema Rofe's case, she had used beauty as a tool to get exactly what she wanted. "My wife's name is Raisa. A wonderful woman that I miss very much," he reminded himself.

"Loneliness is a terrible thing," Frema commented. "No one should have to be lonely."

Deciding that it would be dangerous to provide Frema with a chance to use any of her womanly wiles, Yakov asked her pointedly, "So why did you do it? Why marry a man more than twice your age if you knew that it was a marriage without love."

Frema's smile spread across her face, revealing two rows of perfect white teeth. "You are as wise and clever as they say you are Mar Kahana. The Wisdom of Solomon they claim. And you obviously can see through my little pretense. Why? The answer is obvious. Look all around you; the wealth, the luxury, the power that goes along with being the wife of the wealthiest man in the city. What woman doesn't dream about such a marriage?"

"A woman that seeks love," Yakov reminded her.

"Life is about tradeoffs," she rebuked him. "Surely you can understand that. I had my daughter and she was all the love I needed. But now I have nothing and I fear I will die a lonely and bitter woman."

"It is never too late to change that," he advised.

"It is!" she insisted. "He will never let me leave, and if I did he would make certain that I didn't have a single florin to my name."

"You're an intelligent woman. Young, smart, creative, able to manage a set of accounting books, you could make your own life."

Frema looked piercingly at Yakov, grey eyes boring into his skull as if trying to read his thoughts. "You obviously have made an effort into investigating my background, Mar Kahana. May I ask why?"

"You may. And I certainly have no reason to withhold the truth from you. I know about the bank. I know about the theft of millions that was transferred into your husband's accounts. I've seen your signature on the receiver records. I know about it all. But what I don't know is why you did it? Why were you willing to take that risk?" He could see that he had caused a crack in her public mask that she wore for protection. Behind it was that woman in the kitchen. She did have a soft underbelly that could be pierced.

Changing the topic for the moment, Frema became philosophical. "Makhir, do you believe in divine retribution? That God would punish me for my sins by taking away my daughter; the greatest love in my life."

"God is not about retribution. God is about forgiveness. The sinner is to be forgiven as long as they acknowledge the sin and are willing to correct any grief or suffering they have caused."

"I'm afraid it is too late for that," she wiped a stray tear that appeared at the corner of her eye.

"With God, time is inconsequential. It is never too late. I can help you if you're willing to admit to what you have done."

"You have seen what I have done. I worked in my uncle's bank and helped him cover his arrangement with Mordecai."

"But the issue is more your marriage to Mordecai Maisel, than your signatures on record sheets. How does one lead to the other?"

"I was young, I was poor, and I had dreams. If those are sins, then I was the worst sinner of all," she explained. "I knew what was going on with the accounts, but my uncle had warned me; no threatened me to remain quiet or he'd have me sent back to Odessa. So I did as he instructed. Nine years ago, Mordecai's first wife had died. He had no children. All he had was money. More money than anyone could ever imagine and my uncle was ensuring that his wealth would continue to grow every month."

"And what was your uncle to get out of this."

"Half! Half of everything that was on the records, which would have been a vast fortune in itself."

"And the marriage?"

"It was my suggestion. I had stirred suspicions in my uncle; suspicions of being cheated by Mordecai. I impressed upon him that if I was to become Mordecai's second wife, it would ensure that he wouldn't be able to cheat my uncle. And if I was to have children, then it also guaranteed that once Mordecai passed away, almost all of the money would return to us. Don't look at me that way. Nine years ago Mordecai was still a very handsome man. I was honored to be his wife. I felt that with time I could make him love me."

"But that never happened."

"He always resented the fact that my uncle blackmailed him into the marriage. But even more so, I think he resented me for being what I am, a Karaite. Makhir, how can they hate us so much? How can they view us as something different when we're actually no different from them at all?"

"How can man hate another man because of the way he looks, or talks or believes? I think when we have the answer to that question it might be too late to do any of us any good." Yakov looked on the wall behind Frema at a small framed painting. "Is that your daughter?"

"Yes, that's Rebecca."

"She was very beautiful," he commented. "She had your smile."

"So what will happen to me and my husband now?" she inquired.

"The money is actually inconsequential to me. As I told you that day in the kitchen, it's the killer that I'm after. It just happens that the two crimes are connected."

The look that appeared on Frema's face was one of complete shock and surprise. Until that time, she had never contemplated that there could be a connection. "Are you suggesting that my uncle's death was in some way the result of his arrangement with my husband?"

"I'm suggesting all the deaths have to do with your husband. But he has not been working alone. There are a group of men responsible. You know that a great portion of the money stolen has been poured into the construction of the new synagogue."

Frema acknowledged the fact with a brief nod.

"But you probably don't know that your uncle was about to be audited by the treasury. They would have uncovered the forged treasury notes. I think your uncle was pressuring your husband to return some of the money so he could replace the fake notes with actual cash. But Mordecai didn't have the money. Either that or he couldn't bear to part with it. Your uncle threatened to expose their arrangement, and the only way to see that never happened was to arrange your uncle's murder."

Frema covered her mouth with her right hand. The stifled cry was a mixture of horror and disbelief. She had no idea her husband was capable of such a crime. "He'll do the same to me," she cried, "if he finds out we've been talking."

"You haven't really told me anything I didn't already know. And your husband is aware that I have uncovered his illegal activities. That is why he arranged to have me arrested. But as he's finding out, I am in the least, the equal of whoever is guiding his hand. That is the person that I am after."

Frema's eyes glazed over in fear when Yakov mentioned Mordecai's mentor.

"You know who that is, don't you?"

Frema pulled her arms in close to her body and began to shiver. "He's too dangerous, even for you Makhir. He has powers. He can do things to your mind. Believe me. He is someone you should fear."

"You're referring to Judah ben Loew, aren't you?"

"Don't go near him," she warned. "He's not like other men. He can control you with his eyes. I'm warning you."

"I appreciate your concern. But I must stop him before he kills any more people. Do you know of anyone that he associates with that could be actually performing the murders?"

Shaking her head, her eyes practically pleaded with him not to confront the Maharal. "I've met most of my husband's acquaintances. I can't think of any of them that could actually commit murder. But the Maharal, they say he can do such things merely by pronouncing mystic words over people. They say he can cast the evil eye!"

"People believe a lot of things when they're afraid. The killer I'm looking for is flesh and blood. Of that I'm certain. I believe I've already experienced Judah ben Loew's mystic words when I first arrived in Prague and I must admit, although they did cause me a restless night, if that is the best he can do, then I am not impressed. Have you ever known the Maharal to be in the company of a deformed person?"

"I don't understand."

"A giant, but extremely disproportionate."

"No, I don't know of any such person," she shook her head.

"You wouldn't be able to converse with this person. Their mind is crippled; damaged in some way."

"No…wait!" Frema glanced back at the picture of her daughter. "Rebecca used to talk of someone. A big child she would say. Her father would take her sometimes to the Maharal's home and while the men would go off to talk, they'd first take her to a room where the big child lived. I never really paid much attention. I assumed it was just her way of playing make believe. She had a wonderful imagination."

Yakov leaned over Frema and kissed her tenderly on the top of her forehead. "You have helped more than you could ever imagine," he confided in her. "Please don't let you husband know that I was here."

"I've already told you," she smiled back. "We don't talk. You need not worry. Makhir," she hesitated. "Be careful."

"You too," he replied as he made his way out of the room.

23

Resslova: L'hotel Cheval Blanc

"What do we have?" Bruno attempted to sum up everything that they knew to that point. "We know the primary criminals involved. We know why and how they did it. We know what it is that's committing the murders. So tell me again why we can't take this all to the Emperor and have him arrest everyone involved?"

"Because it's our word against theirs and right now anything we have to say is not going to be readily accepted. We are the prime suspects because of those letters and your breaking me free," Yakov hammered home his argument.

"Are you suggesting we would have a better chance if I let you rot there in prison," Bruno challenged in return.

"No, I'm only saying that without the Golem we have no argument. Maisel can still claim he knew nothing about the money being moved into his account. Judah ben Loew would repudiate us if we even tried to suggest a prominent rabbi was the instigator of the murders. I'm afraid that without a witness either living or dead, we have no way of proving our account of the facts."

"That stinks," Caesar stated.

"That's very profound," Bruno was quick to comment.

"No I mean what my father had to say stinks. I'm afraid there aren't any options except to destroy the Golem."

"Why do you say that," Yakov wanted to hear more.

"It's from Century II, Quatrain twenty-eight. *'The penultimate one who's surname is prophet, must take Diana for his day and then to rest, A long wandering he has taken upon his frantic head, in order to deliver his great people from the imposition.'* You have to battle the creature in the end."

"I'm beginning to resent your father," Bruno was furious with the latest prediction. "What's even worse is that I'm beginning to understand everything he had to say as well. But there's a chance this might not be about us. After all, he referred the prediction to one whose surname meant prophet. So what does Kahana mean anyway Kova?"

Yakov did that little nod he often did to say quietly that it was right. "It's not only Kahana he was referring to, but to Karaite as well. As the Kahana, it indicates the penultimate priest. Karaite translates as the one who's been called by God. A prophet is one that is called by God."

"Damn your father, damn his stupid little games," Bruno shouted. "You know what he's told us here?" Giordano was furious, his closed fists striking out at the air. "Diana for his day. Diana the huntress. Diana who kills her prey with her bow. No rest until Kova brings this Golem down with an arrow. This is not happening to us! We're not letting our lives be determined by a dead man that stared into a bowl of water and predicted the future."

"But I will do this," Kova grabbed Bruno around the shoulders and held him close. "I will deliver my people. That is why I am here. That is what I'm supposed to do."

"Well what about this resting part? I don't like the sound of that. What kind of rest is Nostradamus talking about?" Bruno became very melancholic thinking about Nostradamus's prediction. "What if he means rest as in death? What then?"

"I made my decision when I first came to Prague, Giordano. Succeeding in the mission was everything, whether I returned on not was unimportant. I am reconciled with my fate if that is what it's supposed to be." Yakov broke the gloom by donning a happy-go-lucky visage. "But see, I'm not worried about it. I'm certain if Nostradamus had foretold my death he would have been perfectly clear in pointing it out to Caesar. And Caesar's said nothing of it."

Caesar became quite quiet and reflective for the moment. He then lifted his head and squared himself in front of Yakov. "I think he did have something more to say. In Century VI, Quatrain eighteen, my father described what it would be like when it was all over. *'They all shall be kept alive by the power of the Great King alone, and not by the art of the Hebrew. He and his people shall be raised to the heights of the Kingdom, and Grace will be granted to the people that deny Christ in life.'* I think he's saying that we're all going to be fine. Obviously it turns out the way we want it to. Can you interpret that too?"

"I see more riddles," Bruno's face was flushed, desperate to find a way to end the crisis without placing himself or Yakov in any further jeopardy. "Why don't we let the new constable deal with the killer? It's his job, not ours. We can take what we know to Rudolf, he'll protect us while they investigate. We can bring this to an end. Let's play it safe Kova. None of us needs to get hurt!"

"Think Giordano," Yakov wrapped his arms around him even tighter. "What position would we place the Emperor into? It becomes a choice between his friendship for you or the threat of an accusation from the Church that he's protecting and harboring criminals. Not necessarily us, because they will just as likely accuse the entire Jewish population of this city. He cannot win either way, because the fact is he has been protecting us and collaborating with us. And if we were to provide the evidence of the cabal, and it's learned that it's comprised of some of the leading figures within the Jewish community, then he will be obliged to protect them as well from the mobs. I've seen this before. It's the innocents that are sacrificed; in the hundreds, in the thousands, even the hundreds of thousands because they're the easy ones to punish. A tossed firebrand through a window, a stampeding horse through the marketplace, it doesn't really matter who, as long as the thirst for revenge by the mob can be quenched."

"So what are you saying Kova that we cover up everything as well? We let the one's responsible go free? Is that the grace that's being granted in that quatrain? A pardon for the crimes they committed."

"No," Caesar interjected. "The quatrain is referring to the pardon for Kova's town. But my father has sent us clear instruction that the stopping of the murders, the salvation of Prague has to be attributed to the Jewish community. That in the end it might not even be clear to the people that it was Kova that saved them. In order to avoid a massacre, it may be necessary to let them think that the spiritual leaders of Prague's Jews saved them."

"What? Give credit to men like this Judah ben Loew, while we risk everything including our lives? Never!" Bruno was furious, hammering his fist on the table.

"So, I get to see this hot Italian temper after all," Yakov mused. "Listen to me Giordano. What we do is not about personal glory or honor. That is what other men yearn for. We have been given a mandate from God. We are to save this world, even if we have to do it one person at a time. We do it because it is right and that should be enough."

Bruno hung his head ashamedly. "Sometimes the burden is more than any man should have to bear. But you are right, Kova. Our purpose in life is to protect those unable to protect themselves. Please forgive my outbursts. And Caesar, please pardon me for anything offensive I might have said about your father."

Holding out his open hand for Giordano to grasp, Caesar accepted the apology. "Trust me Giordano, you didn't say anything that I haven't said about him at least a dozen times already. But he understands. He said in a quatrain that you'd be very skeptical of him."

Once he grasped his hand, Bruno pulled Caesar forward to his chest and embraced him in a hug. "So I'm a skeptic. Well gentlemen, let's do it! What's next?"

"What's next is you putting on your priest's frock once more and playing the part," Yakov instructed. "I learned quite a lot from the mayor's wife and I want you to see the parents of the kidnapped girl tomorrow. I need to know everything about her. Age, hair color, eye color, everything! Caesar, I need to know if you felt anything last night. Could you sense the Golem? If we manage to draw him out I need to know that we can find him before he finds us."

"I don't know yet," Caesar replied. "I knew he was in that house and I knew he was kept in the attic room, but I don't know whether that's because I felt it or whether it's just because I think I heard him howl. I'm not certain yet."

"You are able to do this, I know you can. I am prepared to place my life in your hands. I believe in you." There was a sense of pride when Yakov spoke these words to Caesar. The same pride a father showers on his son, when his boy takes his first steps. "I need you to go back to the Castle. You're the only one of us that can still move freely about town without being arrested. Explain to the Emperor that we are intending to catch the killer and provide him with leverage so that he need not fear the Cardinal. If he asks how he can help, then tell him I need to have Holeckova cleared of any of the constable's men for at least three nights. Tell him to send a squadron of palace guard in their stead. Also, none of Calabrese's men can be there either. But whatever you do, if he asks, you can't tell him whom we think is behind all this. Can you do that?"

Caesar nodded in the affirmative.

"Giordano," Yakov continued. "Is there anything of religious significance in Holeckova?"

"There's a small church that is said to house a holy relic, St. Michal, but I've never been there. Why?"

"I need to know if there's anything or anyone of significance that would make it a target for the Golem. Is there a reason the relic is there?"

Bruno began to laugh loudly. "I'm such a fool." He laughed some more at his own expense.

"Stop stating the obvious," Caesar criticized, "and get to the point."

"Jan Hus," Bruno stated between mirthful gasps. "He was the priest almost two hundred years ago at both St. Michal's and the Bethlem Church."

"And this is important because…" Yakov held his hands out in front of him encouraging Giordano to get to the point.

"He threatened to destroy the Catholic Church! Of course they had him tied to a stake and were roasting him at the time, so he might be excused for being a little resentful."

"Get on with it."

"A little touchy, are we? Okay, so Jan Hus was a reformer priest that began his oratory in St. Michal's, writing his first treatise on why the Church needed to change, while he was there. At first he was not considered a threat, suggesting positive changes that were popular with the general populace. As a result they gave him a larger church to be the rector of which in turn meant larger audiences, and he became more critical of the Church as time went on. They expulsed him, later imprisoned him, and finally burned him as a heretic. While tied to the stake he pronounced that in a hundred years there'd be one from within the Church that would tear it apart and create a new religion for the masses."

"One hundred years," Yakov reflected. "Martin Luther."

"Yes, as predicted, Martin Luther tore the Catholic Church apart, establishing a new denomination that now rivals the Church in power and authority."

"So what was so funny?"

"The Church leaders believe that St. Michal's was cursed, that there was a demon dwelling in its rafters. How else do you explain the change that came over Jan Hus, one of the finest and brightest? The only explanation they could arrive at was that he became possessed and in order to fend off the demon they placed the relic in the church where it all started. So I was laughing because I asked myself, assuming that the rabbi will target St. Michal's next, why would you go after two churches where Jan Hus had preached?"

"And you concluded..."

"In order to spread the fear that the spirit of Jan Hus had come back in order to destroy Catholicism. Perhaps you noticed, we Catholics tend to be a very superstitious lot. Demons in the rafters. Holy relics to ward off evil. In other words, very easy to manipulate through irrational fear. Killing the priests in both of these Churches would immediately reinforce amongst the people how powerless the Church is to protect its own. Fear would be used to generate new fears until control of the masses becomes completely lost. Catholic leaders would point their fingers at the Protestants, and in turn the Protestants would release their pent up hatred against the mother church and before you could even blink they'd be at each other's throats in a civil war. It's happening everywhere else in Europe, why not here?"

"You would be suggesting that Judah ben Loew has a far more sinister goal than we even contemplated," Yakov concluded.

"Well, why not? I'm suggesting that his are far greater intentions than we gave him credit for. We've been guilty of thinking on too small a scale. Revenge for a little girl, a cover-up for ill begotten funds, the desire to govern from his own synagogue. These are nothing compared to what he could be actually contemplating. He could very well be the initiation of Armageddon and all this time we've been dismissing the sole reason we've been brought here. Do you see it now; the predictions could actually be true."

"Even more reason why we must be the ones to stop the Golem," Yakov interceded. "If you really do believe that the cabal could be promoting such a heinous plot that would result in the conflagration of this city into an inferno of self-perpetuating destruction, then we have no choice but to stop it."

"Wait," shouted Caesar, "this is making sense."

"Another message from the past," Bruno said somewhat sarcastically, then caught his tongue, remembering that he had just apologized to Caesar for criticizing his father.

"Century I, Quatrain thirty-seven," Caesar quoted. "I can see it clearly. *'A little before sunset, The battle is a given, since the majority of people are dubious, But to foil it, the sea-port cannot be made to answer, because the bridge and the grave lie in two strange places.'* I think I understand it now!"

"You're certain your father is telling us how we can stop this from happening," Yakov questioned.

"I'm positive, Kova." Caesar confirmed.

"What's he trying to say?" Bruno scratched his head. "It's almost as if it sounds familiar to us but I just can't place it. Why does this sound so familiar?"

"Let's look at it line by line," Yakov suggested. "A little before sunset could refer to the End of Days, meaning the coming of Armageddon."

"Or it could refer to the attacks in the city always occurring at twilight or in the early night," Bruno added.

"But either way we know he's referring to the threat in the city. Correct?"

"Correct," the others agreed.

"The battle is a given, since the majority of people are dubious," Yakov continued.

"Dubious could indicate the fact that the population is unaware of what's going on," Caesar offered.

"Could be a comment on the state of Christianity right now," Bruno thought aloud. "Which side is correct? Catholics, Anglicans, Lutherans. Perhaps none of them, but they will go to war and kill each other, even if they're wrong. War between the factions is inevitable."

"I think you might be right," Yakov agreed. "It sounds more like what Nostradamus is referring to. Next line is critical. He's telling us it can be stopped. It can be foiled. But why at a seaport?"

"He doesn't quite say that the seaport is the key," Bruno interjected. "More like it's not involved. He refers to it in the negative."

"Opposites! My father always used to play a game with me of opposites. He'd give a word and I had to tell him the opposite word."

"Opposite of seaport?" Bruno questioned.

"Obviously land," Yakov answered.

"More than that," Caesar corrected. "That's not how we played the game. Seaport implies an egress into the ocean. The opposite would involve being locked into the land. So to lock into the land would mean buried."

"And if buried, then that would explain the reference to the grave in the last line," Yakov tapped his forefinger against his forehead.

"And the strange place would have to be Josefov," Bruno immersed himself into the game, "because if we look to the bible for a clue, you Jews described yourselves as strangers in a strange land."

"Very good," exclaimed Yakov. "And the reason this all seemed so familiar to us…"

In unison they answered. "Because we crossed the bridge to enter a strange land that first day we ventured out into the city and the place we went to visit was the cemetery."

"And what's there?" Yakov threw out the question for them all to answer.

"The buried."

"The gravesite," Yakov pointed at Bruno specifically. "What did you say about it again?"

"Bodies are interred in layers there. Some families are buried three or four deep from the headstones I read."

"The Maisel grave had been recently turned over. What if there were two bodies interred? Like the quatrain stated. If we remove the reference of the bridge from the last line, then it would read, 'the grave two strange places.' It could just as easily be saying that in the grave are two strangers. Where better to hide a body than in a place where dead bodies are expected to be?"

"It all makes sense to me," Bruno agreed.

"Me too."

"So as we planned. Giordano, you go to the family and find out everything you can about their little girl. Caesar, you visit the Emperor. I think we have the leverage to offer him now. Tell him only what we suspect about the cemetery, but he is not to exhume the gravesite. All I want is for him to post a guard and prevent anyone from accessing the site. Even Maisel is not to be permitted to visit. As long as we have the grave under our control, we can manipulate the situation to our advantage. Make him understand that."

"What am I to tell the parents of the girl, Kova? We'd be concealing the fact from them that we know her whereabouts."

"We only suspect that we know. That's why I don't want the body exhumed yet. If we were to confirm it, all hell would break loose. Can you imagine the 'war cry' if it was to be revealed that a young Christian girl was dead and buried in a Jewish cemetery. All the blood libels would be renewed. It would unify your different Christian factions and stave off Armageddon, but at the cost of destroying every last Jewish household in this city. I don't have to be a prophet to see that happening. It would be inevitable. We'll get the body back to the parents, but not this way."

"Do I provide Rudolf with any other details," Caesar asked after hearing Yakov's view of the future if the whereabouts of the girl were to be exposed prematurely.

"Rudolf has to be bound to us. But providing him with the truth will not do so. He will know himself what the outcome would be if word of the girl was to be circulated. Just let him know that we suspect she lies there but nothing else. He'll know what to do."

"For all our sakes I hope so," Bruno said ruefully.

"One more thing, Giordano, I'm going to give you a letter to take with you. I'll write it in Hebrew, so should it fall into the wrong hands then it will take some time to translate. I don't know exactly how you'll get it to him, but I needed it to be delivered to the Maharal."

"I don't believe he'll welcome me with open arms if I arrive on his doorstep."

"I agree. You'd be clasped in leg irons and chains before you even got close to his property. Maisel knows what you look like. He'll be on the lookout for you. Arrest must be avoided at all cost since Calabrese I suspect is fluent in Hebrew as well. I'll leave it to your own discretions on how the delivery will be made."

Bowing in compliance, Bruno thought to himself, 'he knows.' How he knew that he was capable of committing possible atrocities in order to achieve an end, he couldn't imagine, but he had come to realize that Kova was far more than an ordinary man. Able to tap into unworldly forces that beggared description, Kova could peer into the book of knowledge that God had written at the beginning of time, but concealed from mankind at the fall of Adam. He already knew what he was going to do; hopefully Kova would forgive him.

24

Josefov: Kanprova Avenue

Having just completed his visit to the young couple living in Vinohrady, Bruno traversed the couple of kilometers distance to Josefov under the influence of a darkening cloud. From what he could establish, they had absolutely nothing to do with this entire affair; their daughter appeared to be chosen completely at random.

When he first knocked at their door they were reluctant to let him even pass over the front stoop, assuming him to be just another priest wishing to perform the last rites for a daughter that they were not yet ready to let go of. It took some time for Bruno to convince them otherwise. His saving grace was when he boldly told them that he would promise them that he'd find their daughter, alive or dead, but he would not return to their house without finding her first. That was sufficient to get him entrance into their parlor where he had the opportunity to explain that he was there on behalf of some very special people, including the Emperor. It was the first time that they had heard that their plight was even being discussed at such a high level. Prior to this, the only word they had was from the constable that he was still looking but they shouldn't get their hopes up. That was some time ago, and they hadn't heard from anyone since, except the monks and priests that they felt were only there to collect a thaler or two for performing the rites.

Bruno could appreciate their being bitter. No parent wants to admit their child is gone forever. No one wants to be told over and over again that for their own sakes, part of the healing process requires them to acknowledge that fact. Why not hold on to hope as long as you can? It was not his intention to give them false hope, but as he explained, he would return with her alive or dead, but either way they would be able to end their grief. This was acceptable and a promise they were going to hold him to.

He asked for a description of the child so that he'd be able to recognize her when he saw her. The level of detail they provided was astonishing. Every scar, every hair out of place they could describe effortlessly. So this is love, Giordano thought to himself. The ability to close your eyes and paint a picture of the one you love with absolute precision. The heartache they must be suffering had to be excruciating, numbing to the soul. If there was to be one last thing he would do with his life, it would be to find their daughter and return her body to them so that they could say goodbye. In a world gone mad, these people deserved at least that much.

Now that he was nearing Josefov, he had run though the checklist of features that Yakov had provided describing the Maisel child. From the notations, it would have appeared that the two girls could easily have been sisters. Steel grey eyes, soft auburn hair in tight curls that fell across the shoulders. Even the description of how they both smiled, crinkling up their noses as they did so proved identical. Two girls, each a world apart, that never would have met by their own design, but now brought together through death.

His thoughts kept him so preoccupied that he almost missed the turnoff onto Kanprova, walking right by. The street was filled with hundreds of people moving back and forth from market stall to market stall doing their daily shopping. Normally a priest would draw attention in such a predominantly Jewish neighborhood, but the recent increase in activity at the Tyn Church just a few streets away made Bruno's presence quite routine to anyone that noticed him.

If anyone had questioned the recent increase in Catholic clergy in Josefov, it obviously went unanswered. Particularly in a Jewish neighborhood, if there was anything newsworthy to report, then it would have been widely circulated as gossip. All this activity at the Tyn Church and still no ridiculous reports as to what it was about. They considered it to be a non-event. So when Bruno made his way down the road and entered the shoemaker's shop, no one even gave a second glance. Above the door the little set of brass bells rang as soon as he had opened it. Bruno reached up to silence them and then slowly he closed the door while staring outside the window, looking up and down the street in both directions to confirm that no one was watching.

"Can I help you?" the man behind the counter inquired but in a tone that was neither pleasant nor welcoming; a fact that did not go unnoticed by Bruno.

"That all depends," Bruno responded slowly turning to face the man.

"Depends on what?" he said gruffly, the words really signifying state your business or get out.

"Depends on whether or not you're the one I'm seeking?" Bruno smiled menacingly. Having raised his cowl over his head, all that could be seen were his teeth beneath a heavy outlined shadow.

"You're the priest," the shoemaker cried out. "You're one of them. One of the three!" Sweat started to bead on his balding head as he moved left a step or two, then right, then left again, frantic to find a way out from behind the counter that would steer him clear of the hooded figure.

"Again that all depends on which three you're referring to," Giordano toyed with the man, whom was now becoming extremely agitated, evident by his uncontrolled movements.

The only exit was the one directly behind Bruno, and that was strategically being blocked by Bruno who crept closer, spreading out the furrows of his cassock so that he appeared twice as large. "Stay back," the shoemaker warned. "I know you are a wanted man. Both you and your companions! If I yell out, I will have you arrested. They will lock you away. So you better leave now while you still have a chance." The threat was hollow; Bruno could tell that there was no one else in the shop. The stairs to the upper apartment were off the street and there was no internal staircase directly into the shop.

"Scream then, why don't you?" Bruno challenged him to go ahead.

"I will if you come any closer. Not even your friend the Emperor is willing to protect you now."

Bruno laughed in a manner that frightened the shoemaker even more. "And how would a lowly shoemaker even know who I am, let alone my friendship with the Emperor. You must have some friends in high places."

"I do, and I'm warning you, when they find out, there's no way in this world you're going to escape prison."

"Not surprising for someone who calls himself a master cobbler, so as not to be confused with the rest of the saddle makers." Bruno taunted him with his own words that he had bragged to Caesar. "I think I'll call you a butcher instead. I just left the home of a little girl that did not deserve to die, master butcher. Two parents that loved her very much, grieving endlessly, innocents that had nothing to do with you and your band of butchers. That's what you are; you know that, nothing more than a butcher of the innocent." Only a few feet now separated the shoemaker from Bruno.

"I had nothing to do with that girl," the shoemaker's voice cracked as he spoke. "She was an accident. She wasn't supposed to happen. It was a mistake!"

"A mistake? You killed a young girl by mistake. That makes the world of difference. Wouldn't you agree?" Bruno mocked the pretensions of the little man.

"Yes, yes, it does," he warbled. 'It was his fault. He mistook her for a playmate. He didn't know better. She was screaming. He didn't know what to do. He couldn't get her to stop screaming?"

"So he killed her. Not you! He did! It was completely beyond your control!"

"Yes, that's right!" The shoemaker grabbed the awl in his hand as Bruno continued to approach. "That had nothing to do with me! Ask the others if you don't believe me."

Giordano noticed the change in demeanor and tone and knew instinctively that the shoemaker had firmed his resolve. The moment was at hand when all men make the decision to either fight or flee. "What makes you think the others are any less guilty than you?"

The shoemaker lunged forward, raising his hand with the awl above his head in order to bring it swiftly down upon his assailant. In the blink of an eye, Bruno had opened the vial and threw its contents at an imaginary target on the shoemaker's chest. The impact of the white powder caught the man by surprise. For the moment he stopped the descent of the pointed awl in midair.

"What nonsense is this?" the shoemaker started to say as he stared down at the substance sticking to the fabric of his shirt. He raised his chin up to continue the attack but it was too late. The moment he looked down at his chest he had inhaled the powdery substance, his nostrils stinging from the faint almond scent. He collapsed over the top of his counter, the awl still tightly held in his closed fist.

"Wild cherry stones mixed with acid then ground and dried into a powder, to answer your question," Bruno explained before the shoemaker gave his last gasp. "You were an angry man, but no one had a right to be angrier than the parents from whom you stole the life of their young child. Wrath is such a vile sin, spawned from hatred, bred in contempt. For you to have vented your sin against a mere child is unforgivable. May the Lord not have any mercy upon your soul." Bruno reached into the folds of his robe and withdrew the sealed document that Yakov had asked him to pass on the Maharal. "At least your death will serve a good purpose. I am certain you will deliver this message to your leader most hurriedly." Bruno placed the letter under the body sprawled over the counter, ensuring that it would be found as soon as the shoemaker was moved.

Retreating to the door, he looked once more on to the shop street to see if anyone was walking in his direction. Seeing an opportunity to slip into the street unnoticed, Bruno exited from the shop appearing nonchalant as he did so. His work done for the day, it was time to head back to the inn, but first he'd find a small, insignificant tavern, away from any commotion, where he could spend some time to contemplate the direction his life had suddenly taken.

§ § § § § §

Bruno slipped quietly through the crack he made in the door off the second storey hallway into his room, closing it silently behind, and sighing with relief as soon as he fingered and twisted the bolt into the locked position. Searching blindly for the flint that lay on the table, immediately to the right of the door, he struck it until it sparked briefly but long enough to light the oiled wick protruding from the chamber lamp. The faint glow illuminated what little of the room there was; just enough space for the table holding its lamp and washing bowl, a bed frame and mattress lying on the floor, and a chair up against the furthest wall. Spartan by anyone's definition.

"Late night I presume," the voice whispered from behind. "We had been expecting you back much earlier. But from the smell of your clothes I can tell you must have been out celebrating your efforts."

Bruno could feel his heart bursting as it leaped and hammered against his chest wall. He swung around to confront his late night visitor, still dizzy from the sudden rush of blood coursing wildly through his veins.

"You are not my keeper," he attempted to remind Yakov, trying to sound more perturbed than frightened.

Yakov sat upright in the winged back chair, looking very accusatory but not saying a word.

"This is still my room you know. I never said when I would be back. I still believe I have the right to come and go as I please. Why are you in here anyway?"

"Your door wasn't locked. The hour was growing late. Something may have gone wrong, so I thought I'd wait up until you returned."

Bruno could feel his hands still trembling from the shock. "Oh, well thank you for your concern but I needed some libations after talking with the parents. It was very difficult discussing their daughter with them. They are suffering tremendously. Afterwards I was walking the streets until my head cleared."

"You don't owe me any explanation."

"No, but in case you were wondering, that is what I was doing."

"And if that is what you choose to tell me, then I have no reason to doubt you," Yakov let him know.

"But you don't believe me."

"As I said, if that is what you choose to tell me, then I will believe you."

"What kind of answer is that?"

"A truthful one. Isn't that the kind that good friends provide to each other?"

Bruno felt the knife being twisted slowly in his gut. How was Yakov constantly able to make him feel like he was nothing more than a waif constantly needing to be scolded? Even now he knew he was being interrogated, not by what was being said, but by what wasn't.

"There are things that I have to do Kova that you don't want to know about." Bruno walked over to his bed and threw himself into it. "You wouldn't understand."

"The truth is, I do understand, probably far more than you suspect. The world is not a wonderful place where everyone lives happily ever after. I am not that naïve. But neither does it have to be as bad as it is. You have always wondered what the dividing line that separates me and my fellow Karaites from the Rabbinical Judaism. It's what I've just told you, that this world can be a better place. I don't expect you to fully understand, because the concept is so foreign, even though your faith was essentially derived from the same teachings by Jesus. He even describes it in one of his parables you Christians hold so dear."

"Are you saying that Jesus was a Karaite?"

"No, he wasn't because Karaism didn't come into being until much later. Like the rest of his family, my family, he was a Zadokite. Much the same thing except the priesthood really did have power and authority at that time."

Bruno sat upright on the edge of the mattress, attentive to what Yakov had to say. "So which parable are you referring to?"

"It's the candle under the basket one. He's talking about the Pharisees of his time, the forerunners of Rabbinical Judaism. You see, God had one primary command to my family and it was that we were to be 'ha-or ha-oylum.'

"The light unto the world," Bruno translated.

"Exactly! It was never the Lord's intention that Judaism should be made exclusive to only the Hebrews and that it would not be shared with the rest of the world. We were to light up the world with his love and teachings. In order to make the world a better place, it was our mandate, our duty to bring the religion of the one true God to the world. But like most things, there are those that wish to covet, preserve things precious only for themselves, refusing to share what they have in their possession. And as a result the antagonism that has divided the world arose and is now responsible for what the world has become today."

"So the light under the basket parable was Jesus' way of reminding everyone of God's purpose for them?"

"Yes, that is what it was all about. He was determined to live his life as an example for others to follow. Problem is that so very few people have even tried to live that life. I am certainly not the one to condemn any of them for trying. But the ones that have never tried, those will be held accountable."

"And how do you see me Kova?"

"It is not an easy path to walk. Many try, most fail. But it's the ones that are willing to try again, those are the ones that will eventually succeed. You are definitely not a quitter, Giordano."

"So there's hope for me yet."

"I do not think God has given up on you. But don't try his patience too much."

25

Josefov: Kozi Street

The atmosphere within the room was growing more restless by the minute. Everyone that had been gathered would have preferred to been somewhere else, somewhere safe, preferably outside the city. It was the first time in almost two months that the entire cabal had been assembled. Not since that night last November had a request that all of them meet at the Maharal's home been delivered. That time it was to discuss the arrival of the three strangers that had come to Prague by request of the Emperor. An informer inside the palace staff had leaked to them the purpose of their summons. A decision had to be made regarding what to do about these interlopers that would meddle with affairs that were none of their concern. The solution seemed simple enough. Use kabalistic forces to terrify their dreams at night and frighten them away. It should have been easy, but no one had informed the Maharal that one of the strangers was the Kahana. Now it was months later and those around the table were beginning to question who wielded the greater magic.

The letter was unfolded on the table's surface and all eyes suddenly were drawn to it. Seated at the head of the table, the Maharal never said a word as he moved the lamp closer in order to read the hand written message. He cleared his throat, a sign for everyone to stop their bickering and sit down. The other members present took their appointed seats and waited in silence. Rabbi Judah ben Loew still refrained from saying a word.

Finally one of the members could tolerate playing the Maharal's game any longer and spoke out boldly what was on his mind. "Melling was right," he exclaimed. "Nothing good could ever come from you. The congress had been right in electing him Chief Rabbi of Prague and dismissing you." The words were angry but shared by others around the table. Arguments broke out almost immediately between those that still supported the Maharal blindly and those that now had their doubts.

A candlestick flew across the table and struck the one who first protested across the brow, knocking him backwards with the force of the blow. It was enough to bring silence around the table once more. "Don't you ever mention the name of that man in my house again! A curse upon Rabbi Isaac Melling! He has been nothing but a thorn in my side and I will not tolerate your sniveling cowardice. Do you understand me, Menachem? Never say his name again to me or I will show you which one of us is the more powerful."

Doctor Philip Mendes, another of the cabal members helped Menachem, the baker back into his chair. The Maharal looked from one person to the next, meeting their eyes with a cold dark stare that made them squirm uncomfortably. "You are all aware of why I called this meeting together. I need not remind you that Eidelman is dead. He died to protect us, to protect our cause, and I will not have you shame him by your whining like little frightened girls."

"What are we going to do?" Maisel for one of the few times in his life sounded helpless. "They will kill all of us."

"Sit down and be quiet," Judah ben Loew instructed. He slid the letter over to his brother Rabbi Sinai ben Loew. "Here, you read it. This man angers me."

Sinai ben Loew held the letter between his hands and began to read slowly. "To my spiritual brother, I give a warning. The game you are playing is a double edged sword. It has come to an end. Your intentions perhaps noble at first are now no different than those you have fought against. You have become the evil that plagues a city. Your spells have no effect on me. My dreams now are as sweet as they've always been. But yours will begin to haunt you. The Golem resides in your attic. The body of the girl lies in the grave of Maisel's daughter. Your synagogue is being built on the blood money from those you have sacrificed. To expose you now would result in the deaths of hundreds perhaps thousands of innocents. Is that what you want? To be responsible for the massacre of your own people because you have been too proud and too ambitious. Let me right this wrong. We will find a way to return the girl's body without implicating the community. In return you must deliver to me the Golem, so that justice system may have its sacrificial lamb. In three nights I will be waiting at the tenth point of your star. Send him to the Church of St. Mikhal, as you intended at midnight. It is time that we end this."

"He knows everything," Menahem the baker cried out. "We're doomed. We're all going to pay the price for your failure."

"He's right," the voice from the end of the table agreed. "It was fortunate that Eidelman's wife contacted me when he didn't return home. If anyone else had found him, they also would have found the letter. Then we wouldn't be having this discussion. We'd all have been arrested by the constabulary by now."

"Well, of course she contacted you, Oram. You are the Jewish Quarter's resident policeman," Maisel commented. "But they killed Eidelman. How can we ignore that?"

"I'm not even certain he did do it," Oram Hershorn replied. "I examined the body. Couldn't find any trace of an injury. I think Eidelman's heart just gave out."

"No, no, do not be fooled," the Maharal berated them. "This Karaite priest is a danger to all of us. He has no reason to be lenient towards us. Remember that we harbor an enmity from a long time past. Do you think that the Kahana could so easily forget the hundreds of thousands that were slaughtered because they followed his ancestor? Would you not seek revenge? It is in his heart, just like any other man's. He must be eliminated before he destroys us."

"You were the one earlier saying we could not lay a hand on him. Remember, the Cardinal is willing to overlook everything as long as we can deliver the Kahana to him. He doesn't know about any of you, believing that I'm totally responsible for the events thus far. Let's let him believe that. We deliver the Kahana to him, we ensure that there are no more victims of the Golem and all will be as it should be."

"You are deluding yourself," Mendes criticized Maisel's plan. They have already told the Emperor. How else do you explain the guards posted at the cemetery?"

"There are guards at the cemetery? We're doomed. All is finished," Menahem the baker wailed.

"Listen, listen to the Maharal," urged Isaac Katz ha Cohen, Judah ben Loew's son-in-law. "There is a way out if you just listen to what he has to say."

"We have listened all this time and look at the mess we're in now," Doctor Mendes dismissed Isaac's plea. "How are you going to make the girl's body disappear? How long do you think you can keep the Golem hidden? I say deal with the Kahana and forget everything else. At least he's offering us a way out. Gentlemen, know when you have been out maneuvered by your enemy."

"Ari, tell me there's another way to get the girl's body without the guards observing," Rabbi Loew's brother Sinai asked Ari Gruenberg, the caretaker of the graveyard.

"I wish there was, but that's the new section. There aren't any catacombs dug yet. That takes years to develop."

"Enough," the baker cried out. "We cannot escape our fate."

"Menahem, I have put up with you long enough," Maisel reached over the table to grab him by the vest. "So help me, if you say one more word, I will see that you get buried alongside Eidelman."

"What, you'll now have us killed too," Mendes jumped to the defense of the baker, "just so you can keep your stolen wealth. That's what this is Mordecai; just an attempt to hide what you started. And the Rabbi's added a list of murders to the crime with the Golem that was yours in the first place."

Once again the members of the cabal divided their ranks and began bickering bitterly between themselves.

"That will be enough," the Maharal commanded in his thunderous voice. "Our enemy is out there, not in here! We cannot make a deal with the Kahana. You all know that. He knows too much and that should concern you most. With that knowledge he can destroy all of us. The Cardinal has offered us an olive branch, and even should he turn on us, it is only Maisel that he is aware of."

"What," Maisel exclaimed. "You'd sacrifice me if you had to?"

"If we had to, yes! Better you than all of us. You would do the same in our position."

The rest of the cabal was of the same sentiment as they nodded their heads.

"But it won't be necessary," Loew continued, "Because the Cardinal will be satisfied when we hand over the dead body of the Kahana along with the remains of the girl. He was found with her, caught red handed, and killed in the struggle that followed when our very own policeman, Oram uncovered his horrific crime."

"Why not just let the Cardinal know where to find him in three nights," the ninth member of the cabal suggested. He was a seedy looking individual named Kuba, known to control much of the illicit activities in the Jewish Quarter but that only made him indispensable for his contacts and information to men like Maisel and the Rabbi.

"He can do our dirty work then. There could be terrible repercussions if we kill the Nasi. You said so before. He has divine protection. We wouldn't want to stir that hornet's nest."

"The stakes have risen well above that opportunity now," Judah ben Loew explained. "With his escape from prison, Yakov Kahana has made a name for himself amongst the populace. Even non-Jews that hear the story are thinking that he has special powers. Those fools for guards that they had posted swear he was escorted from the prison by angels with flaming swords. He may have grown well beyond the Cardinal's control. We can't afford to have him taken to trial. If what he knows should happen to be made public then the entire community would be held accountable."

"But what of the others?" Oram questioned. "Those other two obviously know the full story as well. They're as much a threat as Yakov Kahana is."

"I would not think the Cardinal would think twice of meting out similar justice to those two. Through the inquisition he has the authority to bypass the civil courts. Not even the Emperor would dare question the authority of the inquisition's tribunal."

"And what do we do about the Golem? They will want to be certain that he will no longer threaten the city," the policeman advised, certain that the Cardinal would raise the bar on his demands, now that he'll have more deaths to conceal on our behalf."

"He must be eliminated as well," the Maharal replied, bereft of emotion.

"He is still my son!" Maisel protested.

"He stopped being your son the day you rejected him, Mordecai. The day you brought him to my house, ashamed that this was the only offspring of you and your first wife. That God had cursed you with such a fate, to have a child neither beauteous of body nor complete of mind. Your wife could not even bear to suckle him. Or do you forget that day, Mordecai. 'Take him Reb, take him,' you pleaded for me to remove the blot upon your household. And I have raised him for twenty years, shielding him from the world, concealing your shame from the community. Now tell me that he is your son!"

Maisel hung his head in shame, his mind flashing back to the day he disowned the flesh of his flesh. He had nothing more to say. He was a beaten man. All the riches of the world at the tips of his fingers and no one left to carry on his name. What did it matter? Let the Maharal carry out his plan.

"Then it is decided, we will agree to the Kahana's request but not exactly as he expects. We will send the Golem to remove him as a threat to us." Judah ben Loew looked to his left where his son-in-law sat recording everything he had just said. The Maharal's hand slapped the writing implement from Isaac's hand. "Fool, know what to record of things I say, and know when not to. When you do record the events of this time, it will be as I instruct."

Isaac Katz sheepishly folded his hands together and didn't even bother to bend down to pick you the stylus.

"Now then, are we all in agreement? It ends at St. Mikhal's in three nights."

There were no voices of dissent. There were no other suggestions. The motion to eliminate the Kahana had been carried.

"Good, then that is settled," Judah ben Loew summed up the meeting's outcome. "Mordechai, you'll let the Cardinal know that we'll be apprehending the Kahana for him and that you'll see to it that there is no further episodes involving the demon. Ari, you'll be prepared to remove the girl's body as soon as the opportunity arises. I think we should be able to get the Emperor to pull back his men once we hand over Yakov Kahana's body. After all, he'll see there's no point in trying to pursue the truth any longer. Mendes, as soon as we have her body we'll need to make arrangement to have her transferred to her parents. We'll need a sealed coffin and a medical examiner's report. You need to describe the body in horrific detail so that they will not even attempt to embalm. Whatever it takes to ensure they keep the casket closed. And make the injuries inflicted sound as if there something Yakov Kahana could have easily done. I want the parents satisfied that we've not only apprehended the culprit but exacted justice on their behalf."

"When does this stop Judah?" Mendes challenged. "When do the lies and deceit finally come to an end? I'm a doctor, not an accomplice to a murderer. But you have made me so."

"It stops when I say it's over," the Rabbi blustered. "I will let you all know when that time is and not a moment sooner. But just remember this, when it's all over and the people are hailing you as heroes, and saviors, that it was I who made it possible for you. The stories they will tell of these times will be singing your praises. That is my gift to you ungrateful miscreants!"

26

St. Mikhal's Church: January 1589

The Emperor's men were in their positions, ensuring that no one could approach the Church without being detected. It was a wall of protection more against the Cardinal's men rather than to assist in the capture the Golem. Yakov was certain that if the Cardinal became aware of what was transpiring he'd try to intercept their plan before it came to fruition. It was clear to him that the Golem had taken on a much lower priority for the Church than his own arrest had become. With the Emperor's help, he'd see to it that Cardinal Calabrese didn't succeed.

Having been neglected for quite some time, the little church was badly in need of repairs. The gold leaf had either been deliberately stripped and pilfered or else had naturally succumbed to flaking with time, and the painted murals were being slowly obliterated by water stains that had seeped through porous concrete. Ever since Jan Hus had uttered his now famous curse, the Church of St. Mikhal's had been considered to have been desecrated by his presence there. Under the custodial care of a friar, regular services were no longer conducted and talk of constructing another St. Mikhal's on the other side of the river was quite prevalent.

Yakov noticed that Caesar had grown considerably uneasy as the night wore on, as if he knew something but he wasn't ready to reveal it. On the other hand, Giordano was humming away to himself and had been for most of the day as he prepared his globes in readiness for the encounter. They had gone over the logistics, reviewed the stratagem, and analyzed the variables. The small size of the church would make it difficult to maneuver. They had no false illusions to think that the Maharal was going to send his Golem to quietly surrender. They were calculating on the cabal remaining true to form. To catch a rat, it was necessary to bait the trap with cheese. Yakov knew full well that he was the cheese that night. Hidden in the narrow cloisters that ringed the building as an upper balcony, Giordano had placed four of Rudolf's best men. Each one of them held on to a drop cord in readiness. Concealed in the rafters was a net made from braided hemp just waiting for the precise moment. Yakov would stand by the altar facing the front entrance. As soon as the Golem would make it halfway from the entrance to the altar the net would be dropped by Rudolf's men. Then it was up to Bruno to use his ether globes to render the creature unconscious. At that point, the rest of Rudolf's men would emerge from their hiding spots, secure the net and cart the Golem off as their prisoner.

"You're still looking troubled," Yakov commented to Caesar. "Care to tell me what's wrong."

"It's nothing, Kova," Caesar reassured him.

"For nothing, you still appear perplexed."

"It's silly. Just a gut feeling that just won't go away."

"Caesar, for anyone else a gut feeling might be considered foolishness, but in your family that is never the case. Anything that can help me at midnight should be expressed. Even if it at first appears negative, there are always ways that it can be turned around."

"Not everything has a silver lining," Caesar defended himself.

"But we won't know that until you tell me, would we?"

"My father was quite an amazing man, when you think about it. He managed to turn his aptitude for mysticism into a respectable and desirable business, catering to the cream of European society. They paid dearly to have him provide a line or two that they would interpret in a hundred different ways in order to make it fit the circumstances. He explained it to me once. He said, 'In order to be precise, be vague.' And he was, but they lapped it up like a cat to cream. They could never get enough and so he kept pouring it out, almanacs, horoscopes, sonnets, anything they wanted. Do you understand what I'm saying Kova?"

Yakov smiled at Caesar's dilemma with a kind expression that was more reminiscent of a parent to his child. "I know perfectly well what you're saying Caesar and I appreciate what you're trying to do, but you don't have to pretend with me. I know your father wasn't a charlatan and I also realize that not all his predictions are going to be favorable. You don't have to try and protect me. Whatever God has in store for me, it will happen, whether you try to conceal it from me or not."

"Then why bother to know? Perhaps things occur because we implant the suggestion. If that's the case, then the future can be changed if you don't know what it's going to be."

"A valid argument, but I think both you and I know that whatever your father has said is going to happen, will happen, whether I know it or not." Yakov presented his argument in impeccable logic. "So why not tell me and let me at least try to prove him wrong."

Caesar trembled at the thought of what he was about to reveal. "It came to me just a short while ago. Century VIII, Quatrain seventy-seven, my father said, *'By the Antichrist the three good become the three annihilated. Twenty-seven years in blood, the duration of the war. The heretics are dead, the prisoners exiled. His body made human from red water and compacted earth.'* I fear it is our doom that my father was talking about."

"I must admit that it does not sound favorable," Yakov agreed, but it does not necessarily mean that we fail."

"Then how do your interpret it," Caesar questioned.

"I agree that we were brought here to face what the Church described as the herald of the Antichrist, and therefore this affair will result in the three of us being brought down, but remember that could be long after we resolve this matter. Otherwise your father would have said the Antichrist's servant caused our annihilation. There is a lot of latitude in what he said. He could even infer that some or all of us survive for a further twenty-seven years after we defeat the Golem."

"Or he could be saying that we are killed now and a war breaks out at the same time through some connection with this event and it goes on for that length of time."

'That's possible. I don't deny that but from what you have taught me about your father thus far, I don't think it would be that simple.

The dead heretics could just as well be our enemies as well. After all, we are not the only heretics assembled in Prague at this time."

"And the prisoners exiled?" Caesar was worried by that line thinking that it might imply that he never returns home to Southern France.

"My gut feeling, if I have such a thing," Yakov proposed, "is that once this is all over, those responsible are going to be banished from the Empire."

"Exactly whom are you implying."

"I think your father is telling us quite precisely that it will be the Maharal and some of his group. The last line ties in with the third. The red water and compacted earth is the Golem, or at least how the kabala describes the making of a Golem. Hence the exiled ones and the Golem are tied together."

"I hope you're right Kova because right now my instincts are telling me that this may not go down well tonight."

"Instincts or something more that your father might have said?"

"Right now," Caesar felt himself being burdened by more and more stray thoughts from his past, "I think there is very little difference. Even when my thoughts tell me that we're going to succeed they're always followed by an afterthought that somehow we are not going to be permitted to enjoy our success."

"I have no such illusions, Caesar," Yakov explained. "Each of us is here because the consequences of what the Church is prepared to do were far worse than our personal sacrifice. If we succeed then everything else is inconsequential as long as they observe and keep their promises to us. We are left to their whims in regards to everything else."

"Do you really believe that they will keep their promises?"

"I believe in you," Yakov pointed at Caesar. "I believe your purpose here is far more significant than you originally imagined. I've told you that already but I think it has still taken you quite some time to realize that. I think your father wasn't only protecting you, but ensuring that you would be sent on this mission."

"Why would he do that?"

"Because there was no one else that could protect Giordano and me. You are the only one that has any leverage over the Church once we succeed. You have in your possession the material to guarantee that they do not break their word to us. I don't have it and neither does Giordano; only you. I think if you search through your father's teachings, you'll find that he agrees."

Shutting his eyes momentarily, Caesar flashed through the litany of phrases his father had taught him as a key to memorizing all of the quatrains. He reopened his eyes with a slight look of puzzlement showing in his expression. "How did you know?"

"I think I am comprehending your father's abilities far better than I thought possible. He loved you far more than you even realize. This was his way of saying so."

"It's funny how I only find out after his death that he actually cared for me far more than he ever let on."

"Not that unusual. I think if you were to ask most men you would find that they never truly felt their father's affections until they had passed on. Sad as that may be. I think back to my own father and I can't remember if we ever said how much we loved each other. I think we tend to take it for granted but even so, we're never quite certain. And then one day we wake up and they're gone and we can never ask them."

By this time Bruno had taken a respite from his preparations and had overheard part of their conversation. "I don't know about you two but I think we have far more important things to deal with right now than your reminiscing. We have two sentries posted on the roof, four up in the lofts in charge of the net, and the captain will wait with Caesar and me in the rear vestibule for your signal. From the moment the Golem enters through the front door, until midway down the central aisle, you're all on your own. No one can reach you in time if he doesn't move to the midpoint in the chapel where the net can be dropped. So you have to remain in front of the pulpit and not stray from it in order to lure him up the path. Are we clear on that?"

"Crystal," Yakov responded.

"Good, because I'm not one hundred percent certain how well this will work." Giordano rubbed his hand through his black locks as usual whenever he got nervous.

"It will, it will!" Caesar exclaimed with a degree of alarm. "Century V, Quatrain ninety-seven, it just appeared to me as soon as you made your comment Giordano. *'The one deformed at birth that spread horror shall be suffocated. In the city where the Great King lives. And the edict against the ghettoed ones will be revoked. The hail and thunder at Condon is inestimable.'* We succeed. Do you see that?"

"I guess," Bruno replied questionably. "I can definitely see the first three lines. I don't really understand the fourth. Do you understand it Kova," he turned to Yakov to hear his explanation.

Yakov was quiet at first, choosing to ignore the question. "Yes, it looks like we will definitely succeed." But he chose not to answer Bruno's question directly, instead his expression forcibly blank so as not to betray his innermost thoughts. "Well, I guess we better get into position," he added as he walked towards the dais at the front of the small church and took his position at the pulpit.

"Did you see that?" Bruno commented to Caesar. "Kova was distressed by what you said. I don't know why I know it, but there's something he interpreted from your father's prophecy that he's not telling us."

"What do you think it was?" Caesar questioned. "I thought it was a foretelling of good fortune. I don't see anything threatening."

"Neither do I. Maybe I was wrong. It certainly wouldn't be unusual to be a little apprehensive on a night like this. So Captain," Bruno shouted towards Rudolf's officer. "I guess it's time we get into position and wait."

The captain clicked his heels and turned towards the vestibule in the back where they would lay in waiting. He was joined by Caesar but Bruno remained behind in order to talk with Yakov a little more.

Giordano reached out and grabbed Yakov's forearm. "This plan is far from perfect."

"I'm well aware of that Giordano but it's the best we could come up with."

Bruno was reluctant to leave. "You know, there's no reason that I couldn't stand here right with you. If he's going to surrender, then it makes no difference whether it's just to you or to the both of us."

"Both you and I know that if he shows, he's not coming here to surrender." Turning to face his friend, Yakov placed his free hand over Bruno's arm. "We've come too far to fail now because we suddenly fear for our lives."

"Wanting to live is not necessarily a bad thing," Bruno cracked a smile.

"No it's not. But ensuring that others live is an even better thing."

Bruno felt ashamed that he had let his fears get the better of him. Yakov was right. Yakov always seemed to be right. "I'll be in the back room. As soon as you feel something is wrong, you yell for me. Promise me!"

"I promise. Now get in the back before you spoil the plan."

Reluctantly, Giordano turned and retreated to the vestibule leaving Yakov all alone in the central hall. Waiting patiently by the pulpit, Yakov flipped through the gold leafed pages of the open bible left on the podium. The colored plates of biblical scenes were done in breathtaking water colors. Such beauty, Yakov thought to himself, how something so beautiful could be responsible for so much anguish in the world. Where had the world gone wrong? The bible had come into the world to give man a better life, to provide a moral standard that would create a heaven on earth, and now here he stood, prepared to face a demon spun from the very hatreds and prejudices that this book of beautiful pictures and delicate pages had created. If there was some logic to all this then it certainly had escaped him. In the distance he could hear one of the town clocks strike midnight. He had lost track of the time as he looked through the bible. Still no Golem. Perhaps the Maharal had decided not to accept his challenge; he began to second guess himself. He had calculated on the Rabbi's pride and arrogance to offer no other choice but to send his creature to eliminate the threat. Everything that he had postulated regarding the Maharal suggested that this would be the venue he would select. Not showing was not even an option considered. Yakov began to doubt his own instincts. He took a few steps away from the pulpit thinking that perhaps he should just have a look outside the entrance to see if anyone or anything was in the streets.

Just at the moment he stepped down from the dais, the body came crashing down from above landing awkwardly along the back of a row of pews. Yakov took a quick look at the mangled figure and identified him as one of the guards; one of the guards that was supposed to be operating the net from the loft above. It was then that he looked up, the sudden shot of terror forcing the bile to rise in the back of his throat. Hanging from the net he saw it. Black like a colossal spider the way it seemed to grip the web of netting with its hands and feet, hanging suspended at least twenty feet above the floor. It was watching him, assessing him, looking for the best way to launch its attack. Yakov backed his way up the dais towards the pulpit. If he could move back just far enough and fast enough, the Golem would have no other choice but to swing down to the floor before it could reach him as the loft only encircled that part of the hall where the congregation sat but did not overhang the pulpit. The Golem scrambled across the net, seeking a better vantage point. Observing the speed by which the creature moved, Yakov stood dumbfounded. He could not yell, he could barely raise his voice above a whisper. He kept telling himself it was a man, but no matter how hard he tried to convince himself of that, he failed. Where the hell were the captain's men? Couldn't they see what was happening? Drop the net, he kept screaming over and over in his mind. Drop it!

Suspending himself from the netting the Golem positioned himself over the central aisle preparing to drop a mere five yards from where Yakov stood. Hanging upside-down, the creature's appearance was unworldly, insectoid with its chitinous armor. Mesmerized, Yakov could not break his gaze away, and then it happened. The long neck began to rotate, perhaps one hundred and ten, maybe even one hundred and twenty degrees until the creature was able to stare directly back at him. His body shielded by the black intra-articulating leather plates, a leather helmet over his head, only the creature's eyes displayed any humanity as Yakov watched him maneuver the ropes. But even then the eyes were cold and lifeless, fueled by an indescribable rage that Yakov had never seen before in any animal, let alone a man.

The drop should have been impossible, the distance too great not to have broken a leg or an arm when he landed, but instead the Golem fell like a cat, sprawled out on all fours, the impact spread evenly across his four limbs. The sound and utterances were now audible. Most of them were unintelligible but the few that Yakov could decipher spewed with venomous hatred. It pronounced one word that was clearly distinguishable. "Ka-ha-na." The syllables were stretched out and Yakov's first impression was that it was more a question than a statement. Of course, the creature would have only been provided with a rough and general appearance, but his adversaries had not anticipated that he'd be wearing apparel from Caesar's wardrobe. The pantaloons, and brocade vest over a velveteen chemise was being scrutinized carefully by the Golem. And then he repeated the word, "Ka-ha-na," but this time it was mouthed with pure hatred.

It was then that he was overcome by the malodorous nature of his adversary. A smell that could only be associated with dead and decaying flesh; a sickly-sweet smell filling the nostrils and subsequently dulling the senses. Yakov felt himself growing dizzy, his head swimming uncontrollably, as he fell back onto the podium, gripping the lectern with his left hand in an effort to keep himself upright. The hissing sound grew closer as the Golem made his final advance.

"Giordano," Yakov cried out with the last of his failing breath. It was neither loud nor piercing but to the ears of Bruno waiting silently in the vestibule, blind to everything that was transpiring, it trumpeted in his ears. He charged into the chapel, blue globes gripped in each hand as he raced to the defense of his friend. His sudden appearance from out of nowhere was enough to cause the Golem to take a step backward in order to assess the situation. Slow of mind, the creature had to recalculate the options, attempt to identify this new assailant, a matter of seconds, but sufficient enough for Bruno to launch the globe from his right hand in its general direction.

The glass globe struck the creature on the shoulder and shattered upon impact, the contents spreading evenly over the leather plates, covering them with its oily nature. The Golem stopped his advance. With his fingers he rubbed at the oily material attempting to analyze it through his limited capacity. Time enough for Bruno to have shifted the other globe into his right hand and hit the Golem square in the chest with it. This time the attack only made him angrier as he set his gaze upon Bruno.

"Get out of here, Giordano," Yakov urged his friend. "It's not working."

"But this will," Bruno moved quickly maintaining his calm. "He pulled a red globe from his pocket and launched it. The trajectory was faultless, bursting into flames as it struck the leather armor. The flames covered the upper torso of the creature surrounding him in a blue-green halo. Half sleepy eyes opened fully with sheer terror. Desperately, the Golem swatted at the dancing flames, then not knowing what to do next, ran down the aisle towards the front doors, bashing them aside with his body, all the time releasing a feral scream reminiscent of a wolf caught in a trap.

Bruno turned to Yakov with a huge smile on his face. "Ether burns. Another victory for science!"

"We've got him then," Yakov allowed his friend to help him to his feet. By this time the captain and Caesar had entered the fray but too late to help.

"Doubtful," Bruno replied. "Did you see the color of the leather?"

"Yes, silver-black," Yakov answered. "What about it?"

"Silver alkali," Bruno explained. "You dip materials into a silver alkali solution to make them fire retardant. The ether will burn off and it's doubtful there will even be a mark on the Golem."

"Oh there's a mark all right," Yakov corrected him. "He's had his first setback. He knows he's no longer invincible. We hurt him and we have him on the run. Now we close in for the finish."

While they spoke about their small victory the captain was examining the broken body of his man, strew across the rail of the pew. He called out for his other men, but there was no reply. Racing up the side stairway onto the balcony, he found three more of his men, as dead as the first. He knew his two sentries on the roof would have suffered a similar fate. Poor souls, he thought, didn't even have a chance to draw their blades. The taste of defeat was souring his mouth. More than even the others in the cabal, he wanted this creature dead, but he wanted the pleasure of doing it with his own two hands.

A hand rested gently on the captain's shoulder. Having climbed the stairs silently, Bruno stood behind the decorated soldier. "Dimitri, we will avenge their deaths."

"They were some of my best," he sighed. "I was like a father to them. He broke them into so many pieces like little rag dolls. I want him dead Giordano. More than anything, I want him dead."

"I understand," Bruno consoled the captain's fury. "It will happen, just not today. "Come on back down. We'll have a team dispatched to clean up the mess. Right now it's important that we report back to the Emperor what has transpired and consider our next move. The next time I think it will be necessary to take the battle to them. They won't be so quick to dispatch their monster again now that they know we can exploit a weakness." Bruno escorted the officer down the stairs.

It was obvious as soon as Yakov and Caesar saw their faces that it was futile to expect any others would be joining them. "My condolences captain," Yakov spoke up.

"Mine too," Caesar agreed.

The captain accepted their sympathies and then unsheathed his sword.

"Master Kahana, I am under orders, I hope you understand."

"Dimitri, don't do this," Bruno warned.

"Try to understand," the Captain enlisted Bruno's help. "It would be one thing if we had the Golem prisoner and could manage to find out who he reported to, but it's entirely a different matter since we have nothing to show for our efforts but six dead soldiers. I'm only acting on the Emperor's orders. He needs Master Kahana to return to custody. Otherwise it would appear that there is no law and order in this country and the Emperor is powerless to do anything about it."

"Dimitri, there has to be some other way," Bruno pleaded. "If you take Yakov into custody, then we will not be able to apprehend the creature. You've seen it. You know what it can do. You know we had no part in the other deaths. It killed your men and now you want to eliminate the one person that has any hope of catching the Golem. It doesn't make sense."

"Giordano, try to understand. My orders come from the Emperor. I bear Master Kahana no ill will, but unless he can clear his name, he will have to be imprisoned."

"And how exactly is he to clear his name if he's locked behind bars. Give us a chance Dimitri to find those responsible. Look the other way and we'll be gone before you can even turn around. You know it's the right thing to do."

"Right or not, I have my orders," the captain was resigned to the fact that he had to bring Yakov Kahana back with him.

"But your orders didn't say that you had to take Kova prisoner, immediately. You could instruct us to keep a watch over him in the meantime. Just give us the chance to uncover the conspirators. We're so close!"

"Where will I find you, if I was to agree to your proposal?"

"We're staying at the Chevel Blanc. Let Ruldolf know. You can find us there!"

27

Resslova: L'Hotel Cheval Blanc

In the darkened corner of the inn's tavern, several men sat hunched over their drinks, whispering in hushed tones, and carefully watching the other patrons of the tavern to insure that they were not becoming too curious as to the strangers' presence. The sword hanging from the left hip of one of the men gave fair warning to everyone to keep their distance, and although it was hard to tell for certain, the dozen or so men sharing two tables in close proximity looked as though their grey cloaks could have easily been concealing weapons as well.

"Are you aware of the pressure I am under," the large cloaked figure at the main table was saying to the others. "At any time I expect the Cardinal to burst through those doors with his men and accuse me of protecting enemies of the Church. How in Lord's name am I going to defend myself against that?"

"You worry too much Rudi," Giordano attempted to put him at ease. "All we need is a little time to clear our names and bring the real culprits to justice."

"Time is something you don't have Giordano," the Emperor reminded his friend. "And pardon me if I consider myself to be the fool here, but it would help if you finally confided in me and told me the truth of what's going on."

Bruno looked over in Yakov's direction as if to say you tell him.

"Your Majesty, it would appear that the numbers involved are far greater than we first anticipated. Yes, it's true that a vast sum of money had been stolen from the treasury, but that crime is only a small part of the overall picture. There is a cabal established. Their leader is a kabbalist and is quite proficient at the art. Whereas Calabrese seems intent at setting the Christian population on a rampage against the Jews of this city, there is equally a plan by the members of this organization to set Christian sect against Christian sect. I'm afraid you are in the middle of two forces intent on turning Prague into a conflagration of hatred."

The Emperor sat quietly listening to the explanation patiently but struggling to conceptualize the entire picture that Yakov had been painting. He tittered nervously before his spoke. "I'm afraid Kova that I can't see how this would be possible. We're talking about a group of people having this trained monkey that does their killing for them and you believe they have the ability to set the Christian factions in this city at each other's throats. I can't see how that would be possible. You know that I have a fascination for the mystic arts and alchemy and things of that nature, but I'm sorry, in all the years that I have been entertained by experts and charlatans in their respective fields, not once have I ever witnessed the level of raw power that would be required to achieve what you are referring to."

"That's because we're dealing with an individual that has meticulously crafted his plan based on existing prejudices. He's not using magic to achieve his goals; he's using the natural emotions present in the populations. Their fears, anxieties, mistrust and prejudices."

"So which man would be clever enough to achieve such a thing," Rudolf still scoffed at the suggestion.

"Rabbi Judah ben Loew," the three of them answered in unison.

"The rabbi?" Rudolf snapped back. "You're not serious…you are serious. If I recall correctly, he wasn't even chosen to be Chief Rabbi of the city. He wasn't qualified enough. And you want me to believe that someone that wasn't even considered good enough to lead his own people is actually capable of setting up this cabal you mentioned."

"Do not underestimate him," Bruno responded on Yakov's behalf. "He would have to be an extraordinary individual if the likes of Maisel will take orders from him."

"You are all serious?" Rudolf glanced back and forth at the three of them to see that they were all very covinced. "So if I understand this correctly, I have a religious leader on my one side that is threatening me with all sorts of punishments from the Vatican if I don't cooperate and hand you over to him, and on my other side I have a religious leader from my Jewish community that is threatening to turn my city into hell on earth. Do I have this correct now?"

"Yes," Bruno affirmed.

"Oh, well then I feel much better," the Emperor became extremely sarcastic. "The irony is that it would appear that men of God are determined to wreak havoc no matter which way I turn. You can appreciate why I am hesitant to become further involved than I already am."

No sooner did Rudolf finish his sentence then Caesar felt compelled to speak. *'Alas a great people will be tormented. And the Holy Laws in total ruin. As well as by other laws all of Christianity, When gold and silver is found newly mined.'*

Rudolf stared open mouthed at Caesar. "Is your father trying to tell me something?"

"Century I Quatrain fifty-three," Caesar informed the Emperor.

"It is a gift that takes some getting used to Rudi," Bruno interjected at that point. "I didn't believe it at first either, but Caesar's father has somehow instilled his prophecies in such a manner as to guide us through this mission. I've been trying to analyze it scientifically and if I'm guessing correctly, then if you say certain words in a particular fashion, or he sees certain things, then it triggers some kind of coded memory from Caesar here."

Caesar glared at Giordano with a look of feigned contempt. "I am not one of your scientific experiments Giordano!"

"It's proof enough for me that you are right," Rudolf exclaimed. "Your father over a quarter century ago told me that this day would come. In exchange for the horoscope he sent me actually. There was a price attached. 'When the time was right,' he wrote, 'my son will let you know that he requires your protection. Through a sign it will be obvious.' I don't know how I know, but I think you just gave me that sign. The quatrain confirms everything that Kova and Giordano have said thus far. It all started with a crime of gold and silver, didn't' it? And now it has turned into a clash between the lawgivers of two great religions. We must work fast if we are going to prevent the inevitable."

"We're open to suggestions Rudi," Bruno advised.

"First we must get these charges against you dropped. The Captain here will go with you. I need one of these cabal members to give a full confession of their criminal activities. The Captain is very skilled in that art. Find the weakest member, get me that confession, and I'll see to it that the charges are dismissed in their entirety against both of you. You'll be free men once again. It will be a major setback to the Cardinal."

Yakov held up his hands, his palms directly facing the Emperor. "That may not be in everyone's best interest, your Majesty. If we obtain a confession, then it will be accusatory of the leadership within the Jewish community. The rest of the population will demand revenge not against the cabal but against the entire community. It could turn very ugly!"

"Only if I were to allow the information to reach the public," Rudolf corrected him. "As soon as I have it, I will only let the Cardinal know that it is in my possession and that I will use it if necessary. And then I will let him know that your false arrest and imprisonment in order to foment civil strife places him in direct conflict with the agreed policies of Church and state. I will send him packing back to the Vatican on that basis. Once he is out of our hair, I will be able to contain the situation."

"It seems reasonable," Bruno bobbed his head repeatedly in agreement. "Just one problem is identifying who will be the one to break ranks and confess."

"Have you identified everyone?" the Emperor questioned.

"We know the Maharal is the head of the cabal and that the mayor also is probably highly placed." Yakov took a moment to run over the rest of the likely members. "The custodian of the cemetery is obviously involved. I also have to believe the village constable was directly involved as well. How else do you explain his being under the bridge at around the time I just so happened to be there?"

"That's four," Rudolf counted.

"And don't forget the shoemaker," Caesar added.

"There is a shoemaker in the Josefov that is quite famous for his shoes. Even I am in possession of several pair." Rudolf stated quiet proudly. "Magnificent shoes! But I've had word that he has just died recently."

Yakov looked askance at Giordano, searching for any hint of a reaction. Bruno tended to keep his line of sight in another direction, refusing to lock eyes with Yakov. "Do you know what he died from?" Yakov inquired of Rudolf.

"I think they say he suffered a heart attack. Found dead in his shop. Why do you ask?"

"Just a thought," Yakov contemplated openly. "If it was necessary for me to cover my tracks in case of murder then I'd certainly need the coroner to be in league with me. Perchance, does the Jewish Quarter have its own coroner?"

"Of course," Rudolf was surprised by the question. "After all, you should know that. You Jews have your own special rites when it comes to handling the dead. If the city coroner was to become involved you'd be screaming blue at him and then probably try to stone him too."

"I just had to know that things weren't any different here in Prague. Now that we've established that, I think we should pay a visit to this doctor. Does anyone know who he is?"

Dimitri had been quiet and attentive and now saw his opportunity to enter the conversation. "I know him. A lot of us tend to use his services." Feeling obliged to explain his self, the Captain continued, "Jewish doctors tend to be more professional than the blood letters that call themselves doctors in the rest of the city. After all, you do want the best when it comes to having yourself treated." The Captain looked for confirmation, somewhat sheepish about his admission.

"Of course you do, Dimitri," Rudolf supported him. "Why do you think so many court doctors are Jewish? No way would I want to trust those butchers from the clerical colleges."

"His name is Mendes," the Captain reported. "Philip Mendes. If he's involved, he'll talk. I'm certain of that."

"Well then gentlemen, you know what you must do," the Emperor concluded as he began to rise from the table, preparing for the return journey to his palace.

§ § § § § §

Opening the door to his office, Philip Mendes was absolutely shocked to find someone sitting at his chair with his feet up on his prized oak desk. Frozen to the spot, he found that his feet would not move an inch in either direction and he could not help but stand motionless before his intruder.

"Doctor Mendes, I presume," Giordano greeted him with a cherubic smile and beckoning gesture. "I'm sorry to have disturbed you at this hour but this is most important."

Bruno's gentlemanly demeanor and his flamboyant attire unmistakably of a wealthy aristocrat provided the necessary signals to the doctor's constricted muscles to relax. He took a deep breath and then the elderly gentleman became quite aggravated with his intruder. "Sir, I do not know who you are, but even if you have an emergency it gives you no right to break into my home and take liberties in this manner. I will have you know that this is highly improper and I must demand that you leave immediately." Mendes pointed to the open door behind him, silently demanding that Giordano leave.

"I'm afraid I cannot do that, Doctor. Have a seat and let's talk."

"I will not," Mendes stammered. "If you will not go, then I will go get an officer of the law and have you thrown out." The doctor turned to exit but precisely at that moment the door to his office swung closed, and slammed shut, revealing the Captain of the palace guard whom had been standing quietly behind it.,

"Will this one do?" Giordano asked whimsically. "I believe you two know each other."

"What is the purpose of this? I demand to know immediately! Dimitri, get out of my way if you have no intention of arresting this man. I will get someone that will."

"Doctor," the captain bowed slightly, "I suggest you do as he says. There's a lot to discuss if you don't mind."

"I cannot believe you would lower yourself to this level Dimitri, to consort with ruffians and thieves intent on who knows what but obviously no good. I thought you were better than this."

"Doctor, if you cooperate, there won't be any problem." Dimitri fiddled with the hilt of his sword, purposely drawing the doctor's attention to it.

"If it's money you're after, then the both of you should know now that I hold very little of it in my office."

"No doctor, it's not money we're after," I voice emanated from the shadows in the corner created by the heavy velvet drapes that were drawn back on each side of the window. Yakov stepped into the weak light that still filtered through the panes of glass as twilight was settling. Though dressed in the same sort of attire as Bruno, there was no mistaking the Kahana. The pointed beard and eastern features that were so discernable were highlighted even more by the heavy Galician accent. Mendes felt his knees quivering as Yakov moved towards him.

"Do I frighten you Doctor? Unless you have something to hide from me, I'm usually not considered to be an intimidating person. Are you hiding something?"

"No…no," his voice quivered and cracked far worse than his knees were doing. "It's just…it's just, I know who you are."

"And I know who you are Doctor. I guess we're even on that account. Now if you don't mind, I think you should sit, we have a lot to discuss."

The captain shifted the wooden framed chair directly behind Mendes and pushed him gently into the seat by drawing back and forcing him down at the shoulder.

"Now isn't that better Doctor? Just so you become better acquainted with all of us, that is Father Bruno sitting in your very comfortable leather chair, and that gentlemen over there is Master Caesar de Nostradame." Upon hearing his name, Caesar stepped forward from the shadows on the other side of the window, becoming clearly visible. But I guess you know all of us already, wouldn't you?"

"I don't understand," the doctor feigned ignorance. "How would I know any of you? Other than Dimitri, I've never seen any of you before."

"That's true Doctor," Yakov agreed, "but I know you would have heard about us from the friends you keep."

"What are you talking about?"

"You know whom I'm talking about Doctor; the mayor, the graveyard custodian, your local police officer, your Rabbi Loew, and your shoemaker. Oh, I should say, your deceased shoemaker. I hear he had a heart attack. Is that not so, Doctor?"

Mendes swallowed hard, his Adam's apple barely managing to permit the reflex action. "Yes."

"Now you know and all of us here know that isn't true, now was it Doctor?"

"I don't know what you mean," Mendes squirmed in his seat.

"Sure you do," Yakov corrected him. "You filed a false report. You know very well he didn't die from a heart attack."

"They made me do it," he exclaimed, finally cracking under the pressure of Yakov's penetrating stare.

"So it was all their idea, nothing to do with you then."

"Exactly. They didn't want an investigation. If there was anything suspicious about the death then someone from the civic offices would have been brought in and they couldn't afford to have questions asked."

"Not you, just them," Yakov teasingly drew out his response. "Why should I believe that you didn't have an equal part in the decision?"

"You don't understand, if I didn't do as they said, they'd kill me too. I told them, I want no part of their plotting but they forced me to participate." And as if the floodgates had opened, everything that had been pent up by the doctor suddenly burst forth. "I had nothing to do with the abduction of that girl. You have to believe me. I didn't even know what they were up to. When they brought her to me she was almost dead. There was nothing I could do to save her. I tried! You have to believe me, I tried my best." The doctor collapsed into the palms of his hands, weeping uncontrollably.

"I believed you did try but when she died, you didn't stop them from killing even more people. What kind of man would let them continue their killing spree? It was a little girl Doctor. A little innocent girl! How could you let her killer go unpunished?"

The rest of the men in the room watched as Yakov worked his skills on the doctor. Giordano was most impressed. He understood a little better how Yakov was able to get the Cardinal to do as he suggested. Something in the voice, something in the timbre of the words that became compelling. It would induce an almost trancelike status that seized control of a person's mind and caused them to reveal their innermost thoughts.

"He didn't know better. He's like a little child. He only wanted to play but she wouldn't stop screaming. He only wanted to make her stop."

"You created your Golem in order to kill. Why would you think he'd behave any differently?" Yakov noticed the change in breathing patterns as the doctor sobbed. Something about his last comment caused an expression of guilt to be intermingled with the tears. Yakov pressed the advantage. "After all Doctor, there'd be no Golem if it wasn't for you." He waited for the reaction to see if he had guessed correctly.

"I couldn't do it. I save lives, I don't take them. How could they have even asked that I sacrifice a newborn baby? When he passed into my arms from his mother's womb, it was obvious that he was different, but he was still their baby. How can parents make such a request that I should leave the umbilical cord open? It wasn't right. It will never be right."

Yakov knelt before Mendes and placed his hand on the doctor's knee. "You did the right thing. A life is sacred no matter how it may differ. All things come from the Shekinah and none of us our permitted to wield power over life and death."

"So I ran with the child from their house and took it to the Maharal. I knew that he would guide me to make the right decision. He agreed, Marcus had no right to have me kill his son!" The doctor broke down even further, gulping lungs full of air between hysterical sobs.

"Doctor Mendes, I want you to listen to me," Yakov advised. The captain will escort you away from here to someplace safe. No one is going to be able to hurt you. You have helped us and now we are going to help you but only if you continue to help us. Do we understand each other?"

With head still bowed, the doctor nodded heavily, practically shaking the chair as he did so.

Yakov stood back up and proceeded over to where the captain was standing. "Do you have enough to prepare a statement?"

"I think we have a good start," Dimitri calculated. "I'll need him to put names behind the events but I somehow think he'll be willing to do so."

"Good. Just make certain nothing happens to him in the mean time. We need him alive," Yakov stated his final comment loudly making certain that Giordano heard him clearly.

"Do I get to ask a few questions at least," Bruno protested.

"I doubt very much the doctor is in any condition to be further interrogated."

"Let me at least try."

"I don't know if that would be a good idea," Yakov was cautious, "Perhaps tomorrow once he's had a chance to rest."

"Kova, you know how much I respect you. I would do practically anything for you, but there are times you have to appreciate my methods as well. I can tell you exactly what's going to happen if we let the good doctor recover from this oppressive guilt he is feeling tonight. Tomorrow he will deny everything and that would be most unfortunate because it would mean that Dimitri would have to apply his trade in forcing a confession. Personally I don't think the Doctor would survive the torture. His age and personality are not conducive for his survival. And where would that leave us? All I ask for is just a little time to save the Doctor from such a fate."

"You are asking me to turn a blind eye Giordano."

"Only if you think you must."

"Let him do it," Caesar intervened, much to the dismay of both Yakov and Giordano. "This is something that Bruno is supposed to do."

"And should I ask how you know that?" Yakov had already guessed.

"My father described this moment. '*The great credit of gold and silver in abundance, will blind honor by lust, The offense of the adul-*

terer will become known, in order that his great dishonor will come to pass.' All I know is that this information is important and Giordano is to retrieve it now."

"Bless your father," Giordano praised. "You see, Kova, even Nostradamus agrees with me even though I don't get it!"

"I think I do," Yakov responded. "You're to find out how they've been getting their information on us. But it doesn't mean I agree to this. We're all staying here just in case."

"Did I ever say you had to leave? All I want to do is make certain that we learn everything we can tonight, and the good Doctor here puts his signature to it. I wouldn't want the Cardinal to be in a position of accusing us of forcing a confession through torture. No offence intended Dimitri. It would be too risky and entirely unnecessary." Bruno removed a small vial from his pocket. "Doctor, this is an elixir made from henbane. I'm certain you're well aware of its properties. The hyoscine I've isolated from the plant is a potent truth serum. I will administer a few drops on your tongue and then we'll have a little talk. Is that agreed?"

The doctor sat upright in the chair and was quite alarmed. "Henbane can be very dangerous. The dose has to be precise or else it can cause delirium and death."

"You know your drugs Doctor," Bruno acknowledged the accuracy of the doctor's assessment of the drug. "That's why I need you to sit perfectly still while I administer it. I don't want any accidents."

"Are you crazy," The doctor became frantic, struggling against Dimitri's hands which were now forcibly restraining him from rising from the chair. "I told you what you wanted to know, what more do you want?"

"Actually Doctor, you haven't. All I've heard is that you tried to save a little girl and failed, you falsified a death certificate, and you saved a young child's life by refusing to kill him at birth. And that it was this child you saved that grew up and killed the girl that was brought to you by the people that Kova named but no where do I recall you saying that it was those very same people that arranged for this deformed boy of Marcus Maisel to kill all those people."

"I have admitted to all of that," the doctor practically screeched. "There is nothing more to say."

"I disagree." Bruno slid a piece of parchment along with the ink well and stylus in Caesar's direction. "Here, you write," he said to Caesar, "while the doctor dictates. Dimitri, can you pry the Doctor's mouth open please."

"No wait!" the doctor pleaded as his tears subsided. "I can tell you what you want."

"I want you to state the names of everyone in your cabal."

"They will kill me."

"What's in this bottle may kill you," Bruno swung the little vial in front of the doctor's eyes. "I think you should worry more about it, than what they might do. Dimitri, open his mouth please."

"Wait! Rabbi Judah ben Loew," Mendes began his list. "Rabbi Sinai ben Loew. Rabbi Isaac Katz. Oram Hershorn, Menahem the Baker, Ari Gruenberg, Mordecai Maisel and Kuba Vogelman."

"You want me to believe that there are only eight others besides yourself," Giordano refused to accept that the doctor had provided a complete list of names. "Let's see what some of these drops will do." Dimitri placed one hand on Mendes's head and the other beneath his chin."

"There were more, but they're dead now. Like the shoemaker. Some were old men. They died over the last couple of years. Their names are meaningless now."

"I guess I can accept that," Bruno hummed and hawed over the answer. "But there had to be someone in the palace that was working with you. You knew of both Kova's and Caesar's arrival in Prague before they came. Who told you?"

"Cornelius." The response was spontaneous. The doctor sounded almost happy to give up that name.

"The cook?" Bruno was utterly surprised. "What would someone like Cornelius have to do with your people?"

"He has a proclivity for young women. He especially likes young Jewish women."

"And you provided them for him?"

"He would come into our quarter. He'd walk the streets until he found some innocent. He could be very physical. We had a choice. Either arrest him or use him."

"So you chose to ignore his crimes."

"No, we put an end to that. We gave him whores instead. Even our community has them. We'd pay them to pretend they were innocent girls. He still thought he was finding girls that had wandered too far away from their homes at night."

"And in exchange?"

"We let him know what we knew. We wouldn't press any charges of rape as long as he gave us information. Anything that was happening in the castle that he thought was of importance to us."

The same thought ran through their minds upon hearing that statement. Of course the cook would have known about their arrival in Prague. With Yakov's special dietary needs, Cornelius would have guessed immediately that someone very important from the Jewish establishment was arriving in town. That's how the Maharal knew when they arrived.

"You're doing very well, Doctor. Just a few more questions if you don't mind. Who are next to be murdered. Whom have you targeted?"

"I don't know."

"Dmitri, hold him still."

"I swear, I don't know," he cried. "They never discussed those details with the likes of us."

"Who are they?"

"The Loews," he wailed their name.

"Why them? How are the decisions made?"

"The numbers, the letters; they're the masters of the Kabala. Only they can read them."

Turning to Caesar, Giordano looked to see if he had written everything down. Satisfied that it was all there, he then demanded that Philip Mendes signed the bottom of the confession. Already weakened by his ordeal, it did not take any further threats to get the signature. Bruno carefully padded the ink dry and then carefully rolled the parchment while the captain escorted his prisoner from the house to a coach he had waiting down the street, hidden in one of the many alleys between the buildings. He passed the doctor over to two of his men that loaded the prisoner into the carriage, each sitting on either side, as the wagon master snapped his whip and headed towards the guard house at Hradancy.

The three companions journeyed into the street to join with Dmitiri who was standing beside a second coach awaiting them. "I think it would be safe to return to the Castle now," he said to them.

"There are still a few things we have to pack up at the inn," Bruno waved him on. "Tell the Emperor we'll return as soon as we know he has cleared the path for us. And Dimitri, thank you."

"As always, Giordano, it was a pleasure working with you." The captain gave the order for his driver to take off, still hanging from the coach door as he waved his farewell to the three of them.

"You two have done this before," Yakov guessed.

"There have been times when the palace guard needed some help in procuring a confession," Bruno winked as he explained, "The gentle art of persuasion, as we call it."

"And you were never going to give him that truth serum, were you," was Yakov's next guess.

"Truth serum," Bruno laughed. "Don't tell me you believe in such a thing?"

"Wasn't that what you said it was?"

"No, it was definitely what I said it was. Whether it would work was a completely different question. As a doctor, Mendes would have been well aware of the risk. He was more afraid of what could have transpired after administering a few drops than any threat the cabal posed."

"The captain was always aware of this, wasn't he," Yakov surmised.

"We've done that little play acting before." Bruno strides displayed a cocky confidence as they walked in the direction of the inn. "The doctor would have probably confessed eventually to the crimes. Dimitri knew him at heart to be a good man. But none of us had the luxury to wait for his guilt to eventually take control. It could have been years. He was slothful, and as you know, sloth is one of the great sins that has to be overcome. We did a service by helping him do so." Bruno was even more pleased that he was able to disguise his own quest within the context of his actions. With only two more of the deadly sins to overcome, he was more confident in their overall success.

"Giordano, don't ever do that again, without telling me," Yakov instructed him. "I was going to intercede until I caught some of the signals passing back and forth between you and the captain. And as for you Caesar, I guess you were part of all this too, with that quote from your father to convince me to leave Giordano to his ruse."

"Actually Kova, I had no idea of what Giordano had planned. Once again, my father's prophecy just appeared and I just knew that it was relevant."

"And he really said that," Bruno questioned, slowly becoming more convinced of Caesar's innate ability to summon guidance from his dead father.

"Century VIII, Quatrain fourteen," Caesar clarified.

"But why the adulterer?" Yakov ran the line over and over in his mind but couldn't find an answer. "Why was finding out about this palace cook so important to your father?"

"Cornelius is nothing but a fat cruel man. He has a reputation of being vicious and a dangerous man with his choppers and knives. He abuses the kitchen staff and now it would appear he takes advantage of the law being less stringent in the Jewish Quarter as well. I can't tell you how many times I've had to prepare St. Anthony's fire to treat the pregnancies of the young kitchen staff because of him. I needed a constant supply of ergot of rye just to keep the palace maids from being in whelp."

"But that still doesn't give us the answer why this cook is integral to our bringing down the cabal. Nostradamus definitely indicated that we had to know of the cook in order to bring the others down in great dishonor." Struggling with the connection, Yakov failed to find the answer. "Somehow he is the key to our ending this and I can't see how."

"I know him Kova. Once we've returned to the castle, let me talk with him."

"Giordano, I don't have to tell you again, do I?"

"I know, just talk."

28

The Castle: February 1589

Now comfortably resettled into the Emperor's palace, the freedom of being able to return to wearing their old clothes was an obvious relief to both Yakov and Bruno. The confession from Mendes had been registered with the Hall of Justice and the Emperor's own secretaries had taken on the responsibility of making certified copies just in case the original somehow became lost or damaged. Rudolf had secretly sent a messenger to the Maharal to inform him that they had Dr. Philip Mendes in safe custody and that he had signed a confession detailing everyone that was accountable. A meeting had been requested of the principals in order to decide on how the guilty were to be punished.

At the same time a private audience was held between the Emperor and Cardinal Calabrese. Few details escaped from their meeting but one that everyone was aware of was that the Cardinal had decided to return to Rome to take care of pressing business there. He had arranged to leave by the middle of the next month, when there'd be less snow on the mountain passes. The usual beehive of activity at St. Vitus and the Lichten Palace was obviously absent, a clear indication that Guillermo Calabrese had pulled in his claws and was no longer in control of the situation.

For several days now, Bruno had been busying himself at the forge in the castle armory. The nature of his business had been kept secretive, and those that worked alongside in the foundry knew better than to ask questions. The priest could be most volatile when he was conducting his experiments and anyone who disturbed his train of thought had experienced a vicious tongue lashing. The nature of his activities weren't even disclosed to his two companions, though they asked repeatedly. "It's a surprise," he would answer each time and that would be the sum total of his disclosure. But on the afternoon of February 14th, Giordano invited everyone to the armory's forge to witness his handiwork.

"So this is where you've been burying yourself for almost two weeks," Yakov jested. "Somehow I pictured it would look more arcane than this."

"You are mistaking me for an alchemist, Kova. I am a scientist and working with alloys is science, not magic."

"I stand corrected," he replied. "So what do you wish to show us?"

"Be patient, I want Rudi to be here with some of his generals. I think they will be interested in this too."

"So since when have I become a military man that is in need of weapons too," the inquiry was genuine on Yakov's part, feeling uncomfortable in a place where implements of death were manufactured.

"There's something I made especially for you." Bruno reached underneath the anvil table and brought out a tray, its contents covered by an oiled cloth.

"Very nice," Caesar quipped, "you've baked cookies for us."

"This recipe is for far more than cookies, my friend. Ah look! Here comes the Emperor with his entourage now."

Rudolf entered the foundry accompanied by the captain of the palace guard and several of his military generals. The acrid smell of the foundry caused Rudolf and one or two generals to place their handkerchiefs over their nose and mouth.

"Welcome gentleman," Bruno greeted them. "I'm glad you could all make it here. What I'm about to show you will make you glad that I had summoned you here."

"Get on with it Giordano," Rudolf urged, the pungent smell near the forges causing his nostrils to burn and his eyes to water.

"I have been working on an old metallurgist secret; one that had become lost to us over the centuries. Damascus steel!"

The generals buzzed with excitement upon hearing the announcement. They were all aware that the original Damascus steel swords were made in the period from 900 AD but the secret had been lost in the last couple of centuries. Damascus steel was renowned for being both hard and flexible, a combination that made it ideal as a sword material able to cut a piece of silk in half as it fell to the ground, as well as being able to chop through normal steel blades, or even rock, without losing its sharp edge.

"So, what is your secret," Rudolf asked.

"I knew that I needed to produce a high-carbon steel of unusually high purity. So I added glass to a mixture of iron and charcoal and then heated it. The glass acted as a flux and bound to other impurities in the mixture, allowing them to rise to the surface at which point I scooped them off the top. That left behind a purer steel once the mixture cooled. The elements of the steel are arranged in sheets or bands within the body of the blade. This allowed me to make an edge which can cut through hard materials, while the bands of softer steel allow the sword as a whole to remain tough and flexible. You'll see a swirling pattern in the blade which I believe is the arrangement of the elements that made this possible. By manipulating the ingot of steel in a certain ways during forging I was able to create these patterns."

"Brilliant" one of the generals shouted. "So which alloy did you use?"

"Vanadium," Bruno answered preening and bowing ever so slightly as he did so.

"Very nice, Giordano, but exactly why are Caesar and myself here?"

"Because of these," Giordano pulled the oil cloth off the top of the tray, exposing a half dozen crossbow bolts made from the material. Bruno picked one up and tossed it over to Yakov. "What do you think about that?" he asked proudly.

"It's so light," was Yakov's first comment. "I can't believe how light it is."

"Not only light but tremendously strong as well. It will penetrate practically anything," Bruno boasted. "I've tried them and they'll slice through any suit of leather armor with ease, no matter how hardened the leather may be."

Rotating the bolt between the fingers, Yakov could not stop himself from admiring the arrow. "You're a genius Giordano."

"Thank you," he bowed, "thank you one and all. Remember the name, Giordano Bruno, scientist extraordinaire. And of course your Excellency, I have not forgotten about you." Another tray covered by a cloth just lay to the right of the furnace on a shelf surrounded by tools of the trade. Bruno retrieved the tray and held it out before Rudolf.

The Emperor gingerly removed the oil cloth between his thumb and forefinger and tossed it aside as quickly as possible. Lying on the tray was the polished blade for a sabre.

"I'm afraid I don't do hilts," Bruno apologized, "but I'm certain there's a craftsman in the city that can make a hilt worthy of a blade like this one." The Emperor and his generals couldn't help themselves but to admire the delicate swirling patterns that ran the length of the blade. The patterns that were apparently the source of Damascus steel's legendary status.

"Well done," Rudolf lauded him. "Well done, Giordano!" The generals applauded their approval. "Of course you will teach your secrets to my armorers."

"Of course, your Majesty. And now I think it is time to celebrate with a little ale."

"An excellent idea, Giordano, but unfortunately I won't be able to join you. Matters of state, you know. But don't let my absence stop you." The Emperor turned to leave but then stopped, remembering he had a letter to deliver. "This is for you, Master Kahana, Rudolf held out the letter in his hand. It was addressed to you personally, and I'm afraid my secretaries took the liberty of reading it first. For matters of public safety you will understand. When you make your decision, I'd be interested in knowing how I can help, assuming you'll wish to respond."

Yakov received the letter graciously, even though he had just been told that it had been opened, while the Emperor and his entourage of officers left the foundry, chattering obsessively about the qualities of this Damascus steel and how they could immediately implement it into the manufacturing of their weaponry.

Though feeling that some of his thunder had just been stolen, Bruno was still keenly interested in the letter Yakov had received, that was so important that it actually had to be delivered by the Holy Roman Emperor. "Well, are you going to read it to us or not?" Bruno asked impatiently.

Mulling over the first few lines silently, Yakov hesitated before his started to read it aloud.

'To my brother, Greetings.

It would appear that God has been with you thus far and guided you well. I applaud you in your determination to find the source of the murders that plagued this city. You have proven yourself worthy of the title of Kahana and I acknowledge your intellect of being worthy of both a great leader and spiritualist. Though if there's anywhere I may fault you, it might be your failure as a prophet. You have not recognized the growing tide of hatred and prejudice that is even now building in waves against the Jewish community of Prague. The pogroms and random pillaging targeting the Jews of this city are becoming ever more frequent and the number of our woman being defiled by our neighbors grows steadily. Murder is in their hearts and we are their reluctant victims. I ask you therefore, who is the one in the wrong when it comes to these issues. Myself, who has only cared for the protection and well being of my people, or you who will dance on the end of a string for the very people that have perpetrated these crimes against us? I know you claim to be here in order to save lives of those you left behind, but would a true leader, a rightful Kahana make the decision to save some by sacrificing others? I at least know that I will be made to pay for my sins with the knowledge that I would do it all again if it meant I had the chance to protect the woman and children from harm. Not just those in my community, but Jews all over the world. How can you therefore make the distinction between your community in Brody and the rest of us? Either we are one people or we are nothing. As soon as you claim that one city's population deserves to survive at the expense of another, then you are disputing the fact that we are all one. So I wish to meet the man that can make such a decision. I want to see the Nasi that holds the power of life and death over innocents. I want to know how you can live comfortably in this world of theirs, while allowing our people to suffer. At least afford me that honor to meet my better. Perhaps an open area will instill you with the confidence that I shall do you no harm. I've always been fond of the park on Stvanice Island. Shall we say on the Friday at noon? I will be there regardless.

Judah ben Loew.'

"Surely you're not considering meeting with him," Bruno pleaded, sensing another of the Rabbi's traps. "Tell me Kova, you're not going to go." Giordano knew immediately that he was pleading in vain from the expression on Yakov's face. "Aw, come on Kova, this is madness. He's defeated, he's been caught and now he's just playing games. An animal is most dangerous when he's been cornered. He is no different."

Yakov ignored the plea, instead turning to Caesar who was standing alongside. "I know what you're thinking Caesar, I can see it in your eyes," Yakov detected the rapid movement upwards that he noticed each time his companion became overwhelmed by one of his father's prophecies. "He knew that this meeting would take place, didn't he?"

"Tell him he's wrong," Bruno urged Caesar to speak out against the scheduled parley.

"I can't Giordano. He has to do this. It has to be settled."

"I don't believe it! Let me at least hear what your father said. I want to hear it for myself," Bruno demanded.

'After the victory a vicious tongue, The spirit of hope and tranquillity will be tempted, The victor's blood by the conflict will be harangued, A roasting of the tongue, the flesh and the bone.' Caesar finished reciting Century IV Quatrain fifty-six off by heart.

"So what?" Giordano threw his hands in the air. "It doesn't say they have to meet. It only says that Kova has to suffer abuse from that man. How much can that hurt? Especially when that someone is about to be charged for his crimes. I say forget about it and let the justice system take care of it. Let it go!"

"But that's the problem," Yakov attempted to explain. "He knows I can't let the justice system take care of it. They would put on a show trial the leaders of the community and that would create turmoil and panic. A situation ripe for their enemies to exploit, leading to exactly what Judah ben Loew has claimed as his justification for his actions. By not finding another way, I will be responsible for the future deaths in Josefov. I will be vilified, just as it describes in the quatrain. What a hollow victory I would have achieved if I let my people suffer because of what I've done."

"Am I the only one that's sane? You haven't done this. They did this. They let that thing loose on the city to kill at its own pleasure. Why should you be guilty for putting an end to it?" Bruno was practically frothing at the mouth as he tried desperately to convince Yakov not to meet the Maharal.

"I know it's difficult to understand but the only way this will be settled is if we find a compromise that everyone can live with; Church, state, the Jews and most of all, us."

"I'm not going to convince you otherwise, am I?"

Yakov shook his head.

"You can be a very stubborn man," Bruno criticized. "Not to mention foolhardy."

"Now you sound like my wife," Yakov snapped back.

"Well at least she has the common sense in your family. I'm still opposed to this meeting, but as long as we're all together, along with Dimitri and his men, then I can't see them being able to surprise us with force."

"I wouldn't go any other way," Yakov assured him. "After the Maharal's last response to my letter, I don't think I'm willing to trust him so naively. Give me some credit!"

"Credit is not what you need me to give you," Bruno shot back. "What you need is more arrows. We'll take the crossbow along just in case."

§ § § § § §

The park at the center of Stvanice Island was considered to have one of the finest botanical gardens in Europe. The largest of the islands sitting in the middle of the river, it surprisingly had not been developed as had most of the other smaller islands. Perhaps it was that it lay too far to the north, and slightly east of the main centers of the city, but already there had been talk of development. Land was getting scarce and with the Emperor turning Prague into the commercial center of the world, land had become too valuable to let it remain pristine.

The central garden complex was done in the English style. A large open compound surrounded by hedges, with expansive views from every direction. The outer ring of trees afforded privacy, but generally traffic was quite light in the park. It was there that they found the Rabbi Judah ben Loew sitting by himself on the intricately carved stone bench, contemplating the wonders of the universe. His high pointed hat and long grey beard made him look more like a wizard than a Rabbi. It only served to remind Yakov that this man was a master of the Kabala, as dangerous as they could come if he really mastered the elements of nature. The long black robe trimmed with ermine stretched the entire length of his frame, hiding a height equally as tall as that of Yakov if he was to stand up. A height which made both of them quite unique in the Jewish community and automatically granted them respect solely on physical attributes. The Maharal patted the seat beside him inviting the Kahana to sit.

Dressed in a brightly colored robe and pill box hat with its Yemenite designs, Yakov looked equally incongruous with his surroundings. Both of them stood out like sore thumbs as they sat together on the bench in the center of the park.

"Are you comfortable if we speak in Hebrew?" The Maharal obviously did not wish their conversation to be overheard by the prying ears of the entourage that accompanied Yakov.

Yakov nodded in agreement.

"I see you have brought quite a few people with you."

"After our last arranged meeting, I thought it would be in my best interest," Yakov responded rather coolly

"Ah, yes. I guess you would think that." The Maharal never even batted an eye when he acknowledged that he had sent the Golem to kill him that night. "Sometimes you have to do evil in order to preserve the good."

'You know, I've been hearing that as an excuse from almost everyone lately. It wears thin after a while."

"The truth is hard to accept sometimes."

"The truth is never hard; it's reality that we try to avoid."

The Maharal acknowledged that Yakov had scored the first blow with a perceptive nod of his head. "I see that some traditions haven't died. The Priest still feels he's in a position to teach the scholar."

"What could I teach you that you don't already believe you know to be the truth? Has that not been the problem between our two people since the fall of the Temple?"

"We could debate the essence of truth for an eternity," the Maharal declared philosophically. "Are my truths the same as yours? I doubt it. Truth is a double edged sword. It's only true when you know how to wield it."

Yakov returned the nod. The score was even. "God is the only truth; the one universal that permeates the essence of life. He cares not for our interpretations, only about our applications."

"Ah, I can see this is going to be a long afternoon," the Maharal grinned. "Are we to wrestle continuously or do we declare a truce."

Yakov laughed along with him. "Under other circumstances, and perhaps a different time, we might have been closer aligned. But today, and with the events you and your cabal have perpetrated, I'm afraid we are poles apart."

"A shame that. Here, I am the protector of my people. In your role you are the malefactor. By exposing us, you have put the entire community in jeopardy. No, that would be too limited. You have placed every Jew in the Empire in danger."

"Odd how you justify theft and murder so easily! Almost reminds me of six hundred and forty years ago," Yakov slid the shame of Rabbinic Judaism onto the playing field.

"I was wondering just how long it would take before you tried to smear my cause with that ancient atrocity." The Maharal dismissed the accusation with a wave of his hands.

"Did you really think that you could slaughter hundreds of thousands of people and it would just be swept under the carpet?"

"How many millions has the world slaughtered of us and never wept a single tear. The numbers you mention are inconsequential by comparison."

"What the world does to my people," Yakov countered holding back the anger in his voice, "is one matter. But what Jews do to Jews is beyond comprehension. It was the vilest of crimes. Inconsequential? Never! Did you think God will so easily forget?"

"Are you trying to say that your condemnation of me and what I have done is somehow retribution by God for what was done by Saadiah? The accusation is as old as the crime. It no longer matters."

"No, condemnation will come in three hundred and sixty more years. And it will be tenfold."

"Ah, yes, the infamous curse of Natronai. How could I forget," Judah ben Loew scoffed. "Your ancestor brought about the death of his own people because he was powerless, and his curse will prove equally ineffective."

"Let me remind you of the refrain, Judah. 'In the end we shall beat Magog, to kill a Karaite, is like killing a dog.' How many of those little children that were beaten over their heads did God consider of no more worth than a dog? Your famous and legendary teacher was no more than a butcher of innocents. Forget? Time has a way of memories to fail but to forgive, never! The curse will come to pass!"

"Then I am glad I will not be here to see it happen," the Maharal remarked. "Surely then, that would be the End of Days."

"If it is, then it is only because you and those like you have brought it to pass. You disguise your hatred through chapter and verse in the Bible. You justify you slaughter of those too weak to defend themselves through the words of the prophets. But what you fear most was that Karaism provides the opportunity for all men to find God on their own mettle. You are no different from the Catholic clergy you condemn. All of you are bloated on your own egos and demands for exclusivity. It is no longer a case of God creating man, but which one of your religions created God!"

"Spoken like a true Karaite!

"That is because there is no other kind of Karaite. Unlike every other religion divided into its sects and denominations. Haven't you ever wondered how one God can demand to be worshipped in so many ways?"

"The right way and the wrong ways," the Maharal offered sublimely.

"We can debate this forever," Yakov offered. "But that is not the reason we are here. What we need to discuss is how we can bring an end to this entire episode without causing any further damage."

"Exactly and the only way this ends is with no prosecutions. Both sides have suffered. Both sides believe they were working in the best interests of the people they represented. We draw a line in the sand and move on."

"You really do believe that you can walk away from all that you've done without any repercussions."

"What have I done that hasn't been in self defense of the community?" The Maharal clearly believed himself to be an innocent.

"For one, let's consider the theft of millions of florins from the treasury. Do you not consider that a crime?"

"When one steals for personal gain, then that is a crime but when the theft is for the purpose of providing charity and buildings for the populace, I would consider that an act of kindness and generosity. Have you ever considered how much money the State donates to the Christian charities? Not to mention the land that they provide to the Church. And let's not forget that they don't tax any of the Christian religious centers, not one thaler. Now, as loyal citizens of the Empire, should we Jews be treated any differently? I think not. Yet we are taxed more than any other population. Not a single coin is provided from the public purse to help our needy, and there certainly aren't any government contributions of either land or buildings for the purpose of our religious centers. In fact they go as far as demanding from us an additional tax, the Jew Tax, which they say we must pay as a levy for the privilege of living in the Empire. So what do you think Kahana, were we entitled to some of the money that we had already paid in to the government as taxes, or do you consider us to be less than everyone else and therefore not entitled to any share of the rights and privileges of our Christian neighbors?"

Yakov knew that he was not going to be able to defend his position on that issue. It was a good argument. In Brody, the dreaded Jew Tax did not exist, as it was considered a Free City, a commercial center that was not ruled by any particular state or Empire. The closest they came to any governance was through the royals of Poland but even that was nominal. To argue that the return of funds that they should have been legally entitled to was unlawful was a bitter pill to swallow. "Even if I was to accept your argument, what about the murders? What about the little girl?"

"The little girl was an accident. It truly was. A shame on all of us." The Maharal sounded genuinely remorseful. "It was not intended to happen. But if we were to put it into context, what about Mordecai Maisel's daughter? Intentionally murdered by a riotous mob of Catholics, bent on killing and destruction. And why? Because their religious leaders stirred the masses into believing that we were killing Christian children in order to make matzoh. Our children die at their hands and it is not even punishable in their courts. One of their children dies accidentally and you want to put us all on trial. So what do you wish to say about the little girl that I haven't berated myself for already?"

"In your defense I admit there have been crimes committed by both sides. I would not let anyone deny that. Give me back the body of the girl and we will return it to her parents without any hint of a crime. We will tell them that she was found dead on the streets, from exposure to the elements. In an act of mercy she was buried in an unmarked grave, with the hope of some day being identified."

"You have your guards posted at the cemetery. You can take her at any time," Judah ben Loew advised.

"We will but on the condition that this is the story that is to be accepted and spread."

"Agreed."

"And as for the other murders, you will deliver the Golem for execution. We will have him declared criminally insane and he will bear the guilt of all the crimes."

"And what of the confession you have obtained from my good friend, Doctor Mendes. Is that going to be made to disappear?"

"The confession won't see the light of day. It was only necessary to secure my release from prosecution."

"And I'm to believe you won't use it against me," the Maharal stated doubtfully.

"From what the Emperor has promised me, the answer is yes."

"But you cannot promise me that it won't happen."

"I cannot promise you what I'm not in control of. I can only tell you that I believe the Emperor is a man of his word. So will you deliver the Golem to us?"

"You are not a bad man, Kahana. I believe you to be a man of your word as well, and though we are never destined to be friends, at least I can admit that I do trust you. You will try to deliver on what you have promised but I cannot deliver to you the Golem."

"May I ask why?" Yakov was astounded by the refusal.

"Because after the night he was sent to eliminate you, he has not returned. I think he may be dead. You would best know what happened that night."

"He obviously did not succeed in his task, but he still managed to kill several of the Emperor's guards. I doubt he is dead."

"Then that is most unfortunate because he could be anywhere. He is a creature of the night; a shadow that haunts the city. He knows how to evade your efforts to find him, how to procure the sustenance he requires, and how to blend in to his surroundings. He had never failed before. Between that and killing randomly, he may have feared more of coming home and being reprimanded than he did of surviving alone in the city."

"Are you suggesting that he had not killed randomly in the past?

"Do you understand the Kabala at all, Kahana?" Rabbi Loew watched the lines in Yakov's face to secure his answer. "I thought not. There is magic in this world, whether you choose to believe it or not. Man did not invent the Kabala, he was given it from God. Those of us that understand that can use it quite proficiently. Fate is determined through the meanings of numbers and letters. All things are predetermined. Nothing is random."

"So how do I catch him then?"

"As I told you, nothing is random. The Golem understands the Kabala too. His entire life has been governed by its application. He knows that in order to free himself of its control, he must first complete the sequence."

Yakov analyzed what the Maharal had just told him, not liking the answer he had provided himself. "The sequence meaning the diagram, correct?"

"That is correct," Rabbi Loew replied. "But I cannot tell you the when or the who. "

"Can't tell me or won't tell me." Yakov became angry at the Rabbi's reply.

"Is there a difference?" was the Maharal's final answer as he stood up and started to walk away from the bench. Having one final comment to make, Rabbi Loew swiveled on his feet to face the Kahana. "Stop him, but stop him for all of us. I've told you how!" With that, Judah ben Loew walked in the direction of the bridge in order to make the long walk back to Josefov.

Once the Maharal had disappeared from site, Yakov was immediately surrounded by his companions as well as Dimitri with his elite guard.

"Is it over?" was Bruno's first question.

"Almost," Yakov replied. "We can dig up the girl now and return her to her parents. If you could please make those arrangements, Giordano. Let her parents know that she was buried accidentally in an unmarked grave when she was found dead in the streets. The good Samaritans had no way of knowing where she came from. They only meant well by her."

"And what about the rest," Bruno pressed on.

"That is where we are going to have some difficulty. The Golem never returned after our encounter at St. Mikhal's. They no longer have any control over his actions."

"And you believed him?" Bruno was furious.

"I know when a man lies and he was not lying."

"He is a master of deceit and lies," Bruno cursed. "Look at everything he's done to us so far. Send Dimitri and his men to chase after him. He couldn't have gone too far. We'll force the truth out of him!"

"No, let him go. This time I could see from his eyes, that he was scared. He is probably far more concerned about what the Golem will do, rather than what he has already done." Yakov was confident that he had assessed his reading of the Maharal correctly.

"And just how do you intend to stop him without having any knowledge of his whereabouts?" Bruno was not wishing to sound aggressive but for the first time since their encounter at St.Mikhal's he felt they had once again lost the upper hand.

"I need to understand the Kabala. The clues are there."

"Well we're in luck then," Bruno patted himself. "I just happen to have a well rounded knowledge of the Kabala.

"Then consider ourselves lucky," Yakov approved as he started his troop back in the direction of the castle.

29

Hradcany: The Castle

Taking advantage of the royal library, the three of them buried their faces into the collection of books dealing with the Kabala. It was already several hours since they began and still nothing that shone any light on the situation.

"Our problem," Bruno commented, "is that we're trying to understand a Jewish mystic art based on notes and books written by Christian scholars."

"I thought you said you were an expert," Yakov retorted.

"I am, but I'm an expert on Christian interpretations of the Kabala."

"So what are you trying to tell me, Giordano?"

"I think this may be more difficult than I first anticipated."

"Oh great," Caesar threw up the pile of books before him into the air and let them fall back on to the table with a thud.

"Let's think this out rationally," Yakov encouraged both of them. "Christian scholars or not, they must have some idea on how the diagram works. Let's look at this carefully. We have a six pointed star, made up of two intersecting triangles. There's got to be a correlation to something in the Kabala."

"Like this," Caesar pointed to the picture in one of the books that had fallen open on the table after he had tossed them. The others gathered around to stare at the picture.

"That will do," Bruno fingered the page in the book.

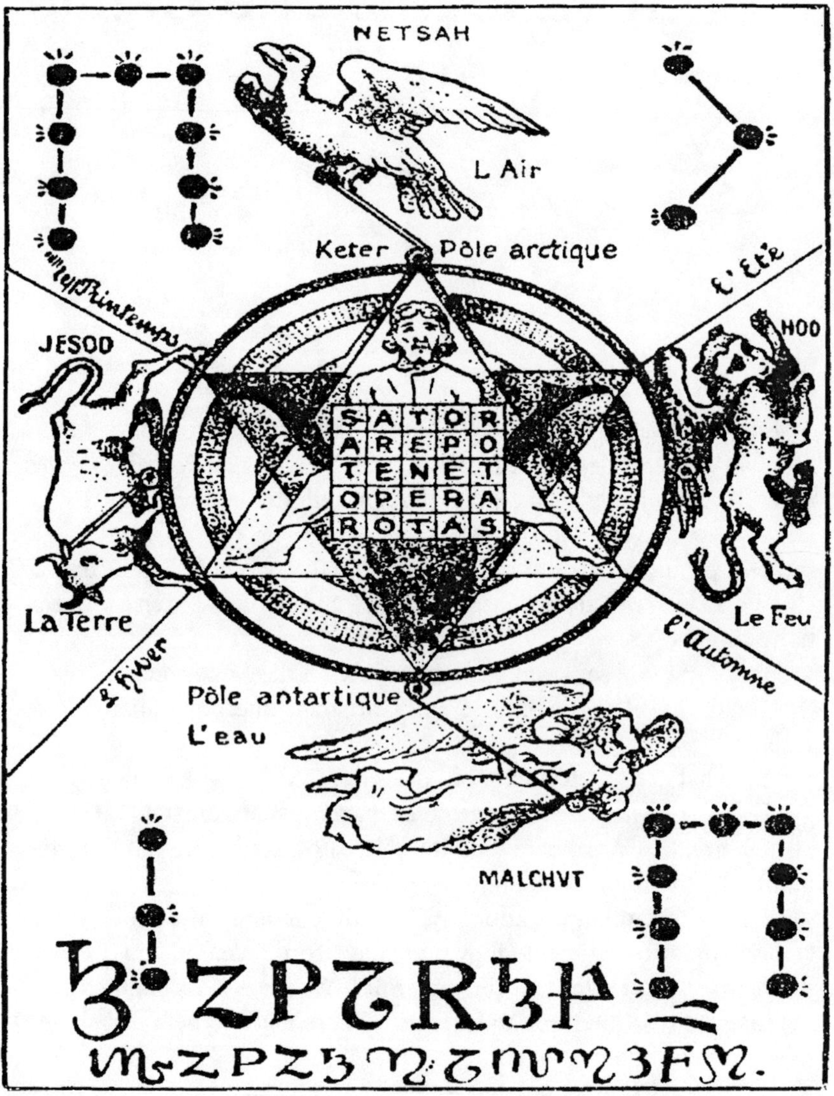
NETSAH
L Air
Keter
Pôle arctique
l'Été
HOD
JESOD
le Printemps
SATOR
AREPO
TENET
OPERA
ROTAS
La Terre
Le Feu
l'Automne
l'Hiver
Pôle antartique
L'eau
MALCHVT

"Seen anything like it before," Yakov inquired.

"It would appear to be a combination of multiple beliefs,"

Bruno examined the detail and wording on the diagram. French, Latin, Hebrew and alchemic symbols. Overlain with the elements, astrology, and religion, "It's a very complex picture."

"We can see that Giordano, but what's it mean?"

"I don't know." Bruno looked at his friends hapless, wringing his hands repeatedly.

"It's familiar," Caesar stared at the diagram. "I think my father had something like it in his sanctum."

"Do you remember how he used it?" Yakov was excited by the news.

"It would rotate. The central star would rotate on the wheel. But that's about all I can remember."

"That makes sense. That would explain the Latin word ROTAS in the central box. It's telling us it's a wheel to be rotated." Bruno was satisfied that they were on the right track.

"Then what?" Yakov pushed for an answer. "Where do we start?"

"I think I know," Giordano pointed to the top of the diagram. "The man's head is called the northern pole. I would think that should be placed over the first victim's site."

'No, you're forgetting one thing," Caesar jumped in, "remember my father riddled in opposites. Place the southern pole over the first site."

"But this isn't your father's diagram," Giordano objected. "This is from the Kabala. The rules of how it would be used were in place long before your father used it," he argued.

"Wait!" Yakov shouted. "I think you both might be right in a way. Look at the Hebrew. NETSAH means eternity. You don't achieve eternity when you're born; you only achieve it when you die. So we still start with the northern pole but we place it over the twelfth site when all things will end."

"So in this case, my father would still be half right!"

"If you insist," Bruno conceded. "We'll do it Kova's way. So the twelfth murder site will be the northern pole."

"Correct me if I'm wrong Giordano," Yakov requested, "But the central anagram is Latin for an understanding. Is that not so?"

"That's right," he confirmed. "TENET is the word for an understanding. And as the only word that reads in either direction it would suggest that it governs the central core of the diagram."

"Understand what though?" Yakov tapped his head as he contemplated the riddle. "Understand the diagram…too simple. I sense it's telling us to look for a deeper understanding but I don't know where we should look. There's just so much!"

"Well, OPERA translates as labor and tells us that we have to work at it. That it's not going to be easy." Bruno picked out the word as if it was personally challenging him. Then he began trying to analyze the significance of the word SATOR. "Why use that word for Creator and place it on the outermost ring of the square. You'd think that whoever designed this would have placed God at the center of it all. I agree everything is mixed up, turned upside down! Absolute chaos if you ask me."

"Say that again," Yakov encouraged Bruno.

"What? That it's all chaos."

"Chaos! That's it," Yakov was jubilant. "I think I understand it now. It's telling the story of the creation but how that one story is a universal truth for everything else. Are you following me?"

Both Caesar and Giordano shook their heads.

"Remember what I told you about the three that became one. Well this is it. Whoever designed this wheel was familiar with everything that was passed down through my family. The Creator, the Avenger and the Fool. The square places them in their order of context. The Creator was there for the birth of the universe. But it was empty and void. Spinning, exactly like a wheel but without any life; without any purpose. Just a meaningless creation. And just like the rows in the square would be if they didn't become filled in by a purpose. Along came the Avenger, also known as the Destroyer. He looked upon the vast emptiness and decided to give it structure. He formed the celestial bodies and set them on their axis. He gave the planets form and the sun its light. But as the Avenger, he failed as well, because he did not know how to make anything of value that wouldn't ultimately be destroyed. The sun burnt so hot that what little life he did create could only survive by creeping and crawling along the surface and on the bottom of the seas. AREPO, correct. Those that crawl or creep. So though the Avenger works hard to create something of value, the OPERA, he is not successful. Thus your second ring of the square. But along comes the Fool and he has TENET or understanding. He knows what is required to bring purpose to the universe, so he creates man. But in his foolishness, he gives man the power to think and understand for himself. But man is of two natures, the two triangles. He can be good or he can be evil."

"Hence the picture of the man superimposed over the devil," Bruno was beginning to see where Yakov was heading with his explanation. "But then I don't understand the destinations that each triangle points to. As you said, the one with the man is being pulled up towards the NETSAH or eternity. But the one with the devil is being pulled towards the MALCHUT or kingdom."

"I see you do understand your Hebrew concepts well," Yakov commented. "Did you overhear much of my conversation with the Maharal?"

Looking sheepishly, Bruno tried to bury his chin on his chest. "I was too distant to hear all of it Kova. But on occasion I did hear some of it."

"And?"

"I can only state that good men can do bad things for the right reasons. Once again the rule of opposites suggests that we will never live in a perfect world."

"This diagram is a testimonial to that," Yakov confirmed but failed to repeat his usual refrain that performing evil to do good was never acceptable. "At first I didn't understand the use of the eagle and the angel. Once again it appeared to be backwards. Angels should be taking men to heaven. Eagles should be delivering punishment and messages. Did you know, as a Karaite, I have no belief in the devil? Man is the author of his own demise and author of his own devices. Rabbinic Judaism and Christianity needed a devil to explain how man can sink to the depths of depravity. As a Karaite I knew that was one of the foibles when the Fool created us. So the more I look at this picture of the wheel, the more I realize that whoever designed this felt the same way. It might seem odd to you, but I think this wheel may have everything to do with Karaism and wasn't a kabalistic creation at all."

"Kova, this was a book put together by a Christian cleric," Bruno reminded him.

"This was a book collecting numerous articles and artifacts put together by someone that probably didn't understand any of it," Yakov sermonized. "Otherwise he would have understood the significance of this diagram and never included it because it goes against everything that's taught in religion."

Bruno looked at the picture and studied it closely. He could see that there were some issues, but nothing to the extent that Yakov was obviously referring to. "I don't see it."

"Look at the letter in the center and what do you see?"

"Just the letter 'N,'" both Bruno and Caesar remarked simultaneously then stared at each other as if to say I answered first.

"But the author of this picture would not simply let a letter be nothing more than a letter. Notice that he wrote his Hebrew using the Latin alphabet. Don't you think that's odd? I think he's inviting you to write his Latin words in Hebrew letters. So the letter 'N' becomes a 'nun' and that letter has the mystical meaning of soul. Do you think it's by chance that he put that particular letter in the center of the square or do you think he wanted us to recognize that the soul is at the center of our existence?"

"Could be coincidence?" Caesar voiced his opinion.

"Is it Caesar? Giordano do me the favor and change the Latin letters in SATOR to their Hebrew equivalents and tell our friend here what it means."

Bruno suddenly turned white as a ghost. His voice became hushed as he answered, "The Destroyer."

"Still think it's coincidence," Yakov gave a smug look of confidence to his companions. "Try AREPO now."

"Headless," Bruno answered.

"Another word for being headless if we were describing someone's character," Yakov revolved his hand in a circular motion as if to pull the word from Bruno's lips.

"A fool," Giordano said softly.

"And then I thought about the word ROTAS and at first I arrived at the Hebrew action to destroy. But why would the author repeat that when I already had the word for Destroyer. It would be of no value. Then I remembered the other spelling and realized it was referring to the action of trembling when one stands before God. Of course OPERA when converted into Hebrew letters tells us about the finality of life. Dust and ashes as it refers to the end state of all living creatures. As we come into this world so shall we leave! We tremble at the time of judgment but for all the good or evil we have done in our lives we will share the same fate. Dust to ashes and nothing more."

"But that still leaves the word TENET and I can't think of any Hebrew equivalent," Bruno declared.

"Neither could I at first, but then I recalled that much of what we have looked for has been opposites, just as Caesar has stated numerous times. This diagram is about opposites. If understanding is at the core of the universe then its opposite must be there as well. The man who designed this wheel was a fatalist."

"So we don't look for a positive but a negative," Bruno mused over the suggestion. "If we don't understand then we have ignorance."

"More words," Yakov challenged. "Give me verbs rather than a noun. Remember the author of this diagram has provided the Latin verb to understand."

"Verb, verb," Caesar rambled. "To confuse. To be indecisive. Unperceptive. Unperceiving."

Holding up his finger as if it was a torch to light their way, Yakov finally decided to help them as they floundered. "So when man grew too smart and had too much understanding, what did God do to stop him from challenging the heavens?"

The light went on within Bruno's head. "The Tower of Babel," he answered. "It's the Hebrew for babbling incessantly. If you don't understand something, the tendency of most people is to just babble unintelligibly and mask their ignorance."

"The diagram tells us that it doesn't necessarily have to be two different people. The same person possesses both attributes. That's why the eagle and the angel are pulling in the same direction. They would be turning the wheel constantly. At any time man can be at the bottom and the devil at top. They interchange positions many times through life."

"You see all this in that picture?" Caesar sounded amazed at the level of insight that Yakov had achieved. "That's something my father could do. I thought he was unique."

"Don't ever think otherwise. Your father was unique. If it wasn't for the similarities to my own beliefs, I would be as blind as most people when looking at this."

"So have you figured out where and whom the Golem's going to strike next," Bruno was eager to move on to the next step."

"I believe so," Yakov responded. "The Maharal let me know that nothing was random. Every victim, every attack was governed by the Kabala. If that's the case, then his pattern that he overlaid on the city has to correspond to everything on this wheel. Then next strike will occur at Mala Stana. The last at Hradcany. If we put the northern pole over Hradcany, then the southern pole overlays Strasnicka."

"So the banker becomes the southern pole," Bruno gestured with his hands to try and understand the significance.

"In that way the devil's head and the kingdom both correspond to Korunni the banker. He was pressuring Maisel, threatening the construction of the synagogue, threatening to destroy all that they had planned. He was the devil to them. But he was their key to tapping into the kingdom's treasury."

"And what about any other connections then?"

"We'll work around the dial. The first assault was on the city councilor. Draw a line from the concavity and it connects to the constellation in the corner."

"Equuleus," Caesar identified the star map for them. The others looked at him in surprise at his quickness to identify the symbol.

"My father was keen on astrology. He had me study star charts since I was a little boy."

"Yes, Equuleus, makes sense," Yakov pondered, "Referring to a little horse, but in Roman times to the Equestrian order. The Equestrian order governed the city. The second attack on the rich man, the point of the star linked to the Hebrew word 'hod.' Depending whether the 'h' is hard or soft make the translation either a sharp point or an echo. I choose the latter. The second attack was similar to the first. There was little distinction between the two men."

"And the third attack on the brigand? Do you see the connection there?" Bruno inquired.

"Again, draw a line from the concavity of the star. It connects to the cherubim."

"You mean the griffin."

"Take a look Giordano. It has a human head. It's not a griffin. I know you Christians like to see your cherubim as little, pot bellied, rosy-cheeked children flying around and resting on clouds, but this is a depiction of the Shedu, the original cherubim; a creature entirely devoid of human emotion. Brutal in the performance of its tasks which usually involved standing guard and preventing anyone from passing that didn't have authorization. What do you think? Similar enough to our bully preying on those crossing the bridge into his territory?"

"How do you explain the young couple," Caesar jumped into the fray."

"A play on the French word feu. Fire. What are young lovers if not impetuous and full of flame and fire? Their hearts burn like an inferno, their passion lights up their lives."

"The little girl?"

"Notice how the next concavity is in line with the constellation. But before you can connect a line between the two, you find the head of the angel swoops in and blocks your effort; an innocent, sweet young angel, fair of face and divine in spirit. What little girl doesn't match that description?"

"So you're saying that the Golem had a specific target in mind, but because the girl accidentally crossed his path, he ended up taking her instead?" The expression of disbelief was obvious on Bruno's face.

"You have to understand the Golem's actions are governed by this Kabala wheel. He was already of the frame of mind that there was a chance an angel could block his path to his intended prey. But if you notice, he has a second chance at this same target because the identical constellation appears at both the fifth point and the eleventh. So it's not a case of the wheel necessarily telling him what to do but instead his belief that all his actions are being dictated."

"Let me see if I have this right," Bruno held up his hand for a moment. "You're now saying this wheel doesn't tell the Maharal or the cabal or even the Golem what to do. They just believe it does."

"It's suggestive. They believe that it's telling them everything but instead they were making their actions fit the wheel."

"But what about all those details you just told us about the first six victims. They match up to everything on the wheel." Caesar had become just as perplexed as Giordano, both of them staring wide-eyed at Yakov awaiting an explanation.

"They matched because I wanted them to match. I knew that if I thought in a similar frame of mind to the cabal, I would see how they would come to their conclusions regarding the wheel's foretelling of events."

"So you're telling us that they have used the kabala and the wheel simply to provide a justification to their own actions."

"The mind is a funny thing," Yakov mused. "People often want to be manipulated. For example, Maisel was being pressured by his partner, Korunni. He was threatening to have him arrested, to pin the crime totally on the mayor. Easy enough to do considering that the only one on record receiving funds was Maisel. So Maisel would probably wish his one time partner dead. If Maisel is arrested then the new synagogue would be forfeited since the stolen funds were used in its construction. The Maharal wouldn't obtain his seat as a chief Rabbi. Although he'd never admit it, he wanted Korunni dead too. I'm certain there were enough members of the cabal that shared similar sentiments. The problem is that basically they are good men, and murder is something they are reluctant to do. So they consult the kabala, and the wheel tells them yes, the banker is going to die. It's not their fault anymore, it's destiny, fate, whatever they wish to call it.

But the truth is that the reading performed by their kabalistic master was controlled by his innermost thoughts and desires."

"Fascinating," Bruno contemplated the concept. "It's a form of mind control."

"Remember what I told you about the principle law of Karaism, Giordano."

"If you read it and you believe it to be right and it is good, then it is right."

"You remembered! So if this wheel is actually Karaite in origin then it's built on that same principle."

"Let me see if I can do it then," Bruno was excited by the challenge of the game. The seventh is a concavity pointing to what looks likes Orion's belt. By legend Orion was a hunter who boasted of invincibility. He could kill at leisure without repercussion. Taddeush felt he could kill without being held accountable. Like Orion he hunted his prey mercilessly. Like Orion, his belligerence had to be punished and he had to die."

"Very good," Yakov congratulated him. "You see, it can actually be quite easy once you master the rules of the game."

"Okay, let me now try," Caesar chimed in. "The next murder is the bishop. But the star isn't pointing at anything." Caesar sounded defeated.

"Yes it is, take a better look," Yakov advised.

"A hoof? What am I supposed to do with a hoof?"

"Treat it like a game." Bruno was already aware of where the connection was leading and danced almost imperceptivity as he urged on his companion.

"Alright, a game. The hoof belongs to a bull. The bull is Taurus. Taurus was the form Zeus took on when he came down to earth to fornicate with Europa. How am I doing so far?"

"Good. You're thinking in the right direction."

"King of the gods came down to earth and impregnated a woman. I'll grant it has a semblance to Christian beliefs." Caesar began to appreciate the power of the wheel. "Christian beliefs are the domain of the Church." He smiled broadly now that he was able to draw a line between the hoof and the Church. "So what part of the Church," he continued. "Not the bull's head, so it can't be the Pope. Hooves are in contact with the ground. That part of the Church that is in contact with the populations is the diocese and the bishoprics." Caesar took his bow before making his pronouncement. "Therefore the next victim had to be either an archbishop or a bishop."

Bruno gave Caesar a loud clapping ovation. "Bravo, bravo."

"You can do the same with the constable and of course even myself. The Hebrew word 'Jesod' makes it a lot easier to draw the connection to myself by referring to the keystone or foundation. That's how they would view my position as their arch nemesis."

"That just leaves us with the final two victims," Bruno pronounced, "and now that we know how the system works, we should be able to fill in the details."

"Easy enough for the twelfth victim, the indicators are obvious, but the eleventh is going to take us some time." Yakov was cautious about jumping to any conclusions.

His two companions had similar thoughts on the twelfth, so they also concentrated fully on the eleventh.

"I recognize the constellation," Caesar announced. "You're looking at Vela which according to the legends represents the sail of the Argo, Jason's ship."

"And Jason of course stole the Golden Fleece," Giordano added. "Now we just have to identify what that could actually refer to."

"Not a what, but a who," Caesar corrected him.

"Don't forget that whomever it is moves between the two locations. That's why he can be at both the fifth and eleventh locations on the wheel. That has to be the significant factor in our thinking. Mala Strana and Vinohrady. What's their connection? Find that and you find our victim!"

30

Riegrovy Park: Vinohrady

The streets were narrow and dark from the shadows cast by the three and four storey buildings that lined either side. From out of one of the second store windows a cascade of wash water was dumped unceremoniously into the street narrowly missing the two travelers as they navigated the winding roads towards their destination.

"Mind what you're doing," Bruno shouted up towards the still open window but the return offering was more colorful and the list of profanities exceeded even his knowledge of any known vocabulary that he was familiar with. "Stupid immigrants," he moaned under his breath. Caesar laughed at the reference, realizing that Giordano had not recognized the absurdity of his comment.

"I thought you would have felt at home walking these streets, Giordano," Caesar nudged his friend in the side as they strode together.

"And how do you figure that?"

"Take a look at the street name. Italska. Most of the people here are immigrants from your own country."

"Better yet, why are we here?" Bruno was more to the point.

"That is my surprise," Caesar responded. "Kova is with the Emperor at the other site, and we're here to find the clues to the eleventh victim at this one. But I think I've already solved the mystery."

"Well that's so very good of you. So why have we walked all this distance if you already know what is going to happen. You could have just told us all back at the castle."

"I needed to confirm my suspicions. Unless you see it with your own eyes, there's no way you can do that."

"So let me hear this theory of yours so we can get this over with and return to the others."

"Aren't we in a cheery disposition today?" Caesar mocked him. "If you behave yourself, I'll even let you be the one to tell Kova that we solved the riddle."

"And let me take all the credit. That's so kind of you. Why would you do that?"

"Considering you'd have to explain that the clue came from my father, he'd know immediately that I was instrumental in solving it."

Bruno gave a playful shove to Caesar's shoulder, knocking him a stride or two off balance until he recovered. "Okay, what did your father say?"

"First I have to tell you how I was able to trigger the quatrain. That's the fascinating part."

"Don't' tell me you started staring into bowls of water in front of candles and mirrors like your father." Bruno couldn't help himself from having a barb or two at his friend's expense.

"I didn't think of that. Perhaps I should try it next time," Caesar mocked in return, a huge grin wrapped across his face. "Keep walking, the entrance is just up this road."

"How do you know where we're going? You aren't familiar with Prague."

"I made a point of studying the model in the Lichten Palace this morning. I've memorized the entire route Even though it may not seem like it, it's practically a straight line since we left the castle and crossed the bridge."

"How very astute of you. But back to the clue if you don't mind."

"I was thinking about what we last discussed regarding the Kabala wheel. You know the Vela constellation and how it represented the story of the Argo when Jason sailed after the Golden Fleece. So I started thinking about the crew on the ship, the Argonauts and who were some of the members of that crew. Did you know that the Vela constellation is often confused for the Gemini constellation because there's a strong similarity in the way the stars are laid out in the pattern of an open ended rectangle?"

"Is this going somewhere?" Bruno sounded irritated but Caesar knew that he had already caught the priest's interest.

"The Gemini or Discouri as they're also known were Castor and Pollux. They were members of the crew of the Argo. And it's when I suddenly remember that, that's when my father's quatrain practically leaped into my head."

"Okay, I admit it, you've caught my interest. So get on with it! What did he say to you?"

Caesar recited the verses from Century II, Quatrain fifteen. *'Shortly before the Monarch is killed, Castor, Pollux and a ship in fear of the stars. The public arena, by land and sea are emptied, Pisa, Asti, Ferra, Turin, prohibited land.'*

Bruno scratched his head. "Explain it to me."

"I can't believe you don't see it."

"Don't get smart with me," Bruno warned him.

"We are all in agreement that the twelfth point indicates an attempt on the Emperor's life. That much was obvious between the Eagle and the use of the Hebrew word 'keter' for crown. But it also tells us that can only happen once the eleventh victim is attacked. And we know that the eleventh victim moves back and forth between this hill we're about to climb at Riegrovy and the Petrin Hill over at Mala Strana."

"And how pray tell do you know that?"

"Because of my father's play with words. The interchange between fear and awe is quite common. One can be struck with fear but is also said to be awestruck. The wheel told us that studying the constellations are the focal point of this person. He goes to those places so that he can observe the stars. Empty places. Where there are no lights, no buildings, nothing to interfere with the observation of the heavens."

"Hence the reference to emptying the public arena, but why then talk about Italian towns and call them forbidden places."

"That I'm about to show you." Caesar paraded confidently towards the gates ahead as they turned into the short side alley.

They approached the entrance to the large stretch of land known as Riegrovy. There were several guards posted at the central gates to the area. Caesar waved an official looking document in front of the face of one of the men that appeared to be in charge and he let them pass.

"Did I just miss something?" Bruno asked his colleague.

"I had the Emperor's office prepare that letter this morning. Access to the hill is restricted."

"They've restricted access to a hill?"

"No, they've restricted access to what is grown on the hill."

Once Caesar and Bruno had walked past the outer ring of trees that demarcated the limits of Riegrovy, they had a clear view of the terraced gardens, neatly tended by the hordes of people milling about like ants on an anthill.

"Welcome to the government owned vineyards," Caesar spread out his hands indicating the vast expanse of vines that spread in every direction as far as their eyes could see. "Everyone's pretty busy treating the vines now that spring is almost here; removing dead growth, any winter disease, and a whole host of other conditions. But you'd know that Giordano. Not only are you Italian, but you're a priest as well. Part of your basic training isn't it?"

"I drink it," Bruno's answer was short and curt. "But I never bothered to learn to grow it. There were others in the order that were better suited for that."

"So now you know the government's little secret."

"Why would a vineyard be a secret? And what kind of vineyard needs guards."

"You've lived here for how long, and you didn't even know about this place. How's that possible?" Caesar's tone was bordering on being sarcastic but he knew better than to push the matter too far. "Remember when I told you that my father had spent considerable time teaching me business aspects?"

"Yes."

"Well this is one of those lessons in action. Operation of a vineyard is labor intensive. So in order to cut your costs and maximize your profits, you bring in foreign labor. Pay them practically nothing, let them live in squalor, and because they have no rights as citizens, you don't have to worry about them."

"And the source of this foreign labor force?" Bruno asked but he was already prepared for the answer.

"The street wasn't called Italska for nothing. I think places like Pisa, Asti, Ferra and Turin are pretty likely."

"That explains this site, but what about the other. I know for a fact it doesn't have vineyards because I've actually been there many times."

"And when you were there, did you notice the wall?"

"Hunger wall…," Bruno's voice droned off into silence.

"From what I was told, it was even worse than here. At least here they get paid. The foreigners that built that wall were treated like slaves. They got food and that was it. But who am I to judge."

"I still don't understand why Rudi wouldn't tell me about this place."

Caesar put a comforting hand on Bruno's shoulder. "Personally, I think it's because he cares for you. You're Italian, these people are Italian. Perhaps he thought you'd be upset by that. Business and friendship are never a good mix. He valued your friendship more and didn't want to lose it."

"He still should have told me."

"We all should have done a lot of things. That is the nature of life."

"I think you've been around Kova too much. You're beginning to sound like him."

"If I do, it's not for not trying!"

§ § § § § §

The walk up the thousand and forty foot Petrin hill was as tiring as it was invigorating. The views as one rose higher of the city below were absolutely breathtaking. Each scape was a painting ready to be mastered. Even Rudolf tended to overlook the strain the hike had placed on his sizable frame, refreshed by the glowing panorama of his city.'

"Kova, do you have any idea why Caesar requested that we make this little trip?"

"Something to do with viewing the night skies, I believe."

"But it's daytime," the Emperor reminded him.

"I think he felt it necessary to take in the view as part of his research." Yakov suspected that Caesar had a far more constructive reason for sending everyone trekking through the parklands but he never revealed it. That would happen once the two parties rejoined later in the day.

"Good thing I had my chefs prepare us a meal. I am working up quite an appetite." Rudolf patted his growling stomach. "Captain Dimitri, make certain when we reach the top that you set up a perimeter so that our lunch isn't disturbed by any intruders."

Dimitri nodded deferentially, a half salute as he did so.

"Once we approach the top we'll ascend the wall so I can show you the observatory tower. I've had some of the finest astronomer's in the world view the sky from that tower. They told me that it was one of the finest viewpoints they had ever entertained."

"So, there's an observatory up here," Yakov grasped the significance immediately.

"Oh yes. Initially it was built to warn of attacks on the city, but since our arrangement with the Sultan that is a very unlikely occurrence, I've fitted it out as an astronomical laboratory. I think you will find it quite intriguing."

"I'm certain I will. I'm intrigued already."

Rudolf removed a stone from his shoe and then continued to climb. "I know there are other rulers that think me quite eccentric. But they don't understand the science the way that I do. We live in a fascinating age. Everything is happening so quickly. All our beliefs that we thought were immutable are changing over night. There is no stopping progress!"

"But admittedly we are still in an age of incongruities. In one respect you are taking me to an observatory where man is exploring the heavens. But from what I've been told by some of your palace staff this morning, this is the same hill on which Jan Hus was burned for his views on Christianity. How can we live in an age where we talk about science and progress, yet not too long ago we acted like savages. We don't even have to look that far back. Look at our present situation. We're all here now because we are under threat of our own inhumanity."

"I would like to say that a better world is coming at the turn of the century, but I'm afraid I don't know that for certain. I know that Giordano believes it to be true. That is why he considers science his new religion."

"Giordano is ahead of his time," Yakov offered. "I fear he is well ahead of many lifetimes with his views. That' places him in danger. He needs your protection!"

"And he has it without hesitation!"

"But you know he longs to go home. He doesn't say it, but I can see it in his eyes. You won't be able to protect him outside of your kingdom."

"I will always do what I can, but I swear no one will be safe from me if they do him harm."

"Watch over him, your Majesty. The world needs people like Giordano Bruno."

"And people like you, Kova."

"The world's changing too fast, even for one like me. The old ways don't really count for much anymore. I fear the time of the Kahana is coming to an end."

"I didn't think that was possible," Rudolf reminded him. "I don't wish to tell someone like you what is written in the Bible, but it did state that the rod and the staff would never fall from between the legs. I would think that in some way guarantees you family's immortality. Wouldn't you think so?"

"Ah, but therein lies God's little joke. What good is immortality if no one bothers to pay you any attention? The meaning and purpose are lost and you can't lead if there's no one to follow."

"Let's not talk about melancholy subjects" Yakov's comment had coincidentally hit a chord in Rudolf's reflection of his own ability to rule the Empire. "I much prefer to talk about why we are here. You said you would fill in the details once we reached the top and we're almost there."

"I did say that," Yakov agreed. "It's not easy to explain. As you are aware there is a definite pattern to the attacks and from that pattern we were able to determine that here in Mala Strana the next attack is going to occur. But our research in your library provided valuable information as to how the attacks are planned. We were able to decipher that there is a connection between the intended victim of the fifth attack and the one who will be attacked at this site. The little girl unfortunately became a distraction to the Golem and he abducted her and abandoned the original target. For the two points of the pattern to be interchangeable meant that physically there had to be identical evidence between the two. It was Caesar that pointed out the obvious, that they were each demarcating a large hill."

"The highest in the city I might add," Rudolf inserted his comment into the explanation.

"This hill is over a thousand feet high. The other is not as tall, but stretches over a greater distance. So our challenge is to discover what is unique about these two hills that make them similar and different from anything else."

"Why didn't you just say so," the Emperor guffawed. "I can show you that right now!"

"You can?"

"Of course I can. Follow me." For a big man, the Emperor moved nimbly up the side of the hill towards the peak of Hunger Wall. His guards followed close behind with Yakov trailing last. Inside the wall was a door that led to the upper tower that crested the hill.

"Welcome to the Quarter Mile," Rudolf addressed Yakov. "That is the height of the tower observatory. And this man over here," he pointed to what had to be the resident astronomer sitting in the far corner working over a series of calculations, "is David Gans."

The name failed to register with Yakov, the stranger smiling back politely at the mention of his name.

"David Gans, our most prominent astronomer in Prague," Rudolf explained, surprised by Yakov's lack of recognition. "He's one of you," he then added, thinking that would achieve the desired response.

"One of you what?" Yakov still hadn't drawn the connection.

"You know," Rudolf shuffled his feet slightly, feeling somewhat embarrassed, "One of you Jews. I thought you'd all be familiar with each other, especially with your leading scientists."

Yakov and David looked at each other slightly amused and shrugged their shoulders as if to say, 'what can you do?'

"No, your Excellency, I cannot say that I've had the honor or the pleasure, until now," Yakov deftly maneuvered Gans and himself out of any further embarrassment. Holding out his hand he walked over to the scientist and grabbed his arm in a strong greeting. "I am very pleased to meet you. I am Yakov Kahana."

David Gans released his grip almost immediately upon hearing the name, an act which was immediately noticed by the Emperor.

"See," Rudolf commented, "he definitely knows you!"

"I'm sorry," Gans apologized. "It's just that your presence here took me by surprise. No one had told me you were coming."

"No apology necessary," Yakov assured him. "But I am surprised that an eminent scientist would know of me. I'm not a man with any scientific achievements of note."

Gans felt compelled to explain. "In a previous life, I was actually being trained to be a Rabbi. But once they exposed me to the sciences, I knew that was where I had my true calling."

"Ah, so you would have heard all the stories about me from the Rabbis. I'm afraid I don't have horns upon my head, despite their insistence that I do."

Gans found the comment quite amusing releasing a series of pleasant laughs which were met by Yakov's warm and friendly smile.

"They actually said worse about you," he added once his laughter subsided.

"I bet they did," Yakov laughed in return. Rudolf looked a little perturbed that he was being left outside their conversation which had now taken on a very personal tone. "But tell me," Yakov inquired, "You've adopted a German surname. Not exactly customary for a Yeshiva trained Jew."

"Most of my time now is spent outside my Jewish heritage. For David ben Solomon ben Seligman to exist and contribute within the Christian world it was necessary to change my name."

"And you're place of birth?"

"Lippstadt in Germany," he replied. "But I did my studies in Poland and then afterwards came to Prague. That would explain my accent being different from most."

"I could not place it. But I would guess not sounding too Jewish benefits your movement within the scientific community." Yakov turned his head and gave Rudolf a sly wink

Rudolf cleared his throat but didn't have a remark to come back with, so instead waved for his guards to set up the food in the picnic baskets they carried right there in the observatory.

"I believe his Majesty has brought us some dinner. If it's not too great an interruption in your work, would you care to dine with us?"

"Yes, please David," Rudolf pleaded. "I'd like to hear so much about what you're working on now."

Thanking his host and benefactor, Gans sat down around a large map table where the food had been displayed. "I'm still working on the same issues, your Majesty that we had discussed before; the identification of the center of the solar system."

"And have you changed your mind yet?" The Emperor reached over and tore off one of the drumsticks from the roasted duck.

"Master Kepler has been trying very hard to persuade me to his line of thinking," Gans admitted. "But I'm still not convinced. His mathematic calculations still haven't proven to me that the stars are moving in different directions and different speeds. Until he does so, I still believe that they are nothing more than a concentric ring moving at a predictable speed around the earth. At least I can support that theory with my own calculations."

"You correspond regularly with other astronomers?" Yakov stated as a rhetorical question.

"It is the only way we can actually develop the science. By our being spread out over such wide expanses, any variables in movement of celestial bodies would be detected since our perspectives of the stars and planets will be at slightly different angles. Johannes Kepler is insisting that his measurements when compared to mine show an increased degree of separation between several stars. On that basis he is supporting his heliocentric theory that everything is moving around the sun."

"Which Copernicus had already theorized a century ago," Rudolf pointed out.

"But never proved," Gans was even quicker to point out.

"You'd probably find one of my colleagues far more interesting to discuss such matters with," Yakov mentioned.

"Who would that be?" David Gans inquired.

"Father Giordano Bruno."

"He has been my guest here quite a few times. We do have some lively discussions. But I do find that he has taken a far more esoteric approach to astronomy."

"How so?"

"He keeps asking me if I've seen God in my observations yet."

"That does sound like him" Rudolf poked fun at his friend.

"And have you?" Yakov in turn asked quite seriously.

"Have I what? Seen God? Of course not!"

"And if you don't mind me asking, is that why you left the yeshiva, and your rabbinical training?"

"They were right about what they said about you, Master Kahana," Gans curled his lips in a half smile. "They talked about your ability to size up a situation with an almost unworldly perceptibility."

"But nonetheless, I would suspect your current interest in the stars has placed yourself at a crossroads."

"Only because I wrote a treatise on the importance of the liberal disciplines as a means to mediate between Christians and Jews," Gans explained. "By being theologically neutral they bring us together in a common pursuit and as a result harmony. Interdenominational discourse and respect would be unavoidable."

"Brave words," Yakov offered his encouragement, "but words which will also win you the enmity of many in power on both sides."

"Not will, Master Kahana, but has!"

"I am not surprised. I believe Father Bruno shares a similar reaction from within his own peers of his religious community. I am safe to presume that you would not be immune from the contempt of your own rabbinic teachers."

"He has asked me to refrain from publishing much of my material for fear that it would persuade others to leave his classes. It never bodes well for a teacher to have one of his prize students writing articles that suggest possibilities outside of biblical creation."

"So you're former teacher is still alive then."

"Oh, very much so! When I first came to Prague I was under the tutelage of Bezalel Loew. But later his son, the Maharal, took me on as his student. I was one of his best."

"I bet you were," Yakov commented. "I bet you were!"

31

Hradcany; The Castle

As they sat around a table in Rudolf's study, they all partook in a thick porridge being served that morning. It was the first opportunity for them to reassess the information they had obtained from the day before. Still, there had been no discussion of the last victim with the Emperor. Consciously, the three of them had mutually agreed not to raise the subject for fear that Rudolf would react irrationally. For anyone, let alone a man with supreme power, the natural reaction to a threat against their own life would be to preempt any event by eliminating all those that had planned to carry it out. Realizing that this would only achieve what he was trying to prevent; the wholesale slaughter of the leaders of the Jewish community and the unavoidable massacre of the innocents that would inevitably follow, Yakov was adamant that they should avoid revealing the intended twelfth victim at all costs.

So, when the Emperor raised the subject once again at their breakfast meeting, Yakov was quick to label the identity as being irretrievably unknown until such time that the eleventh victim had succumbed to the Golem. And then, for good measure, he just as quickly dismissed the possibility of the eleventh being harmed, because they were now aware of whom it was. Without an eleventh, the Golem would be unable to proceed onto the twelfth under his own initiative. All would be safe!

"And you quite certain of all this?" Rudolf wanted confirmation that what Yakov had promulgated was a fact.

"I am absolutely positive. Based on what Caesar derived from his father's prophecy and the confirmation of the vineyards as being the selected sight for the fifth attack, then we know for certain that the intended victim was to be David Gans. Even the season on the wheel agreed with that. During the autumn season David admitted as much that he did all his night observations from the hill at Vinohrady. Now that spring is coming he has moved his observations back to the observatory at Petrin Hill. There could be no other person by fact or coincidence that would meet those specific criteria as established by the Kabala wheel."

"Yet you did not warn David of the danger he is in," Rudolf pointed out, having disagreed previously with Yakov's decision not to do so.

"Of what advantage would that be, Excellency? It would only make Master Gans paranoid that every shadow moving in the night was a sign of impending doom. We are able to protect him without his knowledge far easier than if he was constantly panicked. We have time to prepare; spring is still a week away. The Golem will not make a move before that."

"I hope you are right, Kova."

"I believe I am."

"I'm certain of it too," Bruno piped in on Yakov's defense. "When Caesar explained the quatrain to me, I thought it was impossible that it would be in reference to a specific person. Having known David Gans personally, I still had no idea that in the fall he was relocating his observation point to the eastern part of the city. And in all the discussions we've had on his personal life, not once has he mentioned to me that he was a student of Judah ben Loew. Now that I know this to be true, there is no other person who could have been the object of that wheel."

"But it makes no sense," Rudolf shook his head. "He's a brilliant astronomer, but surely that is not a reason for anyone wishing him dead. It makes no sense at all!"

"It's his presence in Prague as a brilliant astronomer, as you have so aptly described him that makes him very much the object of murder. He's an embarrassment to the Maharal. Perhaps if he had gone away, back to Germany or even farther afield, then he'd be less threatening, but by staying in the very city where his rabbinical teacher resides, he is a constant reminder to the Maharal of failure. No different a situation I might add from Giordano's situation. They are like two peas in a pod. In both cases their study and pursuit of the sciences has placed them in direct conflict with their religious institutions. Their existence, in both cases, is a statement that their religious training was weighed in a balance, measured, and found wanting."

"But to plot the murder of your former student only because he no longer agrees with your teachings. I find it difficult to believe the esteemed Rabbi ben Loew would consider such a thing." Rudolf scooped up another spoonful of the porridge and placed it in his mouth.

"As we've already discussed, the Rabbi is capable of many things that would not have been thought possible. The Golem alone is proof of that. But the wheel, it is an entirely different level of logic. It provides the perpetrators with deniability. How can they be held accountable if the fates have already been set and sealed? Even though it is their own hidden desires that they read into the wheel, they can still excuse themselves from the outcome." Yakov frowned at the thought that if the Kabala wheel was Karaite in origin, that it may have been his own ancestors that had gifted the tool to the rest of the world with which they could justify their evil intentions.

The Emperor had to repeat his question in order to snap Yakov out of his brooding thoughts. "I say again, Kova, what do you intend to do now?"

"We'll make certain that we don't leave David Gans alone in the observatory at any time. The Golem will not attempt to attack him anywhere else. He is unable to think outside of the wheel. As long as there are always guards present, and they're prepared for the worst, then I think we'll be able to keep the Golem at bay."

"Think is not good enough! This is the same creature that killed six of Dimitri's best men in a matter of minutes," Rudolf reminded him.

"Only because we were not prepared for an attack from the rooftop," Yakov reminded everyone. "The Golem had the advantage of surprise. We had underestimated him. We had no idea that he could move across rooftops and climb like an ape with such a high degree of agility. That is not a possibility now. The observatory stands alone at the top of the hill. He must approach like everyone else. On foot and exposed."

"And when he does approach…?"

"Dimitri's men will contain him with fire. He will be deathly afraid of it now from our last encounter. It will give your men the advantage they need to defeat him."

"You mean to kill him, don't you," Bruno wanted that point clarified.

"Yes, kill him," Yakov agreed. "He is too dangerous to take captive. He must die." Regretfully, Yakov had to admit that Giordano was right.

"Then it's imperative that we plan now how this is going to be done," Rudolf stated quite imperiously, puffing out his chest as he did so. "I'll need Dimitri to set up a rotation of troops to guard the observatory. At any time, there will have to be men stationed inside the observatory with David Gans. We'll inform him that there's been a threat against the observatory itself. There are always threats against government property. That should explain the presence of the troops without alarming him too much."

'It is he that is given the charge to destroy. Temples and sects changed by way of fantasy. More to the rocks than the living will come harm. By a smooth tongue the ears are constricted.' The quatrain poured out of Caesar automatically no sooner had the Emperor completed his sentence. "I'm sorry, I can't stop myself," Caesar apologized.

"Another quatrain I suppose," Rudolf cocked his head sidewise in Caesar's direction.

"Century I, Quatrain ninety-six to be exact," Caesar replied. "I don't know why, but as soon as you mentioned protecting property instead of his life I felt compelled to say it."

"I think it's a good sign," Yakov reviewed the contents of the quatrain. He went on to explain, "Obviously David Gans is the one having the ability to do harm to the tenets of Judaism as is being taught by the Maharal. And if astronomy isn't the world of fantasy, then I do not know what else could be described in that way. So as we have already discussed, his scientific exploration is quite disconcerting and threatening to his old teacher. But Nostradamus is telling us he won't come to harm. More damage is done to property than to any actual person."

"And what about the last line?" Rudolf insisted on knowing how it could be accounted for.

"It can be taken in several ways," Yakov insisted. "Being out of context, it can be accepted from almost any point of view. If we think of it being in reference to the Maharal, then it is telling us that no matter how compelling the arguments might be from David Gans, it will fall on deaf ears. The smooth tongue of Rabbi Loew will see to it."

"And the other ways in which it can be interpreted?" Rudolf desired to examine the line from the variety of available perspectives.

"I think it might even be talking about you, Rudi," Bruno offered his opinion. "You'll be able to keep Gans from knowing what your men are really doing by telling him several well placed lies. You smooth tongued devil."

"Or perhaps it's talking about David Gans himself," Rudolf offered his own opinion ignoring Bruno's quip at his own expense. "Maybe it's a reference to the state of science in the future. Perhaps scientific discovery will become the glib tongue that turns people away from the Church completely."

"Possible," Yakov acknowledged the viability of the Emperor's analysis. "Whatever the case may be, it's fairly certain that we'll be able to protect the astronomer. And should that comes to pass then the threat of the twelfth victim is eliminated."

The expression of Rudolf's face changed suddenly and turned sour. "And the threat within my own castle, when do we plan on doing something about that"

"We've been over that," Giordano reminded him. "As long as Cornelius is free to roam about, he can still serve as a conduit between us and the leaders of the Jewish community. They still have no idea that Doctor Mendes has informed on him. We can provide them with false information if necessary just in case they still have a way to contact the Golem."

"But from what you have told me, it would no longer be necessary. You know the Golem's next moves." Rudolf did not like the idea that he still had a traitor working on his staff.

"True," Yakov agreed, "but it never hurts to have an extra piece on the chessboard."

"Do you play chess Kova?"

Yakov nodded in the affirmative to the Emperor's question.

"Then I'll remind you that the goal of the game is to remove your opponent's chess pieces." Rudolf swallowed another spoonful of the cereal.

Bruno looked up from his bowl and across to the Emperor, giving him a barely imperceptible wink that the two understood completely.

§ § § § § §

It was in the evening that Caesar caught Giordano, creeping through the foyer on his way outside the castle. He could sense from

Bruno's quick steps and far reaching strides that this was very much a man on a mission.

"Hey, where are you off to?" he shouted after the fleeting figure before it exited onto the palace porch.

Caught completely off guard, Bruno practically stumbled and fell as he brought his legs abruptly to a halt and swiveled about to greet his hailer. His cloak twirled in the air as he revolved on his toes and that's when Caesar heard an all too familiar sound. The sound of the little glass orbs as they strike against each other, the same sound that he had heard in St. Michal's Church.

"Where are you going with those?" he referred to the hidden globes that had clearly rung from their concealed place in the inner lining of his cloak.

"Trust me Caesar you are better off not knowing."

"Probably, but since when has that ever stopped me from asking. If you are going to place yourself in danger, then it might be best if you do not go alone."

"There are some places I must go alone. Things I must do, without endangering anyone else. Bear with me brother; what I do is in the best interests of all of us."

"Is that your polite way of telling me to mind my own business?"

"Kova was right, you are intuitive!" Bruno laughed at his own joke, but his good humor was infectious and Caesar felt compelled to laugh along with him. Donning a more serious visage, Giordano then took a more somber tone, "You would not wish to be with me tonight. Sometimes, even I have to wonder about what kind of person I am."

Bruno could see that his last comment had triggered a response in Caesar. The same faraway look that appears each time his father's prophecies beckon from beyond while the hands massage the temples for relief. But this time even Caesar seemed frightened by whatever he had heard.

"What was it Caesar. What did he say?"

"It was a warning Giordano. A warning to you!" Caesar started to recite the sixtieth quatrain of Century V that had manifested itself into his consciousness. *'By a shaven head comes good and bad choices, More so because he goes beyond his permission, His great fury and rage makes it dire, that by fire and blood both sexes will be cut.'*

"Tell your father he worries too much. I know my limitations. I will see you on the morrow."

Caesar watched as Giordano disappeared out the castle's portal into the concealing darkness of the night. "Be careful, my friend," he whispered into the emptiness.

Once beyond the flickering lamps that lined the main paths to the castle, Giordano turned towards the servant's entrance at the rear of the kitchens. He knew it would only be a matter of time before the last of the kitchen staff would head to their rooms having finished preparing for the next day's meals. Time moved swiftly as he waited, hidden in the bushes, watching for the door to open as the last shaft of light in the kitchen was extinguished. Though it may have been easily an hour, it only felt like mere minutes once the hunt began. As expected, the last one in the kitchen left the castle rather than head to his rooms. Bruno was aware of the pattern. The few inquiries he had made of the other kitchen staff were enough to establish Cornelius's routine. Always a Wednesday night, always after the other kitchen staff had finished their duties. He thought of himself as being discreet but everyone knew he was going out on the prowl. But none could say where he went or whom he saw. That much he did keep a secret.

Keeping at a distance of several hundred feet, Bruno stayed deep in the shadows as he followed the chef onto the streets of the city. Only when it came to crossing the Karlov Bridge was it necessary for Giordano to fall back further into the distance to ensure that he was not seen. The long bridge with its well lit causeway provided too great a threat of being discovered, in spite of all the people that were traversing it in the early hours of the evening. But by increasing the distance between them, keeping Cornelius in sight was proving a difficult task. Once clear of the bridge on the other side, Bruno reassured himself that he would be able to approach his target more closely and not have to worry again about losing him.

Through the gates on the far side, Bruno turned quickly up Krizovnicka, heading towards Josefov. He had lost his view of the chef over the last third of the bridge but was certain that he'd be able to reestablish contact by increasing his pace once clear of the pedestrian traffic. By the time Bruno had reached the crossroads at Plaznerska, he knew he had a serious problem. The number of people on the streets had thinned to the point that he was practically walking on the street all alone and yet there was no sign of the chef. "Shit!," he cursed under his breath as soon as it dawned on him that Cornelius must have gone in the opposite direction once he crossed the bridge. Turning on his heels, Bruno took off back down the street as fast as he could run without tripping in the folds of his priest's robe. He couldn't believe that he had made such an acute error in judgment. Why in the world the chef had gone southwards was not yet clear. Turning south on Smetanova would not take him anywhere close to the Jewish Quarter. 'Think, damn it!' Bruno forced himself to analyze the possibilities. South led to Narodni, Narodni led to the square. Narodni led to taverns. Narodni led to Perlova. Crime, prostitution, anything you could wish to find. Perlova? It didn't make sense, Bruno thought to himself. Cornelius would never pay for sex. In fact that was his most infamous boast that he had never paid for sex in his life. And Bruno knew it to be true. From the number of confessions he had taken over the past few months from the scullery girls and the chamber maids, Cornelius was not beyond physically forcing himself on the hapless girls but he would never pay for it. Too often he had become physical, striking the women in places where the bruises wouldn't be seen by others, until they submitted. Brutal, merciless, heartless, and always without gratitude, that was his true nature. No, Cornelius the chef was not one to pay a prostitute for sex. Now Bruno was even more confused. If not Perlova, where could the chef be heading? Bruno told himself to decide on an alternative but he couldn't think of one. It had to be Perlova. Figuring out the why would have to come later.

Gambling on the destination, Bruno chose to take the backstreets rather than keeping to the main roads. Karlova to Liliova, and then on to Skorepka; small, dark, shadowed streets that most people avoided for fear of the element that resided there. Convinced that no one would attack a man dressed in a religious frock, Bruno pressed on, stripping precious minutes from the journey to Perlova. Turning into the street the smells and sounds assaulted his senses. Amidst the moral decadence of the district dwelled the abandoned and neglected too. All that Prague society chose to ignore and forget were there. Bruno could feel the penetrating eyes of the crippled beggars boring into his flesh, vague and shadowy remainders of the last wars fought against the Turks that left both sides reeling and pursuing a truce. Orphans, the abandoned, the disowned, all searching for nothing more than a shelter in the night against the winter's cold and a meal, no matter how poor to warm their bellies. This was hell and the more Bruno examined the wraiths that darted in and out half closed doors, the more certain than ever he became that he would find the chef here. Whatever his reasons, whatever he was searching for, Perlova would offer it to him. Here existed the denizens of God's abandoned, and none would ever concern themselves with their fate, especially if doled out by men like Cornelius.

Upon first exposure to the pathetic creatures, even Bruno harbored the thought to turn around and head back to the castle. He fought hard against the urge. Weren't these the people that deserved God's protection the most? Those that no longer had a voice, nor anyone to protect them, to even give them a glimmer of hope? And then he thought about his vows and how meaningless they were in a place like this. If Christianity had no compassion for these people, then what purpose did it even serve? What purpose did he serve as a priest? Tonight he would be their protector. Resolving himself to press on, he let his eyes dance from face to face in the flickering torchlight, searching and listening for any clue that would lead him to the chef's whereabouts. Hands reached out for alms but he could offer them nothing more than a short prayer. To desperate people, it wasn't enough.

Moving along the edges of the street, where darkness hung like an awning over the sprawled bodies stinking from the mixed aromas of alcohol and feces, he peered into the alleyways and narrow crawl spaces between the buildings, certain that he would find the chef concealed down one of them, feeding his depravity on one of these poor souls.

The search was frustrating, not a single sign to reassure him that he had guessed correctly. Perhaps Perlova had been nothing more than a stab in the dark and Cornelius wasn't around for miles by now. It was then that the wind carried the faint cry for help to where he stood. None of the inhabitants of the street even blinked an eye if they heard it; they had grown immune to such things. Misfortune and death was in some ways a blessing to release them from their existence. He heard it again, and this time Bruno was able to fix on a location. Not more than twenty yards he estimated from where he stood. Down the little alleyway that angled into Rytirska.

His pulse was racing, and even though he only covered a short distance he found himself breathing heavy as he turned into the alley. It took almost half a minute until his eyes adjusted to the gloom that enveloped the narrow lane. At first sight he made out the rotund form that could only be Cornelius, but as his vision adjusted to the low light intensity he was then able to make out the much smaller outline of the young girl; thirteen, fourteen perhaps, definitely no more than fifteen. One of the street urchins by the way she was dressed in the assorted rags, throwaways from the prostitutes of Perlova.

The chef hadn't even heard him step into the alley, completely engrossed by his sadism as he slapped the girl each time she screamed for help. Blows that were hard enough to make her topple to the ground and then he would pick her up in order to do it again. He tore at her clothing like a savage animal, and for all his size and bulk, she fought valiantly to keep him at bay. It was obvious that Cornelius wasn't use to fighting for his gratification, but Bruno knew that it was only a matter of time that the young girl was either beaten senseless or overpowered from exhaustion.

"Let her go!" Bruno screamed at him.

Cornelius didn't recognize the voice of his intruder, seeing only the hood of the robe pulled well over the face it concealed. "Mind your own business priest, or you'll be next on the menu."

"Release her now while I'm still in a forgiving mood," Bruno shouted back."

The sound of the voice began to register with the chef. "Is that you Bruno? What in hell's blazes are you doing here?"

"I'm here to stop you Cornelius," came the reply. "I'm here to see that you never harm an innocent again."

"Bah! Get the fuck out of here priest! Who do you think you are? You've shoved your dick in as many a piece as I have and no one holds you accountable. Be gone by the time I finish with her or else I'll part your backside too!" Cornelius turned his back on Bruno and returned to his struggle with the girl as he tried to pin her up against the wall.

"Fatal mistake to turn your back on me," Bruno gave a warning just before he launched one of his blue globes at the chef. Striking Cornelius in the back of the head, the globe shattered its oily contents over his nape and on to his shoulders.

Cornelius turned on Bruno in a rage. "What the fuck you think that is going to do, arsehole? I'm going to shove one of those balls down your throat," he threatened seeing the next one in Bruno's hand and about to be thrown.

"One," Bruno counted as he threw the globe hitting the chef square in the chest. "Two," he stated calmly as the chef lumbered towards him. "Three," he barely got the word out before Cornelius crumbled at the knees and dropped to the ground. "Four" as the fat chef fell flat on his face, completely unconscious.

"Don't worry," Bruno held up his hands to calm the girl. "You'll be alright now. He won't hurt you anymore." He couldn't help but wince upon seeing her swollen cheek and battered eye. "Go home now and tend to your wounds. I'll take care of him." She didn't move, just stared blankly at the chef sprawled in the dirt of the alley with the drool dangling from the corner of his mouth. "Go home girl, this is no place for you now!" Bruno ordered her.

Reaching into his robe he pulled out a little rolled up pouch that he laid out on the ground and spread each side outward so that it unfolded evenly. Inside were a series of instruments; siccators, forceps, a scalpel and a few other assorted nameless contraptions that Bruno had personally designed. He looked up to see the girl staring horrified at his little pouch, thinking them to be tools of torture. "Don't worry little one, in my order we all receive medical training. He will recover far better than you would, had I not stopped him. Now go home, you don't want to see this."

"Yes I do," she replied firmly. "He was a bad man."

"This is not something for young children to witness. Now go! I insist."

"I am not a child," she battled back. "I'm old enough to survive on the street, which makes me old enough to stay where I wish."

"Do you not understand? I'm going to do something to him so that he will never be able to hurt another girl again. Trust me; you don't really want to see this."

The girl knelt down on the ground beside Bruno and rested her hand on his. "I will help. My name is Maria."

"Maria, you have to understand that to me this man is known simply as lust, one of the seven deadly sins. I have to punish him for that. Even the Emperor Rudolf wants me to punish him." Bruno felt compelled to explain his actions as if the girl's hand was drawing a confession out from him. Realizing that there was no way he was going to convince her to leave, he quickly set about performing the surgery while the chef was still under the effects of the anesthetic. Completed in less than half an hour, taking care to see that there was no bleeding when he had finished, Bruno pulled Cornelius's pantaloons back up over his waist and leaned him upright against the wall in the alley where he would eventually awaken.

"Thank you Maria, you were a great help to me but you can go now. We are done here."

Her eyes widened into large saucers "I have no place to go. If you leave me here he will come after me when he awakens and he will kill me for what you have done."

Admittedly, she was wise well beyond her age; Bruno had to take her valid argument into consideration. She definitely was right. Though Cornelius might never admit to anyone what had been done to him, he was a hot tempered man that would exact revenge by any means he could. Under the Emperor's protection, Bruno would be untouchable, leaving only the girl that would be made to pay a price. "Come with me then and I'll see what I can do. No promises though. If I can find someone to take you in, then you'll have to go immediately. Do you understand?"

"Yes," she smiled up at him, looking into his eyes like a puppy looks at its master.

32

Hradcany: The Castle

"It's the talk all over the palace," Caesar announced to Yakov whom had just risen and was now rinsing his face in the gold laver that sat in the corner of his room.

"And where is this chef now."

"Apparently he staggered into one of the ministry buildings early this morning and someone recognized him from the castle. They took him immediately to the Wincelas Hospital."

"I presume then that he will no longer be a concern of ours," Yakov stated quite blandly.

"He claims to have been attacked by the Golem," Caesar repeated one of the rumors that had been circling. "But I looked at the map model and where it happened placed it directly in the center of the star. It wasn't even close to either the fifth or eleventh sites."

"Nor should you have expected it to have been, Master Nostradamus," Yakov responded quite coolly.

"You know it wasn't the Golem," Caesar remarked quite sheepishly. "I think…"

Yakov interrupted him. "You don't have to continue, I know what you think. It is not something we need talk about."

"I think we do," Caesar insisted. "I think it was meant to happen. I think my father might have actually seen it happen."

"And what do you think he saw?"

Caesar felt compelled to sit down on the corner of the bed, feeling somewhat uncomfortable with what he was about to talk about, as he actually squeezed his legs together as if he was feeling a sharp pain. "It was the Emperor's doctors that tended to him when he arrived. They say there is a secrecy to be kept between doctors and their patients but it would appear they couldn't wait to report this back to the Emperor."

"And what was that," Yakov was growing slightly impatient with the drawn out answer.

"He was cut," Caesar declared. "He'll be singing like a choir boy from now on."

"Then I commend his attacker's restraint," Yakov applauded. "From what I heard of the man, it was a punishment meted out fairly."

"A right good job his attacker made of it too," Caesar added.

"And the prophecy?"

"It had to do with Giordano last night. I told him that my father had clearly indicated that a priest with his shaven head would do something considered both wrong and right, and that he would do something outside of the law because of his anger. There would be both a man and a woman involved. He would cut them both."

"But we only have a man being cut in this instance," Yakov pointed out.

Caesar hesitated before correcting him. "Actually, there is a young girl in the Castle that appears to have returned with Giordano last night. Her face is quite cut. It would look like someone had been beating upon her."

Yakov smiled as he fastened his doublet. "I see. And what is your opinion of the events. Let's be open about our suspicions."

"I believe that Giordano may have rescued her from being attacked by Cornelius the chef. I also know that many of the orders train their priests in the castration technique. Then they're the ones that have to choose which choir boys have to go under the knife. I think Giordano may have been trained as one."

"Your intuition is growing stronger every day," Yakov congratulated him. "I think you are right about it all. I even think you're father's quatrain is sublimely telling me that sometimes one has to do evil in order to achieve good. But if I was to sit in judgment, then I would think that whoever may have done such a thing to the chef was doing good in order to achieve a greater good. It would have been easy to justify for the chef to have been slain. But his attacker demonstrated restraint and in many ways, compassion. I have no issue if that's what you really desire to know, Caesar. Now pass me my robe, I think it's time we join everyone else."

"Then you are not mad at him?"

"Why should I be? No one has even made the accusation that he did anything. Therefore as far as I'm concerned, he's done nothing wrong. You may tell him so."

Caesar sucked his lower lip nervously. It had been his intention all along to act as intermediary on behalf of Giordano. Caesar started towards the door.

"And Caesar," Yakov called after him. "Next time that Giordano wants to know if I'm mad at him, tell him to come to me personally."

Caesar tucked his tail between his legs like a scolded schoolboy and departed from Yakov's presences. Yakov shook his head once his companion was gone, wondering what things they would be doing next now that he had not vented his displeasure over this incident. He was certain he'd find out once he joined them and equally he knew that it was going to be a very long and tedious day ahead for all.

§ § § § § §

Bruno found out very quickly that undertaking Maria's welfare was going to become a full time habit. Owing him her life, she tagged along everywhere he went, so much so, that Giordano felt he was wearing a second shadow. Yakov had made it clear that day that she had become his responsibility and his alone. At first Bruno resented her constant presence but her equally constant smile and fascination in everything he did and said, soon found a place in his heart. Or it may have been his ego, but either way, the thought of having an eager young disciple appealed to him. Even the Emperor appeared to have taken a liking to the young urchin, providing her with new clothes so that she did not appear totally out of place in the castle surroundings. He made certain to inform everyone that he did it for no other reason but to save his friend Giordano Bruno from the embarrassment the ragamuffin would garner him, but that explanation was betrayed by the frequent smiles and waves Rudolf would shower upon his young guest.

That afternoon, Yakov, Giordano and Bruno combed the streets of Mala Strana, convinced that the Golem had to be hiding in the vicinity. But the possibilities were endless. Over the past few centuries, towering structures had been erected as part of the ever sprawling expansion of the academy. It was impossible to check each one. There had to be another way.

"We need your intuition more than ever," Yakov turned to Caesar for help. "The fact is that we will not find the Golem if we continue to search like this. We have no idea even where to start."

"It does seem rather hopeless," Bruno agreed. "Hopeless," Maria echoed.

"And is that your total assessment of the situation," Caesar turned on her.

"Only if you keep looking here," she added.

"And what makes you so certain of that," Caesar was critical of her impertinence.

"When it comes to hiding in this city's buildings, people like me know every place there is," she stood her ground. "You don't pay any attention to us, but where do you think we go during the times you don't want to see us in the streets. Do you think we just disappear, vanish into thin air?"

"Of course not!" he rebuffed her. "But that doesn't mean you could possibly know every place to hide in this city either."

"Most of them though," she smirked devilishly.

"Better listen to her, Caesar, she is an authority on such things," he cautiously advised his colleague. "And what she doesn't know, I found her to be a very quick learner."

"Still, she couldn't possibly know every place in Prague."

"Maria, where do you think we should look?" Bruno asked her point blank.

"Most of the old buildings in Hradcany have lofts and belfries accessible from the outside. I know of one building where several families reside. No one even knows they're there. They're always under renovation. So there's plenty of scaffolding to climb."

"It does sound like the more appropriate place to hide," Yakov confirmed. "Close enough to Mala Strana that he could move back and forth undetected and perfectly situated for access to Rudolf."

"And how is Hradcany going to prove any easier to search?" Caesar was not about to concede to the young girl.

"Less buildings for one," Bruno defended her.

"And that means when the time is right, you will be able to better focus and point us in the right direction." Yakov was convinced that Caesar would prove to be the solution to their problem.

"Why do you believe in me so much?"

"Because I know you! I know and understand why we were brought together. I know that you are the key to everything we do. You only have to believe in yourself."

"I want to believe, Kova but I am not my father. You all want to continuously confuse me with him."

"Personally," Bruno put his around Caesar's shoulders," I don't believe in your father. But I do believe in you,"

"I believe in you too," Maria added.

"Do you have to repeat everything he says," Caesar asked her.

Peering out from behind Girodano she answered honestly, "Yes."

"The three of us will succeed, Caesar. When we are together, there is nothing stronger. Believe!" Yakov held out his knuckled fist for the others to place theirs against it and to recite their vow of unity. "One heart, one soul, one mind, we three of a kind," they recited together.

"Four of us," Maria threw her hand on top of theirs.

§ § § § § §

The following day, Giordanno was handed a message marked and sealed in strictest confidence that he unceremoniously unfurled in front of everyone, much to the horror of the courier.

"I was instructed that you were to read that in private." the man's voice quivered.

"These are my boon and trusted companions," Bruno lectured the courier. "You've intruded on our meal and now you expect me to run off in secret and read this? Whatever is meant for me is also meant for them. Unless there is something that your master wished to hide, which is even more reason for me to open it in front of them. Now be quiet and let me read, but stay where you are and don't go anywhere, I may have a message for you to take back."

"Good news?" Caesar asked rather doubtfully.

"About as good as this fish we're eating," Bruno screwed up his face in displeasure.

"Well perhaps if the kitchen didn't suddenly have a need for a new chef, the fish would have been better," Yakov added to the discourse.

"Is that humor I detect, Kova," Bruno latched on to Yakov's comment, the first word that Yakov had exchanged with him concerning the incident.

Yakov didn't reply, preferring to return to consuming his meal and avoiding the topic once more.

Holding the parchment out in front, Bruno read certain parts aloud. "Requests the honor of my presence…Now there's humor if I ever heard it. Matters of grave importance…The man's being exiled from the city; it couldn't be graver than that. Concern for my well-being…That would be a first. Oh, this part is good. In possession of documents that represent an endangerment and threat to my life…Now where do you think he got those from? And this last part is very enticing. Come alone if you wish to preserve your life…Now I can't see how there could be a better way to end a letter." Bruno turned on the courier with a fierce look of anger. "Tell you master that I have not yet made up my mind whether I wish to see him or not. I will send him word whichever way I decide. Now get out of here before I show you some of my alchemist tricks and turn you into a frog."

The messenger tore out of the room terrified. Stories of Giordano Bruno's experiments had grown to legendary proportions, especially over the last few months. Bruno knew instinctively the inferred threats being leveled against him by the Cardinal in the letter were in direct reference to accusations of using the black arts.

"Turn you into a frog?" Caesar laughed. "Did you see the look on his face? He actually believed you!"

"Superstitious lot, the whole bunch of them," he answered in a fit of anger. "How dare he threaten me? I've lost my stomach for this meal. I have to see the Emperor."

"I'll come with you," Maria stood up from the table.

"No! You stay here; I must talk to him alone." Bruno was gone from the dining hall almost as quickly as Maria had sat herself down feeling rejected.

"He's not angry at you," Yakov consoled her. "He's angry with those that keep threatening him no matter how much he does to earn his clemency."

"Do you think they will not offer him the pardon if we succeed in our mission?" Caesar felt a wave of compassion for his clerical companion.

"They cannot," Yakov revealed. "He represents everything they must destroy. A free thinker amongst them is the most dangerous of adversaries. Even more so than the plethora of reformists that are changing the face of their religion. They only ask the question of why they do the things they do in an effort to modernize them and involve the people they're meant to serve, whereas Giordano raises the question as to whether there is even a point to their beliefs. He's willing to question the existence of God."

"He's in trouble," Caesar commented, his chin tucked towards his chest.

"Yes he is. And he knows it."

"Kova, do you think it's wrong that I kept the truth from him?"

"You know something?"

"My father's quatrains again. He hasn't given me anything yet to find the whereabouts of the Golem, but it's as if he wanted to tell me about Giordano's future."

"When you care for someone, sometimes it is best not to tell them everything."

"I've known it for quite some time now." Caesar's eyes clouded over with a mist as he thought about it. "I didn't know what to do. So I've remained quiet about it. I thought perhaps it could change. That somehow we could do something to alter the future. But in my heart I know that's not possible. My father always saw what would happen, not what might. I know that Century V Quatrain twenty-nine was referring to Giordano. This is what he said, *'His liberty is not to be recovered, the one who inhabits the black shall be branded a fierce and wicked villain, once the matter that started with the bridge has all been opened and cleared, There in Venice, the republic shall take out its anger on him.'* They're not going to stop once this is all over. They're going to find a way to get him to Venice and then they're going to put him on trial."

"Then as his friend, you must keep him from going to Venice. I would not tell him why. Just do it for Giordano."

"But it's inevitable. My father cannot be wrong! He was never wrong!"

"Nevertheless, he did not say when. It could be a long time from now. You can see to it that it remains a very long time from now." Yakov watched closely the expression on Caesar's face. It did not lighten but instead became more dour. "There's something else you're not telling. You know when, don't you?"

"I didn't want to. But after I received that first quatrain referring to Giordano's death, I tried to do what my father used to do, creating a trance like state where I could access other visions. I shouldn't have. I shouldn't know! I didn't' want to know."

"When," Yakov asked firmly.

"Don't make me say. Please, don't make me."

Maria stroked Caesar's hand gently, understanding well beyond her age the trauma that Caesar was suffering. He tried to flash her a smile but it was hard enough to stem the flow of tears that were swelling up inside.

"I know what you're not trying to tell me," Yakov reassured him. "I know I am not long for this world either. It's okay. You're father hasn't told you anything I haven't already seen."

"You weren't mentioned in the next quatrain, Kova. You were gone by then. There was only Giordano and I left; the Gaul and the Italian. No mention of you. I'm so sorry, Kova."

"Don't be. It's not your fault. It's not anyone's fault. It is fate and no man can stop death when his time has come. I presume it was one of your father's early quatrains."

"How did you know?"

"As I told you, I'm beginning to understand how your father thought. He was very direct early on, providing what would happen and much of his later quatrains were merely explanations of how they would come about. He assembled them like a mason constructs a building. First the foundations are laid, then the layers are added brick by brick."

"It was early in his writing. The first century, the fifty-first quatrain. *'Chief are Aries, Jupiter and Saturn, mutations of the Eternal God, then after the turn of the century the evil times return, and the Gaul and the Italian incredible emotions.'* It's horrible."

Innocently, Maria continued to stoke his hand. "Please explain it to me," she requested.

Caesar took a deep breath and exhaled in an even deeper sigh. "The Greek and Roman gods of death and destruction take over. There is no God of love and mercy left. He's been changed, converted into this vengeful being that plunges the world into evil after the turn of the century. Eleven more years and horrible times begin again. And something horrible happens to Giordano. I know it at that time and it tears me apart inside. I suffer along side of him, even though his suffering is physical and mine is emotional."

With childlike simplicity Maria was able to interpret and analyze Caesar's comments.

"But you live Master Caesar. And you will avenge my poor Giordano. You will."

Another deep breath and Caesar snorted it through his nostrils, firming up his resolve. "Yes, I will."

§ § § § § §

"What do you mean you don't know about any of this," Bruno shouted in defiance at the Emperor. "You know everything that goes on in your city Rudi. Don't tell me different."

The Emperor hesitated before continuing. "It's complicated."

"Complicated? He's threatening my life and you're telling me it's complicated."

"Perhaps next time you'll think twice before you go and castrate someone who knows your identity," Rudolf shouted back. "Did you really expect him to remain quiet about having his manhood severed by some maniacal priest?"

"You were in agreement with me that he had to be punished. I don't remember you telling me not to do it!"

"Since when do I encourage you to leave a trail? I expected you to be more discrete!"

"For God's sake Rudi, he was about to rape a young girl. The man was an animal. I treated him like such."

"The man is a man, Giordano. Exercizing what men do. Do you really think anyone cared about the girl? He knew he'd get no satisfaction from me, so he's taken his charges against you to the one man he knew would give him satisfaction. They have a signed affidavit that it was you. From what I understand Calabrese has gone out and secured letters from anyone you may have harmed. Some bank clerk that now claims you used witchcraft to make him ill. They've tied together the comatose boy with your presence in a tavern that night. He can talk now; did you expect him to remain quiet forever? And God knows what people like Maisel might have told the Cardinal about you? You've placed yourself in a fine mess now."

"I noticed you have excluded yourself from any of this." Giordano paced the floor rapidly as he contemplated his next move.

"Giordano, you know I love you like a brother, but I cannot be your keeper. And I'm certainly not about to place my neck in a noose alongside yours."

"A brother would!"

"I will help where I can, but I can only act in the background. I cannot draw any suspicion to myself. You have to understand that."

"What I understand is that there is no justice in this world. When men of an evil nature can rule over our actions and punish those that stand up against their cruelty, then this world deserves to be damned. And when friends can no longer be friends because they fear more for their own safety than that of others, then what hope is there for it to ever get better."

"Don't try my patience," Rudolf warned. "I have been a friend to you beyond the scope and endurance of most mortals. But you demand an almost inhuman sacrifice of anyone that befriends you. I am sorry if you feel I have deserted you."

"I am sorry that you felt a need to desert me," Giordano threw back the words in the Emperor's face.

Pointing a finger in Bruno's direction, Rudolf gave his instruction. "Do what you must and do it quickly. I will keep the wolves at bay. But I do not want to know about it and I do not want any trail leading back to this throne. Are we clear?"

"Perfectly."

33

Prague: Lichten Palace

There was a knock at the chamber door, which stirred the Cardinal who had been dozing on and off from his New Testament readings. "One moment," he shouted towards the entrance as he straightened his robes and rose from his chair. Proceeding to the door he drew back the bolt and opened the door only to find Giordano Bruno standing there all by himself.

"Giordano," he exclaimed surprised. "I was not expecting you." Calabrese popped his head outside his suite, looking in both directions for any sign of his steward but the hallway was empty. "You are alone?"

"They told me to proceed directly to your room when I announced myself below." It was a lie, but one which Giordano had concealed well. Calabrese could find no trace on his face that betrayed the truth. He had used the drainpipe as a ladder to get back into his old room and from there headed down the hallway to where the Cardinal resided. Sensing no imminent danger, Calabrese relaxed and invited his unexpected guest into his room. The Cardinal motioned for Bruno to take a seat directly across from his chair, divided only by the small low table that stood between.

"I'm glad you came, Giordano, but I had thought you would have at least sent a messenger first agreeing to meet."

"I am here without anyone else's knowledge back at the castle and I want it to remain that way, Excellency. They would be suspicious of me if they knew I had arranged to meet."

"Of course, of course," Calabrese agreed fully with him. "All this time and they still don't trust you. That is the way it always is my son, with those that are unified against the Church. They will never accept you as one of them. I'm glad you have come to see that for yourself."

"I realize that now, Excellency, and I fear that they have grown too powerful. In some respects the Frenchman is more dangerous than the Jew."

Calabrese thought he detected a hint of disdain in Bruno's voice as he mentioned the others.

"Ah, so you have come to recognize the younger Nostradamus's ability. Most thought it was the father that had to be considered dangerous, but the son is a far greater a threat. He can actually make sense of that gibberish his father generated."

"It's incredible to hear him. Everything he says comes to pass. I swear it's almost satanic. And he talks of nothing else but the destruction of the mother Church. I might have my disagreements, but never have I sought its annihilation. You must believe me, Excellency. That never was and never would be my intention."

"I know you to be a good man at heart, Giordano, but you have done so many things of late that I have been forced to question that opinion." The Cardinal held his handkerchief to his cheek as if to suggest he was heartbroken by the revelation.

"Only in an effort to gain their trust, Excellency you must understand that. But I see now that was never to happen."

"It is never too late to gain wisdom, my son. God can forgive you for your sins if you truly repent."

"And my sins have been many," Bruno confessed. "I will need absolution for them; I cannot deny them any longer."

"I will hear to your confessions myself." The Cardinal was most pleased the Bruno had come to him in this state. Desperation made him malleable and the Cardinal was an expert in influencing others to his will.

"No, Excellency, you don't realize how long the list of sins actually is."

"I do, Giordano, and I was grieved at the length of that list when it was made apparent. I feared we had lost you completely."

"I need absolution for all of them," Giordano pleaded. "Each and every one if I am to retain my soul."

"Fear not, my son." Calabrese patted the little wooden box that he kept on the low table. "In here I have kept all the matters pertaining to your sins and whatever grievances have been lodged against you are merely words on paper that are contained within. If necessary we will deal with each one separately. I promise you that."

Falling to his knees, Bruno lowered his forehead until it touched the shoes of the Cardinal. "Thank you, father, thank you. I don't know how to convey my sincere gratitude for your act of kindness."

Calabrese placed his hand on the back of Bruno's head, acknowledging his acquiescence. "All will be taken care of my son. But first we must discuss another situation that has come to my attention." Placing his hands on Bruno's shoulders he helped the wayward priest back on to his feet and then steered him back to the chair.

"Certainly, Excellency, if I can help by any means."

"It is a most serious grievance that has been brought against the Kahana."

Bruno pricked his ears as soon as he heard the mention of Yakov.

"I will need a second witness to confirm the accusation and I believe that you should be that man, having known his movements and whereabouts better than anyone these past few months."

"In any way I can be of service, Excellency. I am you humble servant." Bruno kept his head bowed as he responded.

"Good. Good. It is a strange charge but one that I can understand totally why the mayor of the Jewish Quarter had to bring it to my attention. It would appear that his wife and the Kahana were engaged in an adulterous act. They were alone together for some time in her house and only by the observations of a dutiful neighbor has the truth been revealed. I never thought it possible that a man of that nature would succumb to the weakness of the flesh but obviously he is a sinner at heart."

"But surely that would be a matter for their own religious court," Bruno inferred that the Church had no jurisdiction in the matter but did not press the point.

"Normally it would have been," the Cardinal agreed, "But it would appear that neither the wife, nor the Kahana are considered Jews by definition of their courts. They are both Karaites and therefore not subject to their rulings. Therefore the case is passed on to the state legislators, and since this man is here only because of a special request of the Church, he is entirely under our jurisdiction. We have the ability to pass sentence upon him and the unfaithful wife."

"Quite a serious charge, especially considering the penalty under our code is death." Bruno did not display a shred of concern or agitation, even when acknowledging the death sentence, a fact which pleased and impressed Calabrese greatly.

"Yes, it would be," he confirmed. "But all I have is the neighbor's sworn statement in that box. That is not enough! I need a second witness whose testimony would be beyond scrutiny. You must have known that he went to see her. I need your testimony Giordano to seal his fate. Do this for us and all is forgiven. We will welcome you back with open arms, a free man to do as you please."

"It is not as if he doesn't deserve it," Bruno testified. "I do know he went to see the wife with lust in his heart. He had talked about nothing else after the first time he met her. She was young and beautiful, and he knew he had power over her since she was one of his own subjects. I pray though that you show the woman some leniency, Excellency. She would have been powerless against him, and unable to refuse his advances. Please promise me that you will take that into consideration."

"Of course, of course, my son," Calabrese reassured him. "You may testify on her behalf, just as you have done now. I'm certain the judge will have clemency under the circumstances and not punish her with death. You will have done a good thing by defending her. We do not want the blood of innocents on our hands."

"Only the guilty, Excellency, and there is much that Yakov Kahana is guilty of."

It was an open invitation for the Cardinal to rant endlessly about the evil that the Kahana represented to the Church. Bruno sat attentively hanging on every word the Cardinal spewed out his disdain for the man. The venomous hatred he bore him knew no bounds and it poured from his mouth like a river heading to the sea. Every so often Bruno would throw in a word of consent and agreement, confirming and endorsing what the Cardinal had to say. Once Calabrese had completed his rhetoric, he asked for Giordano's opinion regarding his accusations.

"Excellency, if the man is truly in possession of the knowledge you have stated, he is clearly a threat to the existence of our Church. With a word he would have the power to extinguish our flame. That is power far beyond the limits of comprehension and not even God would ordain such a thing. Only Satan himself would have sent such a man into the world."

"You understand Giordano. He is the greatest danger we have ever faced and for him to rise in glory and esteem once the city is saved from this creature that has been threatening it, would finally provide him with the platform from which he would begin his preaching to the world. And like sheep the people would listen to him. That is the nature of the masses. And all the good we've done would be swept away. He would rise above us all. He is the Antichrist! He is the one we must fear and destroy!"

"Imagine all that knowledge and power in one man. Inconceivable that it would be placed into the mind of an unbeliever. Just think if you were in possession of that knowledge, Excellency." Bruno dangled the carrot in front of the Cardinal.

"Even in one as dedicated as I am to our Lord, Jesus Christ, I would not know how to deal with the truths that would be revealed to me. But I do know that I would not betray the Church. I would have acted far more responsively and been far more deserving than this Jew with his ancient blood lines."

"Yes, it should have been you, Excellency."

"You're right Giordano. It should have been me! Will you pledge to me to right this grievous wrong. Will you guarantee that you will stand against this man in a court of law and provide the testimony of his sins to the tribunal so that he may be punished accordingly? For all our sakes he must be executed!"

"I give you my word, Excellency."

"Swear to me in the Lord's name that you will purge yourself of your sinning ways by doing this act of extreme piety in the name of the Holy Church and our Lord. Swear to me Giordano."

"In the name of the Father, the Son and the Holy Spirit, I swear I will do what is right in the eyes of the Lord. I will not fail," Bruno declared boldly.

"Then let us seal our pact; a drink to celebrate your exoneration and return to the fold."

"A drink then," Bruno agreed heartily.

"I will get two glasses, the bottle is over there." The Cardinal pointed to a ruby cut-glass bottle standing on a shelf over by the corner. Bruno stood and went to retrieve the bottle while Calabrese removed two glasses from his desk over on the other side of the room.

Sitting back down in their respective chairs, the Cardinal stretched out his hand to retrieve the bottle from Bruno. "I will pour if you don't mind."

Bruno deferred to the elder, knowing full well that it was a sign that he wasn't fully trusted. There was always the chance he could tamper with the glasses once the drinks were poured.

"No offense of course," Calabrese stated, "Just a force of habit on my part."

"No offense taken," Bruno happily turned the bottle over to the Cardinal.

Guillermo Calabrese poured out two drinks into the glasses and stoppered the bottle immediately afterwards. He carefully picked up both glasses and offered one to Bruno. "To our mutual understanding," Calabrese recited. "May God smile down upon us for what we are about to do."

"To the Power and the Glory," Bruno began, and then completed in unison with the Cardinal, "Forever and ever."

Putting the glass to his lips, Calabrese watched carefully over the top of the glass to ensure that Bruno was imbibing his drink. Only when it was half gone, did he start to down his own glass.

"So tell me Excellency, "Bruno inquired, "how was it possible that this line from which the Kahana stemmed still exists?"

"That my son is one of the major conundrums of our world. For if, as we teach, Jesus was the last to be called the son of David, then how could it be possible that there is another line that makes that claim. It cannot be. And if it is true, then it cannot be tolerated."

"So like others that have made similar claims, it is only befitting that we cleanse the world of their hypocrisy and blasphemy."

"The Albigensian Heresy was such a situation. They denied that Jesus was the son of God. Some even went as far to claim he had children by Mary Magdalene and she brought them to France. Can you imagine, our Lord having children by a prostitute? How were we to be expected to let them live to spread these foul lies. Like the rest of the Cathars, their knowledge was imperfect and threatened the existence of the one true Church of the Lord. And as always, with spiritual guidance, we did what was deemed necessary!"

"And yet, they claim to have had verification of their lies. Documents that proved that the things they said were true?"

"Nothing more than lies and deception, my son; whatever false documents there may have been were burned during the excision."

"So even if they did exist, then we ensured that they were destroyed."

"Of course, we could not have it any other way! You are beginning to sound as if you have regrets Giordano. You care too much for the pursuit of knowledge. It has always been your failing drawing you ever closer to the flames. You must learn that there are some things that man is not meant to know."

"Why, Excellency? Did Jesus ordain that we must be kept in ignorance in order for the Church to be able to control the masses?"

"I know it is you nature Giordano to vex people but this in neither the time nor the place for your obstinacy. I thought we were of an understanding?"

"We are," Bruno assured him. "I merely am agreeing that there are matters the people shouldn't know. They would not know how to handle the information. It is best that we spoon feed them only enough to keep them satisfied and to let us deal with the issues that are beyond their comprehension."

"Yes, I agree with you there. Another drink, my throat is feeling awfully parched."

"I'd love another, Excellency. Most generous of you!"

Calabrese thought he may have detected a hint of a mocking tone, but dismissed it and poured another pair of drinks into the glasses. Bruno raised his glass in a salute then quickly downed his, smacking his lips loudly as he put the glass down.

"A good brandy is made to be savored, Giordano. One should drink it a little more slowly."

"I will keep that in mind for the next one Excellency."

"I don't recall this bottle having such a burning sensation as it goes down. That is a good sign that a fine draught is aging nicely."

"It does warm as it goes down," Bruno agreed.

"So where was I?"

"You were talking about how it wasn't fair that the truth and knowledge was possessed by the wrong people. That it should only be you and not them in possession of it!"

"No, I wasn't saying that at all. You're confusing me. Where was I? Why can't I remember? This brandy is much stronger than I recall." Calabrese finished his glass then poured himself another. "I can even feel the sensation in my stomach. Do you feel that Giordano?"

"I can't say that I do," Bruno responded.

"I'm feeling so dizzy. Not like a couple of glasses of brandy should do this to me. Help me to my bedroom. I must lie down."

Giordano helped the Cardinal to his feet and tucked his shoulder beneath Calabrese's arm. Supporting most of his weight, Bruno helped the faltering Cardinal into his bedroom where he laid him gently down upon the four-poster bed, with its white lace filigree.

"I don't understand it," Calabrese apologized. "I feel so weak. I usually don't react this way, even to strong drink."

"It's perfectly understandable." Bruno helped the Cardinal out of his red frock which he then laid neatly on the chair beside the bed. With some difficult he was able to pull the sleeping gown over the Cardinal's head and then unroll it down to his knees. Pulling the covers out from underneath the prone body he was then able to tuck Calabrese neatly into his bed and prepare him for the long sleep ahead.

"Giordano?"

"Yes, Excellency."

"I think I am dying?" he stated and questioned simultaneously, his mind no longer able to discern what was real.

Bruno watched as the old priest's eyes fluttered and dimmed; the pupils becoming dilated and confused. Death was impending. "Yes, you are," he answered, sounding detached from the events taking place. "Forgive me father, but I am no Judas. You were wrong to think that you could make me into one! Those are good people that you wanted me to condemn and though my life may be of little value, the Kahana's is worth far more than you would ever understand."

The word slipped with some difficulty from the Cardinal's lips; the saliva beginning to pool at the corners of his mouth. "How?"

"Arsenic. I slipped the powder into the bottle when I retrieved if from the shelf."

"But you drank from it too. I saw you." The words were becoming slurred and hard to differentiate.

"An old apothecary's trick that I learned long ago. If you take a little bit of arsenic every day, you become immune to its effects. I knew you wouldn't drink unless you saw me doing so."

The eyes that peered up at him were now hollow, devoid of any semblance of consciousness, though the Cardinal was still breathing.

"Forgive me father, for I have sinned." Giordano made the sign of the cross across his chest and forehead. "I pray that you will understand that in order to save many, the death of one can be justified. You were envious of Yakov and you coveted his birthright. And envy is the deadliest of all the sins. Because of envy, a man will easily commit the other six. And as you revealed, in order for our mission to succeed, it was necessary first to defeat the seven deadly sins. I have done as you advised and now this city will be saved through our efforts." Bruno closed the bedroom door behind him as he left the Cardinal in a semi-comatose state. Within the hour he would be dead and by morning when the coroner filled in his report it would only say that

Guillermo Calabrese died peacefully through the night while he slept. Moving through the formal room of the suite, Bruno eliminated anything that could point to his visit. The glasses were returned to the drawer in the desk. The remaining brandy was poured over the balcony and the bottle returned to its place on the shelf. And finally all the papers were removed from the little wooden box on the table and shoved into one of the inner pockets lining his robe.

Nothing remained that could be used as incriminating evidence against himself or Yakov.

Locking the door to the suite from the inside, Bruno sauntered over to the balcony where he found a rose trestle within arm's reach that he could scale down to the gardens below. In the morning they would have to break down the door in order to discover why the Cardinal had not responded to their morning call. They would find him dead, lying peacefully in his bed. There would be no suspicion of murder. Everything had proceeded as planned.

34

Mala Strana: Petrin Hill

It had been a week since the death of Cardinal Guillermo Calabrese had been announced. As Bruno had anticipated, no mention of foul play was even hinted at. It took them almost the entire morning to batter down the solid oak door to the Cardinal's suite once his steward had raised the alarm that his master had not come down for morning prayers. Death through natural causes was the verdict. Finding him neatly draped under the covers of his bed, the royal physician could not come to any other conclusion. His heart had simply stopped.

Bruno refused to comment on the death, not even discuss how fortunate the timing had proven, though the amazing co-incidence of events was lost neither on Yakov nor Caesar. Easier to believe that although Giordano's relationship with the Catholic Church had become somewhat strained, he still could feel some remorse for one of the elders in the Holy See. The two of them respected Bruno's silence on the matter and decided not pursue it further.

Even the Emperor avoided raising the subject not only with Bruno but anyone that may have dropped the untimely event into conversation. That alone was a clear sign to everyone that knew Rudolf's penchant to go on for hours discussing anything that there was a good mystery behind the Cardinal's death and that the diagnosis of a simple death was anything but simple. Rudolf's behavior around Bruno had even become uncharacteristic, almost as if the two of them were purposely avoiding each other.

Though committed not to investigate further, Caesar more than anyone had knowledge of what may have transpired. The same night that the Cardinal had died, one of the quatrains practically bounded from his skull, so great was its pounding within his head that he screamed in agony when it appeared. But by morning he had made the decision that Century I, Quatrain thirty-nine would remain buried in his mind forever, never to be spoken of. Not even Yakov would be told about it. Whatever role Bruno may have played in the death, Caesar concluded it had to be done. Just as it had been foretold by the Quatrain, *'By night in his bed the Supreme one strangled, Deserved for he had corrupted too much the fair elect, By the three the Empire would substitute the glory, but he with neither card nor packet would put him to death.,'* Most of it was quite clear and Caesar knew that one of them had been responsible for the death. He could not decipher his father's intimation to the card and packet which would have eliminated two of them immediately from suspicion, but he knew in his heart that Yakov was incapable of such an act and he, though he certainly may have wished it, had certainly not done it. That just left Giordano without an alibi. But at the same time he concluded had his father wanted the murder to be stopped then he would have had his vision long before the actual event occurred. That not being the case, then it was inevitable and nothing more would be gained by pursuing it. Some things were just meant to happen. Who was he to say it should be any different?

So life in the castle continued normally and during the interceding days Bruno had made a point of having the body of the missing girl returned to her parents, fulfilling his promise to the mother that he would find a way to return her. Even the explanation seemed to satisfy the family, that she had been found in the Jewish Quarter and thinking her to be nothing more than another dead street waif, she was provided with a proper burial through the generosity of the mayor of the district. When she was finally buried in her family plot, Maisel had attended as an invited guest of her relatives, who wished to express their gratitude for all that he had done on her behalf and how he had gone to the trouble of having her exhumed at his own expense once he was made aware that she had parents that were eagerly awaiting her return. Bruno had decided judiciously not to stay long after the funeral, fearing that he would not be able to restrain himself from confronting Mordecai Maisel as he watched the girl's family lavish the mayor with their gratitude.

Leaving Yakov and Caesar to convey the Emperor's condolences, he and Maria took a coach to the park at Mala Strana, where he could clear his head and soothe the urge in his stomach that continuously tried to reflux the bile into the back of his throat whenever he thought of Maisel. As they rode through the city streets, Bruno turned his attention to his young protégé, as he started referring to Maria, beginning with her teachings in basic astronomy. If they were lucky, David Gans would already be at the observatory and he'd be able to point out the finer aspects of the heavens that Bruno felt completely unqualified to even touch upon. David had already earned a reputation as an excellent teacher and Bruno was eager to see how he'd fair with a female student, since among the circles of astronomers it was forbidden to teach the fairer sex such things. From Bruno's perspective it was a challenge to his friend to see if he was as open minded as he claimed to be.

Slipping the driver a few coins once the carriage reached the end of the road, Bruno led Maria up the hill, towards the observatory building which stood at its summit. They started to race each other at first, but attired in his priest's gown, Bruno quickly retired from the competition long before he was at the half way point. Whether it was the fact that he was beginning to feel his age, or that the thousand foot ascent was a miscalculation on his part, as the strain on his legs made it feel twice that distance, he wasn't certain but proudly acclaimed Maria as the winner and then settled into a much more leisurely pace. Maria fell back into stride until he came along side and they were able to walk together.

"Do you think that you will be able to find a home for me?" she asked once Giordano's breathing had returned to normal.

"I haven't been too successful, have I? I guess it will be necessary to double my efforts."

She stayed silent, not responding to his comment.

"You do want me to do so, don't you Maria?"

At first she squared her jaw and sealed her lips as if forcing herself to say nothing, her hands clenched as she did so. Then as if a damn had burst, the words shot from her mouth. "Why can't I stay with you?"

Bruno looked at her askew, as if too suggest she didn't know what she was saying. "Have you noticed something different about me?" he asked sarcastically. "Do I not look like a priest to you? Would that not suggest to you that I wouldn't be the most appropriate person to take care of you?"

"I don't care," she refuted his concerns. "It's not as if we would have to marry. I know you can't do that!"

"Wait a minute. Who said anything about marriage or anything related to that matter? Maria it would simply be inappropriate. A priest and a young girl would be frowned upon by everyone. And even though nothing would be happening, people would prefer to imagine everything would be happening and at some point they would find an excuse to lock you or me away on some trumped up charge. Trust me, over the years I have found myself to be an easy target for them. You don't want to have the same done to you!"

"I am fourteen, you know; almost fifteen. I'm old enough to be considered womanly."

"And when the time is right, I will work very hard in finding you a proper husband, and that is part of the reason I'm teaching you as much as I can, so even though you won't be entering a marriage with a dowry, at least you can bring with you knowledge and an education. To someone that already has money that might be exactly what he's looking for in a wife."

"I don't need some stuffy old fart."

"Who says he has to be old? I said wealthy. I never said old."

"Most men don't have any money until they're old."

"How do you reason that?"

"Just look at you or Master Kahana or Master Nostradame. The three of you aren't that old and none of you seem to have much of a pot. You're all friends of the Emperor and still you don't have any wealth to speak of."

"That's not exactly true," Giordano argued. "Caesar is actually quite well off from what I understand. Perhaps he'll take a fancy to you."

"I doubt that," she pierced a hole quickly to that thought.

"And why not?"

"Sometimes men can be so stupid," she shot an icy glare towards him. "Haven't you noticed how he looks at me?"

"Why would I do that?" Bruno was beginning to wonder who was teaching who by this point.

"Because if you looked, you'd see it was very different from the way you or Kova look at me."

"Is that so," Bruno now pretended to know what she was talking about, "But he didn't have a clue."

"You don't understand, do you?"

"I guess not," he finally admitted.

"When you look at me, you see me as a young girl, but still with the knowledge that I'm growing up quickly and you may not be able to be seen with me too much longer."

Bruno was surprised at her degree of insight. It was exactly how he viewed her. A girl at the threshold of blossoming and that was exactly when their relationship would become difficult.

"And when Master Kahana looks at me, he suddenly feels himself restricted; not knowing exactly what he can get away with saying or doing. Sometimes I catch him reaching out to me with an arm and then he quickly pulls it back in case his familiarity would be misinterpreted."

"I can understand that," Bruno defended Yakov's actions. "He is placed very high in his community. He can't permit any sort of scandal even if it wasn't the truth at all."

"But still, you admit he recognizes me as a young woman. But Master Nostradame, he looks in my direction but it's as if he's looking right through me. As if I'm not even there. It's as if in his mind he can reduce me to something that he doesn't have to deal with."

"Oh, I think you might be exaggerating," Bruno dismissed her comment.

"No, I'm not. It's true. I see it all the time."

"So what are you saying that he's not into women? I think I would have noticed that. Men have this natural ability to spot other men of a different persuasion."

Maria blushed as she watched Bruno struggle with the suggestion and knowing that he still hadn't understood her at all. She thought his fumbling with the thought was quite cute.

"That's not what I was talking about," she stopped him before he went any further. "I meant that he can look through people as if they don't exist. Other than you and Master Kahana, I don't think he sees or bothers with the existence of anyone else. Something has happened to him a long time ago, and I don't believe he can love. It's as if that part of his heart has been torn away and there's nothing but an empty space left behind."

Giordano thought carefully about what she had to say and went over his past conversations with Caesar. He especially thought about the nights at the inn when he was encouraging him to take a greater interest in the twins. Even then, it was as if he couldn't acknowledge their presence. He would squirm wildly to avoid the conversation. At the time he thought perhaps Caesar was merely a very private person when it came to that part of his life. He had never thought about the possibility that Caesar was incapable of feeling any sort of attraction to someone else. The though almost seemed inconceivable to Bruno. It could explain why Caesar didn't have anyone waiting for him when he returned to France. He never even mentioned having someone in the past. Now that he was paying particular attention to the facts, the only people that Caesar had ever made reference to in all the months they had been together were himself, Kova, and of course his father. That was strange!

"How did you ever get to be so clever," he demanded to know from Maria. "I seem to have missed the part where you grew out of being a little girl."

"I was never a little girl," once again she tried to explain to him, feeling somewhat exasperated. "No one on the streets is ever a child. You grow up immediately, or you die. There is no in between."

"Let me at least continue to delude myself in viewing you as an innocent child. Is that still permissible?"

"For a while," she nodded.

Bruno was relieved that they had reached the summit. He feared where the conversation may have led had it continued. Waving to Dimitri's guards posted at the entrance, he held the door open for Maria. They were in luck. David Gans had decided to spend most of the day at the location working on the star charts that he had spread over the three long trestle tables laid end to end.

"Look at this Giordano," he waved the arriving priest over to his side of the table. "I've been tracking this particular comet for just over three years now. It's just come back into view recently and now it's almost exactly in the same position as when I first observed it."

"David, take a moment to look up a second. I've brought a guest."

Gans looked in Bruno's direction and saw the young girl standing to his side. He quickly assessed her attributes; slim, attractive, with brunette hair that fell off her shoulders, and very young. "This one is a little younger than the rest, wouldn't you think," he chastised his friend.

"This is my student, David! As in protégé. Maria isn't a paramour if that is what you were implying."

Maria flashed a curious look at her self-stylized tutor. David Gans had only confirmed what had been one of her suspicions. Giordano was afraid of his feelings for her. When Bruno finally turned in her direction he found her wearing the broadest smile he had ever seen on a woman.

"Whatever you say, Giordano, now get over here and look at this."

Maria tagged along closely behind, and at the time, Bruno thought she may have been standing closer to him than normal. In fact it felt as if she was practically underneath him as he peered over the star charts.

"I've sketched the arc of the comet as it moves around the earth during the month that it was visible to the eye last time it was here."

"You know, the Muslims talk about a device using glass lenses that allows them to observe the stars much closer. If you could manage to secure one of these from the Sultan's connections, you might be able to watch these stars for much longer periods than you can, using the naked eye."

"Yes, and they believe in genies too!" Gans dismissed the invention as nothing more than another middle eastern legend. "But look. I've calculated the degrees of the comet's arc, and it's not a circle at all. It moves in an ellipse. Now that I know to complete a full trajectory the comet takes thirty-nine months, I merely had to extend the ellipse by a factor of thirty-nine in order to plot the orbit through the heavens."

"Assuming that the comet is always traveling at the same speed," Bruno argued. "And you have no way of knowing that."

"But I do," Gans insisted. "After twenty-seven years of observations I believe I can definitely state that everything in the heavens revolves around the earth at a uniform speed. Each object has its own set velocity but they remain constant."

"I think Kepler would defeat your argument right there," Bruno challenged Gans's calculations. "He'd simply state that the earth is not the center of the universe and therefore if the earth is in motion itself, then there's no way you could possibly measure the speeds of other objects because they would not be moving in the same direction of the earth at all times."

"And that is why Kepler is wrong! I've gone over the mathematical calculations hundreds of times. Everything is where it's supposed to be in the heavens at the times calculated. Therefore, that could only occur if the earth was stationary. The math does not lie!"

"But the universe does," Bruno pointed to the trajectory of the comet. "From the arc you've drawn on these charts, there is a substantial portion of its path that suggests it has sped far beyond the sun and even some of the constellations. In order to do that, there would have to be a celestial sphere beyond the stars. Right there you are challenging current dogma that says there's nothing beyond that sphere. Either your math is wrong, or we've been lied to!"

"Dogma taught us the earth was flat too. We've put an end to that belief a hundred years ago. I choose to believe there are more spheres beyond the seven we've been taught."

"And what do you choose to believe, Maria?" Bruno addressed his young companion.

"I believe we have enough problems on earth that need our attention without trying to resolve those in heaven."

"I think she's put us both in our place there, David. "Care to elaborate for her sake."

"Well, young miss, as I have explained on numerous occasions to Father Bruno there, you can only solve this world's problems if everyone is willing to believe in the same things and share a common understanding. Since there's nothing on this earth that's going to unite us in that manner then it behooves us to look towards the stars. Not only do they remind us of our own insignificance, they require us all to work together, Jew, Christian, Mohammedan, Buddhist or whatever else anyone might believe in, in order to comprehend the true nature of existence. And once we learn to work together, then we will be able to solve the problems of this world."

"See, Maria, it's as simple as that. Finding the answers up there gives us the answers we need down here."

"I really do believe you have to walk the streets that I came from, and spend some time living in the real world. Unless you can find food and medicine up there in the sky, nothing is about to change in my world."

"Forgive her David; she's not had the easiest of lives. I'm hoping to introduce her to a somewhat better world."

"Forgive her? There's nothing to forgive. She just proves my point that I have always lectured to my students. Women have no place in the sciences. It is a waste of time. They cannot understand nor comprehend the unfathomable mysteries of the universe. They lack the imagination required. Imagination is the key to unlocking the universe. That is why the mastery of the world will always be the domain of men."

Giordano braced him for the conflagration that he knew was about to be released.

Maria started moving towards the table, and Bruno quickly grabbed her by the hand to halt her advancement. Her eyes darted around the room looking for anything she could use as a projectile. "I am amazed that you have managed to live this long David," Bruno found himself needing both hands to restrain Maria. "If you could kindly find it in your heart to say something nice to appease her, it would be very considerate and in your own best self interest."

"Don't let her lay a hand on my charts, Giordano. If she damages them in any way there is going to be hell to pay!"

"I'll teach him what hell is," Maria unleashed a side of her personality that Bruno had not witnessed before.

"He didn't mean anything by what he said," Giordano tried to calm her down. "He's always saying stupid things like that. Why do you think his own community is trying to have him silenced?"

"What!" Gans screamed at his colleague. "What are you talking about Giordano? Who's trying to silence me? Is that what all these men posted around here are all about? This has nothing to do with an attack on the observatory, does it? What's going on Giordano? I demand to know right now!" Gans's screams and outbursts raised an alarm that brought Dimitri rushing into the observatory followed closely by the rest of his guards.

"What's going on," Dimitri raised his voice above the din, screaming louder than anyone else in order to command their silence.

"She's trying to destroy all my research!" Gans pointed an accusing finger at the girl. "Get her out of here. I don't need this kind of interruption right now. Everyone should just get out of here!"

"You're right David," Bruno couldn't agree more. "We should all get out of here at once, but not for the reason you're thinking. Because Dimitri, if you and all your men are in here then we have a serious problem."

Dimitri was about to answer that he still had one man posted outside when they all heard what sounded like the tormented wail of a wild animal caught in a trap.

"What the hell was that?" Gans questioned everyone in the room.

"I think that's him," Dimitri mobilized his men to rush back outside.

"I don't think it was," Bruno suggested an alternative. "I think he's out there but if you still had any men outside, I'm certain that was one of them sounding his death rattles."

"I demand to know what's going on!" Gans was appealing to anyone that was in a mind to talk to him but at the moment everyone appeared to preoccupied with other matters.

"Everyone back to the far wall," Dimitri ordered, his men having drawn their swords as he prepared to open the observatory door.

"Don't open it!" Bruno tried to dissuade him. "We stand a better chance if we all remain together. If we form a circle around David he won't be able to get to him but we'll be able to strike at him."

"Him, who?" Gans kept asking but received no answer.

"You're presuming that he'll find a way inside. I think its best we encounter him before he has a chance to get that close." Dimitri was still thinking like a military man. Rush the enemy on an open field and overwhelm him with sheer force of numbers.

Bruno was still adamant that they don't separate. "This is an observatory. It's made to open up in a hundred different ways. I'm certain if he tries every door and window on the roof he'll find one that isn't locked. He'll be in here with us while you and you men are searching outside. That's the truth of it!"

"Will someone please tell me what's going on," Gans repeated, nervously shaking from head to toe as he watched the guards scramble about the room checking for the presence of some unknown adversary.

Dimitri looked at Bruno as if to warn him not to tell Gans. He had been under strict orders from the Emperor to not let the astronomer know that he was being stalked.

Bruno chose to ignore the haunt of Dimitri's piercing black eyes. "It's not as if he wouldn't figure it out for himself once he had a look at the creature."

"What kind of creature is everyone talking about?"

"One that your former teacher and mentor would have been predisposed to create if he really had any power." Giordano had purposely been quite cryptic with his answer, just to see how David Gans would react.

"Are you referring to Rabbi Judah ben Loew? Why would he have anything to do with this?"

"Maybe because you're an embarrassment to him," Bruno snapped back. "Have you ever thought that your presence in his city, while expounding your one world, one people philosophy might be offensive to him? Or do you just think he'd overlook everything you do because you're just like a wayward son that doesn't know any better?"

"He was my teacher…he knew I had a greater love for the sciences than I did for religious teachings. He wished me well when I left. Why come after me now?"

"Of course he wished you well. What did you think he was going to say? That you're a fool! That you've slapped him in the face with your scientific arguments and are continuing to do so? That you wasted his time and then turned your back on him. That you deserve to be dead! I can go on if you'd like!"

"But why now?"

"You're about to release your major treatise on the universality of mankind and man's place in the universe, aren't you? That could be reason enough if you make your statement that there's no place for the old religions. You might as well have stabbed him in his heart; you'd have the same effect!"

"People don't kill people for making astronomical statements!" Gans still couldn't accept that he was being targeted by his old master.

"Have a good look around you David, of course that is if we manage to survive this day. People are constantly being killed for promulgating beliefs that run contrary to today's religions. You've angered some awfully important and powerful people."

"I hear something moving up on the top floor," Dimitri voiced his concern that they still couldn't pinpoint the exact location of the Golem. "How many ways can he get into this room?"

"There may be a dozen or more," Gans replied. The walls were built hollow with numerous passages so that the astronomers could move up and down freely without disturbing each other."

"Great. He could be using any one of them." Dimitri realized that he did not have a very defensible position. "We need to draw him out and deal with him then and there."

"That's why we should form a circle," Bruno insisted. "He won't be able to penetrate the circle if we keep it tight."

"But that means letting him get close before we can use our swords."

"What choice do we have?" Bruno awaited an alternative but none was forthcoming.

The captain ordered his men to encircle the target while Bruno and Maria stood off to one side in a safe corner that harbored no doors. Gans was still protesting when they pushed him into the center for his own good, still not fully comprehending the dangerous situation.

Swinging through the glass paned window, well over seven feet above the floor, the Golem landed on top of the trestle tables amongst the broken shards of glass that sprayed across the room. The move had caught everyone by surprise. They had been so fixated on watching the numerous doors that existed in the walls of the observatory that they had forgotten about all the other ways to enter that were more readily available.

"Don't break the circle," Dimitri ordered. "Stand your ground. He's not to get past us."

Standing like a giant beast on the tables, completely covered in his silver-black metallic leather armor, the guards looked small and ineffectual by comparison, waving their swords in the air while attempting to draw the Golem towards them. The Golem beat his chest and roared in anger, seeing his target crouched within the circle of steel blades, cowering with his head tucked between his forearms. The creature had failed to notice Bruno and the girl, compressed into the corner trying to remain inconspicuous, its focus entirely on the astronomer for the moment.

He walked along the top of the tables looking for a better vantage point from where he could snatch his prey, but as he moved the circle of soldiers rotated as well, always maintaining at least three men between Gans and itself. Another roar of anger, but this time it was terrifying enough to make some of the men quiver in their boots. From the corner came a sound like a whimper; not very loud but quite distinct from all the other sounds of the commotion. Maria suppressed the urge to scream in horror at the dark imposing sight of the creature but she was unable to stifle all but that little whimper that managed to escape from her throat.

The Golem turned and noticed the two of them cowering in the corner for the first time. All that they could see were the black soulless eyes peering at them through the split between the high collar of the armor and the bowl shaped cap he wore on his head. It took the creature several moments to register where he had seen Bruno before but once he had made the connection the expression in those eyes changed to absolute unbridled hatred. It was the same man that had tossed fire at him in the Church. The first man that had caused him to fear for his own life and at that moment the Golem forgot completely about the astronomer and only had one though on its limited mind. The priest had to die!

Lunging from on top of the tables, he had hold of Bruno in what was a seamless, fluid single motion. Bruno found himself being raised off the ground his feet dangling in mid air. The shock of the attack caused Maria to faint and slump to the ground but even that wasn't enough to draw the Golem's attention away from the priest that he held trapped in his huge gloved mitt.

Bruno could feel the air being crushed from his throat and knew time was running out. He acted instinctively, kicking repeatedly at the groin. No matter how competently plated the armor appeared to be, the fundamental law of tailoring was that you had to leave the seam between the legs free to move. It could only be lightly protected at best. He couldn't tell whether he had hurt the creature but he definitely knew that he had angered it plenty. Treating him like a rag doll, the Golem hurled Bruno several feet across the room into the wall. The impact knocked the wind out of him and he fell to the ground. The Golem was moving towards him quickly and he feared that at any second the final blow was about to be delivered.

The sound of the shot echoed through the observatory chamber as if it had been from a cannon. The smoke and burst of flame that swirled from the muzzle was enough to terrify the creature, even though the shot itself like most wheellock pistols missed by several inches. When it hit the plaster wall to the left of the Golem, it sprayed up enough cement dust that it stung sharply in its eyes and the Golem let out a howl of pain. Bruno used the opportunity to roll away from his attacker where he could see Dimitri with his outstretched arm, holding the weapon in his hand.

The momentary blindness of the creature provided the opportunity for Dimitri's men to charge towards the Golem, breaking their protective circle in order to do so. But once again they had underestimated the quickness and agility of the Golem as he leaped from where he was standing, bounded off one of the tables, and in one graceful motion scooped up the unconscious body of the girl and swung back out the window from which he originally entered. The soldiers were hapless to stop him. Even the most athletic of them would have been unable to match the jump to the window ledge in order to follow.

Dimitri charged to Bruno's aide, helping him back on to his feet. Giordano was still dizzy from the attack, not realizing yet what had transpired.

"Giordano," Dimitri snapped him back to full awareness. "He's got the girl! He's got Maria!"

"What are we waiting for? Let's get after him!"

"You heard the man," Dimitri shouted to his men. "I want that girl brought back alive. Go, go, go!"

"What's happening," Gans continued to ask annoyingly.

"Oh shut up already," Bruno hollered his voice cracking from the crushing force of the Golem and the resentment he was now feeling for his colleague whom was now safe while his Maria was in jeopardy. "Track him whatever way you can," he pleaded to Dimitri. "I need to go back to the castle. I have to get the others. Please find her. Please!"

"I'll do whatever I have to, Giordano," Dimitri clutched Bruno's shoulder. "My men will track him down to the ends of the earth if need be. You get your friends. We'll join up when we can." The two men raced out of the observatory and down the hill, each with a single purpose; save the girl.

35

Prague: Cathedral of St. Vitus

"Kova, Caesar, help me!" Bruno screamed as he came bursting into their quarters at the Castle. The desperation in his voice was obvious and he began to panic when they didn't respond immediately. He called out their names again and this time they appeared, the doors to their rooms opening simultaneously as they rushed to his aide.

"What's wrong, Giordano?" they asked, knowing immediately upon seeing his face that whatever it was it was extremely serious. Bruno tried to catch his breath to speak, but he was so overwrought that he was finding it difficult to say anything that made any sense in between his gulping lungs full of air.

"Calm down, speak to us," Yakov tried to comprehend what was happening. "We can't help you if you don't tell us what's going on!"

Bruno took in a massive breath trying to steady himself. "It's Maria," he was finally capable of saying. "He got her."

"Who's got her?" Yakov still couldn't make any sense out of what he was trying to say.

"The Golem," his voice shuddered. "He took her and we don't know where."

"This is crazy," Caesar offered his comment. "Why would the Golem want to take her? This doesn't fit in at all with what was on the Kabala Star."

"I'm telling you, he took her," Bruno repeated once more furious that they weren't responding to the urgency of the situation. "We have to do something!"

"Of course we'll do something," Yakov assured him. "But first I need you to settle down, tell us what happened and then we figure this out together."

"We went to the observatory. Gans was there. There was a commotion and all the guards came inside to see what was happening. That's when the Golem struck. He must have been waiting all that time, in a tree or somewhere close by, just waiting for the opportunity. Dimitri and his men encircled Gans. The Golem couldn't' get at him but he attacked me instead. There was a shot, everyone was shouting, they were all hysterical, and that's when he grabbed Maria and escaped from the observatory. By the time we got out of the building he was already gone and out of sight. I came running here. We have to do something."

"So he was shot then."

"No, Dimitri missed. The creature must have become frightened and escaped taking Maria."

"That would explain it," Yakov analyzed the events. "The Golem responds on primal instincts. The firearm would have scared him and he had to find an alternative to his instructions. He was going after Gans for the second time. The first time he was stopped by a young girl because he knew the Kabala Star contained a diversion with the intercession of the angel. He wouldn't have seen any difference this time either. Another angel, another diversion, thereby stimulating a change of tactics."

"He killed the last girl," Caesar blurted out.

"Was Maria staying calm?" Yakov needed to know.

"She had fainted," Bruno explained.

"Good, hopefully she'll stay that way. As long as she doesn't panic and start screaming like the other girl, then there's a good chance he won't kill her. With a little luck she'll stay unconscious for some time or at least feign to be so."

"She's a smart girl," Caesar tried to reassure Bruno. "She'll figure out what she has to do."

"But what are we going to do?" Bruno pleaded with them for their help.

"Caesar, we can't do this without you," Yakov reminded him. "I don't know how you do it, but right now we need you to focus on your father's quatrains and tell us where the Golem has been hiding out all this time. That's where he's going to take Maria. I'm certain of it!"

"Do it, Caesar. I know you can do it," Bruno beseeched his companion.

"It's no good! I can't call upon it on demand. I don't seem to feel or see anything."

"You have to," Bruno started shaking Caesar hysterically. "Even if you can't do it for her, you have to do this for me!"

"I'm trying Giordano. I really am," he tried to restrain Bruno from assaulting him further. "Wait! Wait! I think I see something. Yes, yes!" Caesar became excited by the sudden appearance of the quatrain. *'When the beast that is part of mankind, After great exertion and leaping shall come to speak, the lightning shall be harmful to the virgin as she's taken from the ground and suspended high in the air.'* It's got to be about her! I know it is!"

"But what's it mean," Bruno could no longer think straight so overcome was he with fear and anguish.

"What were the numbers," Yakov insisted on knowing.

"Century III, Quatrain forty-four. But why?"

"Your father was a clever man," he answered. "Even his numbering has a hidden meaning. Three and forty-four. What could forty-seven have to do with this? Why forty-seven?"

"What did you just say?" Bruno snapped out of his sense of helplessness.

"Forty-seven," Yakov repeated.

"I think I know where she is!" he exclaimed. "You said something about suspended in the air, right? Exposed to lightning. I know those words. Matthieu d'Arrus said them back in 1352. Don't you see, Arrus, Air, your father was playing with phonetics. Things that sound the same. I could kiss your father!"

"For God's sake, Giordano, what are you talking about," Yakov needed him to take a step back and to explain what he was referring to.

"The first architect that designed and worked on St. Vitus Cathedral was Matthieu d'Arrus. When he was dying he was concerned about the exposed metal structures in the roof. He said they'd attract lightning, so he made certain that the next architect would concentrate on the roof and towers, otherwise one storm and they could lose everything they had constructed thus far. The next architect was Peter

Parler. Don't you see, his last name, the French verb 'to speak.' Just like in the Quatrain. The beast will come to speak. It's not saying he'll literally talk. It's saying he'll go to where Parler spent the next forty-seven years of his life."

"My God! I think you're right," Yakov was overwhelmed by the evidence.

"You did it! You did it!" Bruno started shaking Caesar by the shoulders again but this time it was through sheer elation.

"And he'd have no problem moving in and out of the tower since the construction was never completed," Yakov was still thinking about the cathedral. "All that scaffolding in place for the last hundred years with so little work done that no one even pays any attention to it any longer. It's perfect. Right by the Castle, he's been able to watch the movements of the Emperor undetected. What better way to be close to his twelfth victim and not even be noticed?"

"Let's go!" Caesar urged them to start moving. "We have to save Maria."

"And she didn't think you cared about her," Bruno commented.

"What?"

"Nothing. Long story. I'll tell you about it later. First we must get some materials from my chest; the crossbow, the arrows, some globes and Brunon. It's the only thing that will hold him after we take him down with the arrows. I've seen and felt him up close. His strength is incredible. It will have to be my thickest Brunon."

"Let's get going," Caesar urged them once more.

"Don't worry Giordano. We're going to save her and we're going to end this once and for all. I don't know how I know but I know!"

"I believe you Kova. I do!"

§ § § § § §

St. Vitus stood dark and brooding before the three companions as they stared upwards at the unfinished tower and steeple on the southern wall. From their viewpoint they could see nothing but the scaffolding that encircled the tower for the last fifty years since the great fire that almost destroyed the cathedral.

"He's up there, I can feel it," Caesar half whispered to his two companions. "Perhaps we should wait until the Captain arrives with his men."

"No time," Bruno chastised him. "We have to go in now if we are to save her."

Yakov just kept staring upwards towards the top of the steeple. "Must be at least one hundred and eighty feet to the top," he commented.

"Phew…" Caesar blew the air through his lips, "Wouldn't want to be scared of heights."

Yakov remained silent, trying not to think about Caesar's comment. There was little he feared in life, but he always had a problem with heights. Ever since he was a young child climbing trees. Vertigo would onset rapidly and before he could stop himself he'd be scrambling to the ground, much to the amusement and laughter of the other children. He swallowed hard. This was not going to be like those days. His friends were depending on him. Maria was depending on him.

"There must be a way up to the top inside," Giordano waved them to follow as he held open the large wooden door into the cathedral.

"You mean other than hundreds of winding stairs," Caesar frowned at the thought. "We'll be exhausted by the time we confront the Golem."

"Try not to think about them," was all Bruno could suggest.

"Come on Kova," Caesar had to encourage Yakov to follow.

Haltingly, Yakov forced his legs to move forward, a step at a time. They felt like massive lead weights, impossible to lift off the ground, but he fought the sensation until he was ascending the stairs with some difficulty but a lot more determination. The cross bow hanging across his back felt like an anchor but he ignored it as best as he could. He found that closing his eyes while he held on sweatingly to the rail helped him overcome the trepidation.

"Are you okay, Kova," Caesar asked, noticing for the first time the beads of sweat that were rolling down Yakov's forehead.

"I'll be fine," Yakov stiffened his resolve. "Just adjusting to the altitude," he explained.

"Well good, because you better open your eyes because we've just run out of stairs!"

Yakov forced his eyelids to separate until he could make out the open platform that the three of them were now standing upon. They were at the same height as the vaulted ceiling with its crisscrossed supporting beams, almost one hundred feet above the ground. Yakov kept his eyes focused on the beams, refusing to look down.

"I don't get it," was Caesar's reaction to their inability to climb any higher. He could see that there was another platform directly across and perhaps ten feet below from theirs on the other side of the tower, and it was only that one that appeared to have any framework of lad-ders and trestles leading up to the cupola. "How are we supposed to ascend the rest of the way from here?"

"We can't," was Bruno's answer to that question. "There's obviously another set of stairs built into the tower and they're on the other side. We'll have to go back down and start up again."

Yakov felt his heart rising up into the back of his throat. He wasn't sure if he could do this a second time. He kept his eyes focused on the metal struts that supported the tower's dome, the same ones that the architects must have fretted about in the lightning storms. "Quick, against the wall," Yakov shouted as he dived straight into Bruno and flattened him up against the boards. The bag Bruno had been carrying flew against the surface of the platform and they all froze momentarily, but there was no sound of breaking glass. 'Lucky,' was their first thought. Before Bruno could even utter a word of shock or surprise, a massive beam, a hand's breadth square and at least six feet in length came smashing down upon the platform on which they stood, splitting right through one of the flooring planks and continuing on its way down to the bottom of the tower a hundred feet below.

"He must have heard your voice," Yakov confided to Bruno, whose eyes were as big as two thaler coins as he stared at the hole in the platform where he had been standing just moments before. "I don't think he likes you."

"You think?" were the first words Bruno uttered upon regaining his composure.

They watched as the creature swung from the interlaced beams and wires that braced the inner walls of the tower approximately thirty feet above their heads.

"My God," Caesar exclaimed. "I've never seen anyone or anything move like that before in my life."

The simian movements came naturally to the Golem as it hung by one hand from a girder and hissed its disapproval at the intruders. Yakov saw the opportunity and swung the crossbow off his back. Bruno reacted almost instinctively, opening his bag simultaneously as he pulled one of the metal bolts he had made using Damascene steel and handed it over to Yakov.

In the excitement they had forgotten that the creature they were dealing with still possessed human traits and as soon as the Golem saw the crossbow elevated in its direction it knew exactly Yakov's intentions. The frail trace of humanity that it retained still knew how to counteract a threat. With amazing speed and precision accuracy the Golem was able to perambulate from one crossbar to the next. Displaying faultless agility, it somersaulted through the air, landing on a ledge that appeared to be no more than a couple of feet wide at most. Yakov lined up the bolt with his target. That's when the Golem unleashed a surprise of his own. Picking Maria out from the shadows, where she had been curled up in fetal position on the ledge, the creature held her under one arm, while he ranted and railed with the other, roaring his outrage and challenging Yakov to shoot.

They could see that Maria was fully conscious but she didn't struggle, didn't even try to resist the Golem's own movements as he swung her back and forth over the precipice.

"Smart girl," Bruno thought to himself. "She knows how protect herself."

"Don't shoot," Caesar begged Yakov. "Even if you don't hit the girl, he'll drop her for certain."

"If I don't shoot, he'll drop her anyway," Yakov replied. "We didn't give him enough credit. He knows our weakness. It's up to you Bruno. You're the deciding vote."

Bruno reached over and withdrew several more bolts from his bag. "I'll pray, you shoot!"

In his head, Yakov started to count the swinging movement, timing the number of seconds from when the Golem held Maria fully over the edge until the pendulum motion swung her back completely over the ledge. He estimated the time the arrow would take to reach the target, and then he pulled the trigger. He targeted the right shoulder and chest, at the joint of the arm, the same arm in which the Golem clutched Maria. The joints in the armor plates would be weakest there, the overlap minimal in order to allow the Golem freedom of movement. His aim was as true as ever, striking exactly where he intended. The howl was unlike anything anyone had ever heard before. Not human, not animal, but demonic in nature. Penetrating through the plates and into the flesh, the Golem could not help but release the girl, and she fell safely onto the ledge, Yakov's timing had been perfect.

"He's going to grab her again," Caesar shouted as the Golem swung around, ignoring his attackers and obsessed now with punishing Maria for the pain it was experiencing.

"Another bolt quickly," Yakov reached his hand out towards Bruno who slapped the metal arrow into his clenching fist. Within the blink of an eye, Yakov had cocked the bowstring and loaded the bolt into the sliding track. The Golem stood sideways to them not offering much of a target. Its thigh was the most obvious location as the

Golem crouched over the girl preparing to pick her up and hurl her over the side of the precipice. It was also the site that probably had the heaviest plating of all, where the skirt of the armor's vest, hung over the leggings. There were no other options and Yakov pulled the trigger a second time. It was the impact more than hitting anything vital that caused the creature to howl in a venomous rage. Yakov could see from the length of the bolt protruding it had barely penetrated but it was enough to dissuade the Golem from daring him to fire a third bolt. Scrambling up the lattice work of scaffolding on the inner surface of the tower, the Golem disappeared into the Gothic crevices of the cupola.

"We have to get Maria out of there before he comes back," Yakov instructed.

"How exactly do you propose we do that," Bruno challenged him to provide the answer.

They could see from Yakov's expression he was searching for the answer. Analyzing the possibilities, awaiting some form of divine inspiration. "Giordano, how much weight can that Brunon of yours take?"

"If you're thinking what I think you're thinking, you're crazy," he replied.

"We don't have time to argue about which one of us is crazier than the other. Will it hold my weight?"

"I don't know, I guess so."

"Don't do it Kova!" Caesar became alarmed by the conversation passing between the other two. "This isn't a good idea," Caesar cautioned him. "I'll go! I'm the lightest."

"But you can't fire a crossbow and neither can Giordano. I can't protect her from here and the person lowering her down at the same time, unless I'm the one to do both. Unless you have a better idea, this is the only chance she has."

While Yakov was trying to assuage Caesar's fears, Giordano was busy tying one end of his Brunon cord to the mid shaft of the crossbow bolt. Yakov took the bolt and loaded it into the bow.

"Where do you intend to anchor it?" Bruno looked up into the rafters but couldn't see a suitable location.

"In the grill work," Yakov pointed the tip of the arrow in the direction of a small circular grill that would serve as an air vent to keep the humidity under control and the timber dry once the tower was completed. The vent was located at a point where the tower narrowed and the walls vaulted to the point where the bell cap would be placed.

"That little grill up there?" Bruno pointed at it location in the curvature of the wall perhaps fifty feet above them. "That's going to be one hell of a shot." Bruno set about unwinding close to a hundred feet of cord, and then cut it with the knife he had in the bag, tying the end to the support beam in the wall.

"What kind of way is that for a priest to talk? Just watch!"

Yakov lined up his target, the rosette at the center of the grill. It would be like threading a needle, the rosette about half a foot in diameter but from the distance they were looking, to be no larger than a thumb's width.

"Ready?" he asked Bruno.

"Ready," came the reply.

The missile was launched on its way and stayed true to its path. Passing through the center of the rosette and rising into the sky, until it lost momentum and pulled sharply on the cord which was now fully extended but would not break free. They waited until it had fallen back to the roof, at which time they wound in the cord until the bolt rested tightly across the rosette, its shaft longer that the diameter of the opening.

"Well, at least we know it's pretty strong," Yakov commented, noting that the cord didn't break under the massive pull of the arrow when it was stopped mid flight.

Bruno wrapped fifteen feet of cord around Yakov's waist then cut off the remainder. "That will get you across to the other side and then once you're on the ledge you can unwind the cord. You and Maria can then climb down to the platform."

"You make it sound so simple," Yakov treated the situation with humor.

"Done it a hundred times myself," Bruno lied. "Just remember that the swing will take you into the wall on the other side perhaps ten feet below that ledge. Be prepared to hit it awfully hard."

"I could see as much," Yakov confirmed the obvious.

"You'll be totally unprotected from the time you hit that wall until you climb on to the ledge."

"Tell me something more I don't know."

"I'd do it myself, but like you said you're the one that knows how to use the crossbow." Bruno helped sling the bow over Yakov's back and then handed him the last remaining two bolts he had in the bag. "Be careful Kova."

"I still think this is insane," Caesar protested. "There's got to be another way."

"I need you both to find the Captain and his men. Once Maria is safe, he'll be able to concentrate on getting the Golem. We have him trapped in this tower and he's not getting out of it alive."

"You get to Maria first, then we'll start heading down," Bruno insisted. "You may still need us."

"What, you think you could hurl one of those globes that distance in case I do need saving?"

"No, but I can stand here with one in my hand and that might be enough to make him think twice about attacking you."

"Kova…" Caesar's voice trailed off into silence.

Yakov wrapped his arms around Caesar's body. "You don't have to say it. I already know." Confirming Caesar's worst fears only brought tears to the young Nostradame's eyes.

"Hey, don't forget me," Bruno piped in.

"Never!" Yakov smiled. "I will never forget either of you." Holding out an outstretched fist, Yakov signaled for them to recite their vow. They placed their clenched knuckles together in the shape of a triangle. "One heart, one soul, one mind, we three of a kind," they recited in unison.

Stepping to the edge of the platform, Yakov prepared to make the leap of faith.

"It will hold," Bruno reinforced his waning confidence.

"It better," Yakov turned to him with an expression of mock anger. "Otherwise I'll be very mad at you!" As soon as he completed his statement, Yakov pushed off from the edge, his body swinging like a pendulum across to the other side until he crashed heavily into its brick and timber framework. Clinging to the framed pieces of wood, he refused to look down, concentrating only on the short climb to the ledge above him. Meanwhile Caesar and Bruno congratulated each other on his success with jubilant slaps on each other's backs.

Bruno reached into his bag of tricks and pulled out a couple of his fire globes, holding them aloft for the Golem to see, where ever he might have concealed himself. "Come and get it you overgrown sack of shit!" Bruno's voice roared and echoed inside the tower.

On the other side Yakov steadily made the climb to the ledge until he was able to pull the upper half of his body over its lip. "Are you certain you're a priest?" he called back to his friend.

"You serve God your way," Bruno yelled back, "I'll serve him my way!"

Now completely on the ledge, Yakov quickly checked over Maria for any signs of an injury.

"I'm all right," she insisted." not wishing for Yakov to make a fuss over her.

"That's a miracle in itself," Yakov caressed her cheek, the first time he had displayed any physical familiarity with her.

"I just treated him like any man that would get rough with me. I'd just lie there. They soon lose interest."

"Smart girl," Yakov smiled at her, appreciating how difficult life on the street must have been all those years. "Now let's get you down from here." Yakov unwound the length of cord that Bruno had circled about his waist. "I'm going to put one turn underneath your shoulders and then you'll place one hand on the rope here, and the other one here like this." As he explained the procedure he helped fit the Brunon around Maria's chest. "You'll be able to slowly lower yourself by releasing a bit of cord at a time with your left hand." She nodded fully understanding how it was to be done. "And when you get to the platform, I don't want you to wait. Just take off down the stairs and get out of the tower as fast as you can. Bruno and Caesar will be waiting for you below. Now, ready?"

She nodded once more as Yakov helped her over the edge, using one hand to steady the cord so that there was no unnecessary jiggling. With his other hand he freed the bow from his back and using his knees cocked the string into the locking mechanism. Pulling a bolt free from inside his chemise, he loaded it into the track. 'Come and get it you overgrown sack of shit,' Bruno's words played over inside his head and he could not help but laugh at his friend's mastery of the language.

"She's down!" Bruno shouted from the other side, as Maria released the cord and began to race down the flights of stairs towards the bottom. "Now start lowering yourself," he instructed.

Wrapping the cord under his arms and around his chest exactly as he had explained to Maria, Yakov began his descent. He was over the edge and perhaps a full body length lower when he suddenly appeared to stop.

"What are you doing?" Bruno questioned upon seeing the cessation in movement.

"I'm not doing anything," Yakov yelled back. "It's not me." The cord started to jerk, and with each pull, Yakov found that he was moving upward, several feet at a time.

"He's got me," Yakov stared up towards the grillwork and could make out the dark shadow of arms, reaching out to the cord and reeling it in, length by length.

"I can't see him!" Bruno screamed. "I can't see him! What should we do?"

"Get out of here," Yakov shouted. "Get Dimitri and his men. You can't help me. Save yourselves!"

"We aren't going to leave you!" Caesar screamed back.

"Go! There's nothing you can do for me!"

Bruno pulled at Caesar's jacket. "Hurry, we must get over to the other side. There might be just enough time for us to get over there and grab that cord."

Caesar looked at Bruno as if he had lost his mind. There was no way in the world they could descend one flight of stairs and climb the other in time. But there was nothing else they could do. Tearing off like banshees, they raced as fast as their balance would allow them, descending the stairway.

Yakov surrendered to the fact that he could not stop the Golem pulling him to the top. All he could do was wait patiently, crossbow in hand, waiting for the opportune moment to release another bolt, a killing bolt this time. Higher and higher he was dragged towards the cupola, towards the darkness that hung above his head.

Dangling one hundred and seventy feet above the tower floor, Yakov could now make out the shadowy form of his adversary. He was not afraid. It was as if his entire life had led to this moment. The Golem was now reaching out, practically seizing him in his huge mitts. He targeted the slit through which he could see the coal black eyes burning brightly with hatred. There'd only be one chance to make the shot. He pulled the trigger. The Golem's reaction was equally as fast, raising one hand in front of his face before the bolt could strike. It ripped through the glove and into his hand. Yakov could see both ends of the arrow protruding from each side of the leather mitt. The creature looked somewhat dumbfounded at its own hand, not registering or recognizing the pain it should have been experiencing. Last chance, Yakov thought to himself, and it had failed.

Ignoring the barb, the Golem dragged Yakov onto the crevice where it had been concealed all this time. The slackening of the cord caused the bolt from which the Brunon had been suspended to fall harmless through the rosette grill so that it dangled far below from Yakov's chest. And then the cord slackened even further so that it now fell the full distance to the tower floor far below. Yakov didn't even think about the fact that he'd no longer be able to climb down from the cupola. At the moment, it was the least of his worries. The Golem pounded the tail end of the bolt against the metal bell cover, forcing the greater portion of the shaft through his hand and out the other side. It was now easily removed and tossed over the ledge, no evidence of any effect, as the Golem apparently ignored that it had even pierced him.

Yakov had a moment to gauge his situation. It looked hopeless. The crevice on which he lay was nothing more than an alcatrave designed to hold statues of the saints that could be viewed from the outside; a window into nothingness but the empty sky above. "Ridiculous design' Yakov thought to himself, as if anyone could see the statues at this distance from the ground, and then he was furious with himself that this was all he was thinking about as he was about to die.

Turning on his adversary with animal-like ferocity, the Golem raised Yakov to his feet, dragging him upwards by his head. The huge hands were wrapped around his throat, squeezing the last breaths from his beating chest. He tried to resist, struggling like a fish on the hook, but the height and strength of the Golem was enough to keep his feet off the ground and he had nothing against which to brace himself. Yakov could feel the blackness reaching out to him. It reminded him of the dream that he experienced when he first arrived in Prague. The dream that Judah ben Loew had sent to haunt his spirit. He was no longer anchored to this world; he was parting from it without ever achieving his destiny. Falling into a black abyss while failing to fulfill his one purpose in life. And it was then that he realized that the Rabbi had not sent them nightmares to frighten them like little children but instead had delivered to each of them glimpses into their own futures. Using the fear of what would be, in an attempt to defeat them.

And then he heard it. At first it was faint, unrecognizable, until it grew, as if it were a living, breathing thing inside his head. A voice, a thought, perchance words that may have been spoken, empowering itself with a sense of well-being and renewed strength that defied even human limitations. Not a glimpse of what would be but instead of what could be if he didn't resist, didn't fight to make the future his own. Then he beheld the rare reflections of forgotten ancestors eagerly awaiting him. He had proven his worth and now they beckoned him. 'Aryeh-Zuk' he thought he heard them calling. It was the realization that he had finally earned the most coveted and illustrious title within his family, voices so soft and delicate, and so comforting. The entitlement to the familial peerage was finally his and instantaneously the realization set him free.

A smug smile of confidence spread across his face and he could feel the resurgence throughout his body and the vigor that took possession of his limbs. He reached out and seized the bolt protruding from the Golem's left shoulder and then twisted it, driving it forward with every remaining ounce of strength he possessed. The Golem screamed in agony, his fetid breath burning across Yakov's face but in its pain it loosened the death grip around Yakov's throat. Sucking the air into his lungs, the Kahana pressed his advantage. Arching backwards, contorted like a scythe, he grasped his assailant behind the base of its bull-like neck and interlocked his fingers in an unbreakable bond. Yakov stared directly into the creature's dumbfounded expression. "God has a message for you!" The Golem looked even more panicked and perplexed. "He said, 'Die Monster!.'" Applying leverage, Yakov braced his feet against the framework of wooden girders, tightening the hold he had on the Golem's neck even further. As soon as the Golem felt the pull of gravity trying to drag him over the precipice, he immediately reacted to the danger and exerted even harder backwards against the drag. Yakov's legs coiled like massive springs with the Golem's attempt to retreat within the safety of the tower. He smiled even more when he saw the startled pale look of horror in the Golem's eyes. For the second time in its existence, the creature had come to understand fear. The Golem panicked, releasing his stabilizing grip with which he held the cornice, raising his hand behind his own neck in an attempt to break Yakov's hold. It was the advantage Yakov had been waiting for. Off balance, the Golem was no match for the raw kinetic power that had been building within Yakov's thighs. Silently, mechanically, Yakov uncoiled his legs, propelling himself and his captive into the sky, far from the safety of the tower.

Once again the Golem screamed. Not in fear or pain but in absolute unbridled rage. A monstrous, unearthly howl resonated above the city, shaking the bricks and mortar of the surrounding buildings like thunder. A sound that those whom had gathered in the streets, witnessing the titanic battle high above their heads in the waxing approach of twilight would never forget. Caesar could do nothing but watch haplessly from his position far below, his head aching with another quatrain that swam around in his mind, as if his father had seen this all before. *'They shall hear the cries from the sky the battle between the combatants, Between the divine enemies that same year that, The holy laws will be debated unjustly, and by thunder and battle the true believer shall die!'* Century IV, Quatrain forty-three he recounted the number. Once again the number forty-seven in total, and no matter how he tried to dismiss it, he knew that this was the time Yakov was meant to die.

But what some would remark later which was most unforgettable, was not the screams of the creature, but what they thought they perceived as a serene laughter, a calm gentle sing-song of contentment, so totally incongruent with what was transpiring high above in the sky. That was the sound they would never be able to wipe from their memories.

Caesar was first to reach the base of the tower, racing towards his stricken comrade. Bruno with Maria's help tried desperately to keep the townspeople that had been drawn to the site as far away as possible. In their struggle, Yakov had managed to twist the Golem beneath him as they plummeted, so that the creature took the full impact of the fall. It had bought him some time. Not much, but enough to say what he had to before entering the darkness.

Caesar winced as he gazed upon the bludgeoned body of his companion. As he carefully laid Yakov's head upon his lap, he felt his forearm in Yakov's weakening grasp. Blood oozed steadily from Yakov's nose and mouth. "Keep them back," he shouted to Giordano whom was now running towards them. "Keep them all back. Don't let anyone touch him!" Caesar screamed.

Yakov pulled weakly on Caesar's arm, his mouth parting silently from the words that began to form. Putting his ear to his friend's lips, Caesar strained to make out what was being said, the blood spurting from Yakov's throat with each new word. "Promise me…Promise me! Tell Raisa, I was the eighteenth. Tell her I love her." Caesar placed his arm behind Yakov's neck, elevating his head higher in an attempt to make him more comfortable and prevent him from choking on his own blood. Yakov smiled at his touch, as if to say thank you, and calmly, quietly, closed his eyes. "You did it Kova," Caesar cried, his voice sobbing as he feared it was too late too late to be heard. Briefly Yakov's eyes flickered open again, the fading smile still on his lips. "Yes, we did it," he corrected him. "Remember all that I have told you. Do not be afraid to be who you are."

"Don't exert yourself," Caesar counseled. "There will be a doctor here soon."

"It matters not. Just remember." his voice weakening by the second until he closed his eyes once more.

"Kova, Kova! Don't go!" Caesar gasped as he shook his friend ever so slightly in an effort to arouse him. There was no response.

"What did he say," asked Giordano, as soon as he was able to hand over the duties of crowd control to the Captain's men who now ringed them safely from the in-surging crowd. Caesar still caressed his friend's head in his arms, the tears now flowing uncontrollably down both cheeks. "I must go to Brody. I have a message for his wife."

"Then I will go with you."

"No, no, it is more important that you return to Rome. Get us those decrees that they promised. Then have a courier deliver mine and Kova's to Galicia."

"Why don't I bring them myself?"

"For God sake, Giordano, once you have yours, run! Just run. As far and as fast away from any place and any one you have ever known. Run like you have never run before."

"You're over reacting. I'll have my Papal amnesty. Rudi has the signed confession from the doctor. I'll finally be protected. I won't have to hide any more. I can go work at the universities. Why should I keep running?"

"Because I can see things! Do you understand? My father's final gift to me! It's very much alive in me now. I'm not afraid to use it any longer. I can finally see and it is clear that no piece of paper is ever going to protect you from them. In many ways you are more dangerous to them than that poor creature ever was." Caesar indicated towards the Golem, lying twisted on the cobblestones, surrounded by the Captain's men, who every now and then would give the creature a sharp prod with their pikes to ensure that he was not suddenly going to revive and take them unaware. "Don't be fooled Giordano, whereas the Golem only killed a few people, you on the other hand are in possession of knowledge that could destroy the ignorance from whence they draw their power. You are their greater enemy. You always will be!"

"But I still don't understand."

"I have seen your end Giordano. Now just do as I say. Run for the rest of your life. Far away from their reach. Go to the lands where the Church doesn't exist. For your own sake, listen to me!"

"Tell me what you saw."

"No man should have knowledge of when and how his time should come. I'm sorry Giordano, but for my sake if not your own, please do as I say. But whatever you do, don't set foot in Venice!"

"Shall we never meet again, my friend?"

Caesar shook his head. "They will be watching me to see if you should try to visit. We must not give them that opportunity. Go to Rome and get the decrees while the Pope still remembers his promise to us and the Emperor has a hold over him. But he is not much longer for this world and his memory and his promises will be short lived.

So get them while you can and then leave Rome as quickly as you came. Now go!"

Kneeling together the two men embraced, each with the other as they cradled the body of their fallen comrade between them. They sealed their farewells with a kiss upon each other's cheek, holding tightly to the memories that they had shared together.

"One heart, one soul, one mind, for we three of a kind," Caesar uttered.

"One heart, one soul, one mind for we three of a kind," Giordano repeated as he steeled himself for the journey he was about to take.

Caesar still cradled his fallen comrade as he watched Bruno disappear into the mingling crowd. And as he watched he recalled the quatrain that had flared in his mind. Six eighteen the numbers flashed before his eyes. He could hear his father's voice reading the verse to him, like he had done every night when he was just a child. *'The highly learned one in the universal sciences, Shall be reproved by the ignorant Princes, Who will pass a punishing edict and chase him across the globe, Until where they find him and put him to death!'* Run Giordano, run and never stop! He closed his eyes and prayed. And then he wept.

36

Brody: September 1589

It had been several months since those fateful last days in Prague. The cooler days of summer had already taken hold of the night, as the townspeople of Brody busily prepared for the coming autumn. Great preparations were made for the arrival of the Jewish New Year matched with great hopes of what the coming year might bring. In a town where sixty percent of the population was of Jewish extraction, over four hundred major families at last count and countless subfamilies, the festival season was evident everywhere one looked in the city that had become known as the New Jerusalem. Still, there was no word as to their fate, the community still under the threat of the Papal decree that threatened them with extinction, but after several hundred years of expulsions, exterminations, and forced conversions, the Jewish populace had become numbed to the threat, continuing to live life as if nothing would ever change.

So in a city where distinguished emissaries and foreign potentates frequently visited, the arrival of one more caravan hardly raised an eyebrow, until it turned towards the bridge leading to the Jewish Quarter. Then the only thought that crossed everyone's mind was the year had ended. And just as the papal emissary had promised almost one year ago to the day, the Jews of the city would not see the coming of another New Year if Yakov Kahana failed. The magnificent gilded carriage was surrounded by an elite guard that marched effortlessly alongside the paired grays in their belled harnesses.

Surely this must be his holiness, the Pope himself to travel in such a regal fashion the townspeople commented upon the passing of the conveyance. No one could ever recall such a splendid vehicle appearing in Brody before. Though the Gentiles of the city bore no hard feelings towards their fellow Jewish citizens, they could only give thanks to God that it was better them than us. The children swarmed excitedly in the trail of the entourage, laughing and dancing but never distracting the fifty armed soldiers that paraded in unison. The shutters were thrown open as the people peered sheepishly from their second store windows. No one could be certain what the fanfare was all about, but morbid curiosity still drew them to watch every movement.

"Make way for Caesar de Nostradame, Counsel to his Royal Majesty the King of France," the herald shouted exuberantly, well above the clatter of hooves and feet against the cobblestone street. It had cost Caesar a sizable mountain of ducats but nothing he couldn't afford following his Papal amnesty, which freed up all the funds in his accounts that his father had left him. It was far more important to keep his promise to Yakov and in order to do so, no expense would be spared. This he swore would be his friend's moment of glory, a day that Yakov would never have the pleasure of enjoying in life, but that none would ever forget in death.

"Where are you going,' someone in the gathering crowd cried out towards the carriage as it passed by.

"His Excellency, Caesar de Nostradame seeks the home of Rabbi Isaac ben Shakna. Show us the way," the herald replied. As if on cue, the peopled parted in a fashion that left a bounded route directly to the Rabbi's house. The excitement of the townsfolk amplified exponentially with every turn of the carriage wheels towards the synagogue that dominated the Jewish Quarter. Well ahead of the carriage, the rumors were running rampant. Some even claimed that it was Yakov Kahana returning in a golden carriage and was now proclaimed as a Prince of France. But in no one's mind was there any lingering doubt that the mission had been successful. The city would be spared.

Rolling to a stop in the front courtyard that lay beyond the huge stone walls that surrounded the synagogue enclave, the herald accompanied by two guards made their way to the front door. There they banged heavily against the wood with the hilts of their sheathed swords. "In the name of his Excellency, Caesar de Nostradame Counsel to the King of France, I hereby summon Rabbi Isaac ben Shakna to meet his eminence.

"I am but an old man," a voice responded from behind the closed door, but it did not open. "I am too feeble to enjoin your Excellency and therefore suggest he enters my parlor where we can partake in a refreshing drink."

"Poppa, what are you doing?" Raisa's voice could be heard from behind the door.

"Quiet girl!" her father tried to hush her in a muffled tone. "We don't want a circus at our doorstep. Let me deal with these gentlemen in the seclusion of my home, rather than in the midst of a frenzied and boisterous crowd."

"But Poppa, my Kova could be with him. He could be waiting outside for me right now. Let me go out! Please!"

"Be quiet girl. Any reunion with your husband must be done discretely. Otherwise you would shame this household in front of those people."

"But Poppa…"

"But poppa nothing! You will do as you are told!"

Caesar was not surprised at what he was overhearing. Yakov's stories about his father-in-law had educated him well. He had come prepared for such a contingency and there was no way he would permit this old man to steal the thunder from his son-in-law. Opening the door to the carriage, Caesar grabbed the outstretched hand of his aide and stepped down to the ground. He then turned and walked towards the entrance of the courtyard where the people stood eagerly awaiting the good news. As soon as they saw Caesar in his white robes trimmed with gold, they were awestruck. Young women swooned in admiration of this princely vision of perfection walking towards them.

"Your Rabbi has claimed he is too weak to come out and greet me though I bear this gift of amnesty which I have been requested by Yakov Kahana to deliver to his people. Is there anyone else that speaks for his people that can accept this gift from me? Where is your burgermeister? Where is your town secretary? Surely there is someone prepared to accept your amnesty on your behalf. Show me your spokesperson for this most momentous day!" Caesar shouted.

The door to the Rabbi's home flew open and Isaac ben Shakna hobbled out onto its portico. "Your Rabbi suddenly feels better," he announced to the assembled crowd. "God has heard this great news and blessed me with his healing this very moment so that I may have the strength to rejoice in our delivery."

The people cheered for the Rabbi's fortunate turn of health. Unbelievable, Caesar thought to himself. No wonder Yakov had been so excited to leave his community behind. By now news of his arrival had spread through all the other sectors of the city and more and more people were flooding into the Jewish Quarter. Caesar never turned towards the Rabbi, always speaking directly to the people as if Isaac ben Shakna didn't exist. Reaching inside his vest, he pulled out a roll of parchment and held it high above his head for all to see. "Good people of Brody," Caesar shouted in his fluent German though heavily accented by his native French. "I bring you good tiding from his most Holy Excellency, Pope Sixtus. He bids you all well and good health. As a token of his appreciation of the great service that was performed by Yakov Kahana, I have been requested to deliver this epistle signed by His Holiness's own hand to the chief magistrates of this city and especially to the leaders of the Jewish community. Let all men know that Yakov Kahana has earned the respect of all mankind, both Jew and Gentile, for he fought against Satan's champion for possession of the world and he won!"

A thunderous ovation, crowned with a resounding chorus of Yakov's name being praised in 'glory hallelujahs' reverberated back and forth through the assembled masses. Caesar held up his hand in a gesture for silence. It took some time in coming.

"There was a time your city had been accused of being a vile and unholy place."

"No, no," the people repeated in a ripple that seemed to drone on forever.

"Oh yes, it is true. A virtual Sodom and Gomorrah! A place that God had measured and found wanting."

"Say it isn't so," one person shouted, only to be echoed by a hundred more.

"It was, and I could not lie to you. In the papal decree of a year ago, it was said that the Jewish community was to be extinguished should Satan's champion prove triumphant. But what you did not know that along with the Jewish community, every other quarter of this city was to be razed to the ground as well. In that way the Church would be certain that no Jew escaped their edict. But one man stood up for you. Like Abraham of old, a deal was struck between a man and God. And whereas Abraham said, let me find ten good men in Sodom but failed, Yakov Kahana said, let me take on Satan's champion and he won. A man of God against a demon from hell! A battle so amazing, so unbelievable, that even those of us who witnessed it still cannot believe what our eyes had seen. But as you know, Yakov Kahana was no mere man. He was the Davidic Prince, the Scion of

Aaron, the Kahana and he dwelled amongst you. And without betraying a single ounce of fear, he accepted the mantle as the Pope's envoy, to go to Prague and release the city from the demon that gripped it in its talons of terror. Without a thought of his own life and safety, he wrestled with Satan's creature, a horrible thing which tore the flesh from all it encountered and devoured the city's children. High above the city they fought, the creature screaming like a banshee, and in the air they turned and rolled, a hundred feet above in the sky, but Yakov would not release his grip nor could the creature beat him off. And knowing that the only way he could be certain to destroy the demon was to plummet himself and his adversary into the ground from such a tremendous height, he crushed the demon into the depths of the earth."

A tumultuous cheer was released by the crowd. Everyone broke into rapturous applause.

"And as reward for his bravery, this Papal decree swears that Brody is now and forever under the protection of the Vatican. No hand shall be lifted against it. Nor will divine wrath ever assail its walls. His eminence, Pope Sixtus extends clemency to all whom live within its boundaries. Praise be Brody, praise be Yakov Kahana!"

Once again the crowd applauded and sang out the Kahana's name in tribute and adoration.

"Wait, wait," Isaac ben Shakna interrupted. "Where is my son-in-law now? Surely he can tell his own story."

"Certainly you were listening to me when I told these good people of the epic battle between man and beast? With our own eyes, all of whom were there saw a clash of titans that defied the laws of nature. And I say to you again, only by placing his foe into an unbreakable grip, and then plummeting headlong into the bowels of the earth was Yakov able to return the demon to the kingdom of Hell which spawned him. No man, not even Yakov Kahana could have survived such an effort. His Majesty, Emperor Rudolf the Second laid to rest whatever remains of Yakov his garrison could find with great fanfare. And he said these words as he did so, "Let no man forget what great things Yakov Kahana has done for the love of his people."

The fresh roar of the people silenced whatever challenge ben Shakna was thinking of raising. But no matter how loud the cheers of the people seemed to be, the horrific wail of grief that assailed their ears from within the house pierced everyone's heart.

"Is that Yakov's wife," Caesar asked the Rabbi.

"That is my daughter," he responded. "Pay her no heed."

In a soft yet firm tone, Caesar beckoned the woman to come out. "Have no fear Raisa. I bring you a missive from your husband. I bear his final words that he parted through me to you."

In a matter of seconds the boisterous crowd grew silent as the widow of their new sung hero stepped out of the shadows into the light, her face strewn with tears and her clothes rent in grief. "Do not hesitate, Raisa," he urged her forward. "Not even his battle with the demon could make him think of anyone but you with his dying breath. He asked me to pass on these two messages to you. He said that you would understand. The first was that he wanted you and the children to know that he was the eighteenth and therefore there was no doubt about his destiny. He did what had already been foretold that he would do. But his second and last request was for me to let you know how much he loved you. A love that was so beautiful that it gave him the courage to overcome the fear of death itself."

For a moment there was the faintest smile on Raisa's lips but it faded immediately when the last words of her husband made her realize that she would never hear those words from him again. The tears began to flow like a river and she fell to her knees, her head in the palms of her hands.

"Cry little one," Caesar consoled her. "Cry for your husband, but while you weep, mix them with tears of joy. For how many men could love their wife so much that they would be imbued with the courage to save a world. No man could have loved any woman more." With that said, Caesar handed the parchment over to Isaac ben Shakna, whom stood silently beside his daughter, unable to put a hand on her heaving shoulder, and daring not to say anything that might incite the crowd against him.

"Let no man forget the sacrifice that was made to save this city. Let no man forget Yakov Kahana," Caesar shouted while looking sternly into the eyes of the Rabbi. Leaning over the Rabbi, Caesar whispered into his ear, "do not let his sacrifice be forgotten or I will come and see to it that your memory improves."

Never one to be threatened by any man, even one that held the entire population in the palm of his hand, Isaac responded, "What need have dead men of tribute? Only the living can make use of it."

"I will not let you steal this day from the greatest man I have ever known."

Isaac ben Shakna smiled with the sneer of a venomous snake. "Be assured, this day is definitely his. Of that there is no question. But the future, who can say what time and failing memories will do to any man's reputation?"

"I have already been warned of the things you will do. Just so you're aware, my father wrote about this day, he wrote about you." Caesar recited the thirty-sixth Quatrain from Century II. He had been prepared for this moment. *'The letter presented to the great prophet will be intercepted, Falling into the hands that he considered a tyrant, He will try to undertake the role and thereby deceive his King, but this efforts will not go well and they will come to trouble him soon.'*

"What nonsense is this?"

"The type that says you will be made to pay for if you try to steal the glory from your son-in-law!"

"They will all forget, you will see!"

"We shall see old man, we shall see. Now smile and wave to the people, your lives have just been saved."

37

Venice: 1592

It had not been a good day for Giordano Bruno. It now marked several months that he lay in the dark dampness of his cell. He remembered the words that Caesar had engraved into his consciousness three years ago. "Run, run for your life!" He should have listened and never come to Venice!

But he had become tired of running. Helmstedt, Frankfurt, Zurich, none of these places felt like home. None could even come close to reminding him of Naples. No matter how far he strayed from his origins, the call to return grew stronger and stronger. He had kept himself busy even while on the run. Two more books had been written. One of them was on magic and the other on the origin of matter and the order of nature. Not to mention the further editing of his previous works. With such a productive authoring schedule, it was no surprise that when the offer to return to Venice and teach in the household of Mocenigo, a councilor of the Republic was made, that Bruno jumped at the opportunity. He had forgotten Caesar's warning or at least allowed it to fade. He knew it would be difficult but convinced himself that there might exist a slim chance that the Church and the Inquisition could accept a scholar-priest.

Several months later, when Moncenigo handed Bruno over to the Inquisitors of the Venetian Tribunal, he realized just how wrong he had been. A new Pope was now sitting on the papal throne; Pope

Clement VIII. There was still the faint hope that this new Pope would respect the letter of clemency he received from Pope Sixtus.

The tribunal stated its mission clearly. "Giordano Bruno, you are accused of being a heretic, of having commented against the Church and its ministers; of denying the Trinity and questioning the divinity of Christ and of teaching that the universe is infinite and eternal. You deny the virginity of the Virgin Mother. You teach of the existence of some form of energy that binds all living creatures and which transforms easily between the species upon death. And most grievously, you are an ordained priest that has repeatedly engaged in carnal pleasures. How do you plead?"

Bruno immediately recognized the trap. To deny the truth would instantly brand him a perjurer. The books he had written promoted the statements which they had spoken. And as a perjurer, he would burn just as readily at the stake as he would for a confession to heresy. "I humbly request that your Excellences consult with his Papal Excellency, Pope Clement. He should be made aware of the papers that have been bestowed upon me by his Excellency Sixtus V. To act in a manner contrary to what was therein stipulated would call into question the infallibility of the Papacy. For if one Pope was wrong in what he has done or said does that mean that the next Papal Father to rescind such an ordination is necessarily correct or could it brand him as being fallible? One must certainly be in error if the other was correct. And should the Holy See be culpable in any manner, does that then mean that a shadow and pallor is cast upon every Papal decree, past, present and future?"

"And this is your answer, Giordano Bruno, a trickery of words!"

"Actually, it is just part of an answer."

"Then let us hear the rest of it," the Inquisitor encouraged him to speak further.

"I met a man, if you could call him that. For most men are limited by soul and spirit. But this man was not. He could clearly see that which blinded most men and he could feel for those he had not ever met. And he taught me of the infinite nature of the universe and how pretentious we are to even imagine that we can fathom the works of the Almighty Creator."

"So you are saying Brother Bruno that you have found God."

"Let me continue kind sir, for the things I have learned are beyond human consideration. He showed me how all life is interconnected. But know this, most of all he taught me not to fear death, especially if such self-sacrifice is freely given in order to save many."

"And when did you encounter the Savior, Brother Bruno?"

"He was with me in Prague, good sirs."

"And did you encounter him again once you left that city?"

"Most certainly not. The memories of his life and death shall be borne by me forever. And from the very first time my eyes were opened and I understood the Glory of Christ, for I witnessed what he would have been like as a man, and I knew all things were possible, even for a derelict soul like mine."

"I'm afraid I do not fully comprehend," replied the Chief Inquisitor.

"Nor is it likely you ever will Monsignor. You were not in Prague."

"So tell us all then."

"As I said, he was a man if you could call him that. A man whom would question how someone could find the true path to God if they considered that path would include the beating and torture of anyone in the name of His love."

"And that is your answer?"

"Is it not the answer to all things?"

"We are to discuss this Brother Bruno and what we are to do next with you. In the meantime, you will return to your jail cell until such time that we summon you here again." The inquisitors closed their books, tucking them under their arms and briskly exiting the room.

They would do so in a repetition of events for a further eight years until such time that Giordano Bruno was brought to Rome and they could no longer tolerate his insistence that he met the Lord in Prague. And in February of 1600 they sentenced him to death for a new heresy that was not pardoned in the papal decree given to him by Pope Sixtus V. He was charged with contempt of God, for he claimed that he had communed with the Lord and had been told that life on earth was more sacred than everlasting existence in heaven. They took this as a denial of the existence of heaven as the reward for embracing Christ. His pardon had forgiven him for numerous denials regarding Christian principles but nowhere was it written that he would be pardoned for denying Christ.

On February 17, 1600, Giordano Bruno was led to the pyre they had erected in the center of the Campo dei Fiori. He neither came willingly nor resisted. He recalled one of the quatrains that Caesar had shown him that his father left behind. Caesar was positive that somehow it was meant for Giordano but he never quite understood its meaning. It was labeled as Century VI Quatrain Two and it read, *'In the year five hundred and eighty more or less, one will await the arrival of a very strange century.'* This February morning Giordano understood it completely. It was the compelling reason why Caesar had urged him to run and keep on running. The 580 represented the decade in which the three of them had come together on a mission to save the world. It was common practice to leave off the numeral indicating the millennia. There had never been a more exciting time in his life, nor had he ever met two friends that he loved so much and with whom he shared an eternity in such a brief moment of time. With Yakov's death and Caesar's departure, he had done nothing but await this latest event. Most of his lethargy was excusable, he had been locked in a cell. But reflecting back on the last eleven years he realized that he had died along with Yakov that day. And as the quatrain indicated, with the turn of the century his suffering would finally be over.

Tied to the stake, he felt the flames surging and dancing all around him. It didn't hurt as much as he thought. It was the smoke that bothered him the most. He looked up at the Inquisitors that all sat broodingly on the balcony facing the square. And then he smiled and said, "God has a message for you. Die monsters!" And as the fire licked at his clothes those that had assembled to witness the burning swore that they could hear a calm and gentle song of laughter rising from the flames.

Epilogue

"So John, what did you think?"

"I think I'm at a loss for words Doc"

"That I do not think will ever happen," I contradicted him.

"I really don't know what to say. It's definitely different from anything you've written before. But it was so…so, melancholy."

"Dark?"

"Dark's one way of putting it! Couldn't you give it a happier ending?"

"My ancestor didn't have much of a life when you reflect upon it. His greatest moment was achieved in death John, what would you like him to be happy about? You can't really have happy thoughts when your climax is pretty morbid."

"Does everybody have to die? Couldn't you have your heroes go on to another adventure or something?"

"You obviously didn't understand what I told you when I started telling the story John, this wasn't the myth version. That is already in circulation when you read up about the Golem. That one has everyone living happily ever after. But that story has nothing to do with the truth. It was a cover-up, a fabrication to conceal what really occurred; a fictitious attempt to hide the identities of those responsible for the deaths of so many innocent people. What I gave you was reality! Reality doesn't have happy ever after endings."

"But you said you weren't certain if your story was an actual recounting of the events or not."

"No, I said that it may never be possible to find the supporting evidence to prove my family's version is the truth. I know that there are private accounts of the actual events locked away, but they may never see the light of day. So all you have is my word against the myth that has been circulated. But which story are you going to believe? A creature created from clay and brought to life through kabalistic hocus pocus, or some sad, unfortunate deformed and mentally deficient human being, taken advantage by a sadistic individual comfortably sitting in a seat of power and hiding his own true nature behind a veil of religious glorification. The fairy tale or the real thing?"

"Is there another choice?"

"I'm afraid not John. That's what's been put on the table. You have to now choose! Obviously the masses were fed the clay man version so that the people in high places weren't suspected of murder and intrigue. Easy enough to do! You told people what to think back then, and unfortunately, at that time the majority of people were happy not to have to use their brains to any great degree. In that way it was far easier for them to deal with the misery of life."

"So you're saying it was easier to accept a clay man," John guffawed at the thought.

"Oh, they did. Most definitely! Even erected a statue to him which stands in Prague today. You can see it there for yourself. But then they went ahead and erected a statue to Rabbi Judah ben Loew as well. The legend claimed that he saved the city when he was able to rub one of the sacred letters off the Golem's head which caused the creature to die. Trouble with that is he was the same person that released the Golem to terrorize the city in the first place. Bit ironic, don't you think?"

"Well, maybe they felt the Rabbi was genuinely innocent of the Golem going bad and therefore by stopping him he did do a great thing." John knew his argument was sounding a bit naïve as soon as he completed his statement, letting the last of his words trail off into nothingness.

"Let me give you metaphor to think about John. There's this man, supposedly an intelligent man, but he gives his ten year old son a loaded gun and sends him outside to play in the streets. Well, the boy does exactly as one would expect. Having shot and killed all the other children in the neighborhood, his father runs outside and takes the gun away. I guess as one of those parents of the children shot, you're so grateful that you want to see that this boy's father is given a medal for his actions. Does that sum up your feelings accurately."

Pearce laughed. "Got me there Doc."

"Thought I would."

"Okay, so why then such an obvious sham of a cover-up?"

"Has that not always been the way? I once told you, that the victor's will always write the history, no matter how distorted it might become. And people will always forget the truth and tend to believe the lies instead. And the more ridiculous and illogical the lie, the easier it is for everyone to accept."

"The rule of history according to Goldenthal," Pearce made fun of my assessment.

"People don't want the truth. It's too depressing!"

"Very cynical Doc."

"But very true. Do you know the legend version of Rabbi Loew actually claims that he named the Golem, Yosel."

"Is that important?"

"Yosel is the nickname for the savior. From the Hebrew for 'God's Has Saved.' Don't you think it's a truly strange coincidence that the myth version says that Rabbi Loew was responsible for stopping or killing so to speak, the Yosel. If one was skeptical, you'd almost think the teller of the story was trying to say cryptically that he was responsible for the death of the savior in this case, Yakov Kahana. But most interesting is the fact that very few scholars are willing to speculate about. That fact being that he was later summoned to the palace to have a conversation with Emperor Rudolf. The details from his son-in-law would have you actually believe that the Emperor wanted to discuss mysticism with the Rabbi. That was on the 23rd of February 1592. You'd think an event of that magnitude, if it really was a cordial visit would have been celebrated in the Prague Jewish community and that Rabbi Loew would have felt bound to be their spiritual leader until the day he died. Instead, after the meeting he packed up his bags and moved with his family to Posen. He didn't come back to Prague until he was close to dying in 1609, after Rudolf had already been removed from power. Even when there was the opportunity to be the Jewish spiritual leader of Prague in 1604, the community didn't offer it to him; instead they gave it to Rabbi Shlomo Ephraim. The community didn't even want him back!"

"That does sound a little suspicious Doc, I have to admit. Sort of like, hit the road Jack!"

"You think? You do the math John. Does it really sound like he was the hero of the story like the myth would like to portray him? Admittedly they say that no one knows exactly what was talked about at their meeting. But do you truly believe that the Emperor wanted to be taught the Kabala by Rabbi Loew. He had enough problems with the Catholic Church without adding another bullet for them to fire at him.

And for his biographer, being Rabbi Katz, whom he supposedly shared every detail of his life with, why wouldn't he tell his son-in-law the details of the meeting to record in full. Unless, they didn't want those details released because they weren't very favorable to the Rabbi and if he were to print a bunch of lies he'd be in even more trouble with the Emperor. I think I can tell you exactly what they talked about, and it sort of went like this, 'leave town or I'll expose your role in the Golem affair,' because at that time, Rudolf was aware his good friend Giordano Bruno had been placed in prison and he would not have been too happy about it. He'd want to strike out at anyone that he considered responsible."

"But it wasn't like the Rabbi got him thrown in jail."

"No, but the Rabbi created the situation that led Giordano to believe that he was safe to go home after he successfully completed the mission. Had there been no Golem, Giordano Bruno probably would have stayed with his good friend Emperor Rudolf until a ripe old age. So there was an obvious reason to hold the Rabbi responsible."

"Would that have been enough to make him leave?"

"Well, not to mention that he got out of town a couple of years after Yakov's death. You can't overlook that fact that people actually died. The Golem was just the loaded gun. It was still the Rabbi that pulled the trigger."

"But remember, the Golem was created to protect the innocent," Pearce insisted taking the standard line that has been promulgated for centuries.

"You see, that's where it starts falling apart. Because if Judah ben Loew's intent in creating the creature was to protect the Jewish community in Prague, then he could have done them no better service than stay in Prague having destroyed the creature, and obtained as many concessions as possible for his community as a reward for his heroic action. More importantly, without the Golem, there was nothing to stop the persecutions beginning once more. Only the threat of another Golem would have done that. And without Judah ben Loew that was an impossibility."

"You're right, it wasn't logical but as a reporter, I have to say that it's all supposition. Not enough for me to go on. You have to provide indisputable truth."

"The persecution of the Jews in Prague never stopped. Judah ben Loew had no effect and in 1611 they were massacred. Is that proof enough?"

"But he was dead by then. Maybe they waited until after he died?" Pearce suggested.

"You're really trying to annoy me now, aren't you? Try this one. In 1601, on his death bed, Mordecai Maisel divorces his wife Frema of twenty years."

"So the guy's a bastard, what about it. We knew that already. What's that prove?"

"The witness for his divorce is Rabbi Judah ben Loew. Problem is, the Rabbi's not even in the same country. Sounds suspicious, let alone illegal! The document had to be prepared long before in order for Maisel to have the Rabbi's signature on it."

"Okay, so he's a really big bastard!"

"You have to look deeper Pearce. He divorces his wife and cuts her off from all his worldly possessions. He discredits her, shames her. What my people would refer to as the 'shunda.' The rest of her life she would be treated as a leper for something that wasn't even her fault. No one would go near her, talk to her, believe anything she had to say after that. You have to ask the question, 'Why.'"

"I give, why?"

"Because they were afraid of what she'd confess about them; she was too dangerous. It didn't matter though. Rudolf was too smart for them and he had the crown seize all of Maisel's assets. He took everything! Left the family without a cent. But Rudolf did give the synagogue and the religious items to the Jewish community of Prague, just like Yakov had advised him, so the people weren't harmed at all by his actions."

"So let me get this straight. The guy dies and the Emperor takes everything from him. That would mean that he had to be guilty of stealing it all I the first place, I guess, just like you said."

"Well, the apologists for Maisel would prefer you believe their version that the Emperor in his hatred of the Jewish community felt empowered to steal the money from this poor innocent family unjustly and without provocation."

Pearce thought about it and realized, "But history demonstrated that the Emperor's policies were quite liberal when it came to the Jews. Therefore their version wasn't likely."

"Aha! Exactly! Why suddenly get greedy for the wealth of one individual. Take it all. It's a rich community. Spare no one. Why just take it from one family? That is what was normally done when you look at other rulers in history."

"But it could happen," he still protested, "No rule that says you couldn't take just from one family."

"There's more. There's a letter dated April 5, 1601 that has been circulated for the last few centuries as well. The apologists claim it was written by David Gans."

"The astronomer?"

"The same one. Interesting, don't you think. In the letter he describes the horrible doings of the Emperor and how he perpetrated this terrible crime of stealing the Maisel family fortune not only in one raid, but twice. Even names the president of the Bohemian Chamber, Von Sternberg as personally leading the attacks under the Emperor's instruction. Goes further describing the torture of one of Maisel's nephews in order to have him reveal where the family treasure was hidden. Pretty damning evidence if you ask me. Now tell me what's wrong with this story?"

"Seems like a stupid thing for Gans to do, considering he was the court astronomer."

"A very stupid thing to do," I added. "His entire income was based on his solid relationship with Rudolf. How long do you think he would have survived if he actually accused the Emperor and the Bohemian President of being criminals?"

Pearce thought about it and found my argument sound. "A forgery?"

"A poor one by all accounts! No, Mordecai Maisel was not the innocent they'd like us to believe."

"And the Emperor wasn't obviously the tyrant they'd have us believe either," Pearce conceded.

"I guess there is some divine justice after all. Maisel may have ruined his wife's life, but he wasn't able to get away with his crimes even in death," I continued. "He knew that Frema was going to confess once he was no longer there to bully her into inaction. After all, she knew what her role in the entire affair had been, and her silence resulted in the death of several people, including the Prince of her own people. Do you have any idea how the level of guilt of such magnitude would have weighed on her."

Pearce was about to say something but I cut him short. "Of course you don't. It would have been tearing her apart. After all, she never intended to hurt anyone when she became involved with Maisel. She was only looking to advantage herself through the marriage. And then all hell broke loose. Probably in some ways she may have thought the death of her daughter was God's retribution for her misdeeds.

Whether she came forward and told the supreme justice of the court, or whether Rudolf acted on his own, the fact is that everything was confiscated. And that is recorded, though some historians overlook that fact. And here's something even more interesting. After Maisel cut Frema out of his will, he left everything to two nephews. Once Rudolf had been removed from power, several years later actually, they appealed to his brother, Matthias and were awarded with some of the confiscated fortune. An obvious pay off I believe because they would have known the details of the entire Golem affair and the Church's involvement as well. Matthias wanted to keep all that very hush-hush."

"So once again justice was perverted," Pearce quipped.

"Not exactly. It's also recorded by reliable sources that the nephews were treated as pariahs by the Jewish community. Weren't even allowed to be buried in the cemetery plots that Maisel had purchased for his dynasty. That information appears to be once again overlooked by those writing the history of the Maisel family but you don't get that kind of treatment if you're a stalwart upstanding citizen. Fitting, don't you think?"

"If you're right, then just one more example of historical cover ups," Pearce acknowledged. "I should be getting used to them by now after I talk with you."

"Of course I'm right," I argued. "Now if your editors do their homework, you'll be able to dig up even more information that supports my version of the events."

"Anywhere in particular we should look?"

"I think one of the key sources is Rudolf. He had contact with all the people involved. In a way, he was the lynch pin to everything that occurred. He even knew Caesar's father, whom had prepared a personal horoscope for the young prince, don't forget. You'd have to wonder why Nostradamus thought the prince worthy enough to spend the time doing so. After all, Nostradamus was already dying, swollen with edema, unable to move about, and the Prince was nothing more than a boy whom was considered frivolous by most. Nostradamus had to think it very important to do so at the time."

"You think he had to tell him something about the Golem?" Pearce eagerly speculated.

"More than that, I think just as my story indicated he thought it necessary to tell Rudolf about his own son Caesar and request that later in life the Emperor had to protect him."

"Oh, if only we could be certain," Pearce groaned, pained by the fact that he might never know the true reason.

"Michel de Nostradame can actually help us in that respect. There are his prophecies after all."

"Not that anyone can make any sense out of most of them," Pearce was quick to add.

"And not that I'd like to believe that I can do better than most, but when it comes to my family I might have a better handle at sorting those particular quatrains out."

"What makes you so special?" Pearce said flippantly.

"I think Nostradamus does," I responded positively. "I think he knew that the events of the Golem were going to be buried in lies but he also knew that someone like me would come along and uncover the truth. He could see the future after all!"

"He said this or are you just making this part up?"

"Pearce, you should know me by now. The stories I tell usually end up being well supported by the facts. But figure this one out for yourself if you think otherwise. In his Century V Quatrain ninety-six, he says, *'On the middle of the great world, the rose. For a new deed, blood shall be publicly spilt. To say the truth, everyone shall close their mouths. Until there comes the one that will attend to it later.'* Okay, give it a shot."

Pearce thought about it in the context of the story. His furled brow and pensive stare meant he was trying hard not to disappoint me. "Okay, okay, I got some of it. Great World is the same meaning as the Holy Roman Empire. Right?" I nodded my head in confirmation. "Then the middle of it would be the center, but in this case center means the commercial or municipal center, so in other words, the capital. In this case, Prague." I nodded again in agreement. "The rose? I can't sort that one out."

"Think the Rose of Sharon," I told him.

"Oh, your ancestor."

"Right."

"The new deed is a great deed, and the spilling of the blood was obvious. A lot of murders and eventually Yakov and the Golem die in the public square. So that part was pretty easy. But even though the truth is known, everyone was sworn to secrecy and they presented this false tale of the events. The lie became a major cover up. They buried the truth with their silence."

"Very good," I congratulated him.

"And the last line is saying that it will all be revealed but not till well in the future. Not until you come along."

"See, that wasn't so difficult, was it? But the numbers he used for his quatrains also meant something," I advised. "There's a pattern but it's not always clear. Sometimes he's referring to years, sometimes it's a numerical code. Five ninety-six definitely has a significance but I haven't cracked it yet. But there are so many other clues that Nostradamus left regarding this story that I can leave the numbers for a later time."

"Such as?"

"You remember the one that Caesar read out to Yakov. About the Great King that doesn't live by the art of the Hebrews but because of him, his people are pushed to succeed at a great level, which results in their being pardoned."

"Yes, I remember that. That was where Caesar knew that Yakov was going to succeed."

"It's actually longer than what Caesar told him. The number of the quatrain is Century VI:18 and it reads '*Par les Physiques le grand Roi de laisse. Par sort non art de l'Ebriewu est en vie. Leure et son genre au regne haut pousse. Grace don nee a gen qui Christ en vie.*"

"Thanks Doc. That really made a lot of sense to me. Like I was going to understand that? Care to translate."

"Let's start with the numbering. This one I think I can figure out. Most people feel that Nostradamus was referring to actual centuries when he numbered his prophecies. So with this one they expect to relate to something six hundred years after Nostradamus's death. I think it was a lot simpler than that. Century VI: 18. Six and eighteen or twenty-four. Twenty-four years after he died or between 1589 and 1590."

"Clever."

"Only if its right of course. But assuming it is then Nostradamus knew the three of them would be there and they'd end the nightmare at that period of time."

"But what did the rest of it mean?"

"Caesar left out the first sentence which loosely translates that the Great King is let go by the physicians. Or in our present day language, the doctors couldn't save him. Caesar knew that Yakov was going to die he just couldn't bring himself to admit it until later."

"And the rest?"

"That part about the Great King not living by the art of the Hebrews was certainly correct. It implied that Yakov practiced a different form of Judaism, not the Rabbinical Judaism of the day. As a Karaite or Zadokite he was considered worlds apart. The 'pushed to succeed at a great level' reads more that he was challenged to take on a great task in order for his people to meet a challenge. In this case the push would be more like forced; exactly the situation that Yakov faced when the Church threatened his community. Nostradamus specifically mentions him as separate from the people in performing this task. So he was doing it for them, not with them. And the rest pretty much reads like Caesar told him. Grace, signifying a pardon to a death sentence is given to the people that deny Christ. In other words the community is not exterminated."

"Wow," was Pearce's immediate response. "I can't believe that was all in there. It's almost as if the entire story is summarized in that one quatrain. Now that you've explained it, it seems so obvious."

"Of course to make it even more complicated there are two versions of the quatrain. In an altered version the people that deny Christ has been changed to the people that envy Christ. Guess it wasn't politically correct at that time to suggest that there could be a people that benefited even though they actually denied Jesus."

"Were there any similar prophecies?"

"In regard to the particular event resulting in the sparing of his community, no. But that's very much like Nostradamus. Four lines for a specific prophecy and then on to the next. But I did find Century VI Quatrain fifty-six particularly interesting when trying to understand Nostradamus's numbering system."

"Let me take a guess, six and fifty-six, making it sixty-two years after his death or the year 1628. What did he say about that year?"

"He refers to it as the year of the dreaded army of the Narbonne enemy."

"He was calling his own people in the south of France the enemy."

"I'm glad you remembered where Narbonne was, John. But think more carefully in the lines of the book, *Blood Royale.* That book was very clear in telling you who resided in Narbonne. And even though Yakov was from the Kahana line out of Baghdad, it was still the Kahanas that ruled Narbonne for over a century."

"That being the case, then the year 1628 would have signified a big event in Jewish history."

"You got it John. You win the prize. It was a great year! Denmark granted formal protection to the few Jews that resided there, giving them the right to hold private religious services and Albert Dionis became the Danish Royal Court Jew. The English let the Jews settle in Barbados and for the first time you have a Jewish community that was free of European persecution. It was the year that Jewish musicians set up an Academy of Music in Venice. In retrospect it was a year of liberation. The migration of Jews into the New World probably being the most significant event of the ones I mentioned. But for us, we have the advantage of hindsight and can look back at a turning point in Jewish history. Nostradamus didn't have that luxury."

"Okay, I think I have a starting point for my investigations. Anything else I should know about Rudolf?"

"Yes, find out why Rudolf changed his mind about going to war against the Turks. That would be significant. Originally, he considered them his commercial benefactors and allies. Suddenly, in 1592, the same year he apparently turfs Judah ben Loew out of Prague, he decides to go to war. Why would he suddenly change his mind you must ask? It was what the Church always wanted him to do, but he certainly didn't want to."

"You think he was trying to cut a deal, Doc."

"Definite possibility! Defeat the Turks, save the life of Giordano Bruno. Wouldn't surprise me. Trouble was, he couldn't defeat the Turks and ended up plummeting his empire into a decade of war."

"What about Caesar?"

"He fared the best of them all, but then he went and broke his promise not to publish his father's quatrains that condemned the Church. So why would a man that had everything he wanted suddenly decide to go after the Church and risk everything? Besides it being predicted by his father I also think he considered it sweet revenge for their burning Giordano. Like I said, his father did tell him that he'd do so."

"Did I miss that part?"

"Perhaps, but Yakov didn't. It was when he was in St. Mikhal's Church. Remember when he became very quiet after Caesar told him the quatrain."

"I think so. I don't remember the number but I do remember something about hail and thunder."

"*The hail and thunder at Condon will be inestimable.* Yakov knew it immediately. It was about Caesar in the future. About his exacting divine punishment, or in this case, since Nostradamus liked playing a game of opposites, punishment of the divine."

"I'm not following you."

"Condon in the past was a big diocese in France; a center for Catholicism. The quatrain was foretelling the future when Caesar would attack the Church through his father's prophecies. Since Yakov knew the only reason Caesar would do such a thing was if they had been betrayed and the Papacy failed to fulfill its promise to them. It only talked about Caesar's revenge, suggesting the other two weren't around. He knew then that he wasn't going to survive the mission."

"I didn't see that. It does make sense though. Too bad there weren't any easier quatrains that talked about Caesar in his old age"

"But there were," I corrected him. "Just take a look at Century III Quatrain Fourteen. That was about Caesar in his later life. *'By the bough of the valiant person, The weaker Frenchman, the one who's father was unusual, Honors, riches, workers will be his in his old age, All because he believed in the wise counsel of that gentle man.'* He had a promise of greatness for having been allied to Yakov."

"And Marie?"

"Caesar took care of her afterwards but as she had elucidated, he never had a love interest with her?"

"So what was his story?"

"He never had a love interest with anyone. She was right. That part of his soul was dead for whatever reason."

"Looks like we have a lot of homework to do."

"We? I've done my job John. The rest is now up to you!"

"That could take forever!"

"Maybe not as much as you think John. Get the book published and get it out into the public. Like I said, someone's sitting on vital information that confirms my story."

"Gonna put a lot of noses out of joint. It's not like you pulled any punches."

"My ancestor was right. The use of evil in order to achieve some good should not and cannot be tolerated. The only thing that evolves from evil is more evil. Jew, Catholic, it didn't matter. What they did back then was wrong. And Yakov Kahana paid the price. If I make them uncomfortable, then so be it. They deserve to feel some heat even if it is over four hundred years later. My ancestor deserves to rest in peace, and I shouldn't have to be tormented by his memories any longer." I could see a wistful and faraway look in Pearce's eyes. "What are you thinking about now, John?

"At four hundred years after Yakov, I was just wondering what that would make you generation wise," Pearce calculated out the numbers.

"I know exactly what you're thinking about but just so you know, I'm only the thirteenth generation. Both you and I will not be around to see what's in store for the eighteenth. By my estimate that won't be until around the year Twenty-one Twenty."

"So, did Nostradamus have anything to say about that particular generation," Pearce asked, half jesting and half serious.

"A matter of fact, he did. There does appear to have been a definite link between his prophecies and my family. In Century III, Quatrain Ninety-four he actually talks about it."

"You're kidding," Pearce was shocked by my revelation. "What does he say?"

"Here's what he wrote. You do the interpretation yourself. *'For a little more than five hundred years, no account shall be made. Of the one that becomes the ornament of his time. Then suddenly his head will be given a great light, Then he will render that century to be content.'* As you can see, he is expected to live up to the family tradition."

"Aw, shucks. Would have been interesting to see," Pearce reflected remorsefully. "So what now?"

"Now, I think I'll focus a little more time on my young protégé."

"Mandy?" The way Pearce said her name he was still baffled by my story of how she and I came together but he was willing to accept that it was more than mere coincidence.

"Someone's got to teach her how to use her abilities. And once she learns, I think she'll have some great stories to tell of her own," I insisted.

"But they couldn't be anything like yours Doc."

"Different! She's a restless spirit. That much I know."

"Meaning?"

"Meaning we're two of a kind, her and I."

"I don't know if the world's ready for two of you!"

"We'll see John, we'll see!"

CPSIA information can be obtained at www.ICGtesting.com
Printed in the USA
LVOW111955230512
283009LV00001B/236/P